LOOKING FOR ROMEO

CARMINA ESQUIVEL

OLIVE MOON BOOKS

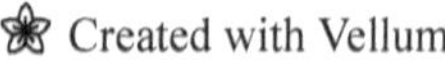 Created with Vellum

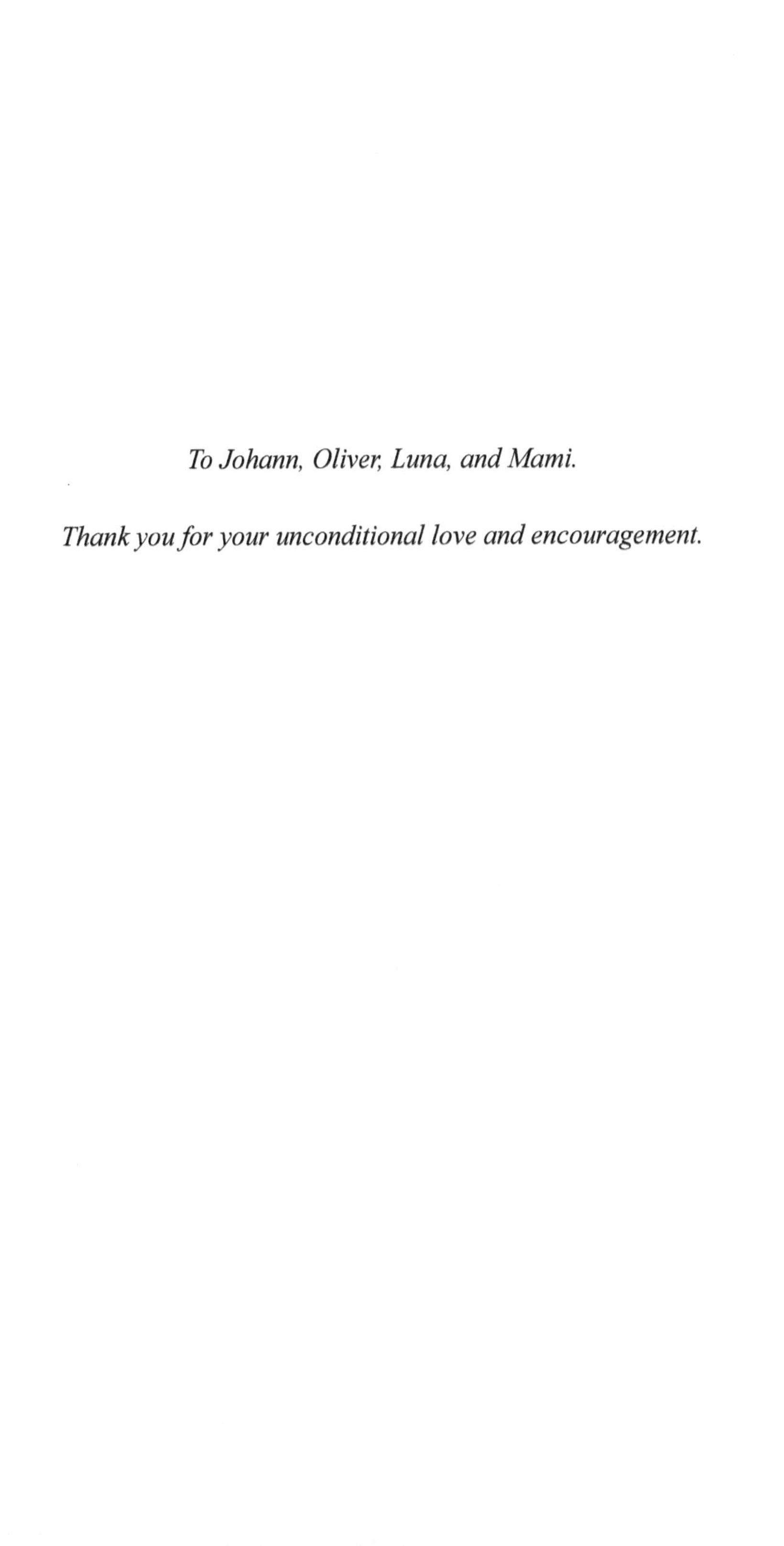

To Johann, Oliver, Luna, and Mami.

Thank you for your unconditional love and encouragement.

CHAPTER I
THE CUTE SCALE

There was something magical about finishing a book, especially a love story. In that moment the heroine's happily-ever-after felt fresh on my skin. As if the love I hoped to find was there for me to take, made out not of words but of flesh and bone. Would it be possible to find the guy of my dreams? I wanted so badly to live a love story that would pull me into a romance so tornado-like that life itself would never be the same again.

But I wanted it to be real. I'd read enough fiction.

It all started when Mrs. Lib, the senior children's librarian from Storybridge's public library and my favorite ever, introduced me to my most cherished love-story boyfriend of all time, Romeo Montague. Mrs. Lib always said that readers didn't just read books; they *lived* through them, and I was such a firm believer of that.

The guy from the book I'd just finished, whom we were about to dissect in the teen book club tonight, landed a solid six and a half on my cute scale. That was the imaginary scale I used to measure how likely I'd fall for a fictional guy. Still, there was no comparison to Romeo Montague, who had obviously earned a ten. But as my best friends, Maggie and Alex, constantly reminded me, meeting someone as perfect as Romeo was clearly impossible. But still, I liked to dream. Dreams didn't hurt, they pushed us toward what we really wanted in life.

I pushed my glasses up the bridge of my nose and checked the time. Any minute now the STAFF ONLY door would open, and Mrs. Lib would come out ready for the teen book club. She was never late.

I walked down to the second floor, leaving my favorite reading spot behind. Mrs. Lib was nowhere to be found so I looked for Sarah, my second-favorite librarian. I found her behind the adult reference desk, helping a patron. Her blonde-and-silver bob was visible from behind the big guy she was helping. She always wore stylish glasses, and they always matched the color of her accessories. After the man shifted and her face came into view, I saw that today they were green.

Meanwhile, I stared at the Summer Reads bulletin board in the glass case next to the staircase. The book-cover posters were falling apart, and many things in this library needed an update. I wondered if Mrs. Lib had heard anything else about the grant this library could win when suddenly I had the feeling of being watched.

Through the reflection on the glass of the bulletin board, I could see someone far behind me. A tall guy with long hair seemed to be looking in my direction. I couldn't see him very well, but he looked cute.

It would be a first to find a hot guy at the library. Most of the young people who frequented the public library were . . . nerds like me. Trying to be discreet, I took my time turning around, but when I finally did, he was gone. I should stop hoping to find my real love story at this library. My dreams were now clouding my judgment.

I approached Sarah and tapped my foot on the carpet, because she was taking too long. I hated being late, and the book club would start any minute now. I got a little closer to the information desk, hoping my presence would make Sarah look my way. I urgently needed to ask her where Mrs. Lib was. But she didn't even glance in my direction.

I felt observed again and looked around me. I couldn't shake the feeling or find who was watching me. I frequently found peculiar and entertaining characters at this library, but nothing out of the ordinary was going on.

Across the information desk, I recognized classmates inside the study rooms. I could see them frowning at each other, confused about what they were studying. Maybe they were trying to learn in a few hours what they'd missed during the whole school year. I was proud, for once, to be a nerd. It had its perks, such as less stress and free time at the end of the school year.

My eyes met those of a guy I'd never seen before. He sat with his legs apart, as if he were lying on a beach instead of sitting on a library chair. Openly staring at me, he was simply not interested in whatever the rest of his group was saying. I suspected he was the one in the reflection, and he seemed to be obsessively interested in me. I looked away, trying to ignore him focusing on Sarah instead.

She finally looked my way and said, "She's not here," then handed me a paper. The book club must have been postponed, since Mrs. Lib was in charge of it.

Out of the corner of my eye, I glanced back at the study rooms, and the guy was still looking at me. His stare was becoming uncomfortable. My first impression of him had changed from mysterious to annoying—definitely not a good change. He had the looks, I'd give him that, but by his attitude I knew that he was not my bookish type. I decided to read the paper instead.

It was not any normal piece of paper. It seemed to have once been a pretty envelope, but several notes had been crossed out.

Mrs. Lib was famous for reusing even the smallest scrap of paper, so this didn't surprise me. She had circled a series of numbers and letters, which I immediately recognized as a call number. Mrs. Lib was sending me on a quest, some sort of scavenger hunt for a specific book. She used to do that a lot when I was her volunteer a couple of years ago, leaving me notes or messages to figure out.

I looked around, trying to find the aisle that contained the call number. It was nerdy but at the same time so exciting. Of all the libraries I had visited in the surrounding cities, this was by far my favorite, and not only because of the awesome librarians. Contrary to others, I could check out a great number of books, and there were no fines if I returned them a day late. But above all the building was inviting and beautiful, with dark-blue walls and huge tinted windows that let me see the flower garden from the inside.

I found my aisle and enjoyed immersing myself in the beauty of the identical navy spines, a great selfie backdrop or wallpaper for my phone. The Timeless Literature section was my favorite, especially for the smell of old books. Some people liked to stop and smell the roses. I liked to stop and smell books.

There was something unique about being surrounded by big ideas and stories from people who may or may not be alive. The stories could be loud, controversial, or sweet, yet all of them stood in silence, neatly organized. As I passed my hand over their spines, I whispered to them, "You guys are gorgeous."

My little brother, Will, called me a weirdo for talking to books, but they communicated ideas to us all the time. Why couldn't I respond and make it a conversation instead of a monologue?

There! The book that matched Mrs. Lib's note was *Tristan and Isolde*. I was not familiar with the title, but I knew it must be good. I grabbed it and headed back to my special reading spot on the third floor.

My lime chair, as I liked to call it, was a light faded green and was in the perfect location. It was right by the window, with tons of natural light, and it was next to the storage room, which nobody ever used. The only bad part was that it was directly underneath the AC vent. The inside of the library resembled a never-ending winter. Colder temperatures might be good for books, but they weren't as good for a skinny sixteen-year-old like me.

Exuberant cleavage and curves had never been in my gene repertoire. I found it annoying when people counted calories and worried about their weight. I was flat from all angles, with a metabolism working on overdrive. Will had once called me a straw with legs.

At some point I gave up on stressing about filling cups in a bra, or not being able to wear tight clothing. My jeans will always be a couple of sizes too big, like I got stuck in the nineties with a baggy-cargo-pants look. But I cared more about the thoughts and ideas in my head than the vessel that contained them. I crossed my legs, sitting on the lime chair with space to spare. Life hadn't given me lemons; it had given me this precious comfy lime.

Today was cloudy, so I couldn't sunbathe like a cat in the rays that often fell over my lime chair. I took my favorite scarf from my bag. It was not any common scarf. It had my favorite passage of literature printed all over it, the balcony scene from *Romeo and Juliet*. I wrapped it twice around my neck and got comfortable, ready to smell the book first, as I always did before I started reading. Now I was ready to dive into the world of *Tristan and Isolde*. Perhaps I'd find a new book boyfriend and fall in love with him too.

"June?" Sarah's voice took me out of Ireland, where Isolde was falling in love with Tristan. "Did you read the letter? Don't tell me you thought it was canceled."

It took me a few seconds to realize what she was talking about.

"Oh, my word! Now you are really late for book club."

I could sense the frustration in her voice.

"Come on, follow me," Sarah said, sprinting toward the stairs.

I looked at the envelope again. Not only did it have a classification number, but it had a letter inside that I had totally missed. I ran to catch up with Sarah, but it was challenging to focus on getting to the letter when my glasses were jumping up and down on the bridge of my nose. I was trying to open the envelope to find the letter when I bumped into someone and fell flat on my butt. I looked up, and the stalker guy was right in front of me, taller than I expected.

"There are chairs around to read, you know?"

His mocking tone irritated me. He held out his hand, but I chose to ignore his help.

He was sort of hot, with his long blond hair and blue eyes. But he looked rather shabby with ripped jeans that had so many holes they would hardly be considered a piece of clothing.

Maybe if he hadn't acted like a brat, he would have gotten a solid eight on my cute scale, but he had slipped down the list with his presumptuous tone. That was why I never gave guys any scores until I heard them speak.

I walked away, trying to catch up with Sarah, who was already down the stairs on the first floor. I reached her a few feet before the teen room entrance. She summarized, in the fastest way possible, what Mrs. Lib's letter was about. But I had a hard time concentrating on her words, since we were really late.

Sarah was about to open the teen room door but stopped and turned to look at me. Perhaps I wasn't good at dissimulating my stress, because she put her hand over my shoulder and said, "I'll talk to her and say you were helping me with something."

Her? Her who? I peeked at Mrs. Lib's note and read something about her daughter being in labor and her taking a last-minute plane. That sounded impossible. Her daughter still had a couple of months before her due date. She must be so stressed.

Wait, if that was true, who would be my mentor for the summer? Mrs. Lib was not only my supervisor but also the reason I wanted to become a librarian. I had gotten an internship with her this summer, instead of my usual part-time job. I got paid less than half time, but I didn't care, since the point was for me to follow her around and learn. Besides, she'd said that if I did a good job, I'd get a letter of recommendation for library school at the end of the summer.

Sarah quickly reminded me to take a deep breath, since I was about to meet my new boss. I had heard little about the new librarian who was coming from New Jersey to work here. Rumors said she was coming from a high position and was not necessarily happy to join Storybridge Public Library. The odds were not in my favor since I was late to make a good first impression. If I had learned anything about working with librarians, it was this: don't break the rules, don't damage books, and don't be late.

I tried to keep calm, knowing I had Sarah to back me up. We stepped into the room, and I felt all eyes on us. Definitely not a nice feeling for an introvert like me, who loved to hide behind books. The new librarian seemed far from pleased with the interruption. Once she noticed the badge hanging from my neck, she frowned. I clasped my hands together, trying to stop them from shaking, as Sarah asked her for a moment to introduce us.

"Please make it quick, Sarah," she said as she approached, "we are running behind since the projector is not working."

Sarah smiled politely. "This is June Capehart, one of the most amazing interns and volunteens we have ever had."

Her support was very much appreciated. I was hoping her flattering words had some positive effect on the new librarian whose name, according to her badge, was Nora.

"Part of her internship requires assisting a librarian," Sarah elaborated. "Now that Alice is away, she's all yours."

Nora seemed to be unsure of whether she liked me. "Yes, Alice Libbengood told me about the girl whose obsession with a certain Shakespearean play was *beyond compare*."

I smiled uncomfortably, distracted by Mrs. Lib's real name. For everyone at this library she was Alice Libbengood. But to me she was Mrs. Librarian, or Mrs. Lib for short. She'd given me my first library card when I was five, and I'd genuinely thought that was her name. She'd let me call her that ever since, and the rest was history.

Nora's curling lip remained unchanged. "I assumed my assistant would be here early and ready with the handouts for the book club."

I quickly hid Mrs. Lib's letter in my bag, trying to avoid Nora's disappointed gaze. I took out the folder with the handouts for the book club and gave her my most polite smile. I walked around the tables, handing out the copies to the attendees. I had come prepared. It was not my fault Nora had had bitterness for lunch.

"June," Nora called, "are you able to fix the projector after this interruption?"

I shook my head, overwhelmed by all the attendees staring at me again. As an assistant I should be almost invisible, but it didn't feel that way. Besides, I hated when older people assumed

I knew about technology just because I was younger. Sarah volunteered to help Nora, and I felt relieved.

When I was done, I sat in the empty chair next to Nora's. A few seconds later someone sat in her place, but the person did not have her long black hair.

"Why are you stalking me?" I asked the annoying stalker guy.

"You do know it's seventy-eight degrees outside, right?"

It didn't surprise me that he'd found a new way to mock me. I pushed my teal glasses up the bridge of my nose. "And?"

"You can't possibly be cold in this amazing weather." He pointed at my scarf.

I hated having to elaborate on why I was always cold. "It's not really that warm, since it's made from cotton."

He stared at me, clueless.

"Cotton has cooling and heating properties because it is a natural fiber. You'd know that if you read more rather than stalking strangers," I said dismissively and turned away. He unsuccessfully held his laugh.

I looked at him defiantly. "Do you find me entertaining? Or you just can't find anyone else to stalk?" He was getting on my nerves.

"I find you as pretty as a picture."

I sighed with frustration and looked away realizing Sarah had left.

Nora tapped his shoulder. "Excuse me, sir. Do you mind moving to that empty chair over there?" She pointed at the opposite side of our table.

He winked at me and obeyed. It was ironic that, of all the guys I could have imagined to meet at this library, he was the one to approach me.

"Where were we?" Nora said, looking more pleased now. Perhaps the broken projector had been the cause of her bitterness.

She continued the session and managed the discussion in such a boring way that I stopped paying attention. If Mrs. Lib were here, people would be laughing. She always made the discussion entertaining. And people adored her because the teen book club was full almost every month.

Even as I tried to ignore the stalker, his incessant stare became aggravating.

"June?" Nora called.

I shook my head and turned to her.

"Let me repeat the question." She folded her hands. "Thinking of the main characters from this novel, do you find any resemblance to other famous couples in literature who went against their families to be together?"

There was something passive-aggressive in her tone, but maybe it was her weird way to make peace.

The stalker murmured something inaudible to the guys next to him.

"*Romeo and Juliet,*" I said, thinking of the joy that love story brought me.

The stalker and his new friends laughed softly. I tried to let it go—he was not going to get to me.

"Perhaps you might want to share your thoughts, Mr…?" Nora asked him.

"Tyler." The stalker finally had a name. "With all due respect, Miss Nora, I think we are losing focus here." He rearranged himself in the chair with an air of grandeur. "Look, I like Shakespeare. I really admire the guy. But let's not compare this book to *Romeo and Juliet,*" he said, and pointed at the handout in front of him.

He was such a phony. I was sure he hadn't even read this month's title.

"Besides, Romeo has got to be one of the worst and most boring characters of all time," he added.

"Why the heck would you say that?" My thoughts were not

just mine, but words I actually spoke out loud and at high volume.

Nora looked at me, unpleased since I hadn't raised my hand before speaking, like she'd repeatedly asked us to. I'd normally feel the heat rising to my cheeks as everybody stared, but I was not going to let a jerk like *him* say anything against my favorite book boyfriend.

Nora stared at him, waiting for an answer. He gave me a cocky side smile. Perhaps I had unconsciously taken the bait.

"I think Romeo is a moron. He's reckless, stupid, you name it," he said as he looked at Nora. "Unlike the character we are discussing, that is." He pointed at the handout again, completely insufferable.

"So you see the resemblance in yourself?" I added with a cocky smile of my own.

The guys around him whistled, but Nora cut it short and called my name right away. I looked at her in panic. Perhaps I shouldn't have said that in front of her.

"I'm going to have to ask you to leave." Nora pointed at the door.

I tried to justify my answer. It was clear he hadn't read either book.

"This is a book club. Discussions are allowed. However, personal attacks are not," she said, waiting for me to leave.

I stood up and grabbed my things. Tyler kept staring at me, a grin on his face. I bit my tongue to avoid saying anything that could make me lose my job.

I walked upstairs, needing to calm down. As soon as I reached the second floor, Sarah called to me. "Everything OK?"

I shook my head.

"Is something wrong with the projector again?" she asked.

She had a point. Why else would I have left the teen room? I knew I could be honest with her, and I knew I had stepped out of line. It was one thing to talk like that as a patron, another as a working member of the library.

"I messed up. This annoying guy insulted Romeo, and I got carried away."

She nodded. "People mocking our favorite characters never ends well." Sarah, like Mrs. Lib, was always understanding, especially when it came to a reader's attachment to a book or character.

"Perhaps you can help me with something else," she said, and I genuinely smiled.

"We have a little bit of a situation here," Sarah said as she unlocked the multipurpose room on the third floor.

The temperature was colder than the rest of the library, and I was glad to be wearing my scarf. Several acrylic display cases filled the room, with small square columns underneath. Each one contained an old collectible book. Except for the last display, which was empty.

"Alice's contacts with library associations allowed for the loan of these collectible books for our upcoming summer exhibit —hoping to get the grant we desperately need." She turned the lights on and dimmed them right away. "But I'm guessing you already knew all of that."

I nodded politely.

"Well, perhaps you also know she's an expert at handling old books, since she has a few in her personal collection."

I knew that too. I had been to her house, since she and my mom had become close friends, but I didn't want everyone else to know that.

Sarah continued, "Since she had to rush to the airport this

morning, she left one book unpacked." Sarah took out a paper, unfolded it, and adjusted her glasses. "She told me over the phone how to do it, and I wrote it down here."

"Do you know how much books like these cost?" I asked, looking at all the old books around us. I had an idea, but Mrs. Lib had never revealed how much she had paid for one of hers. Mrs. Lib's husband showed her his affection by getting her rare books.

"Certainly more than any of us can afford," Sarah said as she opened the box. "Let's just say that if anything happens to any of these books, we can kiss our grant goodbye, and people might lose their jobs."

I was not worried about the safety of these books. Jim, the superintendent, made sure the library remained locked at night and everything of value was locked away. Besides, with security cameras and the smart cases, it would be impossible for anyone to even attempt to steal a book.

"Once the exhibit opens in a couple of weeks, Jim will be in charge of opening and closing this room every day."

Jim was super fun. He was always in a good mood and, without fail, up for a good joke. He could retire, but he refused. I still remembered when his characteristic goatee and long ponytail were black instead of gray.

"Make sure to wash and dry your hands before handling the book," Sarah read out loud, then looked up. "I forgot my phone on my desk. Let me go get it. Alice texted me the lock combination before her plane took off. Please look out for these books, and I will be right back."

"That would be an honor," I said, smiling.

As I waited, I stared at the open box. MLA was stamped on it. I had no idea what it meant, but Mrs. Lib had talked about so many library associations that I had lost track. I looked at the other books, trying to get a sneak peek ahead of the exhibit inauguration. I recognized most of the titles and realized many were classic works of literature. Fingers crossed patrons would love this exhibit.

These cases were much more modern than the ones I remembered Mrs. Lib had at home, but they still seemed familiar. They were the only pieces of technology, besides my computer and phone, that I enjoyed using. One time Mrs. Lib got a new collectible, the second edition of *The Adventures of Sherlock Holmes*, and invited me over to see it. Like a hawk, I had observed her put it in its case, and I still remembered every detail.

Sarah came back and took me out of my thoughts. "I just washed my hands. Why don't you go and do the same so we can get started."

I ran to the closest restroom, immensely grateful that Sarah would let me be part of such a special ritual.

When I came back, Sarah had already taken the book out of the box, but it was still wrapped. I stood by her as she unwrapped the plastic and unfolded the cotton fabric covering it.

"Oh my, you are going to love this," Sarah said.

Perhaps when this book had been bound, it had been firm and a bright royal blue. But the brightness of the leather cover had faded to reveal patches of brown. At the center a crown sat atop a faded red heart, surrounded by two faint gold letters. The elaborate calligraphy made it hard to read the letters.

Sarah looked at me excitedly, waiting for my reaction, but the low light made it difficult to identify the book. She turned and handed it to me.

I held it like a newborn baby, afraid to damage it with my warm hands. I opened it slowly, noticing the faded blue marbled endpaper. Even if it was a little damaged, it was gorgeous. But the smell—that struck me the most, so different from the smell of ink on the brand-new paper found in the New Books shelf. If a spice rack and a library shared a smell, this would be it.

Like many other books I've seen, it had gilded edges. But as I fanned out the pages, a hidden fore-edge painting of an old castle's balcony appeared. The book itself was a work of art.

I turned the pages with care, as if they were made of glass; then I reached the title page: *The Most Excellent and Lamentable Tragedy of Romeo and Juliet.*

I almost fell backward. "No way!" I said loudly.

Sarah laughed.

"Is this for real?" I said, looking at the year, 1734.

This was by far the oldest book I'd ever held. I turned the pages and reached the prologue. That strong introduction set the mood for the whole play. I needed to admire this book as much as I could, since it would be locked in its case until the exhibit was over. A happy tear escaped. I wanted to spend hours admiring each and every page.

"Did you know *Tristan and Isolde* was the predecessor of *Romeo and Juliet*?" Sarah asked.

"I know now." I smiled. That must be the reason why Mrs. Lib sent me to read that book. To set the mood for this beautiful collectible.

"We should put it in the display now," Sarah said softly.

I couldn't believe I had been so lucky as to hold this book.

"Let me read the display instructions before you place it, dear," Sarah said, reading the manual.

"Which page do you want it open to?" I asked.

"You decide, just not too close to either the beginning or end so the spine is not stressed by the weight of the pages," she replied.

Just like the picture on its edges and the one printed on my scarf, the balcony scene seemed to be popular. I imagined myself as Juliet, having Romeo saying those beautiful verses to me. But I quickly realized that would mean I'd be dead, since I was already sixteen, and Juliet was thirteen at that time. I'd rather be alive to enjoy this book.

I set the book inside the display, and Sarah fixed its position so the spine was centered with the wedge underneath. She closed the lid and clicked a few buttons. I glanced at the screen and saw the combination before Sarah closed the case, 1987 a set of numbers I was sure I was never going to use.

Beeps sounded as the case locked, and I never realized technology could make me feel so sad. The LED lights transitioned from orange to yellow to green as it checked the humidity levels, temperature, and light exposure. The glass turned a little darker, lightly polarized for extra protection against artificial light.

The book was safe and far from my touch.

As we left the room, Sarah turned to me, "You can still catch Nora if you'd like to talk to her about anything regarding your internship." She rubbed my arm as we reached the elevator. "The book club will be over any minute now."

She had a point. If I wanted to smooth things out with Nora, I'd better talk to her.

As I approached the teen room, the door began to open. I stood to one side to let people out, but the first person coming out of the room was Tyler. He stopped and winked at me, and I sighed heavily, waiting for him to move out of my way. Then I waited for Nora to finish talking with patrons.

She looked at me with no decipherable expression and pointed at the tables. I rearranged them back into rows, instead of in a big rectangle. Once the room was all organized, she came toward me.

"You might have done things differently with Alice, but I expect more professionalism from you." She crossed her arms.

I was aware of the perks of being Mrs. Lib's protégé, but I had never taken advantage of that. I had just enjoyed being around books and behind the counter of a library, as any other bookworm would have.

"You can't address anyone the way you did that poor boy. Even if you disagree, he was just expressing his opinion," Nora said.

I tried hard to keep my emotions to myself. He was not a victim. He was a moron.

"Besides your normal duties at this library, you will have to assist me with closing every evening."

What? That was torture! Closing time was *the* worst. Having to somehow politely push people out of the building and check every corner of the library, including every restroom, was not my definition of fun.

How much I missed Mrs. Lib! I nodded and swallowed my pride. "I'm sorry for what I said to . . . that guy. It won't happen again." I tried to sound sincere.

With my friends many miles away for the summer, I expected this internship to be my biggest adventure. But with Nora as my mentor, it seemed like the only fun was going to be shelving books and reading something from my TBR summer list.

After checking out *Tristan and Isolde* and leaving for the day, I faced the awful reminder of needing to get another bike lock. It had gotten stuck again. As I was struggling with it, I heard the library's main doors open and a not-so-friendly person approaching. Now was definitely not the time for the lock to give up on me.

The lock slipped from my hands for the third time. The evening heat of mid-May was already giving a glimpse of the

Southern summer ahead. I squeezed my hands into fists, as if I could get the lock to work with my frustration.

"Are you a damsel in distress? I'd offer help, but I'm sure you won't take it," my stalker said with such an annoying tone I wanted to slap him.

I took a deep breath. If he was looking for me to fight him, he was not going to succeed. I ignored him.

"We should go out this Friday." He raised his eyebrows. "No, wait. I have another date. Make it Saturday."

I laughed. "You gotta be kidding me. Are you actually hearing yourself? Why on earth would I want to go out with you?" Nora was not around, so I didn't care about my blunt honesty.

Sweat dripped down my temples as I turned the key again, and I unwrapped my scarf, remembering I hadn't taken it off.

"I can bet anything cotton doesn't feel cool *now*," he said with a somehow triumphant tone pointing at my scarf.

I wanted to slap him, but I gave him a fake grin instead and wrapped it around my neck again. I never understood why guys thought the way to get a girl's attention was by being annoying. It was so immature.

My glasses slid down the bridge of my nose as I looked down. I thought about Maggie, who usually complained a lot about the heat. How would she scare away a guy like him? Surely she must have dealt with her fair share of overconfident guys, being a social butterfly. But, realistically, she would have already agreed to go out—*just for fun*.

The key finally turned and the lock opened. I shoved it in my bag and hopped on, but Tyler blocked my way.

"Can't you just move out of my way?" I said, exasperated.

"I think I already deciphered you. It took me a while, but I think I nailed it." He held the handlebars with both hands. "You are a goodie, a hot one, who would never get into trouble. You hide behind books and fantasize all day long about guys that don't exist, like that dumb Romeo."

I looked at him, annoyed and puzzled.

"Nora mentioned something about your *little obsession* with him after she kicked you out."

Who did he think he was to say all that to me?

He continued, "Maybe you buy all that love-at-first-sight crap and are waiting for some Prince Charming to give you your first kiss." His lips pouted. "Don't worry, hot bookworm, I'm right here." He opened his arms.

At least he had let go of my bike, but I didn't know whether to feel offended or revolted. I put my foot on the pedal and it slipped. He leaned closer, and I placed my opened hand in front of him.

"Just don't," I said. His excessive confidence was making me want to throw up. It was clear he was not used to losing. Nora walked out the door and looked our way.

"Please disappear from the face of the earth," I said, hoping that even if Nora had heard me, my words wouldn't incriminate me.

My foot searched for the right place on the pedal, and I pedaled away as fast as I could, leaving him behind.

When I was far enough from the library, I stopped at a lamppost to take my scarf off, sweating profusely. As I stuffed it in my bag, I stared at Romeo's dialogue printed on it. My feelings somehow caught up with my thoughts as I realized some of Tyler's words were true. I wished for a person who didn't exist. I ached for a guy who was impossible to meet.

Tyler's words should be meaningless to me, but just as words had the power to heal, they also had the power to hurt. And for the first time outside of a story, I felt them bruise me.

CHAPTER 2

STORYBRIDGE'S GOSSIP

Whatever was going on outside my room was definitely not a pleasant way to wake up. I stretched under my sheets, feeling unusually rested even after staying up late reading. As I moved the sheets away, *Tristan and Isolde* fell. I'd grown used to sleeping with books, so their sharp edges didn't bother me anymore. I was barely remembering what day it was when someone knocked incessantly on my door.

"Honey, it's really late. Maggie will be here soon," Mom said.

I put on my glasses and checked the time. *Damn it!* I had forgotten to set my alarm last night, and now I had like ten minutes to get ready and have breakfast. I opened the door and rushed for the bathroom but stopped when I heard Will shouting my name, stomping up the stairs with Haiku, our dog, barking and wagging his tail behind him.

"This is all your fault!" He passed me on the way to his room and slammed the door.

What did I do now? Haiku, stared at me naively, tilting his head. Will getting mad at me was not uncommon, and his threats would dissolve in a few days. But I didn't have time to ponder why my eight-year-old brother's life was so miserable. Besides, getting Will's silent treatment every now and then was a nice break from his nonstop talking.

After washing my face and teeth, I did my hair in its usual side braid. Now looking more decent, I went back to my room and opened my drawers. There was nothing worth wearing to school. Old tie-dye shirts, workout clothes I never used, and outgrown pj's were the only things available. Then I remembered—this week was my turn to do laundry. Damn it, not again! Laundry and me were each other's nemesis. Whether I left a red sock in the white load or shrunk Dad's wool sweater in the dryer, it was like I couldn't get it right. That must be the reason Will was so mad at me. I'd hate me, too, if my soccer uniform was dirty. It was not something you can wear again without washing.

I ran to my ex-sister Marian's room. She wasn't really my ex-sister. She was my half-sister who had decided to move to Australia for her master's program. Between the time difference and the 8,581 miles that separated us, it had been impossible for us to be as close as before. It wasn't like I could easily drop by or call anytime to say hello.

I dug through her closet, searching for something that didn't make me look like a tent because of our difference in body types. But it was pointless. She had taken all the good stuff with her to Aussie land. But at the very far end of her rack I found a big distressed denim jacket. Perhaps I could use it to cover whatever clean shirt I could find. I'd look like a rapper with oversize clothing, but I'd have to make it work.

I ran back to my room. I had only a few minutes left. Will's outburst was still going strong inside his room. I dug through my closet and found a pair of skinny jeans that were stained and made me look like a malnourished giraffe, but shorter. I put them on, along with my favorite colorful sneakers. I just needed a shirt. I desperately pulled out all the contents of my drawers.

Why did I have to keep so much useless stuff? No wonder Mom constantly asked me to get rid of old things.

I'd have to skip the earrings and grab breakfast on the go.

Finally! A clean swimming competition T-shirt of the Sea Wolves, our school's swimming team. Miriam, Alex's mom, had them made for his final competition last year. It was a bright neon green with blue letters. The problem was not the wolf silhouette; it was the bold font with *Alex Marquez Is My # 1!* in the front. It was one thing to wear it at a swimming competition along with Alex's family, and another to wear it randomly to school.

Haiku's barking meant Maggie's car must have parked in our driveway. I put the denim jacket on. Hopefully my outfit could go unnoticed for a day at school, but I doubted it. I grabbed my backpack and ran downstairs. Once I reached the bottom of the stairs, I noticed the smell of Mom's lemon blueberry muffins.

Before I headed out the door, Mom stopped me and handed me a container with a blueberry muffin. "One for the road," she said.

I hugged her. "I'm sorry for forgetting to do laundry again," I said apologetically. I knew Mom would fix Will's uniform situation, but it had been my fault.

"Next time I'll put a big note on the bookshelf in your room instead of the fridge. I'm sure you'll see it better there," she said, moving a strand of hair away from my forehead.

"It looks beautiful, Mom," I said, pointing at the tray filled with blueberry muffins and pretty flowers on the dining room table.

Mom smiled. She must be shooting pictures for her food blog. She had been recently named best baker in town by *Storybridge Magazine.* Among my favorite things about Mom were her endless forgiveness and her superb baking skills.

"June, can you please clear out your room before the end of the school year and take the donation clothes to the library?" she asked. After this morning, I was in no position to say no. I nodded.

A horn sounded. I waved goodbye to Mom, petted Haiku and closed the door behind me.

As soon as I walked out the door, it was as if a cloud had suddenly appeared over my head. I had totally forgotten about the *wick-pops* carpooling with us today. Maggie's wickedly annoying popular friends and I were like water and oil—we didn't mix well together. On most days I was pretty good at ignoring their passive-aggressive comments. But by the way both of them analyzed my outfit from head to toe as they lowered their sunglasses, I knew it was going to be a challenging ride. Today was the worst day for a laundry fail. The only free spot in Maggie's car was behind her seat, which was the ultimate worst place to sit when your best friend was the driver.

Having to ride with Alessandra and Mia meant that the only topics of conversation were going to be Maggie's upcoming theme party and the exchange students arriving any day now from our school's summer program. Maggie's birthday coincided with the end of the school year, so it had become the unofficial beginning-of-summer-break party. This year's theme was pure torture. We HAD TO bring a date to the party—not a friend, but a true romantic interest. She'd kill me if I showed up with a copy of *Romeo and Juliet.*

Inside Maggie's fancy new black Audi, the smell of the girls' combined perfumes hit me like a punch in the nose. If only I could open my window, like I did in Alex's Jeep. But since the wind messed up the wick-pops' and Maggie's carefully done hairstyles, it was not an option.

Maggie pulled away from my driveway and looked at me

through the rearview mirror with her haunting green eyes. I knew she had noticed my Alex T-shirt.

"Is that Marquez's house?" Alessandra, who was in the passenger seat, pointed at the house next to mine, while she brushed her brown highlighted hair with her fingers.

"One more to the left," Maggie said as she shifted into drive.

"Do you know who his date is for the party?" Mia, who was sitting next to me in the backseat, seemed anxious to know as she scooted between the front seats. Her big afro didn't let me see a single thing.

We stopped at a red light. "June, besides being Marquez's biggest supporter and best friend, do you have any idea who he's taking?" Maggie looked at me from the rearview mirror. "Cause Mia *really* wants to know."

I hated when she acted more like the wick-pops and less like herself.

"I don't know," I said, avoiding the outfit question hidden in Maggie's sentence.

I was Alex's best friend. I should know, but I didn't. Every year we went together and always had a lot of fun, even though we both hated parties. But this year, if we went together, it would have a different meaning. Besides, I had never dated anyone in my entire life, even as my junior year of high school was coming to an end.

The topic changed to the most boring ever—the countries the exchange guys were coming from. Since Mia was part of the welcoming committee, she knew everything. The exchange students had a reputation of being players who dated as many people as they could. Besides, most were obsessed with having a typical American small-town experience. They seemed to rely on Hollywood way too much.

The wick-pops giggled in a silly yet snobbish way. I would give anything to go back in time and take my bike to school instead. I stared at their outfits, feeling terrible about mine. The wick-pops and Maggie looked as if they were part of a girl band. More like a K-pop group, where all dressed similar, than the Spice Girls, where each had their own unique style.

"Talking about Marquez"—Alessandra looked back at me, taking me away from my fashion dilemmas—"Are you two *a thing*?"

"What? No," I said, offended. Not wanting to relive that time a few years ago when I had a crush on Alex and he kept me in the friend zone.

"So, he's available?" Mia sounded overexcited, staring at me with her perfect cat's-eye makeup.

I cleared my throat. "Look, I've said this a thousand times. Alex is my best friend. He has been since we were—"

"Five," Maggie interrupted, "when he made a bunch of boys at the park apologize for throwing a soccer ball at your head. You've said that story so many times, it's like it happened to me."

"Aw, that's sounds sooo Alex!" Mia sighed.

How could she know if she didn't really know him?

"Besides," Mia continued, "he's so hot with his tanned skin, curly hair, and big black eyes. *And* he plays the guitar."

Mia having a crush on Alex was new, but she had gotten all the details wrong. "His hair is only curly when he doesn't play with it, which is never. And his eyes are not black; they are more like chestnut color," I corrected her.

Immediately Alessandra's eyebrows went up and down, and I realized sharing that had been a mistake. They both laughed in a mocking way.

Alessandra looked back with a devilish smile. "Mia, why don't you date an exchange guy instead? It seems Marquez is *clearly* taken."

"So are the rumors true?" Mia asked, disappointed.

"What rumors?" I jumped in, annoyed.

"You know, that you and Marquez are secretly dating," Alessandra teased.

I rolled my eyes. Just because I spent a lot of time with a guy didn't mean we were a couple. "Why would people say that?"

The wick-pops stared at me like I was an alien. Then Alessandra said, "You don't seem to spend a minute apart from each other at school or anywhere else. You go to each and every one of his swimming competitions, even when they are out of state. And your T-shirt today is the ultimate proof."

My fingers were clasped into fists. I knew this ride would be boring, but it was unnecessary to make it so uncomfortable.

"I'll ask Alex if he wants to go to the party with you, Mia," I said before I could process the weight of my words.

Alessandra and Maggie opened their eyes wide, and Mia's grin was so big it went to both sides of her cheeks. Then she uncomfortably hugged me. I didn't know which was worse, her perfume rubbing all over my clothes or having to ask Alex if he wanted to date a wick-pop.

We stopped at the last traffic light before school. In just a couple of minutes, I could get out of the car and stay as far away from the wick-pops as possible. But once we entered the school's parking lot, I realized the line to enter was really long. No one other than me seemed to care. I just hoped the wick-pops wouldn't mention Alex again.

We finally found a spot, Maggie turned off the car and looked at Mia, "Can you make sure all the exchange guys get an invite to my party?"

I had no idea why she was so excited for the new guys, all she talked about now was Dane, the captain of the swim team. And last summer's exchange guy had left Maggie heartbroken. I guess the more guys, the better for all of them.

"Definitely," Mia said, holding Maggie's shoulder, "we'll make sure Dane is there too."

I took a deep breath, trying not to get annoyed by that. Before the wick-pops, Maggie and I were together all the time. But since she met them, I constantly fretted that Maggie would ditch me for them. They seemed to have more in common than she and I did.

We got out of the car, and Maggie turned to me. "You should have texted me *fashion emergency*. I could have brought you something," Maggie said in a more friendly tone. Deep under all those blonde highlights and makeup was my real friend.

"I didn't think of it," I lied politely. That might have worked back before our bodies had grown at different rates. In the hot-girl lottery, she had gotten a winning ticket with her green eyes, long blonde hair, and curves to die for. While I was . . . clearly not a winner. So her lending me clothes was not an option.

"Just promise me you'll find a date for my party." She stared at me with puppy eyes that were impossible to say no to. "If not, I can set you up on a blind date!" she said excitedly.

Not that again. I didn't feel ready to date, even less for a blind date. I knew it was her birthday party, and I couldn't miss it, but thinking of finding a date had already cost me enough sleep. Well, that and late reading.

"I promise," I said, thinking I'd do anything for her.

She hugged me tightly, and I enjoyed the jealous stare the wick-pops gave us.

As I walked toward my locker, I stared at different guys walking through the aisles of my high school. There wasn't a particular guy I liked to pick from the bunch. When it came to physical appearances or outfit choices, they were all over the place. Some preferred weird color combinations, or awful outfit choices like wearing white socks with black sandals. *It was a school, not the living room.* Others wore oversize T-shirts that almost reached their knees, giving away the unkempt vibe I hated. And the cherry on top were man buns. I hated man buns! I didn't mind a guy with long hair as long as it looked neat, but messy buns worked only for girls with long hair.

I tried to see beyond their appearance, avoiding the superficial. Some were absentmindedly staring at their phones as they walked. Some were playing football in the crowded aisles, bumping into other people. Others laughed so loud they snorted. I looked closer to focus on the details that were easy to miss. Like if they made eye contact, were kind, laughed often, or if they let other people speak. Perhaps then I could find something in common with another guy. But it was hard to find all that in a single person. Why did it have to be so hard!

Try to find one guy, any guy! I told myself. No one was reading or even talking about books. The bottom line was, no one seemed to actually pay attention to something other than themselves. I gave up, opened my locker, and focused on the pictures that decorated the inside of the door.

There were several images of libraries I wanted to visit around the world. Like the Old Library at Trinity College in Ireland and the George Peabody Library at Johns Hopkins University. I had a picture with my family. Marian was there, just before she left for her master's program. And in another, there was Haiku the day we adopted him from the animal shelter.

Next to an image of the inside of the Austrian National Library, in Vienna, was a portrait I had drawn for an assignment in art class. It was Romeo, or at least what I would imagine he looked like if he were a living person. He somehow resembled the guy from the 2013 movie of *Romeo & Juliet.* But mainly for the costume and hair style, because in my mind he was way more handsome than any actor I'd ever seen.

My whole life and aspirations were in that picture collage.

Even my favorite picture of the JAMs, what Alex, Maggie, and I used to call ourselves, using our initials. We were eating ice cream and sitting on a bench the summer I turned nine. The evening light filtered through the trees and made me squint, while Maggie's green eyes were wide open, her head tilted as she tried to lick her melting ice cream. Alex's wide smile went from ear to ear, his always messy hair blowing out of his face. It was hard to believe that once we were inseparable, and now Maggie and Alex's relationship could hardly be called a friendship.

As I stared at my favorite picture, I realized I had more than one problem. Not only did I have to ask Alex if he was up for a date with Mia, but if I wanted to avoid feeding the rumors, I would have to find someone else to go to the party with. How on earth was I going to do that? The only guy I liked to hang out with was Alex. Well, to be honest, Maggie and Alex were the only *people* I hung out with at school, and whenever both of them were busy, I had my books.

I sighed in frustration. I knew I was asking for too much to find someone like Romeo, but I couldn't help it. Before this stupid party, there was no rush to date, because I believed finding love shouldn't have an expiration date. Whoever was meant for me would come into my life at the right time. But this party's theme had messed everything up, and I roundly refused to have my first kiss with a stranger at one of the careless games of truth or dare that Maggie loved playing.

"Please, just be out there," I whispered to myself, staring down at my colorful sneakers, which always brought me joy. As I took a deep breath, a pair of untied shoelaces stood next to mine. Just by the subtle smell of chlorine that accompanied those shoes, I knew exactly who he was.

"How do you do it?" I asked Alex, still staring at his shoes. "I wear my shoelaces neatly tied, and I still trip once or twice a day, and look at yours!" I said, thinking of how he must trip all the time.

"It's just a hassle to have to tie and untie them, since I go to practice twice a day," Alex said.

I shook my head. "Unbelievable."

"Close your eyes. I have something for you," he said quickly before I could look up. "A package arrived at my house by mistake, I bet you are going to go wild about it."

"Alex, please don't tell me you're about to give me one of those super-spicy candies your family brings you from Mexico. Your obsession with them is too much," I said.

He laughed. "Open your hands."

A small package landed on my palms. It felt like a small cardboard box, definitely beaten by the long travel.

"You can look now," Alex said.

As soon as I saw the Australian stamp, I felt such an excitement that happy tears almost came out of my eyes. Seeing Marian's handwriting was like a warm hug I really needed.

"Thank you, Alex!" I smiled at him.

As I stared at the box, Alex said, "Thank you for your support today." He pointed at my shirt as he passed his hand through his frizzy hair, which added a few inches to his already enormous six feet two.

I closed the jacket as tight as I could. "I forgot to do laundry. I had literally nothing else to wear."

"Seriously? Again? You know, it's not rocket science. The machine does everything for you."

"Oh, shut up." I frowned, turning to my locker to get my books out. My clumsiness made several books fall, and my huge math book landed on top of my foot. *Ouch!*

"Perhaps that bag made your book fall?" Alex pointed at a crammed plastic bag that I hadn't noticed before.

I kept the Australian package in my backpack, since I wanted to open it calmly and not while rushing between classes. I took the bag out and browsed through its contents. Inside was a brand-new shirt, just like the ones I loved to wear, with literary references, and it was my size. This one read *Booktrovert: A person who prefers fictional characters rather than real people.* I didn't have to guess who had fixed my outfit disaster, and also who had my locker combination. I looked around to find Maggie to thank her among the crowd, but she was far away, hanging out with the soccer team girls. It was always like that. Maggie had a lot of friends, and I had a lot of books.

"Do you think we did well in algebra?" Alex asked anxiously.

"Oh, come on. Are you really stressing about math?" I asked, knowing that the lowest score he had ever gotten in anything math related was a B+.

"Well, maybe I'm hungry. Want a snack?" Alex patted his gym bag.

"Yeah, that's more like it," I said.

Even if Alex was second-generation Mexican American, it was funny how culturally he believed food to be the answer to every emotional issue. If he was stressed, anxious, tired, or angry, he ate. Luckily my metabolism could keep up with his enormous calorie intake.

Alex took out a container with trail mix clusters. I took one and was about to close my locker door when one of the wick-pops passed by. I had to ask Alex about Mia before the end of the day, or Maggie would say something about it.

"Have you found a date for the plus-one party?" I asked.

"The what?" he said with his mouth full.

"Maggie's party. The one we usually go to together each year but now makes everyone feel incredibly miserable for being single."

Alex raised an eyebrow. "What do you have in mind?"

"What are your thoughts about Mia?" I asked, looking away to avoid his reaction.

He kept quiet for a moment. "Wait, you want to set me up with one of your enemies?"

I tried to sound as normal as possible. "They're not *entirely* my enemies. What I'm trying to say is . . ."

"Did Will slap a book on your head while you were asleep again?"

"No," I said, offended. "It's just that people—"

"Since when do *we* care about what people say? If spending so much time with me bothers you, then I'll leave you alone."

His eyes gave his disappointment away, and I couldn't take it.

"No, Alex, I just . . . I'm sorry. I do like hanging out with you," I said, trying to reverse the damage. I had enough stress fretting Maggie would ignore me to lose my other best friend.

He pulled me closer and hugged me tight. "All good then," he said.

I could hear his heart beating, a nice sound. By now I was used to Latin people showing affection in a more physical way, and I had grown to like it. His big embrace had a soothing effect on me, which was one of the reasons why I loved being around him.

It was so weird to have such different people as my best friends. While Maggie was a social butterfly obsessed with meeting new people, Alex hung out with the same bunch and avoided crowds. While Maggie tried any new trend on social media, Alex called it *social stupidity*. And when it came to caring about people's opinions, she cared a lot, he couldn't care less, and I was somewhere in the middle.

"Marquez, guess what?" a familiar voice called, and he let go of me. Oliver, his best friend and swim teammate, approached.

"See you in class," Alex said as he walked away with Oliver.

The first bell rang, meaning we had five minutes left before the next class started. I sprinted to the nearest restroom to change my clothes before class.

I hung my backpack and denim jacket on the hook inside the bathroom stall. It felt liberating to change clothes, but as I did, my glasses and hair got stuck in the tight neckband of the T-shirt. Perhaps not taking my glasses off first had been a bad strategy, since they were pressing hard against my nose and making the lenses oily. I tried to pull the T-shirt off a little harder but got distracted when I heard someone say my name. I didn't recognize the voice at first, at least not with my eyes closed in a busy restroom. But as I tried to focus only on that sound, I recognized the wick-pops' voices.

"Trust me, she would never go on a blind date," Alessandra said, laughing softly. "Maggie says she might not go to the party because of her fear of dating."

I pulled my T-shirt down again and peeked through the small gap between the door and frame of the toilet stall. The wick-pops were reapplying makeup in the mirror.

"But she might go with Marquez like every year," Mia said.

"Didn't you see how odd she acted this morning? Whether the rumors are true or not, she doesn't want them to keep going. That's why I'm so sure they won't go to the plus-one together," Alessandra said as she brushed her hair with her fingers.

"That's good news for me and Marquez then," Mia added, applying cocoa-colored lipstick.

"If I were you, I would go for an exchange guy instead. You'll get to know all of them at the welcoming committee, and any of those guys would be way more fun." Alessandra smiled at her reflection in the mirror.

Something in their words stung. Maggie thinking I'd skip her birthday party was a crack on our friendship. Just the idea of wasting my time trapped for a couple of hours with a total stranger in a blind date, who I was sure would be totally incompatible with me, felt more like torture than fun. But she had pushed more than twice for me to go on one. I just never thought rejecting her blind date idea would bother her so much.

"Now that the loser-June subject is taken care of, let's think how we are going to set Dane and Maggie up." Alessandra turned around, facing Mia, and I drew back.

The second bell rang, and the wick-pops left. I suddenly felt cold, like a sadness had taken over me. The same kind of sadness I felt when we dropped Marian off at the airport and I realized our relationship would never be the same. Marian would always be my sister, but Maggie didn't always have to be my best friend. Friendship was a choice in which both parts made an unspoken agreement to try to meet in the middle.

I texted Maggie right away. First, I thanked her for coming to my rescue with a new shirt. Then I typed the words I never thought I would write.

> A blind date sounds intriguing and fun, set
> it up.

At first a heart emoji appeared as a reply to my message, but within seconds my entire screen was filled with excited smiley emoji and clapping GIFs. I was scared about what I had agreed to, but I was not going down against the wick-pops without a fight.

Perhaps my heart hadn't really healed from Marian's departure, because I felt the same haunting loneliness all over again. Maybe with a little luck, dating wouldn't be as bad as I imagined. I just couldn't lose Maggie, and I'd rather go on a million blind dates than risk losing my best friend.

After the stressful info dump, I was looking forward to a distracting and complicated algebra class. But like most classes at the end of the school year, it was mostly about keeping the students busy with an easy activity or movie, while the teachers finished with our grades.

Today it was free time, which I really didn't want. Mrs. Cole was busy switching her gaze between her computer screen and the binder on her desk. My anxiety was rising, and I needed something to keep my mind from obsessing about the wick-pops and the blind date.

Alex, who sat in front of me, was too immersed exchanging soccer stamps with Oliver to notice anyone or anything else around him. I never understood why guys were so obsessed about collecting stamps with the faces of other guys. I mean, they were the best players of every country, but still.

I was familiar with all of that because every fourth summer, Dad would obsess about collecting the World Cup album. Once I no longer cared about it, Will took over and filled it during the months before the tournament. Soccer was a huge thing at my house, and we even got together often with Alex's family to watch the games. Will's, Dad's, and Alex's passion for the World Cup made my *Romeo and Juliet* obsession look like a fling.

Today it had worked out for me, because the last thing I needed was for Alex to see right through me and ask why I was so nervous. I knew I didn't have the mental peace to focus on reading, but as I went through my backpack, I found Marian's package. That was the perfect distraction.

I opened the box and found a cute handkerchief with koalas stamped all over it. I carefully unwrapped the handkerchief and discovered the smallest book I'd ever held. It fit in the palm of my hand, and it seemed as if the pages were actually readable, not like those miniatures that are impossible to read without a magnifying glass. The beaten cover gave its age away. It was clearly a secondhand book with no title on its spine or cover.

I opened the book and looked for the title page, sighing in surprise when I saw its title. It was the most adorable pocket edition of *Romeo and Juliet*. I had no idea how Marian had come to find such a treasure, but I could imagine her excited shriek as she danced in triumph. From now on, I would carry it with me always, as if I had a piece of Marian with me wherever I went.

On the first page I found a handwritten message from her on a sticky note.

> While you are waiting for Romeo, at least have fun hanging out with the Mercutios and Benvolios of the world.
> Love, M.

I pulled the note off the book and kept it in my wallet. Marian had always said that I wasted too much time dreaming about the perfect book guy without actually living life. The blind date still freaked me out, but somehow Marian's message helped me feel more at ease. Maybe this was a sign that it was the right time to break out of my shell.

"Hey, you changed your shirt!" Alex surprised me when he turned around, making me drop my book to the floor. It landed right by Oliver's backpack.

Oliver picked it up. "What is this?"

"An early birthday present from my sister," I said.

"By the look on your face I would say it's something related to Romeo," Alex mocked. "Am I right?"

I nodded excitedly.

"Oh, the famous Romeo," Oliver said, handing me my book back.

Alex blew the hair off his face. "When it comes to Romeo, there is no way to compete against him." Both guys laughed.

"What's that supposed to mean?" I asked.

"Last Euro Cup, two years ago, the final game," Alex narrated. "We were all in your living room, feeling the suspense.

Portugal earned a free kick against France. The ball hit the crossbar, went down, and bounced away. Even with all the screaming and shouting going on, you didn't even flinch."

"Not even once," Oliver added.

Perhaps they had a point. If Romeo was there in print form or in my mind, I would have definitely zoned out and ignored everything else.

"I have some news," Alex said excitedly.

I looked at him, raising an eyebrow, waiting. Then I stared at his eyes. I was right before. They were chestnut.

"I'm going to play at my parents' restaurant the last Saturday in June," he added with a big bright smile.

My eyes widened. "No way. Are you serious? That's amazing!" I squeezed his arm. "Wait, how did you get your dad to agree?"

Alex's dad was bluntly against him wasting his time being a musician. According to him, it was the straight road toward disappointment, failure, and starvation.

"Well, getting into Arthsteen University's summer swim program made him change his mind," he said, confident. "Or perhaps my mom had something to do with it, but anyway, it's one step closer to getting a scholarship there for college."

The information overload kept coming my way, and I thought the last days of school were supposed to be boring. His summer swimming program was the reason Alex was going to be gone all summer. But at least his gig would be a good enough reason for him to come back for a weekend.

"Your summer seems to be getting better and better." I tried to sound happy for him, but I couldn't help feeling like my summer was going to be the worst.

Alex and I had never spent so much time without seeing each other. His annual family trip to a Mexican beach usually lasted less than two weeks, but this was going to be all summer. And I doubted Alex would be aware of his phone while he spent so much time swimming and getting to know new people. The one thing that was supposed to help me stay afloat was my library internship, but now, with Nora, it didn't sound as fun as before.

"When are you leaving?" I asked, not really wanting to know.

"Sunday, the day after the party," he said, trying to seem disappointed but failing at it.

It felt as if I was losing my friends one at a time. Marian had been gone for over a month, and that hadn't been enough time for me to get used to her absence. Maggie seemed to be moving farther and farther away from me with the help of the wick-pops, and now Alex. I didn't know how to show authentic excitement for him when my upcoming months were going to be so lonely.

Perhaps Alex noticed my change in mood, because he said, "I'm going to try to come back as often as I can."

I laughed. "We both know that's not going to happen. Arthsteen U is four hours just one way," I said, imagining all the great bonding activities the university was going to have for them. The past hours of my life felt as if a bucket of ice-cold water had fallen over me.

"There are some important things I don't want to be away from this summer." His reassuring tone created more confusion.

Before I had a chance to ask what he meant, Oliver jumped in. "Your fan at three o'clock," Oliver pointed his head to the right making us all look in that direction.

Nichole Kim, who was part of the swim team too, was staring at Alex. Oliver and Alex mumbled something I didn't get. They exchanged a look that was impossible to read. Whenever I hung out with them, I barely had a clue about what was going on.

"What are those *important things* you want to come back to? Did something happen between you and Nichole?" I was getting upset. I had no idea why Oliver had to point out that Nichole was looking our way. It was no secret that she stared at Alex in every class they had together, since she'd had a major crush on him for a while now.

"No, why would you say that?" Alex asked, as if I had offended him. "I was talking about my brother Edgar. He's learning how to drive during the summer, and I want to be there for him." Alex looked nervous. "Besides, I don't want to be away from my family that much."

"Yeah, right." I was not buying it. I knew Alex was close with his fourteen-year-old brother, but Alex's parents had sent both their boys to driving school to avoid any family fights. And Alex had mentioned how sometimes he needed a break from his family because Latin families could be kind of intense. There was something else he didn't want to tell me. He stared at me with nothing to say. He wasn't making any sense. People said women were complicated, but guys were not far off.

Oliver hit Alex softly on the shoulder. "Marquez, look!" He was raising a soccer stamp.

Alex stared at it and then back at Oliver. He acted as confused as before.

"Another Spanish goalkeeper," Oliver said in a silly tone, and this time Alex nodded and looked down at his soccer album.

I tried to ignore them. Perhaps it was their prolonged exposure to chlorine. I had a lot on my plate to obsess about their weird behavior. I've learned over time that guys were like a different species, and I never truly knew what was going on inside their minds. My anxiety came back when I realized Maggie had texted me.

> Everything is set for your date on Saturday.
> He's super excited to meet you ;)

My heart stopped. Now it was really going to happen. I was going to have my first date ever with a real guy, not a fictional one made of paper and ink. That thought made my stomach churn. I wanted to scream out my anxiety, but it was impossible.

I tried to calm myself, even as my mind wandered from regret to hesitation. Maybe this was what Marian meant by meeting the Mercutios of the world. It was Maggie's friend, after all, so he couldn't be far off from her. Or could he? Maybe with a little bit of luck, it would be fun.

"June?" Alex looked at me.

I stared at him for what felt like forever. Perhaps he had asked me something and I had totally zoned out. There was so much going on in my head.

"You OK?" he asked, raising an eyebrow.

Oh no, he could tell. "I was just thinking about how Nichole is really not your type," I said, trying to change the topic.

Alex seemed confused, since my comment had come out of nowhere.

"Your mom wants you to date a Latin girl, right?" I asked.

Alex nodded.

"Nichole's mom is Colombian, and her dad is of Asian descent," Oliver added. "I don't know if that makes her fit the description."

"I knew that," I lied. No wonder she tanned so nicely during summer. "Anyway, I know you very well, Alex. I'd dare to say I can read you like a book. Well, except when you are underwater —that tends to block my abilities."

The guys laughed. At least, it seemed I was trying to be funny.

I tried to calm down since my signature way of showing my anxiety was by talking faster than normal. "Forget I said that, water and books is not a good combo." *June, stop talking!* I told myself.

"You'll be there, right?" Alex asked. "At El Marqués when I play?"

I nodded, trying to hide any trace of my nerves. "I'll shout and fangirl all over you."

He moved his messy hair to one side and stared at me. "You

don't have to go all the way, you know? I know how much you hate being in the spotlight, and the crowd at El Marqués can get pretty wild," he said in a more serious tone.

I weakly smiled at him, breathing slowly to calm my racing heart. I looked down at my pocket edition to dissimulate. Perhaps if I kept my nose stuck in a book, everything would be OK.

"I wouldn't miss it for the world," I said looking up and then back to my book.

CHAPTER 3

THE ENGLISH ACCENT

The sound of the motorized blinds rolling up at the public library made me look up from my book. The sun was setting and almost gone. It was a nice interruption, since my neck was getting stiff and my eyes were drying out. Reading while standing next to the shelving cart and underneath the air vent had not been a good idea. The morning had been overwhelming, but the evening had turned around, mainly because I had time to read. If it wasn't for the blinds rolling down at sunset, I'd have no clue what time it was. That was one of the coolest things about reading—time passed at a different rate. It made you forget, and that was magical.

Staying until closing time had not been as bad as I had imagined. I would prefer to be home, sitting comfortably, wearing my cozy pajamas at this time of the evening, but at least I had undivided time to read while I reshelved books.

I had almost finished *Tristan and Isolde* and their pain felt like my own. I imagined how awful it must be to know you could never have someone you loved and who also loved you back. I took a deep breath, hoping the despair would go away, and left the book on the upper part of the cart as I pushed it around the aisles.

I had leaned down to organize a bunch of fallen books from the lower shelf when I heard the sound of heavy footsteps coming my way. I expected to see Nora or someone running around in the Adult Fiction aisle, but there was no one. Then I heard a murmur that didn't resemble Nora's high pitch, but perhaps it was a patron looking for help. I stood up and looked around again. I must have imagined it. Sometimes the acoustics were off around here.

When I went to shelve some books, a pair of green eyes stared back at me through the opening between spines. I startled and dropped the books. Even if those eyes were a gorgeous olive tone, they scared the crap out of me. I tried not to step on the books on the floor but stumbled and grabbed the first thing I could, which was the book cart. It hit the closest bookshelf, and books fell over me like a waterfall—at least they were all soft paperbacks.

I heard the heavy footsteps again, but I knew who they belonged to now. I stood up, angry and sore, pushing the books away from me. I looked through the aisles, but I couldn't find anyone. I knew I had not imagined it. I knew books couldn't talk. We were the ones who gave them a voice. When they talked by themselves, they were called audiobooks.

I heard Nora's voice over the library speakers, saying the library would be closing in thirty minutes. I expected someone to run out from the aisles, but there was no movement around me. Now I had more books to organize, and I was getting cold, even while wearing my scarf. That meant the library must be almost empty.

I picked up the books from the floor but felt as if someone was watching me. This was turning into a thriller rather than the romance story I had dreamed of having while working at this library. I placed another book in the middle shelf, and I saw the same pair of olive eyes staring back at me. But this time I didn't move an inch. I'd seen eyes of all colors in my life, but these took my breath away. I couldn't stop staring, not only because I wanted to see who they belonged to, but because I wanted to stare at them forever.

I had to stop this person. I was not going to play games. Especially if it involved working extra. I turned toward the cart for a second, thinking maybe I could use it to block his way, but I heard the same heavy footsteps. The eyes that had stared at me through the bookshelves were gone.

I turned around and saw a guy standing at the end of the aisle. He gave me a peculiar look but still had the boldness to approach me one step at a time. Without thinking, I grabbed the only thing I had handy, the *Tristan and Isolde* hardcover copy. I held it in front of me as the only self-defense weapon I could come up with. If he came any closer, I would throw it at him. He stared at the book, confused, and his expression went from confusion to panic. Then he took off. Apparently hardcover copies were threatening as self-defense weapons, at least to him. Thankfully, for the sake of this pretty edition, I didn't have to use it.

He was heading toward the wall instead of the stairs. I did the same, trying to corner him. If he wanted to escape, he'd have to run past me. It was the only time I was grateful for my skinny genes. Since I was thin, I was good with speed but not endurance.

He must have noticed, because he stopped in the next aisle. He stood still as a statue right in front of me. This time I was not distracted by his eyes but by his attire, which was really odd. He was taller than me and wore tight dark-blue pants with knee-length leather boots. He wore a lace-up ivory shirt underneath some sort of thick tapestry jacket. With that heavy jacket and long sleeves, I was sure he was also cold at libraries. His outfit reminded me more of a medieval costume than anything trendy. But perhaps Maggie knew more about the latest trends.

Apart from his odd outfit, he was the most handsome guy I've ever seen. He seemed right out of a dream, with his fine cheekbones and full lips. His dark-brown hair stopped just above his shoulders. It was wavy but neatly arranged.

I shook my head, trying to focus. "You scared me. Didn't you hear the library is about to close?" A hint of despair escaped through my voice. After looking into his eyes, I knew what *weak in the knees* felt like. He was clearly not from here, and the only thing I could think of, since he looked my age, was that he must be one of the famous exchange students who apparently had just finished drama club rehearsal.

His side-swept bangs swayed over his forehead as he glanced both ways for an escape route. He looked lost and disoriented. Perhaps my interest in catching him had been a little too much for him. An inexplicable feeling grew inside me, like I didn't want him to leave. They say you get more bees with honey than vinegar, and perhaps if I took a gentler approach, he would stop running away from me.

"Where are you from?" I asked in a soft voice.

He only stared at me with his hypnotizing olive eyes.

"What's your name?" I tried again. Perhaps that was a much nicer way to start a conversation.

He stared at my hand. I was still holding the book. Not by my side like a normal person but between us as if it was some sort of barrier. Why did I have to act like such a dork around cute guys? I gave him an awkward smile and set the book on the closest shelf.

Perhaps not holding something in front of him had helped, because he seemed calmer and took a step closer. Thanks to Tyler, I had learned to keep my distance from any guy I met at the library, even one as cute as this one. Before he could get any closer, I put out my hand for him. "I'm June." I hoped my introduction was enough to break the ice. But by his peculiar choice of outfit, I assumed he liked formalities.

"Tristan," he finally said. Even with a single word, I picked up a unique accent. But one word was not enough for me to guess where he was from.

He took two steps closer to me, my hand still in the air. He held my hand, but instead of shaking it, like I thought he would, he gently twisted it and kissed the top of it as he bowed.

"A pleasure, Lady June." His words were the most harmonic sound I'd ever heard. His gorgeous olive eyes had struck me first like lightning, and his voice followed like thunder.

My hands were sweaty. My breathing accelerated. I could not think straight. There was something soothing about no longer playing cat and mouse with him. I didn't want to rush to make assumptions. Perhaps he was not even an exchange guy; maybe he was an actor. I've heard the Renaissance Faire was in town.

We stared at each other as if time stood still. He gave me a subtle smile, and I no longer could remember my own name. I was not cold, not anymore. If anything, I felt as if I were next to the furnace at full power on a cold winter night.

Nora announced through the speakers that the library would be closing in fifteen minutes. Startled by the sound, he looked around, frowning at the lights on the ceiling. Perhaps he didn't know where the sound had come from. He took off and ran past me, heading down the stairs.

Damn it! I had been fooled by his charm, and now he was running away again. Without hesitation I ran after him, even with the whole mess of the books lying on the floor. It was the one and only time I had preferred a guy over books. As I got to the stairs, I saw him going into the lobby and out of the building, toward the parking lot.

I reached the parking lot and ran after him as fast as I could, but he was so much farther ahead—until he stopped and fell as if he had hit something. It was a weird fall, because I couldn't tell what had caused it. Maybe he had tripped over something. He was too far ahead for me to see.

"Hey!" I said as I finally caught up with him. "You gotta stop running away from me."

I was out of breath. He didn't get up but stayed facedown on the pavement. "Are you hurt?"

As I knelt, getting closer to him, I realized he was crying and was covering his eyes, trying to hide it. I was definitely not familiar with guys who were older than Will and cried inconsolably.

"Are you OK? Can I call somebody for you?" I asked, concerned about my newly found crush. "I promise I'm not going to hurt you."

I looked up and saw a car moving through the parking lot. It was not safe for us to be here. The lampposts weren't bright enough.

"Can you stand? We'd be safer if we sat in the library's garden. It might even help you relax."

I had no idea what to do, but sometimes when I felt truly overwhelmed, I came to the library garden and soaked in the beauty of the seasonal plants and flowers. Even at night it was pretty, since it had landscape lights.

He nodded and stood up, wiping his tears with his thick jacket. That fabric must be really rough for his smooth skin. We entered the library garden and sat on a bench. I took out the pocket edition from the pocket of my jeans and unwrapped the koala handkerchief that covered it. I handed it over to him, and he took it without hesitation. Whenever Will was sad after losing a soccer game, I used to comfort him by patting him on the back, so I tried to do the same. He didn't seem to mind.

Then he took a deep breath and cried even harder. *"Niente ha senso, non so chi o dove sono,"* he said, sobbing.

Even though I had no clue what he'd just said, a guy talking in another language turned out to have a noticeable effect on me.

I wanted to ask where he was from, but I didn't want to overwhelm him. I tried to keep my cool and focus on helping him feel better. Perhaps he was an exchange student experiencing a homesick episode.

It reminded me of Marian during the first weeks after arriving in Australia. She'd called me several times a day, wondering if she'd made the right choice by moving thousands of miles away, but I always remained silent. I was not going to beg her to come home, even though I had desperately wanted to. A couple of days later she'd adapted and become obsessed with the Aussie life, especially since she had a local friend who showed her around town.

Maybe Tristan was feeling the same, and if he was OK with it, I could show him around too. I was sure the exchange program committee would take them to the typical tourist places, but maybe I could show him the small-town experience I heard everyone wanted.

"It's OK to miss home." I tried to sound reassuring, but it didn't make him stop crying. "Try to match your breathing with mine," I said as I inhaled slowly and exhaled even more so.

At first he didn't look at me or utter a word, but I kept doing it. He uncovered his eyes and stared at me. The koala handkerchief was soaking wet, but at least no more tears were coming. He stared at my mouth as I exhaled and eventually matched his breathing to mine.

"Are you better now, Tristan?" I asked.

He nodded, the corner of his lips turning up. He blew his nose in the handkerchief, then looked from it to me.

"You can return it later," I said, not wanting to touch it.

"I am in eternal debt to your kindness, milady." He moved to one knee and took my hand to kiss it again.

My cheeks couldn't take that much heat. "You don't have to . . . do all that," I said, nervously hoping he would get up.

He bowed his head in acknowledgment and sat back next to

me. Usually exchange students had unmistakable accents. But he spoke English perfectly, and his British accent was more charming than any actor I'd ever admired.

"I have to go back inside and help close the library. Would you like to come with me?" I asked, trying to sound friendly.

He stared, hesitant.

"There's new fish in the fish tank over in the kids' area. They just arrived a couple of days ago." I felt like the lamest person ever. What was I thinking? Fish? Now I would have to come up with something smart to say about them so I wouldn't look stupid. Underwater creatures were far from my area of expertise.

He laughed and gave me a tiny hint of a smile, and I was melting for him again. It was as if my brain couldn't focus while I was around him.

"After you, milady," he said, standing up.

It was such a relief. Maybe fish weren't as lame as I thought.

Once we were inside the lobby, we crossed the automatic doors. I stepped inside the library and realized I had lost Tristan. I looked back and saw he was standing just behind the automatic doors.

"It's this way," I said, hoping he still found the fish tank exciting.

He stared suspiciously at the doors, then took a step back, and they closed. He took a step forward, and they opened again. I would expect this from a toddler, not a teenage guy. It was a silly thing, but he seemed perplexed and entertained at the same time. I wondered if he lived in a very old European town where everything was quaint and small, and big technological buildings were not a thing. I'd heard people say everything was bigger and more modern in America.

He finally came in, and the doors closed behind him, which made him jump. It was such a funny and odd thing to watch. I didn't have to point him to the fish tank, because he ran like a little kid and stared at it closely.

"Just don't tap on the glass. It freaks them out," I said, feeling stupid for the reminder. He put his hands behind his back. Hopefully he wouldn't ask anything about fish. "I have to go to the back for my things; then I have to quickly go all over the library to check that no one stays inside." I spoke without fully understanding why I had to enumerate everything I had to do to a guy I just met.

He nodded but remained hypnotized, following the fish's trajectory. I expected him to say something, anything, but he didn't.

I went to the back to grab my things. As soon as I turned around, I bumped into someone, which almost made me fall. But I didn't, since he was holding my arm and time stopped. When Tristan was around me, the seconds moved so slow. Almost as if they were going backward.

"Hi." I stared at his beautiful olive eyes, which blinked repeatedly at me.

Nora's voice came through the speakers: "The library is now closed. Please take any items you wish to borrow to the closest checkout desk."

Tristan let go of me and looked around him, unsure where the speaker was.

"It's there." I pointed at the speaker on the closest corner, then moved around him. "I have to finish working."

"Shall I accompany thee?" His British accent melted me. "A righteous lady like yourself shouldn't be unescorted."

"What?" I tried not to laugh. But when I realized he was not joking, I had to bite my cheeks. Perhaps he was into old-fashioned manners, or maybe he was playing a character from one of Jane Austen's novels in his drama club.

"Milady, I understand if you must not trust the hand of a stranger. However, I can assure you, I will do no harm," he said.

I nervously played with my hair, since his words seemed to cast some sort of spell on me. I cleared my throat. "You can come with me if you want. I just have to check all around, starting from the top." I pointed at the elevator.

He looked at it and then back at me. "I prefer the stairs, milady. By far a better option, don't you think?" he said, already heading in that direction.

I tried to catch up with him, but he seemed to be much more agile than me. I considered myself fit, since I rode my bike almost every day, but his conditioning was way better. He was all the way up by the time I reached the second floor.

Once I caught up with him, he looked at me. "Lead the way, milady." He moved away to let me pass first.

We walked together through every aisle and checked every study room in silence. I wanted to know more about him, but he remained quiet, smiling back at me only when I stared.

"So tell me, what's your story?" I finally asked as we opened the door for the quiet lounge to check inside.

He put his finger over his lips, pointing at the Quiet Lounge sign. I felt my insides get jittery. Any normal guy wouldn't even bother about that, but he cared.

Once we were far away from the quiet lounge, he said, "Any guesses?"

"Well, I think you're obviously an exchange student from my school's exchange program."

He raised his eyebrows, unimpressed. Maybe he expected more than the obvious.

"OK, you picked Storybridge High because you wanted to get the small-town experience, like in the movies. I'm guessing you are from somewhere in Europe, but I have trouble placing you for your accent, since it doesn't go unnoticed. Maybe somewhere in the UK?" I hoped my elaborate guess had been enough.

He smiled and I blushed. It looked like he wanted me to keep going.

"Maybe your parents are from different countries, or have

spent several years living in different places. Your outfit tells me you clearly love theater or are part of some drama club. Or maybe you got it at the Renaissance Faire in town?" I said, feeling proud of my guesses.

I had seen all sorts of people at this library, but his costume seemed the most authentic.

"Am I close?" I asked, desperate for an answer, since his expression was unreadable.

Finally he nodded. It was so hard getting more than a sentence out of him. But apparently he didn't need to say much for me to get it right.

As we headed toward the Adult Fiction area, he stopped. "May I ask you something, milady?"

"Ask away," I said, hoping to hear his charming voice longer.

"Why are there pictures of tree houses all over the walls?" He was a good observer.

"Come and see."

I walked to the window closest to my lime chair and pointed at the glass. He came closer, and for the first time I noticed his scent. He smelled a little like leather with some old spices. I could stupidly say he smelled sort of like some old books, but it couldn't be. I guessed I just couldn't figure it out.

"If you look closely, you can see a bunch of wooden boards, very old and almost rotten," I said, pressing my nose against the window and blocking out the indoor light with my hands.

He imitated me.

I stepped away from the glass to explain. "In between the full foliage of that red oak tree, you'll find an old tree house. It used to be a playground for kids at this library until one day a kid fell and broke an arm. They had to close it, but since people were very attached to it, they turned it into the icon of the library."

He squinted, his nose pressed against the glass.

"So you see tree houses all over the library because of that one," I said, thinking of all the fun times I'd had as a kid there.

"Have you gone up since, milady?" he asked, stepping away from the glass.

I shook my head. Perhaps that made me sound boring, but when it came to this library, I was pretty much set on following the rules of my favorite place.

"What do you think you are doing?" Nora's voice came from behind, making us jump.

"I've been looking everywhere for you. I thought you might be checking that the library was empty, but apparently I was very wrong." Nora stared at Tristan.

"I . . . I was doing just that," I stuttered, trying to sound serious.

Nora didn't look convinced. "Look, I'm not going to chase you around the library. It's your responsibility to do a good job. And unless you do so, you won't have a letter of recommendation." She crossed her arms. "Now go fix the mess you left upstairs around the shelving cart."

A mix of anger, anxiety, and panic swirled inside me as I realized my letter might depend on her. Perhaps I had left some books all over the place, but besides that, I had worked harder than any other young person at this library. I was here even though her punishment of closing the library was past my work hours.

I was about to go fix my mess when she stopped me.

"The books meant for reshelving will have to wait until tomorrow. There's no more time today. Just make it look neat, like a library should look like."

Without glancing at Tristan, I walked toward the abandoned book cart I had left behind.

"Didn't you hear the library is now closed?" I heard Nora telling Tristan.

I thought I would have the opportunity to say goodbye to Tristan, but Nora had ruined any chance to learn how I could see him again.

I rearranged the fallen books, grabbed my copy of *Tristan and Isolde*, and headed for the main door. It was past closing time.

"What is he doing?" Nora asked when I was on my way out.

I turned to look her way and saw Tristan walking underneath the AC vent, his hair blowing in his face. I felt hope, and I wanted to ask him if we could meet at the library some other time, until I realized he was playing. He'd step under the AC airflow, his hair flying away. He'd step out of it and rearrange his hair. Then he did it over and over again.

He was cute, but he didn't look as smart as I'd thought while doing that.

"Make him stop, please," Nora said. "But be polite. He's a patron."

Ugh. She just couldn't let the incident with Tyler go.

I walked toward him and tried to pull him away from the vent. "Now is not the time to play games. The library is closed."

He stared at me, confused, and refused to move.

"Tristan, please stop. Whatever character you are playing, which is an unbelievable performance," I added politely, "has to take a break."

Tristan still looked confused. He nodded but didn't move. Perhaps he was still on another time zone, and jet lag had hit him hard.

I turned to Nora. "He's being a little silly." I tried to cover for him, but he wasn't making it easy. "He's not from here, some small town in the UK, I think," I added, and stepped closer to him.

"You have to leave," I whispered.

He nodded and stood back. At least I knew how to talk to him, since he was a true theater fanatic.

"With that, I bid you ladies a good night," he said and bowed with his whole body, then walked out the door. I had again missed the chance to ask if we could meet sometime soon.

As I headed out, I saw him take a turn behind the library and disappear into the night. Maybe if he was a book nerd like me, I'd see him again. But one thing was certain—he was a solid nine on my cute scale, and no other real guy had ever come so close to my Romeo.

CHAPTER 4

THE BILINGUAL GUITAR

Saturday had come faster than I anticipated. I checked the time on my favorite watch, the one Mrs. Lib had given me for my last birthday. It was a simple mechanical wristwatch. I've never cared for watches that supposedly were smarter than me.

The watch face had an open book with the inscription *"Once upon a time . . ."* and delicate yellow hands. It amazed me how a simple opening line held infinite possibilities. Now that the blind date was only two hours away, I hoped that at least the tiniest part of this date would live up to my expectations. Because so far I felt like the upcoming hours before meeting the guy were the most nerve-racking of my life. Maggie had also promised a makeover, and that freaked me out too.

I grabbed my things and locked the door of my empty house behind me. Maggie had just texted that she was running a little late, which was unusual, but I had to get out of my house, or my nerves would become unbearable. Marian was in another time zone, and Mom had taken Haiku to his vet checkup, so I couldn't dump my anxiety on anyone else.

I considered running away and not showing up to this date,

but I had no believable excuse on a Saturday. Since my hands were shaking from the nerves, I took a deep breath and reminded myself the real reason I was going through all of this. Maggie meant the world to me, and that was a big enough reason.

I sat down at the creaky front steps of my porch. I tried to untangle the cord of my headphones, wondering if a song could help me calm down. I could probably get wireless ones, but then I would have only one, because that was the kind of person I was when it came to tiny things that came in pairs. I was also not very good with earrings, but at least they were supposed to stay put.

Before I could connect the earphones to my phone, I heard music. It wasn't hard to guess where it could be coming from. Someone who happened to live two houses down the street loved music more than anything else in the world. I stood up, peeking above the bushes at the end of our yard, and found Alex playing on his front porch.

Listening to him play was soothing, even hypnotizing. I never understood why his dad was so against it. When he sang, I would forget everything around me. He played with such passion that I was sure he belonged on a stage, not in a swimming pool.

I walked toward him and stood by the bushes under his porch. I thought he would see me right away, but he was so immersed in his music, his eyes closed, that even if I had flashing lights on me, like a fire truck, he still wouldn't notice me. His head swayed along with his hair. He was a rock star in the making. He was even wearing the dark-green T-shirt I had given him for his last birthday. It had a grid with four dots, representing the F chord, and it had a guitar under it that seemed to make the letter U. I'd bought it before realizing what it actually said, but it ended up being his favorite T-shirt.

His hand stopped over the strings, and he sang a cappella with so much intensity that I felt chills. That happened only when I read a really good spooky story. I couldn't understand much since he was singing in Spanish, but I felt the pain of the song. When Alex stopped, I clapped and cheered like a fan at a concert, and Alex jumped out of his seat.

"How long have you been listening?" he asked.

"Long enough." I smiled. "This one sounds like a strong contender for your gig. Have you already thought of a set playlist?"

He gave me a side smile. "Still working on it. Have you ever heard this song before? It's an old one," he said, scooting to the side, making room for me to sit.

I shook my head, sitting next to him. "It doesn't matter how much time I spend with your family. I don't understand enough Spanish to know what a song says."

"Well, if you like it, I'll add it to the playlist then."

"How many are you going to play?" I grabbed his guitar, pretending I was a rock star too.

He laughed. "I'm planning on playing twenty hits that my parents asked me to play and ten songs of my choice. I think I can play almost all of them by heart, but I want to push myself and see if I can add a few more."

"That's a lot, isn't it?" I asked, unsure.

"I guess it's like you with your annual book count. You read over a hundred books a year like it's no big deal."

I felt proud and was shocked that he'd kept up with my book count. "If I'm completely honest, I'm kind of jealous," I confessed. "Being bilingual means the things you have access to multiply. Like, I could read the original novels instead of losing precious details in the translation."

He passed his hand through his messy hair. "I never really thought about how cool it was to know more than one language. But you're right. I can find some cool songs that say exactly what I mean and are not in English." He took his guitar back. "I have even found words that have no translation."

He played some chords. "That's the cool thing about music. You don't have to understand it to feel it."

"It'd be nice to be able to know the message," I added.

"Feelings are not restricted to one language, you know? A song is a message or a feeling that needs to be let out, despite the language." His dark eyes beamed just the way they always did when he talked about things he was truly passionate about.

"Now you are talking like Mr. Grooms," I mocked.

"Languages are the key to human understanding." He imitated Mr. Grooms, our literature teacher, talking in class, and we both laughed.

He blew the hair out of his face. "Miguel de Cervantes once said, 'There's a phrase somewhere in a book, waiting to give meaning to our existence.'"

My eyes opened wide. Now he was talking my language.

"I recently found a song that says exactly what I feel. Can I play it for you?"

I nodded, getting comfortable.

He cleared his throat and placed his fingers over the fretboard. If only his confidence was contagious. I could never look that comfortable in the spotlight. His voice started sweet and slow and then grew deeper. I had no idea what he was talking about, since it was in Spanish, too, but he was right. I could get a sense of what it was about.

Maybe he had a point—songs were some sort of poetry. Perhaps we were both poetry fans, just in different formats. I liked them in prose, and he preferred them in verse.

As he played, I got lost in his voice. Then he looked at me through the strands of his messy hair as he swayed with the melody.

I got goose bumps again, and I remembered why I had a crush on him once. There was something hot about a guy singing and playing a guitar. I stared at his eyes and felt as if he was singing the song to me. But then he made a mistake in a chord, and I looked away. Perhaps on stage he could be blinded by the lights, but here in front of me might be too much pressure on him.

Once the song was over, I looked up. "That was breathtaking. Are you sure you didn't write it? 'Cause it somehow feels like you did."

"Nah, I'm just covering the song in my own way. I'm more of a singer, not a songwriter." He moved his guitar away, resting it on his foot.

"You could totally write your own songs. I'm sure you'd be great at it."

He didn't seem quite sure. "I think I'll focus on enjoying music from different Spanish-speaking countries instead. Did you know you can totally know which country the singer is from by the way they pronounce certain letters or words?" he said excitedly, but then he lost me again. Sometimes he got carried away and talked about Spanish as if I could actually understand what he meant.

"Not bad, Marquez, not bad." Maggie's voice made us both jump off our seats. Fortunately Alex was holding on tight to his guitar.

"You scared us, Maggie," I said with a nervous laugh.

"I couldn't pass up the chance." Maggie gave me a devilish smile. "Thinking about anyone in particular when you sang that song, Marquez?"

"No . . . n-no one." Alex looked away from us and stared at his guitar. "No one in particular. I was just practicing to see if this song makes the cut for my live gig."

"I think it was great. You should include it in the final playlist." I tried to help Alex out. "It's kind of romantic."

"Uh-huh, just what I was thinking." Maggie squinted at Alex, then turned to me. "I don't mean to crash on your *rendezvous*, but we need to go. You don't want to be late for your date."

Alex's expression changed completely. "I still don't know how you managed to get her to agree to that," he mumbled.

Maggie raised her chin. "Jealous, Marquez?"

Alex shook his head. "Me? Nah, I'm just not the type of person to push my friends to do something they don't want to."

I could feel the tension rising between them, and I was afraid they'd get into another of their heated arguments where I suddenly became invisible.

"No one is forcing anyone," Maggie said angrily. "June is willing to go outside of her comfort zone to get a date for my party. Something perhaps you are too scared to try."

All the confidence he had when he was playing disappeared, replaced by the anxious Alex I was more familiar with. "Going together is our thing, every ye-year," Alex stuttered. "Why do you want to change that?"

Maggie took one step closer, leaning toward Alex. "Let me remind you of one tiny detail. I want *romantic* couples at my party, not just any pairs." Maggie pointed at both of us. "You two are not a couple, unless you want to confirm the rumors everyone has been saying about you."

Alex looked at me. I covered my face with my hand as I shook my head. Having to dismiss the rumors was becoming irritating. Besides, in recent months, if Maggie and Alex would get into an argument, it was impossible for me to stop them. I just hoped this time I could stay out of it.

Maggie crossed her arms, waiting for an answer, but Alex remained silent. At least the steam seemed to be running out.

"That's what I thought." Maggie nodded, looking happy to have the last word. "June needs a real date, a guy who wants to be with her in ways you just won't. We all want a man, not a boy who thinks he can."

"Maggie," I jumped in. Her mean comments sounded more like the wick-pops than her.

Alex stood up, his knuckles turned white over the neck of his guitar. The steam between them seemed to be rising again.

He took a step closer to Maggie. "So you think you know everything about guys? Do you think Dane lives up to his reputation? Because you should hear the way he talks about girls in the locker rooms."

Maggie laughed sarcastically. "Marquez, I think you are just jealous of his accomplishments, 'cause let's face it, you'll always be second best."

"Maggie, stop!" I stood up. This was heading in the wrong direction. I really didn't want them to reach a point of no return.

Alex's free hand opened and closed several times as he tried to calm down. I knew all about his grounding techniques before swimming competitions, but this must have gotten to him. Alex twisted his neck and stood closer to Maggie. His six feet two looking down at her five feet three. Alex's gaze became intimidating. I wouldn't want to be against him in the water or anywhere else.

"Let's set one thing straight," he said, his tone menacing. "Never ever compare me to that piece of trash, Dane Cooper. I am not intimidated by him, not the slightest."

Maggie rolled her eyes.

"You want to know why? Because I earned my place on the team by my own merit, not because my uncle is part of the school board. And not because I take some sort of performance enhancers. That's just not my style of competing. If that means I'll always be second best, then so be it."

Maggie laughed and crossed her arms tighter. "Marquez, you might think your speech is intimidating, but the truth is, when it comes to individual work, you don't bring the first-place trophies to our school. And even though a few girls might have a crush on you, Dane is the type of guy *every* girl wants to date."

I was so close to pulling Maggie away so we could leave. But she stepped away from me.

"Dane is charming, incredibly hot, has perfect hair, and is the number one swimmer at our school. Save your speech for someone who cares, because you're none of that."

Alex turned away, infuriated, and left his guitar on the bench. If Maggie were a guy, I was sure someone would have already thrown the first punch. But I had learned better than to intervene in their arguments with more than a few words. Maggie was being mean, but the last thing I wanted was for her to turn away and stop talking to me.

Alex came closer to us and raised his T-shirt, showing us his amazing abs. "I'm a swimmer. We all look the same underneath. You should focus on what's inside, 'cause he's full of shit." He lowered his shirt.

"Whatever, Marquez." Maggie turned toward me. "Are you coming?"

I nodded but looked at Alex, impressed. I had never seen him react like that.

"I'll catch up with you in five," I told Maggie, and she waited for me in the car.

Alex sat again on the bench and played random chords without looking at me.

"Alex, I'm sorry for what Maggie said. It's not true."

"You don't have to apologize for her. She's your friend, not mine," he said, staring at the strings of his guitar.

I hated the feeling of being trapped between them, of having to choose a path. "I guess I'll see you later," I said, trying to clear the air before I left.

He stopped the music, passed his hand over his hair, and looked up at me. "June, before you leave, answer me one thing."

I nodded.

"Is this really what you wanted? I mean, do you really want to have your first date with this random guy Maggie picked out for you?"

I didn't want to answer that, and I knew Maggie could be

listening to us. I opened my mouth, but nothing came out, so I nodded instead.

"The June I know, the one with wild book-guy requirements, would have never agreed to possibly kiss someone she's never met before," he said, now looking at me.

I took a deep breath. I had to say something convincing to get out of this. "Well, Marian said I should go out and enjoy the Mercutios of the world while my Romeo comes. Isn't now the time to try new things and make mistakes?" At least if I used Marian's words, I wouldn't have to struggle to come up with lies of my own.

Alex hesitated. Then he nodded. "You are right." He looked back to his guitar. It was time for me to leave.

"What if the right guy for you is out there? Life has a strange way of sorting itself out," he said as he played again. "Besides, you always say love should never be rushed."

The thing about best friends was that they knew you so well that no matter how hard you tried, you couldn't hide your true self from them. He was right, he knew me, and I didn't want to go through with this date. But I couldn't tell him that, not with Maggie waiting for me.

I turned to look at Alex, but his gaze was directed at the horizon. Part of me thought that if I had just waited on my porch for Maggie to come get me, none of this would have happened.

I had turned to leave when Alex asked me, "June, can you promise me one thing?"

I nodded.

"Promise me you'll always tell me the truth, no matter what." His dark eyes stared at me with a mix of sadness and fear. Perhaps the same feeling I constantly battled inside myself since Marian had gone away, since Maggie and I had begun to drift apart.

I nodded. "Always, Alex. I promise."

The silence in the car was uncomfortable. I expected Maggie to talk nonstop about the last details for her party, but she was silently focused on the road for once. As soon as we were out of my neighborhood, I decided to say something.

"Anything else missing for the big day?" At the same time Maggie asked if I had brought my contacts. I told her yes as I patted my bag.

"Am I really pushing you to do this? I mean, for the blind date?" Maggie said. Perhaps Alex's words had gotten under her skin. If I was going through this circus to please her, the last thing I wanted was for her to feel guilty or doubt my motives.

"No, I want to. I do. I'm just . . . nervous. It's my first date, after all. And I guess I've spent too much time inside my literary shell." I wanted to sound reassuring. "Just don't take Alex's words too much to heart."

Her eyes illuminated, and I felt I could breathe again.

She was confident her mystery guy and me would make a great match, including the fact that he was somehow a Shakespeare fan. Perhaps I had underestimated her matching abilities.

"But first, should we talk about him?" Maggie asked.

I was confused now. "Isn't mystery the main point of a blind date?"

"No, you dork! The wannabe rock star that is hopelessly in love with you."

"What? No." The last thing I wanted was for Maggie to ask me if the rumors were true. That wick-pop must be dying to ask Alex as her date. But my frustration turned to fear when Maggie turned recklessly onto the first street she could and parked the car.

"He was not just *rehearsing* the song; he was clearly singing it *to you*." She stared right at me. "He even said he found the perfect song that said exactly how he felt."

I rolled my eyes.

"I'm surprised that you didn't get it right away," Maggie said, typing quickly on her phone.

Not again with the Spanish thing. Just because I hung out with Alex a lot, it didn't mean Spanish would get into me by osmosis. My language skills were nonexistent. As Maggie kept looking for something in her phone, I remembered what happened at that posada at Alex's house a few years ago.

Before we could break the piñata, we were divided into two groups. Outside, we sang to the ones inside of the house to let us in. We were holding tiny candles, trying not to burn anyone or anything around us. Alex wanted me to participate, so he wrote the Spanish lyrics phonetically so I could easily read them.

My accent was terrible, but it gave me the naive confidence to try to talk to his cousins visiting from Mexico City. It all went downhill from there. According to his younger cousins, my pronunciation of words like *hola* and *gracias* sounded more like a drunk lost tourist asking for directions.

Ever since, I promised myself to never speak Spanish again and even chose French instead as the foreign language requirement at school. At least no one would ask me to practice talking to anyone in French.

But the fact that Alex went through all that preparation for me to be part of his traditions had added to the crush I already had brewing for him when we were in ninth grade.

"I found it!" Maggie's surprise made me jump. "Perhaps your old crush for him is gone, but it seems the tables have turned now," Maggie said, handing me her phone.

The lyrics of Alex's song were on the screen, each Spanish verse followed by its English translation. I read the lyrics over and over again. It was about a guy who was in love with a girl who happened to be his best friend. But it was impossible for him to get to her or make her see how he felt about her.

"June, I believe it when *you* say that you have no feelings for Marquez. But he literally declared his love for you using Spanish as a disguise. Please don't act like you didn't notice."

"That's just absurd," I replied, still staring at Maggie's phone. It was clear Maggie had heard Alex's song in a different way than I had. I felt her eyes fixated on me, but I had no clue what to say next. It didn't make any sense that Alex had feelings for me.

"I have a theory, so hear me out," Maggie said, looking serious. "Maybe you couldn't get over Marquez and you built this imaginary Romeo as a stunt. That would make more sense for why you wouldn't date someone who is not book perfect." Maggie looked at the time and drove back onto the main road.

My mind went back to that same posada. I had just tried my luck at breaking the piñata, while blindfolded, but had not even touched it. The Marquez cousins took posadas to a different level. By the way most of them aggressively swung the broomstick from side to side, you'd think it was like some sort of high-risk sport. Or perhaps they were releasing their long-accumulated anger in one evening. As they encouraged everyone to sing the tune louder, I decided it was time for me to head inside, where no one could hear me sing.

As soon as I got in, the scent of *ponche* filled the house, and I found Miriam in the kitchen, talking to her sister. I drank the warm beverage, and through the kitchen window I saw Edgar hit the piñata, some fruit falling to the ground. Then it was Alex's turn, and his cousins held the piñata at impossible-to-reach levels.

I still remember how special he made me feel that day. How he went out of his way to include me in every tradition. When someone made you feel that way, seen and important, you simply didn't forget. Once Alex finally broke the piñata, everyone rushed to grab the fruit scattered all over the floor.

At that same moment I felt Miriam standing next to me. "Here, *linda*, you don't want to wrestle those barbarians." She handed me a bag filled with the nicest fruit.

As we stared at them collecting the fruit, Miriam told me how happy she was that Alex and I had remained such good friends after all these years. She told me she cared for me as if I was part of her family and that Alex would always love me like a sister. Any courage I had to tell him about my feelings smashed along with that piñata. It was as if the spell had broken, and I knew right then that nothing would ever happen between Alex and me.

I could not imagine my life without Alex. I had lived more years of my life knowing him than not knowing him. That posada night, I rode my bike to Maggie's house, and we had a sleepover filled with endless ice cream and rom-coms to help me get over the heartbreak.

A couple of months went by, and I remembered feeling glad to have him in my life, no matter how. He was my constant and that should be enough. The next year, Mrs. Lib introduced me to the play *Romeo and Juliet*, and there was no going back from my beloved Romeo. Everything had seemed like a long-lost dream until now.

We parked in Maggie's big driveway. I tried to get out, but Maggie locked the car.

"June, I'm going to ask you one last time, I promise." She held her pinkie in the air as our childhood peace offering. "If you truly think Marquez should be in the friend zone, I promise I will drop the subject and won't bring it up ever again."

"But?" I added, knowing there was more to it.

"But if there's even something tiny inside of you, just say it, and I can call my friend and cancel your date."

I hesitated. "But Alex is so far away from my Romeo," I said.

"Maybe on the outside. I mean, his hair is always messy, unlike your perfect imaginary guy. But I guess we all have bad hair days." Her tone was condescending.

"He doesn't have bad hair days; he has a bad hair life," I answered.

Maggie laughed. "But you see my point, though."

I had trouble grasping what this all meant. The only thing I knew was that I needed this date to happen. By the way Alex and Maggie had interacted a while ago, thinking of Alex as anything other than a friend would push me even farther away from Maggie.

"I'm really curious about meeting this mystery guy," I finally said.

Her smile was the widest. "OK, then. Let's get you super pretty so we can get rid of those rumors and push you out of the spotlight, like you like it." She opened her door and all the doors unlocked.

CHAPTER 5
BFFS

Maggie's house was unusually quiet, and she rushed me to her room without making our signature stop at the pantry for snacks.

"I'll be right back," Maggie said, leaving me alone.

Her room was the definition of anyone's dream room. It was modern, spacious, and obviously decorated by a professional. It was hard to imagine that this space was once filled with unicorns, rainbows, and books—a place that felt more familiar. Now it had a big white bed filled with cushions in all shades of velvety purple over a comfy lilac comforter. A big glass chandelier hung at the center of the room and matched nicely with the shimmery silver curtains over the windows.

Maggie came back with clothes on hangers and placed them on her bed. We heard a door slamming and someone arguing. I stared at Maggie, but she seemed to act as if nothing had happened. She put on music that came through the invisible speakers in her room. The volume was a little louder than normal, but Maggie started dancing, and I joined her, like the dance parties we randomly started when we were in elementary school.

"I hope my mystery guy is your date to my party," she said once the song was over. "It'd be great to see you date a real guy, not an imaginary paper one."

Suddenly I felt a lot of pressure to like the guy. I smiled and tried to not say anything that would show how uncomfortable I was. She promised me she would transform my look entirely but wouldn't let me see until the end. At least I was allowed to veto some things in what she promised would be an *unrecognizable transformation*. I vetoed the usual things I disliked—animal print, anything too short or cropped, and anything hippie or torn.

"Guess what?" Maggie said excitedly. "There's going to be a photo booth at the entrance. So every couple gets their picture taken, and I get to see the cute couples I helped get together for my party." She separated my hair in sections and wet them with a mister. "There will be fun props too. Perhaps that will be the first of many pictures you'll take with my mystery guy."

I was thankful she was looking at the back of my head. She was putting a lot of pressure on this date, and I thought of Alex's words. What if Maggie chose a guy who wasn't my style?

She grabbed a big black round thing.

"What is that?" I said before it got too close to my face.

"It's my new curler." She grabbed a section of my hair, and just like magic, the curler pulled my hair in and twisted it several times. After a few seconds it came out as a silky curl. It looked incredible, but it made me feel odd. As if sometime in the past years I had lost the memo about what it meant to be a girly girl. Maybe I should know more about this stuff—and makeup.

"So now that Marquez is out of the way, what do you want to know about your date?" Maggie asked, concentrating as she dealt with my vast amounts of stubborn hair.

Just her mentioning Alex's name again felt like a tornado of feelings battling inside of me. Could it be true? Could Alex have feelings for me the way I'd had for him? She looked at my face and readjusted my hair on both sides. I had to say something about the mystery guy even though I already knew he wouldn't be up to my Romeo standards.

"I'll let him surprise me when I meet him," I said, and she smiled at me.

As I put my contacts on, Maggie told me about the movie she had gotten us tickets to, which would please us both. I was more concentrated on blinking several times, trying to adjust my eyesight since I didn't wear my contacts often. Once I could focus, I noticed a framed picture of a pepper on her wall.

"Since when do you love peppers enough to frame them?" I asked, knowing how much she disliked eating them.

"It's a postcard from David. It says, *me importa un pimiento*, which is a common phrase used in Spain that means *I don't care*, not even a pepper."

David was Maggie's last summer boyfriend. He was a Spanish exchange student and the reason Maggie had immersed herself in intensive Spanish lessons. Only to drop them once David went back to Spain and they broke up. It was a shame, because she said she liked it and was getting pretty good at it.

"It's an odd way to say you couldn't care less, don't you think?" I asked, since the phrase made no sense to me.

"Well, sometimes you need a reminder to not care about what other people do or say," she said, now applying eye shadow on my eyelids.

Should I ignore what people said and just go with Alex to the party? I felt a spark inside of me. What if Alex and I could be something more? I felt my crush firing up again, like the feeling of finding a meaningful long-lost item that has collected dust over the years. I stopped myself. My heart couldn't take so many emotions in a single day.

At least now I had a plan. I'd get this date over with, and I'd go with Alex to the party. He clearly wanted us to go together, whether as friends or something else. Or that was what Maggie had made me think. Now that the pressure of liking the mystery guy was no longer triggering me, I could think about Alex. I got excited just thinking about him.

"Almost done?" I asked, feeling restless on the chair as she finished my makeup.

"Don't worry Juny-June, I know exactly how to show off your best attributes."

I could feel the layers of makeup building up on my face. My everyday style was more natural, with just a little eye shadow and mascara on special days. This started to feel as if I was wearing a thin mask.

Maggie's phone beeped with an incoming text. She picked up, and from the smile on her face, I understood that she was texting my date.

"He's on his way, so we need to hurry."

It seemed that every time I had managed to calm my nerves, something else spiked them up again. Before I could look at myself in the mirror, Maggie pulled me up and pushed me into her walk-in closet.

"We just need the finishing touches." She handed over some big oval earrings, way heavier than the tiny studs I usually wore. Then she sprayed perfume and pushed me through the fragrant mist of tiny drops floating in the air.

Maggie helped me change into the final outfit without messing up my makeup. I stared at my body, since she didn't let me look into a mirror just yet. I wore a white eyelet top that I was sure fitted like a crop top on her body but sat just under my navel on mine. She matched it with a pale-pink bomber jacket, because she knew I was always cold. The combination seemed a little retro but was not as eccentric as what I imagined she'd make me wear.

I finally looked at myself in the mirror and saw the final transformation for the first time. The foundation had covered all my freckles and beauty spots. I looked different, but without my teal glasses, and with my hair down in long curvy waves, I could barely recognize myself.

"Wow, I look amazing!" I said, trying to please Maggie. I seemed to be doing that a lot lately.

"So much better than your Halloween makeup last year," she mocked.

I shook my head as I put my white flats on. At least she hadn't made me wear heels.

"I was supposed to be Edgar Allan Poe, a horror writer from the eighteen hundreds," I said, remembering my fake mustache and black circles around the eyes. I was going for a more Halloween style.

Maggie laughed. "Nobody got it. Even worse with Marquez dressed up like a giant vulture next to you."

Alex again—he always came up in all my memories. That was how important he was to me.

"He was a raven. It's a literary pun," I said, remembering how long it took me to glue Alex's wings together.

"Our costume was way better. Everybody got it," she said proudly.

Not everybody, I thought.

She and the wick-pops were supposed to be a sexy version of Alvin and the Chipmunks, but my nerdy mind thought they were a sexy version of the SATs for the letters on their tight dresses. It was not my fault they looked like nerds with those humongous glasses.

Maggie stared at herself in the mirror, our makeup matching now. She did hers like this every single day, yet it looked great on her. There was a time, before the wick-pops came into the picture, when Maggie used to try new makeup trends on me. But one day I got a horrible rash from one of her bronzers and learned to stay away from anything other than eye shadow. Maybe that was when I left the door open for the wick-pops to steal my place. They cared about makeup and boys. While I've never stopped obsessing about books.

On our way to the mall, Maggie acted so cold and weird. After agreeing to the blind date and letting her use me as her life-size doll, doing my hair and makeup, I assumed she would be happy. But I guessed her dad's angry voice coming from the kitchen before we left might have something to do with her mood. Her parents were not the type of people who fought, ever. In fact, they always seemed happy. But maybe I was reading too much into it. Her dad might be in a meeting on his phone or talking to Maggie's brother Nick, who was always a troublemaker.

I tried talking to her about different things to distract her, but all I got out of her was *aha, mmm, yeah*. Now that we had stopped at the valet line, I tried to make her laugh by making silly jokes, but she barely responded, since she was absorbed on her phone, texting nonstop.

I let it go and stared at my reflection in the visor mirror instead. I still couldn't believe that girl was me. Not only did my clothes, hair, and face look different, but seeing my big eyes without glasses was shocking. Even considering that I was one of those lucky people glasses really suited. Maggie got out of the car, and I took a deep breath before getting out too.

We didn't have to walk much before I noticed the wick-pops talking to Dane near the mall's huge modern fountain. Its water springs moved along with the music, and it was the meeting point for everyone from Storybridge High.

Maggie waved and got excited as soon as she spotted them. I wonder if it was too late to escape and hide in the bookstore at the mall. But on second thought, that would be the first place anyone would go looking for me. Maggie pulled instead toward the movie theater.

"He's already waiting." Maggie held my arm, pulling me toward the escalators.

My nerves skyrocketed as if they were on an urgent trip to the moon. I took a deep breath. It would only be a couple of hours, and who knew? Maybe I would even have fun or make a new friend.

"June, promise me that no matter what happens today, you will find a date for my party." She raised her pinkie in the air, just like we were seven again.

I swallowed loudly. "I promise," I said, wrapping my finger around hers.

We reached the top of the escalator, and there was a guy standing there with his back to us. All I could see was his blond man bun. *Ugh.*

"Hey!" Maggie called, and he turned around.

It couldn't be. No, this couldn't be real.

"June, this is my friend Ty," Maggie said, standing next to the stalker guy from the library.

Perhaps Romeo was the lens I used to compare guys, but this guy . . . he was just a nightmare.

CHAPTER 6
THE BLIND DATE

e stared at me. "Is that really you? What are the odds, bookworm!"

He had clearly brought his annoying attitude with him.

"You look . . . hot!" he said with a surprised tone.

There was no possible way I could enjoy the evening. With his attitude and his man bun, this evening was going to be downhill from here. Maggie seemed surprised that the blind date was not as mysterious as she'd thought.

"We met at the library," he said, as if it had been a pleasant experience. "That time my parents forced me to go for study group, remember?"

Maggie nodded.

"I just happened to wander into the book club session and met her at work."

It was anything but wandering. It was plain stalking.

Maggie had a big smile on her face. "I can't believe I found a bookworm for my bestie." She interlocked her arm with mine, and the only thing I could think of was how fast I could run to the bookstore before Maggie caught up with me.

Of all the worst-case scenarios I had imagined, this was by far THE worst. For my own sanity, I had to find something positive, ANYTHING positive about him to hold on to.

Maggie unhooked her arm from mine. "I'll leave you two lovebirds to enjoy your date."

I wanted to hold on to her arm tight and stop her from leaving, but I couldn't do that. Not after everything she had done to transform me for this date. I wanted her to believe this was going to work, at least for the next couple of hours. So I gave her a fake smile instead, the same one I used when the wick-pops said something stupid.

Maggie walked away. I looked at the time, just an hour before the movie. During the movie we didn't need to talk, and then I could leave. I could get through this.

"I can't believe I managed to date you." His flirting gave me shivers, and not the good kind. It was such a bummer that his looks came with that horrible personality.

"You said your name was Tyler, not Ty," I said defensively. For some reason I refused to give him the satisfaction of getting his way.

He laughed. "I knew you liked formalities. My name is Tyler James, but my friends call me Ty. The librarian was clearly not my friend, so she can call me Tyler."

I should have asked Maggie something about this guy. *How stupid of me.* Why did all this have to work against me? If I had known his name, I would have mentioned to Maggie about the stalking at the library. But Maggie was friends with everyone, even people that didn't go to our school.

Even if I tried, there was no way on earth I could change my first impression of him, and with every word he spoke, I regretted ever accepting this damn date. I stared at his man bun. Why that too?

"Do you like guys with long hair?" he asked. Apparently I had been staring at his hair for too long.

I smiled uncomfortably. "I care more about what's on the inside rather than appearances."

He laughed. "I forgot you were the smart kind. I like your type, though, very sexy."

My whole body shivered with disgust, but I avoided saying anything, because I didn't want to get into that kind of conversation. There was nothing flattering about him calling me sexy. If that was his way of flirting, he was in serious need of some classes or a self-help book. Besides, being categorized into a *type* took all the fun away from actually getting to know someone. It stopped you from seeing a person for who they really were. Following stereotypes without reasoning killed all surprises and set unrealistic expectations.

It was less than an hour before the movie, and time couldn't go any slower. His suggestion to eat something before the movie didn't seem like such a bad idea. All the nerves for this date had made me totally forget I was really hungry. Ty wanted to go to a restaurant, but that made me feel trapped. Both of us sitting at a table, at the mercy of the server's and cook's timing, with nowhere to go, was daunting. The food court seemed less restricting, and I could get distracted by the people who walked by, so we headed that way.

We both got pizza, and I chose to sit at a faraway table. I didn't want anyone from school to see us together. I thought about what I'd be doing if I hadn't agreed to this blind date. I'd surely be hanging with Alex instead.

The only positive thing about Ty turned out to be that he liked to talk a lot, especially about himself. That actually worked in my favor. As he talked, my mind drifted away. I nodded every now and then as I ate, but my mind was really somewhere else, imagining Romeo was my real date.

By the way Ty talked, he reinforced my theory that guys confused love with a spike of hormones, just looking for an adrenaline rush instead of real love. I wanted someone smart, someone different. Someone who would speak to me in poetry and maybe even challenge the world just to be with me, like Romeo had done for Juliet. I desperately wanted to find a guy like the ones in my favorite books. Maybe a magician from a circus who would endure years of challenges just for a few moments with me. Or perhaps a knight who would fight enemies or spells to get to me because he had been dreaming about me for so long.

At some point I noticed he was staring at me longer than usual. He seemed to be waiting for my answer. "Say that again?" I acted like I hadn't heard well.

"Tell me something about you," he repeated.

I had no idea what to say, since we clearly had nothing in common. If I couldn't talk about books, my repertoire got reduced by 80 percent. I thought about saying something about movies, but I anticipated we were opposites in that area too. I didn't have much to say other than my love for stories.

"Well, you already know the basics. I work at the library and hang out with my friends, like Maggie." The less information I gave him, the better. "How did you meet her?" I asked, hoping he would keep talking about himself. I had already finished my pizza, but I kept playing with my drink.

"At the tattoo parlor a year ago. I was going to get another tattoo but got a piercing instead—two of them, actually," he said proudly.

The memory of Maggie getting a belly button piercing came to mind, and she did mention meeting a guy. I had a sip of my drink and was about to ask him if he had any tattoos when out of the blue he raised his shirt all the way to the top and showed me his pierced nipples. "Aren't they cool?"

I spit my drink through my nose and coughed.

He lowered his shirt. "I know I can have that effect on women." He laughed. "Was that too much for a first date?"

"You think?" I said, trying to ignore the burning sensation of soda through my nose. He stood up and walked away. Not very gentleman like, but then he came back holding a bunch of napkins, which he offered to me.

I thanked him as I patted my skin, trying not to mess up my makeup. He resumed the conversation with talk about his other tattoos, and he showed me each one, along with the story behind it. Fortunately, when he told me about his butt cheek one, I stopped him before he could show it to me. I never imagined you could see so much of a person's body on a first date.

I tried to change the subject and talk about a Van Gogh exhibit I had seen last month at the science museum. If he was into art, perhaps we could talk about that instead of him for a change.

He nodded absentmindedly, then took a pen out of his jeans' back pocket and wrote something on a napkin. I was intrigued. Perhaps he was making an improv drawing of one of Van Gogh's famous paintings.

"What are you drawing?" I asked when he was taking too long to look up.

"I'm just writing down the things I want to say when it's my turn to talk again," he said without a care in the world, and kept writing.

Why did I have to be here? Clearly a mannequin could be here instead of me. Ty was getting closer and closer to Dane's intellectual level and further away from any alternative version of my Romeo.

We left the food court and walked around the mall instead. I could no longer stand listening to him while seated. How could an hour last that long? We had walked only a few feet when he grabbed my arm and pulled me through the entrance of a clothing store.

"The new collection has already arrived." He stared at the mannequins with excitement. "Do you mind if I look around?"

His question felt more like a request from my little brother or Maggie than from my date.

As long as he stayed occupied and away from me, time might pass a little faster. It was weird for my date to feel more like a random Saturday accompanying Maggie as she did her shopping.

I stared at a mannequin's scarf that had scattered letters printed all over. It didn't have any reference to books or literature, but I didn't know what else to look at. I was not really a clothes-shopping person. I was more of a book shopper. I hesitated, thinking about going to the bookstore instead. But leaving him here would make me look bad, especially since Maggie was still somewhere in the mall. I'd never hear the end of it.

I looked for Ty to tell him I'd wait for him outside the store, but I saw him going into the fitting rooms, so I followed him.

"Hey, Ty?" I called, and the fitting room door in front of me opened right away. "I'll wait for you outside."

"How about this for our second date?" Ty said with overbearing confidence while wearing a long-sleeve net shirt that clearly let his piercings and tattoos show. I covered my mouth to pretend I was deciding whether I liked it, but the truth was that I was trying to cover my mocking smile. His idea of what girls found attractive was so far off.

"You're not sure about it yet." He seemed surprisingly interested in my opinion.

"I'm not a fashion person. Maggie picked my clothes for today." I pointed at the clothes I was wearing while trying to bite my cheeks so I wouldn't laugh at him.

Any other girl would be happy to date Ty. But staring at his piercings constantly felt like a turn-off. I gave him a fake smile and insisted that I valued brains over looks. I walked outside to wait for him, not wanting him to show me anything else.

It was time for the movie, but Ty was still shopping. I knew Maggie had all sorts of friends, but I never imagined she would match me with someone like Ty. Alex had been right about that.

Finally he came out with a bag in his hand. "I got that shirt you liked." He winked at me, and I tried to look the other way. "I'll save it for our second date."

My eyes opened wide, and I tried to clear my throat to hide my reaction. "We should go now; it's movie time."

Part of me wondered if all this overbearing attitude was because he thought I was playing hard to get. I didn't want to be rude, but there was only so much of him I could tolerate. At least the movie would be a distraction, because this would definitely be nominated for the worst first date in the history of ever.

The theater was filled with the smell of salty and caramel popcorn, which made me happy. It also reminded me of a book I'd read a long time ago. It was so special when fiction and reality crossed, and only I could make the connection.

Ty insisted that we couldn't see a movie without popcorn, even after having pizza earlier. So I headed over to the theater while he went to get it. I didn't want to miss the trailers, as they were my favorite part of coming to the theater.

I found our seats and enjoyed being alone for a little bit, with no awkward flirting or the sound of Ty's voice talking nonstop. It was the closest I was going to get to enjoying my first date. I got to watch the trailers for the upcoming summer movies alone. One of them was a historical love story. An actor wore a costume that was somehow similar to Tristan's. Perhaps it would be a good idea to ask Tristan to watch that one with me. Based on his weird clothes, he might enjoy it. And once my friends were gone for the summer, I would not have anyone else to come to the movies with. I took my water bottle out of my bag and took a sip.

The next trailer was a contemporary love story, totally predictable. I had read so many novels that very few storylines surprised me. But the guy wanted to be a singer, and he played the guitar, and I couldn't help but thinking about Alex. I closed my eyes and remembered how Alex was singing. For the first time I tried to think of the memory as him singing the song *to* me. What would he be doing right now? Was he still practicing songs for his gig? Just thinking about him made me wonder if this was what butterflies felt like when it involved a real person and not a fictional character.

"I know what you are thinking." Ty's voice scared me, making me jump and throw water at him.

It was the kind of clumsy situation that you saw in movies or imagined happening to someone other than yourself. The embarrassment was overwhelming. Should I help him dry his hair? Should I run for napkins like he had done before for me? I wanted to hide under my seat.

"I am so sorry," I said, handing him over a few extra napkins I had kept from the food court. Even though he was far from being my favorite person, I felt terrible.

"It's OK, bookworm. I know I can have that effect on people." He took the napkins from my hand and patted his head, going back to his overconfident self.

This was the opposite of what a successful date should be. I had dreamed of sparks and fireworks, but this was all disaster and uncomfortable situations.

He untied his hair, letting it loose to dry. "I didn't mean to scare you," he said.

At least he looked better without the man bun.

The movie started, which was a relief. I could forget about all this for an hour and a half and immerse myself in the superhero world that Maggie had picked for us.

It hadn't been more than twenty minutes into the movie when I felt something tap me. I looked around, but Ty was immersed in the movie. So I ignored it until I felt it again. This time I realized what it was—a piece of popcorn had landed on my hair. Even though my loose hair blocked my peripheral vision, it allowed me to see that Ty was throwing popcorn at me. Another piece of popcorn landed on me again, but this time I looked at him right away.

He smiled like a little kid, caught with another piece of popcorn targeted at me. "Have you ever been in a food fight?" he whispered.

"I don't really like wasting food," I whispered back, and his smile disappeared. Then he looked at his hand and ate the popcorn. If he thought some sort of food fight was fun or romantic, it was because he had never had to clean popcorn or any sort of food from the floor. That was all I remembered doing when Will was a toddler and Mom asked me to feed him lunch while she took pictures of bakes for her blog.

Even though it was an action movie, there was an unexpected romantic storyline, and I was into it. Ty whistled low, as if the movie sounds were not enough for the tension. I shushed him. He was annoying me in a mosquito-in-the middle-of-the-night kind of way.

The first battle scene happened, and I was totally immersed. I ate popcorn, unaware of what was going on around me until I felt someone holding my hand. I zoned out from the movie and stared at it. Apparently I was hovering over the popcorn without actually taking any. I must have sent the wrong message, and I had to be careful. I just wanted to get this date over with.

I looked at him and he stared back at me. First at my eyes and then at my mouth. Oh hell no. I had accepted that my first date would be forever ruined to please Maggie. But there was no way on earth I would have my first kiss with a guy like Ty.

Ty moved his face closer to mine and closed his eyes. I could see him pouting. I faked a sneeze, which released my hand and got me some space back. I had to think of a strategy to create enough space between us and fast. I was sure he would try relentlessly until he succeeded.

I placed my head on his shoulder. It might not have been the smartest move, but I hoped the weight of my head would keep him in place, even if I had to see the rest of the movie sideways.

It worked, but a dark theater had been a terrible idea for a first date.

The movie came to an end, so I raised my head and rolled my neck around. This was going to hurt tomorrow. When the lights came on, I stood up, ready to leave. The end of this date was getting closer and closer.

"Wait! There's always something at the end," he said, pulling my hand and causing me to fall. But instead of landing back on my seat, I fell right into his lap.

"Hello, beautiful!" he said in my ear.

Hell no, I knew where this was going. The more time passed, the worse the date was going. He was getting more and more direct, and I was running out of ways to politely divert him. He was Maggie's friend, after all, and I didn't want him to tell her how rude I had been. This whole date had to look like we were just not compatible, which was for real.

Once any extras were done, I stood up and walked toward the

stairs as fast as I could. I heard his footsteps following quickly after me, so I told him I had to use the restroom. I needed some real space, just to breathe.

"There you are, bookworm." He caught up with me outside of the restroom as I stared at the poster of one of the trailers I had seen earlier.

"The movie was so good. Maybe you could be my own super hero, like Wonder Woman," he said, moving his eyebrows up and down. There seemed to be no end to his unbearable flirting. I swallowed hard, since I didn't want to be anyone's Wonder Woman but my own.

He stared at the poster. The words under the title said, *A modern retelling of* Romeo and Juliet *with a country twist*.

He raised his eyebrows. "Have you ever thought how there are no new stories? Just bad remakes of the old ones? There's nothing new under the sun. I still don't get why you like that cliché so much," he said, pointing at Romeo's name.

For the first time that evening, I agreed with some of the things he had pointed out, but I didn't want him to know that. "What's not to like?" I asked instead.

He laughed. "How about two reckless teenagers and their messed-up romance that ended in double suicide?"

"Have you never been reckless or in love?" I asked, not wanting to know the answer. Before he said anything, I continued, "Besides, you are clearly missing the key point of *Romeo and Juliet*."

"There is no other way to look at it. It's all about reckless teens with naive ideas about love, and endless hate passed through generations."

I shook my head. I had heard all this so many times, and everybody got it wrong.

"Enlighten me then," he said, confident as we headed toward the escalators.

"How about the fact that it's a story that's over four hundred years old, yet it is retold the exact same way? Dialogue, costumes, and all." Before he could say anything, I added, "I admit, not all remakes are good, but still. Can you imagine writing something that lived four hundred years after your lifetime?" I was still amazed by that. "Besides, every person knows who Romeo is, whether they like him or not. Imagine writing something so powerful. Such a universal love story concept."

"Which is?" Ty asked, still not convinced.

"It shows how powerful love can be. It brought their families' hate to an end. And it has something for everyone: comedy, romance, people defying rules and authority, wonderful poetry, and even sword fighting."

"You have given this a lot of thought, bookworm," he said with a side smile.

It seemed like the first time in the evening we were getting to really know each other. But part of me was unsure if he was about to say something to mock me and ruin the moment.

I looked away, trying to avoid him. "We are all passionate about something." Perhaps I looked like a total weirdo, but it was the truth. "You don't have to understand my passions, but I'm sure you have something that ignites you like that. Maybe not Shakespeare plays."

"I am a Shakespeare fan, but more of the bloodbath plays."

"How charming," I mocked.

I had never guessed that I would have a meaningful conversation about literature with someone like Ty. At least I now understood why Maggie would think we were a good match. Although he was full of surprises, the bad ones outweighed the good. It got me thinking how perhaps my nerdy personality was a curse, because boys were always intimidated by girls smarter than them.

As we headed down the escalator, I was relieved that the date was coming to an end.

"So you really are that obsessed with the guy? Like if you could date anyone fictional, you'd date Romeo?" His tone had a hint of mockery, but I was not going to lie when it came to my favorite book boyfriend.

"Definitely, there's no one like him," I said without hesitation. If this was going to be awkward anyway, it might as well win an award for the worst blind date in the history of blind dates. "I think Romeo is smart, chivalrous, would do anything for love, and speaks in poetry. There is no way to compete with someone like that."

Like I anticipated, he laughed softly, then tried to hide it by looking away. I didn't care. I had survived this date while being true to myself. I was even proud.

As we walked off the escalator, I saw Maggie sitting close to Dane by the fountain. The wick-pops were flirting with guys nearby too. I had to make a stop over there for them to see me with Ty. I mean, I had endured this much.

When I headed that way, I felt Ty's heavy arm over my shoulders. Perhaps in his mind, this was romantic, but I couldn't help noticing how heavy his arm was, and how he was pulling at my hair underneath. I couldn't even turn my head.

"How was the movie?" Maggie asked once we were near her.

"Great selection, Mags," Ty said.

Maggie smiled at us and winked at the sight of Ty hugging me by the shoulders. There was no escape this time.

"And how is the date going?" Maggie asked, staring directly at me.

I swallowed hard. Maggie was not the only one looking my way. The wick-pops were also curious, too, and Ty waited for my answer.

"Fun," I dryly said. "Ty is definitely unique." My little white lie seemed to have convinced everyone around me.

"We're all heading for a shake. Want to join?" Maggie asked.

"Lead the way," Ty answered.

The whole way to the milkshake place, I had to endure Ty's heavy arm over me. I thought the date was over, but this had turned out to be an epilogue to today's story. My heart stopped as soon as Dane opened the door for us. I didn't have to wonder about Alex's whereabouts after all.

Oliver, Nichole, and Alex, among others from the swim team, were sitting at a table, and all seemed to turn our way as we walked in. Alex blinked several times in my direction. Without my side braid and glasses, wearing Maggie's clothes, I could easily pass as someone else.

Once we sat down, Ty continued to rest his heavy arm over my shoulders, but I had at least managed to place my long hair to one side. We seemed to be the main talk over at Alex's table, since Nichole and even Oliver constantly looked our way. Perhaps Ty and I were the only unrecognizable pair. All I wanted was for the date to be over and to go home.

The mall was about to close, so we all walked to the central fountain, where we would split up. Alex and the others had somehow become part of our group and followed us to the big fountain too. Alex kept his distance as we walked, but I was sure he was eager to know about the massive failure of my first date.

Once we reached the fountain, Maggie, the wick-pops, Dane, and his gang were making some plans to leave and hang together. Maggie hugged me goodbye and seemed to be beaming from the inside about her evening with Dane, which stopped me from asking her to give me a ride home. Fortunately I could always count on Alex. He seemed to have read my mind, because he came walking in my direction. My cheeks felt warm and tingly.

Ty seemed to have other plans. Once he noticed Alex coming our way, his arm unexpectedly found its way around my waist. Maggie was still around, so I hesitated about moving away, but I managed to edge his arm up to my shoulders, and at least that was more comfortable for me. Freedom had been so brief.

Alex stared at me, blinking several times. "You look so different."

Apparently Maggie's makeover was even better than any costume I'd worn on Halloween.

"I know. I wanted to try something different," I added so he wouldn't say that Maggie was forcing me to do this too.

"You look great," Oliver said, coming closer.

Even Oliver's compliment felt nicer than anything Ty had said all evening. Alex looked at Oliver and then back at me. It was like he couldn't believe it was really me. Alex's stare was so intense it was making me nervous. I tried to put my glasses close to my face, but I remembered too late that I was wearing contacts, and I poked my eye hard. Ty took his arm off me, and I looked up, hoping the contact was still in my eye.

"Contact problem?" Ty asked.

I nodded.

"Let me help. I know how annoying that can be." He held my face with his hands and stared into my eye. I feared this was another trick.

"All good, bookworm," Ty said as he took eyedrops from his pocket and handed them to me.

I was surprised at how helpful Ty was with the drops. Once I was able to see with both eyes, I realized Alex had left. A part of me thought it rude of him to leave without saying goodbye, but the other part realized I would have to ask Ty for a ride home.

Ty offered politely to give me a ride. The parking lot was not as packed as when we had arrived, and Ty's car was nearby. He looked at me sideways every now and then as we walked in silence.

"Is there a book in your bag?" he asked.

"What?" I asked, confused.

"Bookworm, I'm running out of ways to turn you on."

I laughed between my teeth. He laughed too.

"It's true, isn't it? You are carrying a book right now."

I remained silent.

"You have a *Romeo and Juliet* book with you?" He seemed to be about to crack up laughing.

"Don't judge me." I blushed and he laughed. It felt like the pretending part of our date was over, and now we were back at the library, annoying each other.

"I must admit, I never thought I could actually make you laugh," he said.

I stopped laughing and looked at him. "Why?"

"Because you are too uptight. Just relax," he said, taking a deep breath. "I know it's your first date, but you are in the hands of a master here." He pointed at himself.

Unbelievable.

We got to his car, and in a very gentlemanly manner he went to open the door for me but stopped, standing very close.

"This is for you." He took out the letters scarf we had seen at the store and gave it to me. "Whenever you are at the library, you won't look like you lost winter in the middle of summer." He always finished with a punch line.

He put both arms around me on top of his car, trapping me. He stared at me so closely I couldn't escape. I knew he wouldn't give up on a kiss so easily.

"Are you going to let me kiss you?" he whispered in a romantic tone. I was sure any other girl would love this. And maybe I would if things hadn't started so badly at the library.

He got closer, and just when I knew his lips were about to touch mine, I turned my head. His lips landed on my cheek. Maybe if I had been more like Maggie, a kiss would be only a kiss, and dates would be just about having a good time. But I was not her. I was me, and I cared deeply about those things. I cared about making memories that would be dear to me. Ty looked down without saying a word and opened the door for me. If I thought the awkwardness was over, I was still missing the last part.

The ride home was silent, so different from normal nonstop-talking Ty. I had taken my contacts out and tied my hair in a side braid, which made me feel more like myself. I might not have much hands-on experience with real dates, but I had read more than enough novels to be empathic toward him. And no one liked to taste rejection.

"Thank you for the scarf. It was very thoughtful," I said.

He looked at me sideways and smiled.

"I'm sorry I made you waste your time today," I added.

"You didn't. I had a good time. I guess it's just not meant to be."

His words, not mine.

"Firsts are a big deal for you, huh?" he asked, his eyes still on the road.

"They are. But hey, you were my first date. That should count for something."

He laughed. "If I join team Romeo, will you give me another chance?"

I smiled but still shook my head. "You never give up, do you?"

"Friends with benefits then?" he said.

We both laughed.

"That's just not my style," I said.

"Well, it was worth trying. You can't say I didn't try hard enough." He gave me a side smile.

Ty was such a weird guy. He wasn't as obnoxious as I'd thought at first. I was just not interested in the kind of love story he and I could be part of. I felt the entire opposite of attraction when it came to his piercings and tattoos. And our conversations didn't feel natural to me, at least not as natural as my conversations with Alex.

"I have to admit," I added, "no one else has ever put up such a fight trying to dismantle my *Romeo and Juliet* obsession." I tried to somehow clean the air.

"I'll take that as a compliment." He took a right turn on Luna Road, my street.

He stopped outside of my house, but instead of saying goodbye, I got distracted by Alex's blue Jeep parked in his driveway. Just knowing he was there was all the comfort I had craved that evening.

Ty turned off the car, and I looked at him. "Thank you for making me feel wanted. It was nice and new."

"Really? 'Cause you seemed a little uncomfortable."

"I guess I'm just finding my own way to navigate dating," I said, pushing my glasses close to my face. "A friendship is all I can offer."

"A friendship it is." He smiled.

I didn't know if he was talking seriously or if he was about to try again. But at least I was no longer fighting him. And after all, I realized behind his over-the-top style, he was kind and fun.

Before I got out of the car, I asked him, "Can you not tell Maggie about how I didn't let you kiss me?"

He nodded. "No problem, bookworm. I'll say we were both looking for different things." He winked at me. I closed the door, but he opened the passenger window. "Bookworm, can I say something?"

I looked at him.

"Just don't sit around waiting for that Romeo to show up. Make things happen, you know?" His words were not mocking, and were actually sweet.

I nodded and he laughed.

"Thanks for the ride and for the date. It definitely will be one to remember," I said, stepping back.

"Anytime, bookworm." He saluted me with his hand over his forehead and turned on his car.

I watched him drive into the night. Maybe this date hadn't been such a waste of time after all. Ty was using all his cards while I wasn't even playing. If some of Ty's confidence rubbed off on me, perhaps I could find a real love story of my own. Perhaps that was the key. I shouldn't be waiting for love. I should go searching for my own real Romeo.

CHAPTER 7

DOORS, CHAIRS AND SNAKES

A week after my forgetful laundry incident, I promised Mom I'd be more mindful about my family's clothes. Including getting rid of the ones I didn't use anymore. But bringing them to the donation bin at the library seemed an easier task. I was not considering that I'd have to carry three overfilled tote bags throughout the library parking lots.

Mom was running late to Will's soccer training, so she had dropped me off at the very end of the west parking lot, which was the closest to the main road. That meant I had to cross the west parking lot, pass the library garden, and walk through the east parking lot to get to the donation bin. I should have thought this through before realizing the summer heat was rising at this time of the day in the last weeks of May.

Once I reached the library garden, I sat under the shade of the big red oak. With my back against the trunk, I stared at the light filtering through the branches and leaves. Cicadas, the signature summer sound, were not the only thing I could hear. A stressed cat or mating bird or something different was making an annoying noise, and I couldn't figure out what it was. I stood up to throw a pebble at the branches, but no bird flew out.

I couldn't see the tree house but I knew it was there. I wondered if it was still the same as I remembered. I couldn't believe it was once the signature icon of the library, and now it was nothing more than ruins.

I looked around me. There were no patrons, since it was after school hours. Most kids were at sports or other activities and there seemed to be only a few cars in the parking lot. The foliage covered most of the steps up to the tree house, but my feet found the way.

At first I was scared. What if the steps broke and I ended up with a broken arm again? But as I climbed, the excitement fueled me forward. I reached the top of the steps, my head poking just above the floor. The noise was coming from the tree house. Maybe a family of raccoons or mysterious animals was living in here. I stretched and took a peek inside. The surprise almost made me fell backward, as I realize *who* was making that noise.

A guy lay on his side on the floor of the tree house. The noise seemed to be him snoring, deep in slumber. I could see only his bare back since he was only wearing loose white shorts, more like Bermuda shorts with no pockets or shape at all. I wasn't going to make any fuss about it. Who was I to betray a stranger who had found a safe place to nap?

I tried to be as silent as I could while still looking around. I hadn't been here in years, and the tree house was just as I remembered it, but with clear evidence of the years that have passed with no maintenance.

I cautiously took a step down. I could hear the sound of the birds along with the cicadas, but suddenly the snoring stopped. As I looked up, I found Tristan's gorgeous olive eyes looking at me. The fright made me slip, and I lost all balance on the old wooden steps. The next thing I knew was that Tristan was holding my hand and pulling me upward. I landed facedown on the tree house floor next to Tristan's unmistakable long leather boots. How could I have missed those?

I turned around, looking at the top of the tree house. All the commotion was getting me dizzy. From feeling I was definitely going to break something from the fall, to Tristan saving me as I lay safe and sound in the tree house. Tristan reached out to help me to my feet, but as I sat up, I had to cover my eyes, since I was getting dizzy.

"I apologize, milady. I was not expecting any visitors," Tristan said.

I peeked through my fingers, blushing as I realized he had turned around and was grabbing his pants. Apparently those were not shorts—they seemed to be some sort of outdated underwear. Wow, he really got immersed in the role of medieval guy.

I scooted around, trying to give him privacy. The heights still made me dizzy, but I tried to remain steady. I heard him clear his throat, and I stood up and turned around to meet his eyes.

They were still as lovely and hypnotizing as before. And his hair was messier, which made him look even hotter. I stared at his untied ivory shirt, his torso exposed. Perhaps guys like him were the inspiration behind the Renaissance's gorgeous marble statues. The sound of the cicadas made me realize I had been staring at him too long, so I looked away.

"What are you doing here?" I asked, a little embarrassed. Perhaps it had not been a very good idea to tell him about this place. I still couldn't believe why, with all the comfy chairs in the library, he'd still chosen this place for a nap.

"If I'm being honest, milady, I fancied a nap. All the attention has been—"

"Ah, I see," I interrupted. Of course, he knew how hot he was and how many girls would love to be around him. He must be a local celebrity after all, like all the exchange students normally were. I cleared my throat. I was not going to be one more of those. Besides, for such a handsome guy, his snoring was a real charm breaker.

"You shouldn't have come up here," I said, a little upset. "We'll get in trouble if anyone sees us climbing down from here."

My phone buzzed with a text from Nora, who was wondering where I was, since there was an urgent meeting with all the library staff.

"I have to go," I said as I peeked through the branches. There was no one around the garden, so it was safe for us to get down. As long as I could get down quickly, I should be fine. I was not going to bother covering for him.

"May I assist you, milady?" he said, pulling a brand-new rope between the branches. "Perhaps this will make your descent easier." He was still looking at me with his gorgeous eyes.

I thanked him and went down as quickly as I could. As soon as I got to the ground, I stepped all over the totes filled with clothes, and everything spilled out. Now Nora was calling me incessantly.

"Can I ask you for a huge favor?" I looked up as Tristan was coming down. I really didn't have time or energy to carry the totes all the way to the other parking lot. If he helped me, I wouldn't tell anyone about him napping here in return.

He reached the ground and looked at me. "I would be immensely pleased to be of any assistance to a beautiful lady like yourself."

My cheeks were red again, and not from the summer heat. Tristan was a master at getting my heart fluttering. Perhaps he knew how good he was. I'd have to be careful.

"How about you help me out by taking all these clothes to the donation bin over there"—I pointed to the east parking lot—"and I won't tell anyone about your napping spot?"

He smiled, his perfect white teeth showing. I didn't know if it was the bright summer day or his smile, but it was blinding.

"Anything for you, milady," he said.

I smiled back and walked away, my heart racing as if I had

run a marathon. Perhaps the adrenaline rush would be useful for running toward the second-floor staff break room. Because with three missed calls from Nora, I was sure I was in for more drama.

I went in the staff break room door. I tried to go unnoticed while I caught my breath, blending with the rest of the staff at the back. Nora, Sarah, and other librarians were at the front, seemingly preoccupied. Even Jim was here. Meetings were usually scheduled for the whole year, so an urgent meeting was out of the ordinary. I focused on what people murmured, and from what I could understand, something seemed to have happened to one of the exhibit collectibles. The official launching party for the summer reading program hadn't even started, and things were not going well. Things didn't look good for the library to get that grant.

"If I'm understanding correctly, was this the only book Alice Libbengood didn't set up herself?" Nora asked loudly.

Sarah nodded. I felt my heart shrink as I realized something had happened to that gorgeous edition of *Romeo and Juliet*.

"I followed Alice's instructions to the T. The book was fine," Sarah added.

"It must have been a case malfunction." Jim shook his head in disappointment, his long gray ponytail swinging from side to side.

"I already had the display checked, and the technicians said it was fine. Besides, there are no records of the humidity levels or light exposure to have gone wrong," Nora answered.

"Did you personally see the damage?" someone asked.

Nora nodded. "I don't know how to accurately describe the damage, but I'm surprised that an honorable book association would lend such an expensive collectible copy in *that* state."

How bad could it be? It was in perfect shape when I handled it, and my hands were clean. It didn't make sense.

Nora looked worried. "The cover seemed fine and is in good shape, so I made the decision of displaying the book closed for now. At least until the exhibit ends and we send the book back or Alice comes back, whatever happens first."

Sarah seemed frustrated. "I can't believe it. The book was fine when we set it up."

"We?" Nora was surprised. This was definitely not going to work in my favor. "Was there anyone else with you that could verify that it arrived in a good state?"

"June Capehart," Sarah said calmly.

I didn't know which was worse, that gorgeous book being damaged or Nora's penetrating gaze as she pointed at me to come closer while people moved out of my way.

"June, did you do anything to the book while you were setting it up with Sarah? It could be something as silly as sneezing or even drooling?" Nora asked once I was closer.

I shook my head. My obsession with that novel didn't make me drool. A little tear escaped my eye, but nothing other than my hands had touched that book.

"She didn't do such things," Sarah said, jumping in. "I told you already, the book was fine. Didn't the lights turn green when we set it up, June?" Sarah turned to me.

I nodded. I couldn't bring myself to speak. Nora had gotten me into a bad mood. Besides, her way of always making fun, consciously or not, of my obsession with the Shakespearean play was becoming offensive.

Nora took a deep, frustrated breath. In moments like this, I really missed Mrs. Lib. She was always so kind, even when troubles appeared. And she always made us all feel like a big family. Nora and her bossy attitude felt as if she was scolding her minions for not following her evil plan.

"Maybe the book was defective from the start and you didn't

pay close attention. You are an intern, after all, so you wouldn't know. You haven't proven to be very responsible," Nora said dismissively.

Sarah tried to step in, but deep down I knew that no matter what I did, Nora wanted to blame me for everything. Perhaps it was the only way she could cope with failure. After all, she was new at this job, and she was the one in charge while Mrs. Lib was away. I knew better by now. If she had made me close the library almost every night, one more word from me and my internship would be at stake.

"Before the meeting is dismissed," Sarah said, "I want all of you to remember, what happens at *this* library stays at this library. Can I have an agreement from everyone in the room?"

We all nodded, and Nora added, "I couldn't agree more, Sarah. The last thing we need is other libraries talking about us. News like this travels fast, and then we can kiss the grant goodbye."

Her bossy tone was getting on my nerves, but thankfully the meeting was over.

I walked away depleted. Not because of Nora's annoying attitude but because the most beautiful edition of my favorite love story was now destined to be destroyed. Perhaps to other people it was only an old book, but for me it was a real treasure, and I still regretted not having enough time to admire it.

After the meeting, I tried to follow Nora's instructions to the T. I didn't have any room for errors. Even though packing the kits for the summer kids' activities was a volunteer's job, and not an intern's job, I still didn't want to argue with her. While I kept them in containers, I overheard Nora and Jim's conversation. She complained about the library security being defective, since some supplies were missing. Jim sounded even more frustrated, as he explained the security at this library had never failed before.

After listening to Jim saying over and over again that no one would be interested in stealing the summer program supplies, he finally found a way for Nora to agree. He asked her to make a list of the items so he could get them replaced immediately.

As soon as I was done with the kits, I placed them in big container boxes to be stored out of Nora's way, as she requested. And the only place I could come up with for big boxes was the storage room. When Nora was away from her desk, I took a peek as I carried the boxes toward the elevator. The only thing that was on the list was rope.

I unsuccessfully tried to balance two boxes as I made my way toward the elevator, thinking how impossible it was for an old forgotten tree house to have a brand-new rope. I had told Tristan I was not going to blow the whistle for his nap on the tree house, but this was totally different.

Stealing a rope shouldn't be such a big deal. After all, it was a harmless crime. But also, I didn't have any real proof that he'd done it, even if everything pointed at him as the thief. He would have had to go through the library STAFF ONLY door, looking specifically for a rope to steal. And who knew where Jim kept those kinds of things? It just didn't make any sense.

I reached for the elevator button, and one of the boxes was sliding away from my hands when I felt someone stopping the box from falling.

"Are you in need of assistance, milady?" Tristan's voice came from behind the boxes. It was so nice to see him again.

"Perfect timing, thank you," I said, while he took one from me and I placed mine on the floor. "Do you mind helping me taking these upstairs?"

He nodded.

"I'll go for one more. Just take them to the third floor, and I'll meet you there," I said, walking away.

I came back with the remaining box to find Tristan holding both boxes, still standing by the elevator. "You know you have to press the button to call the elevator, right? This is not a smart building or something," I said sarcastically.

He looked away, ignoring me. I called the elevator, and it opened right away. I stepped in and left the box on the floor. "Aren't you coming?" I asked, as I waited for him to get in.

He stared at the elevator as if it was something repulsive. "If you don't mind, milady, I'd rather take the stairs." He slid the boxes onto the elevator floor, apparently not wanting to touch any part of it.

He turned around and headed toward the stairs. I rolled my eyes. It reminded me of a phase in Will's toddlerhood when he refused to get into elevators. Now I was comparing Tristan's attitude with my little brother, but I guessed Tristan was a peculiar guy.

The elevator doors opened, and I didn't expect Tristan to be already waiting for me, but there he was, his chest rising up and down.

"Wow, you're fast," I said, staring at his white smile as he brushed the hair away from his face. I pushed the boxes out, and he picked up two of them. Then I led the way to the storage room.

After I opened the door, I realized the room looked a little dusty, like no one had been there in months. When I tried to get my key out, it got stuck. So I left the box on the floor, holding the door open. I went inside, and Tristan followed me.

As I rearranged things to make space for the boxes, dust floated in the air. I couldn't help coughing.

"Where would you like these, milady?" Tristan asked, and I pointed to a space I had made by the window.

While he left them there, I stared through the window at the gorgeous, swaying oak tree branches, the tree house was barely visible.

"And this one?" Tristan asked, picking up the box that was holding the door open. I turned around and reached for the door, but it was too late. The door had closed, leaving us locked inside.

"You were not supposed to move that one," I said, frustrated.

I tried to turn on the light to see the lock, but the light didn't work in here, and it was dark. I hadn't brought my phone since this trip was supposed to be super quick, but now we were stuck.

"I apologize for any inconvenience I may have caused, milady. My intentions were nothing but noble," he said, leaving the box next to the others.

I felt bad. It hadn't been his fault, and he only wanted to help. I could see now why no one wanted to use the storage room in this condition. The library was in desperate need of that grant.

"What should we do now?" Tristan asked.

I shrugged. There was not much we could do. I stretched to turn the dusty blinds up so a little natural light came in. I then tried to spot anyone passing by through the tiny vertical window on the door, but no one seemed to be in this area of the library, even when I knocked repeatedly.

"May I?" He knelt, staring intensely at the lock and moving the handle up and down. Then he stared at me.

We were really close together. Even with the dim lights, he still was the most handsome guy I had ever been around. It was the first time I realized he was not wearing his theater costume. He was wearing jeans that looked a size too big and a white polo with flip-flops that looked familiar. My stare must have made him uncomfortable, because he stood up, and I looked away.

"Milady, have you ever felt . . . trapped?" he asked, and I chuckled. He didn't laugh, so I assumed he was not talking about our current situation.

"What do you mean?" I asked. It seemed like something was bothering him.

"Milady, you have always shown the greatest kindness, and I believe I can trust you—"

We were interrupted by someone opening the door.

"Hey, June, it's you . . . and your friend," Jim said, staring at both of us.

Seeing him was such a relief.

"The key hanging on the door was a clear sign that someone needed a little help," he said, releasing my key.

I nodded and thanked him.

"I'll get this fixed right now so you can use this room," Jim said, holding the door open for us. "I believe Nora is looking for you, June."

Of course she was. She was obsessed with micromanaging everything and everyone.

"Can you give her something for me?" Jim left his tool belt by the door to keep it open and walked to the very end of the storage room. He opened a dusty box and pulled out two new ropes. "I hope now she can stop saturating my inbox with rope emails."

I nodded.

I could hear Nora's voice asking for me all the way to the third floor.

"I'll catch up with you later," I told Tristan, hoping he'd stay a little longer while I went with Nora.

After a couple of hours, I needed a break. I had been working overtime, and the more time I spent around Nora, the more things she wanted me to redo. So I decided to get a tea and take a break from my tyrant boss.

I got in line for the library café. My phone's battery had

died, which was a good thing, since I didn't want to waste any time mindlessly scrolling through social media, so I took my book out as I waited. A few minutes later, a familiar voice distracted me.

"Greetings, milady!" Tristan looked at me. "What may I serve you today? Would you be interested in hearing the specials? Or perhaps the most amazing item on the menu: a sandwich!" He sounded excited as he stood behind the café counter. He was wearing an apron embroidered with the words *Stories and Bridges Café*, an homage to our city. I still remember when they opened and the library held a contest for the café's name.

"Do you work here?" I asked, surprised.

"Indeed, milady," he answered with a soft bow.

Audrey, the owner's daughter, who was a couple of years older than me, came close to him from behind the counter. "He needed money. I needed help. Plus, he eats everything we don't sell, so we don't have to throw it all away. It's a win-win situation," she said, turning to Tristan and asking him to wrap a sandwich for a customer.

Once Tristan wasn't close enough to listen, she whispered, "I had to teach him basic things, like how to make a sandwich, but he's eye candy, so I can't complain."

As Tristan fulfilled orders, he explained to the customers how much care he had put into making his sandwiches. I couldn't stop thinking that perhaps he was one of those spoiled guys who wouldn't lift a finger. Perhaps his parents had sent him here with a hidden agenda to force him to grow up. Even though his weirdness made him stand out, he did so in a positive way, because people seemed to like him. Every single one of the customers added a tip to the jar, and many seemed to enjoy Tristan's attentiveness, especially the ladies.

Audrey handed me my tea, and Tristan came closer to ask me if I wanted one of his special sandwiches as well. I had no idea what made them special, but I hesitated. No one would get *that* excited for a sandwich.

Audrey told Tristan he could take a break, and he immediately took off his apron and walked around the counter. I almost spit out my tea as I realized he was wearing my mom's old embroidered skinny jeans. It was a terrible mistake for my mom to buy them in the first place. The embroidery was so heavy on the sides that her skin got rashes underneath. But to see Tristan wearing them was disturbing.

"What are you wearing?" I said once I stopped coughing from the tea going down the wrong way. I stared at his flip-flops. Those were my dad's—no wonder they looked familiar.

"I had an incident earlier with a sandwich sauce and had to exchange my garments." He motioned his hands up and down his body. "I consider my clothes a statement."

"You don't say." I had to cover my mouth not to laugh. "Those were my mom's jeans." I had to say something.

"That explains the looks I got earlier." He smiled at me. "Your mom has impeccable taste, if I may add, milady." His confidence was refreshing, even cute.

But the combination of my dad's oversize white polo and my mom's skinny jeans was something I would have never imagined anyone wearing, ever. The flip-flops were just the cherry on top, and I considered myself someone who knew nothing about fashion. Maggie would have a heart attack.

"Milady, would you fancy a walk?" he asked.

That actually sounded nice, and the peak of the heat had already passed, so it should be pleasant. Then I remembered I had something to do first.

"I have to use the library computers to check something, since my phone died. It won't take long. You can come with me if you want." I just had to be careful to avoid Nora. I didn't want her to add more work to my evening, as it was my break, after all.

"It would be my pleasure to escort you, milady."

As we walked to the second floor, obviously taking the stairs, I asked Tristan about the rest of the donation clothes. He confessed to have picked a couple more items from the bags before putting them in the donation bin. I didn't mind. Perhaps he needed them. Could he have come all this way with a suitcase filled only with theater costumes? He had to have researched the Southern heat. Unless he was so immersed in his little-town mindset that he'd ignorantly assumed that the whole world was just like his hometown.

"Did the airline lose your luggage?" I asked, looking away, not wanting to get lost in his olive eyes.

He took a few moments to answer. "Something of that matter," he said with a side smile.

We found a free computer at the middle, and I pulled out an empty chair. He sat and was surprised that the chair moved. His amazement turned to happiness.

"Milady, I am turning!" He said it like a little kid with a new toy, as he spun around the chair's axis and giggled.

He was kind of cuckoo, but I guessed when you were as cute as him, you could get away with a lot. I couldn't help but laugh with him, as he genuinely was having fun. He was simple and funny. So different from any guy I'd met.

I was logging in to the computer when I realized Tristan had bumped into a patron with his traveling chair. She was a regular at the library—and not a very pleasant one. I was afraid I was going to have to do a lot of apologizing, but Tristan's charm seemed to know no boundaries. He was even making her laugh. It seemed like every person who met him was delighted by him. Perhaps I needed to ask Tristan to spend more time around Nora, so that maybe her grumpiness would dissipate too.

I stared at my screen, looking for the updated delivery date for Maggie's birthday present. I had gotten her a handmade wood carousel that was also a music box, very similar to the one she'd had as a little kid. It should've already arrived but seemed to be stuck somewhere on the East Coast, since it had come all the way from Austria. I'd have to get her an in-the-meantime present for her birthday. I was so disappointed. After months of looking for the right present, I would have to look for something else.

"What is the matter, milady?" Tristan asked, pulling his chair closer.

"Something I ordered is not going to arrive here on time. Even when I ordered it a long time ago."

He stared at me with a crease in his brow.

"Do you like buying handmade stuff?" I asked. Maybe he also liked unique things.

"Handmade? There is no other option, is there?" he said, still twirling in his chair. "My page goes to the market often. I assume it's an amusing outing for him."

I shook my head. What the heck was he talking about? He really was a spoiled kid. Maybe his parents were teaching him a lesson by cutting him off. That would explain not having clothes. Maybe he didn't want to take up his family's business and was obsessed with arts and theater. That would explain his way of talking and dressing.

I had gotten lost in my own thoughts about possible stories for Tristan when he suddenly ducked under the desk. I looked around, and the only thing I noticed were the automatic blinds rolling down to cover the sunset that shone straight into the bookshelves.

"Tristan, are you OK?" I asked, but froze at the heat of his hand over mine on my knee. I blushed and looked under the desk, but before I could see what was going on, he jumped out of it, kneeling down.

"A snake! A snake!" he screamed in panic.

The lady closer to us stood fast too. I had no idea what was going on. There was no way a snake could get into the library.

The commotion was such that Nora appeared immediately. "What is going on?"

I looked at Tristan, who was kneeling and brushing the hair off his face. I glanced underneath the desk, but the only thing I found that resembled a snake was a bunch of tied computer cables.

This must look so awkward. "He has . . . he suffers from anxiety and was having a tiny panic attack," I said, hoping my white lie wouldn't offend anyone.

Nora rolled her eyes and stared at us. "A library is not a place for a stunt or prom proposal or whatever it is you two are doing." Then she took a deep breath. "Just stay close, since the library will be closing soon and I don't want to be looking everywhere for you again. Understood?"

I nodded.

Once Nora left, I turned to Tristan. "How about we go for a walk now?"

There was a small trail around the library that started in the garden and ended at the parking lot. It was especially beautiful at this time of the summer, with all the flowers blooming. I could sense Tristan was trying to tell me something, because he would open his mouth but say nothing, and then just smile at me.

"Are you feeling OK, Tristan?" I asked, trying to help him out.

"Milady, have you ever felt that you don't belong somewhere?" he said with his lovely British accent, which was distracting.

I wondered if he was talking about his exchange student situation, or perhaps it was more of a philosophical question.

"To be honest? Many times, at school, with my friend's popular friends. I feel like I belong here, though. At this library, when Nora is not around." I felt the need to clarify, since Nora's presence was tainting my happy place.

He didn't respond and just gave me a side smile.

"I have never been the girl who loves to go out and party all night or not care about school like all the other average people," I added.

"Average can be overrated," he said, and I smiled at him.

He seemed a little off, and I wondered if he was homesick again.

"It's normal to miss your family and hometown. I haven't experienced it, but my sister went through something similar, and it was hard for her," I added, reading between the lines.

Perhaps even if it was one summer, he was just too attached to his hometown, and this experience had been overwhelming. He opened his mouth, but no words came out, like he couldn't find the right words.

"You must miss the places you know and everything that makes your life . . . yours," I added.

"Precisely, milady." His smile was sincere. I kept thinking of the people Marian met when she just got to Australia. They had been so nice to her. I wanted to pay it forward somehow.

"I'm here for you. You know, in case you need help getting around or need more clothes or a place to wash them."

He nodded. "I am in great debt to your kindness, and I will take you up on that, milady."

As we walked around the library garden, I straightened up library signs on the grass. Then someone called Tristan from afar, and as we both turned, we saw Audrey waving in a flirty way as she walked to her car. Tristan smiled back at her. I had no idea what was going on between them, but since he was not from here, I felt that I should tell him something.

"How old are you, Tristan?"

"I could ask you the same question, milady." He seemed to be playing.

"I'll be seventeen this summer," I answered.

"Ah, me too. I mean, sixteen years of age."

"It's none of my business what you do with your love life, but Audrey is an adult, at least legally. You can get her in trouble if you go out with her. I'm just saying." I hated to be nosy, but he seemed so naive.

"There is no need to worry about me, milady. My heart already belongs to someone."

Of course. He was an exchange student, a player. Maybe he had a girlfriend back home and was enjoying flirting on this side of the pond.

I tried to use his flirtatiousness to my advantage. "Can I ask you something and you promise not to make fun of me?" I said as I sat on a bench.

"Mocking a beautiful lady like yourself is something I would never intend to do," he said, sitting by me.

I smiled. "Well, you obviously are good at flirting. Something I'm clearly not. My friend Maggie is having a party. I'm sure you've heard about it." He looked at me attentively, so I kept going. "I have to ask a guy out, and I don't know how," I said, looking away. I wanted to avoid any reaction similar to when Ty mocked me for my obsession with *Romeo and Juliet*.

He looked away, thinking. "Does this man occupy a place in your heart?" His tone was serious.

"Maybe? I . . . I'm not sure." I was not close enough with Tristan to tell him the whole Alex story, especially since I still hadn't figured it out myself. I knew I wanted to ask Alex out as my date for the party, but I was scared of him saying no and our friendship changing forever.

"Loving someone is a wise form of madness. If you ask me, milady, I believe love is not a question but an answer."

I stared at him in awe. I had never heard a guy talk like that. I pursed my lips so I wouldn't drool or do something embarrassing as I stared deeply into his olive eyes. I wanted him to keep talking.

"Do you feel like that for this person?" he asked.

I felt my heartbeat accelerating. Up until now, I never thought parts of what I loved most about Romeo actually existed in someone real. Tristan didn't let me concentrate on my feelings for Alex. I blinked several times and looked away.

"Your silence, perhaps, is the answer that you seek, milady. When true love arrives, it brings no hesitation. For reason is no longer the reign of the body and mind."

Every word that came out of his mouth was poetry.

Nora came out, breaking that special moment and signaling for me to come. I looked at my watch and saw it was almost closing time. I was mad at her interruption, but I knew that if Tristan kept talking like that, I would have trouble stopping myself from kissing him.

"Thank you for being honest with me and for that . . . answer," I said, standing up. "I have to go and help close the library."

He nodded and stood up too. "After you, milady." He bowed.

He was so peculiar. But his uniqueness was making my heart race like no guy had ever done before. I had to remind myself he was an exchange student, and that he might only be flirting. But as we walked toward the library, I let myself be happy. Because perhaps some parts of Romeo might be real, and he was walking right next to me.

Nora switched me from closing to stay at the checkout desk. Which wasn't that bad, to be honest—at least I was sitting down. There weren't many patrons left at the library, but Tristan reconnected with an old toy for him, the automatic doors at the library's entrance. He jumped on the mat, making the door slide open, and took a few steps back into the lobby. He then did it again and again and giggled as if he had just discovered gravity.

"What is he doing?" a young girl asked her mom as I finished checking out their books.

I looked at Tristan and then back at her. "He's a kid at heart, and he's not from around here." I tried to sound friendly, but I was beginning to think that Tristan had been living under a rock since he was born.

Once they left, I motioned him toward me. "Stop it. You're scaring the patrons," I whispered once he was near me.

"Milady, that thing is marvelous. The weight or height of a person does not matter. It still opens at the right time for them to pass and not crash." He sounded like the host of a kids' science show. "And those columns . . ."

"The security sensors? So books don't get taken without being checked out first?" I added.

His eyes widened. "Incredible!" he said.

Sometimes, whenever I was not distracted by his handsomeness, I thought he was out of this world. Or maybe it was the first time he was actually seeing things and not just looking. I had done that when Will was a baby and was impressed by the moon.

Nora's voice was heard through the speakers, announcing that the building would be closing in fifteen minutes. Tristan looked around but then went back to jumping on the entry mat. I had noticed him reading around the library lately. Perhaps he had been reading too much *Don Quixote*, and now it was sticking to him. Maybe the doors were his windmills.

A giggle distracted me. Nichole and two other girls from the swim team looked my way, whispering between them. I had no idea what they found amusing in me. My attire was the same, my hair too. There was nothing out of the ordinary for them to criticize.

They headed toward the exit and ran into Tristan on their way out. He was nice to them, too, even made them laugh. Although he was always super nice to everyone, it annoyed me, because Nichole was far from one of my favorite people. I focused instead on my job, having to take a book to the back.

As soon as I sat back on the chair, Will appeared from behind the desk, calling my name and jumping at me. He scared the crap out of me, making me tumble from the chair. He was cracking up like it had been the most hilarious thing. But Tristan immediately jumped over the checkout desk and helped me up.

"What are you doing back there?" Nora's bossy voice came from behind us and quieted even Will's loud laughter. "You are not an employee nor a volunteer, so please stand back."

Tristan jumped back to the other side of the checkout desk, and I sat on my chair again.

"The library will be closing in five minutes," Nora told me in her usual annoying voice. "Say goodbye to your friend and focus on your job while I go close." Then she headed toward the children's area.

Will stared at Tristan. Perhaps I should introduce them.

"Tristan, this is my little brother, Will, also known as a huge pain in the butt," I said.

Tristan chuckled. "Delighted, mate." He bowed.

"Wow, you do know how to pick them, huh," Will said to me, and I shushed him right away. "You must be the only guy June has ever hung out with, well, besides Alex."

Tristan looked suspicious. "Is Alex the person you were asking me about earlier?"

I looked away. I could feel the heat rushing to my cheeks. I knew what he was saying, but I acted as if I didn't, since I wasn't ready to get into that, and even less in front of Will.

Will took it as an opportunity to mock me about two guys. And even though I was pretty good at ignoring him, somehow Tristan's presence made me unable to. Mom must be around somewhere. If only she'd call him so he'd leave us alone.

"Did you find the soccer stamp you were missing?" I asked Will, desperate to change the subject.

He shook his head and ignored me. Will could talk nonstop about two things, soccer and his favorite book series, about the pirate Captain Jacquotte.

"How's the new book of your friend, Captain Jacquotte?" I asked.

"Stop referring to book characters as friends. No wonder people say you're weird," Will said.

"Well, I heard there's going to be a movie about it," I said, and Will's eyes went wide. He then continued to talk about his favorite character with Tristan. At least I had dodged that bullet.

Tristan was interested in Will's story but kept looking at me sideways, giving me little smiles. Even as I heard Nora's voice through the speakers saying the library was now closed, all I could think of was Tristan's cute olive eyes.

CHAPTER 8

THE COMPLETE TRAGEDIES OF LADY JUNE

It was Friday, the last day of junior year, and also Maggie's birthday. Asking Alex out as my date for the plus-one party had kept me up all night. Fortunately, I had been able to distract myself making last-minute surprises for Maggie's birthday, like making her a handmade birthday card.

Maggie had come to my house for her traditional birthday breakfast, which my mom baked every year, complete with freshly made pecan and cinnamon rolls. My mind had been all over the place this morning when we sat for breakfast together. Mom had given me a suspicious look, since I usually devoured everything immediately.

"Is everything ready for my party?" Maggie had whispered.

I'd panicked, not wanting to tell her that I was going to ask Alex out, not in front of my parents either. I'd simply nodded instead, and she'd seemed happy. I'd kept a cinnamon roll for the road, and we'd headed out the door. I'd tried to keep myself calm on the way, since seeing Alex in literature class was still a couple of hours away.

Maggie and I headed to the last literature class, my favorite with Mr. Grooms. We had arrived with enough time for me to ask Alex out before class started. My hands clasped together as I tried to stop the shaking, since it was getting out of control. I must be overreacting. It would be Alex and me at the party, just like every year. But I knew this time would *feel* different.

I took a deep breath as Maggie and I entered the classroom.

"Surprise!" the wick-pops said in unison, appearing out of nowhere as a bunch of balloons covered our way. They hugged her, acting as if I was completely invisible, even though I was standing right next to her. Once they moved away, we found a huge bouquet of flowers and Dane peeking from behind. He embraced her with a big bear hug, a scene right out of any rom-com.

For a moment I felt like Maggie's in-the-meantime present, a self-care box filled with bath bombs and soaps, seemed insignificant next to those presents. I forced a smile, even though I couldn't stand Dane and the wick-pops. Maggie was truly happy, and that was all that mattered. I walked to my seat while Maggie had a moment with Dane, until Mr. Grooms came and dismantled the group.

Alex was already in his seat in front of me. He stared obsessively at his World Cup album, while Oliver did the same.

"Hey!" I greeted them, trying to keep my nerves at bay. They waved in silence, their eyes still glued to their stamps.

I took an envelope filled with stamps out of my backpack. "Will sent this for you."

Alex looked up, and we met eye to eye. Something felt different, as if I was truly seeing him for the first time.

He smiled and thanked me, then looked through them, and Oliver was also intrigued. I sat at my desk and stared at his messy hair. *Breathe, June,* I told myself over and over. The last thing I needed was for my voice to come out pitchy or to do something embarrassing. We always went together; it wouldn't be such a big deal.

I tapped him on the shoulder. He half turned on his seat, still looking at the stamps.

"Hey, about the party . . ." My voice came out funny. I tried to clear my throat to regain control of myself. He stopped looking at the stamps and turned completely to look at me. "I was wondering if you would like to—"

"He already has a date," Nichole interrupted, leaning on Alex's desk.

I stared at her, annoyed. "What?"

She pointed at herself. "I'm his date. Can you believe he finally ask me out, *and* as his date for the plus-one?" Nichole's triumphant tone was worthy of any Disney villain. Her smile was wide as she leaned on Alex's shoulder, her arm around him.

I shook my head. That was impossible. I looked at Alex, and he looked away, avoiding me. After a second I realized Maggie had been so wrong. I felt as if an ice-cold bucket had fallen over me as I tried to come up with something to get me out of this embarrassing situation.

"I was . . . that's not what I was going to ask." I laughed nervously, looking away from them. I needed a believable getaway. *Books,* that was always the answer. "I wanted to ask if you could bring my book to the party. You know, the one I lent you a while ago, before you leave for the summer," I managed to say before my throat closed completely. At any given moment, Alex always had one or several books of mine. It had to work.

"Sure." He nodded with a sort of gloomy tone. His eyes were not on his precious stamps but looking away.

Nichole stared at me with a devilish smile. I took a book from my backpack and opened it randomly. I stared at the words on the page, but none of the sentences made sense, as I couldn't focus. That must be the reason she was whispering to her friends and mocking me at the library. Alex had already asked her, and he didn't tell me. He was the one who asked me to always be honest with him.

I crumbled into a mix of anger, bitterness, and sadness. Not only would I have to get over these feelings again, but now I didn't have a date for the party. And the plus-one was tomorrow night.

The knot in my throat tightened. I wouldn't allow myself to cry. I undid my side braid and brushed my hair with my fingers as I looked up, which always helped keep the tears at bay. Mr. Grooms asked everyone to sit down, and Nichole walked back to her place in the front row.

Mr. Grooms called the roll, and Maggie walked to her seat next to me, holding her bouquet. The smell of fresh flowers annoyed me. I hated real guys. I shouldn't have relied on school gossip. Why couldn't I have stayed with my fictional book boyfriends like I always had? Why did I have to be such a fool to believe a love story could happen to me in real life?

Maggie smelled each and every one of her flowers. She even took pictures at different angles. I was sure they would be up on social media in no time. None of this would have happened if she hadn't told me about Alex singing *me* a song.

"June Capehart."

Mr. Grooms calling me distracted me from my internal monologue. I raised my hand and looked out the window, at the blue sky outside. My frustration was such that all I wanted was to scribble in a notebook until the ink ran out, until the page was destroyed. This had all been a failed plan from the start. I had put myself out there, but Alex clearly wanted me in the friend zone, again.

Maggie giggled, and I turned to find Dane winking at her from afar. This was all too much, way too corny for me, and I was a sucker for romance novels. Maggie took out a notebook and tore a piece of paper from the last page. I stared as she scribbled a note to pass to Dane. Love did that to people. Love made you forget texts and go for the real thing.

She crushed the tiny paper and ripped another one. There was a similarity between Maggie's crushed note and the way I felt. It was one thing to have a secret crush on my best friend years ago when I was young and naive, and another to feel my heart break for a second time for the same reason. There was only so much silent rejection I could take from the same guy.

I stared at Alex's messy hair. He wasn't to blame. He had no idea how I felt about him, not the first time and not now. I hated that today was Maggie's birthday, and I couldn't bring myself to tell her anything that could affect her day.

"I like your loose hair," Maggie said, and I pushed a bunch of it behind my ear.

Maggie raised one eyebrow. She was my best friend, so of course she could see right through me. The anger had opened the knot in my throat, but I had to keep my cool.

"So how long have you and Dane been an official couple?" I asked in a low voice.

"A couple of days. I told you, remember?" Maggie said.

"No, you didn't," I answered, offended. These were the type of things that you tell your best friend ASAP. Unless I was losing against the wick-pops too.

"I swear I did." Maggie stared at her flowers. "Anyway, doesn't it sound amazing? Dane Cooper, *my* boyfriend?" She sighed. "We'll look so cute with the photo booth props at my party."

Maggie not telling me about her big news added to my despair.

"Students, the class is this way." Mr. Grooms pointed at the screen over the blackboard as he explained to us that we would be watching a movie while he handed out our final essays.

"You will be familiar with this story, and more than a few

will enjoy it." Mr. Grooms stared at me. "I know that asking you to read during summer is almost an impossible task, but I hope you at least remember this movie," he said, leaning on his desk. "We will start next school year with this play. It is a close adaptation. I invite you to focus on the richness of the language as well as how the series of events trigger the conflict of the story."

Some students talked too loud, and Mr. Grooms cleared his throat. Then he turned to put the DVD in the old classroom player.

The screen lit up, and the title appeared on the screen. I couldn't believe my eyes. It was a very old version of *Romeo and Juliet*, from the late sixties, one I hadn't seen before. At least I could easily get distracted by something other than school drama. I just wanted to forget the world around me.

The amazing prologue started, and I soaked in the words. No matter how old the movie was, that love story was my obsession. Mr. Grooms walked through the aisles, handing out our graded final essays. Once the hypnotizing prologue ended, Mr. Grooms stood by my place.

"Miss Capehart, I was a little disappointed in your selection of literary character, totally predictable. The assignment was about pairing up with a classmate and describing the same character as hero and antihero."

I nodded.

"But, nevertheless, it was a remarkable essay." He handed me my paper.

I had gotten an A-. I honesty expected an A+, but I guess choosing Romeo as a hero was way into my comfort zone.

Mr. Grooms turned to Maggie. "Miss Hathaway, your essay was . . . surprising." He paused. "And by that, I mean good. Congratulations."

Maggie turned over her paper. Not even she could believe it. It was an A+. I knew my grade was good, but I was not expecting the punch in my ego when I saw Maggie's grade was better than mine. Especially when she never even read the required readings.

I had beaten myself up a couple of weeks ago when she said she didn't need my help for the literature assignment, when usually I wrote all her literature papers.

"Did you really write this?" I whispered once Mr. Grooms was away from us.

She shook her head. "Juny-June, I knew you would have to dig really, *really* deep to write an essay pointing out Romeo's flaws, and I'm on your team, remember? But, like always, I found a way to make it happen."

I took it from her desk and began to read.

The words felt familiar, and right away I knew who was behind them.

"Tyler wrote your paper?" I asked.

She winked at me. "Stop calling him Tyler. It sounds weird." Maggie seemed totally immersed in her flowers.

I wanted to argue that Tyler was his real name, but then I thought that maybe he could be my date to the party. I would be miserable, but I needed someone, and it would make Maggie happy.

"Why didn't it work with Ty?" Maggie asked out of the blue, still staring at her bouquet.

Damn it, I couldn't go with him now to the party.

"Was he too much?" Maggie asked, and this time I faked being completely immersed in the movie. I knew the plot by heart, scene by scene. I could recite the lines in my sleep, but I didn't want Maggie to read me like a book and discover how miserable I had been on that date.

"His obsession with piercings and tattoos was a little too much."

Maggie laughed. "Wait, did you kiss him?"

"What? No!" I said loudly. "No," I repeated more calmly.

"So you didn't get to enjoy his tongue piercing?" Maggie stuck her tongue out, and I shook my head immediately. "Piercings can be sexy, you know?" Maggie added.

"In that place?" I whispered as I pointed to my boobs. She laughed silently, and it was so contagious I did, too, trying to hide from Mr. Grooms.

"Sorry if he was so bold. I thought you two would have something in common. He can talk for hours and hours about art, and books are some sort of art. I assumed you'd hit it off."

I didn't know what else to say. Telling her that it had been unbearable was not the way I wanted to steer our conversation.

Maggie blew out a breath. "So now that Ty found a date for my party, are you happy you are going with . . .?" She motioned her chin toward Alex, but I shook my head.

Mr. Grooms shushed us, and the class went more silent than usual as we listened to the dialogue in the movie. Maggie went back to staring at her flowers.

"Can I get a hint of who you will be taking to my party, then?" she whispered. "I thought I could wait for the surprise, but I can't."

Alex sat up straight in front of me, and I realized that he was listening to our conversation.

I focused on Juliet instead, mouthing the words along with her: *Romeo oh Romeo.* I stared at the way he dressed. *That's it!*

I looked at Mr. Grooms. Once he was looking away, I whispered, "I already have a date." A white lie, but Maggie wanted an answer. "I met him at the library. He's an exchange student, in fact," I added, hoping my words would be somehow prescient, and Tristan would say yes.

"Really?" Maggie's high pitch was anything but sneaky, and her smile was wide. She jumped up and down in her seat, making it impossible to go unnoticed. "I can't wait!"

Mr. Grooms cleared his throat. "Miss Capehart, am I interrupting you?"

He chided me even though no one paid attention at the end of the school year, even less so on the last day of school. Still, I didn't want to make my favorite teacher mad. I shook my head and apologized.

I kept my eyes glued to the screen, getting lost in Verona. Then I saw Maggie texting nonstop, using the huge bouquet as cover. News traveled fast, because the wick-pops couldn't hide their shocked faces as they turned my way. If an antisocial nerd like me was going out with an exchange student, it was sure to be the juiciest gossip.

My phone buzzed right away, and I let my hair down to cover the text from Alex.

> Are you really going with an exchange guy?

I didn't want to talk to Alex or have anything to do with him right now. I ignored his text and focused on the movie instead. The last thing I wanted was to discuss my love life with him.

Once the bell rang, I said goodbye to Mr. Grooms and ran away from the classroom. I wasn't going to let the wick-pops interrogate me or Nichole display her territorial attitude with Alex like some wild mating bird. I didn't care if I would miss my next class. I just couldn't stand spending one more minute around a guy who had forever exiled me to the friend zone.

CHAPTER 9

STORIES OF WOE

Instead of heading to my last algebra class, where Alex would be, I hid in the restroom, at least until the next class started. Once the second bell rang and most of the students were in their classrooms, I headed toward my locker to empty it before the day ended.

I always checked out more books than I could read from both the school *and* the public library. Now was the time to sort them and return them to their respective places. Besides, the library was my safe place, and I needed a big dose of quiet time, because my thoughts about Alex were not getting any quieter.

I quickly took away all the interior decor from my locker. The last thing I wanted was to look at a picture of Alex, even if it was not a recent one. I hadn't brought an extra tote to carry the books, and my backpack was not big enough. I was stuck carrying a bunch of paperbacks and hardcovers.

The school library, like apparently all libraries, was colder than any other building. I put on my hoodie and returned the school library books. It didn't do much to lighten my heavy load, since most books in my locker had been from the public library. I was now stuck carrying a bunch of books for the next couple of hours.

I needed to find a way to relax, and the tension of my shoulders was pinching the nerves in my neck. One thing that almost always worked was to write my sorrows away. Especially after I finished a book that had devastated me emotionally and left me with a literary hangover.

All the library cubicles were empty, so I could pick wherever I wanted to sit and write. I didn't journal every day, only every now and then, but info dumping on a notebook soothed my soul. Once Marian left to an unreachable time zone and I could no longer vent to her, notebooks became the next best thing.

I opened my notebook and looked for an empty page. Doodles scattered through the pages, along with my favorite book quotes, made me realize I needed to get new notebooks. I took a cute glittery pen and wrote away. My mind worked way faster than my hand. Even though I wrote nonstop, my pen had trouble keeping up with my racing thoughts, and often my hand went numb after a while. Once I finished, even if my fingers were sore, my soul felt lighter, and no one would judge me for what I had written.

Several text messages arrived at the same time, distracting me from my writing. Apparently my phone hadn't had reception until now. Nora, like always, wanted to know if I was at the library. It was fun to keep her guessing. Once she got used to me working overtime, she expected me to be there at all times, as if I was a full-time staff member. But since I wasn't getting paid enough, I'd decided to not answer her messages during schooltime.

Her message was from over two hours ago. I'd have to get back to her to avoid any extra sassiness from her later. Then I realized I had other unread messages, all from Alex.

Where r you?

R u not coming to class?

U ok?

Want 2 talk?

I need to talk 2 u

I had written so much about my feelings, yet Alex's message made me feel like I hadn't released enough. Why did everything have to be weird between us now? We were fine before that stupid song, more than fine. But now I couldn't help feeling some sort of despair and hopelessness when I read his name. The three dots on the screen blinked, meaning Alex was texting again. Those blinking dots were like anxiety on steroids.

Let me give you a ride to the library.

I was still hurt and mad at Alex. But I had no other way to get to the library after school, since I hadn't brought my bike. There was no way I could walk all the way to the library in this heat and with all these heavy books.

K

My sour mood showed through my response. Alex's only reply was a thumbs-up emoji. I would have to talk to him, and I needed to be as chill as possible. I needed to act as if all this mess was in my head, because it was. He had no idea my crush on him had risen from its grave.

I'd had to wait for him to finish his afterschool practice. Unlike other sports where athletes could take a break once competition season was over, swimmers had to constantly train and keep up so they didn't lose the progress they'd achieved. I had more time on my hands than I had originally planned, but as long as I was surrounded by books, it was fun. Even though the school library had a smaller catalog than the public one, I still liked spending time here. And this time, since there was no hottie like Tristan roaming the aisles, I could focus on my reading.

I walked around and browsed the New Books section. Even as my TBR list was infinite, any book nerd knew there was no harm in adding a few more titles to it. I only needed to scan the book's barcode on my phone for it to log in to my app. I loved this kind of technology, because it saved me so much time typing, especially after my fingers were sore from writing.

A noise distracted me, the mix of a soft laugh and a moan. I looked around me, but there was no one. Something odd was going on with me and strange noises in libraries—it was getting creepy. As I returned a book to its place, between the bookshelves and a couple of rows back, I saw someone. In fact, there were two people. A couple was making out in a dark corner at the back of the library. It was the less-visited section and a famous make-out spot as long as you didn't get caught.

At this time of the year the library was deserted. I didn't care about other people's business, but the guy looked strangely familiar. I moved a couple of aisles closer to identify the couple, acting as if I was looking for a specific book.

I recognized the girl first. It was Amy from the swim team. Then she moved a little to the side, and I saw clearly who the guy was—Dane. Oh crap! He was cheating on Maggie AND on her birthday! I tried to get closer to make sure I wasn't imagining things. Maybe Dane had a doppelgänger wandering through school. I wasn't mistaken. It was the real Dane Cooper. The despicable dude Alex had warned Maggie about.

I grabbed my phone to take a picture so I could have proof to show Maggie, but the light was wrong, and I was too far away to get a good shot. As I walked a little closer to take the picture, I got an incoming call. The buzzing scared me, and I dropped my phone. It bounced on the floor and landed on the lower level of a bookshelf, in a hard-to-reach place, then vibrated loudly against the metal. I tried to bend down to get it, but it was too far for me to reach without walking to the other side of the aisle. I couldn't do that, because Dane would see me.

The buzzing stopped, and I felt relieved, but then it buzzed again. The sound was amplified even more by the silence of the empty library.

I lay on the floor, stretching as much as I could, trying desperately to reach it. When I finally did, the call had gone to voice mail. I checked the screen. This was the worst time for Marian to call. We had missed each other's calls so much lately, and I really wanted to talk to my sister. But this ruined my chance to take Dane's picture. I stood up fast and looked through the aisles, but they were gone.

I sat on the floor, trying to make myself small and process what I had just witnessed. Marian called again, but I rejected her call, sending her a text instead. How could it be that after that amazing bouquet Dane was making out with someone else? Alex had said Dane was a horrible person, but I never thought he could be *that* shameless. I had to find Maggie right away. These were not things to do through a text. I waited a little more to make sure I wouldn't bump into them, because that would be really awkward.

After what felt like forever, I headed toward the main aisle to gather my things, but as soon as I turned the corner, I bumped into Dane, who immediately let go of Amy's hand. I wanted to become tiny so I could hide between books, but all I could do was push my glasses up the bridge of my nose.

"Hey, June." Dane spoke to me for the first time ever.

He looked anxious, something that seemed unfamiliar to him.

He looked around and above me as if talking to me would put his popularity at stake. It was really the other way around, the library's image diminished with every couple who came only to make out.

"Dane. Amy." I mimicked his attitude, saying their names. This was incredibly uncomfortable, considering I had experience in awkwardness with guys. I tried to act in the most peaceful and polite way I could, even if my blood was boiling. Anyone who would betray my best friend was automatically on my dead-or-alive list.

"I know what you are thinking," he said with annoying confidence, trying to outsmart me.

I hid the words *doubt it* as I coughed.

"This is not what it looks like. Amy and I were . . ."

"It's none of my business," I interrupted. I didn't care about whatever he had to say. I just wanted to leave so I could find Maggie ASAP.

"Look"—he took a step closer, trying to intimidate me with his height—"if I were you, I'd keep my mouth shut." His cocky smile was shameless. "Unless you want to be responsible for making this the worst day of her life."

I frowned. I disliked him more than Nora. And that was saying something.

"Besides, whatever it is you *think* you saw, it would destroy your friend's heart. And I'm sure you don't want to do that on her *birthday*."

Wow, he was low and manipulative.

"How about this?" His tone lowered. "I'll tell her first thing tomorrow. It's the right thing for me to do, don't you think?" His cocky smile returned.

Guys like him were even worse than villains in books. Dane was just a spoiled rich kid who played people for his own agenda.

He stared at me, waiting. I took a deep breath, considering

his words. Somehow he had a point. No one would want to hear that kind of news on their birthday, and I had seen the way Maggie stared at her flowers. I couldn't do that to her, not today.

I agreed, hoping a person like him would keep his word. If by first thing tomorrow he hadn't told her, I would. Hopefully with Maggie's luck and charm, she would find a summer fling during her upcoming trip, and it would make her forget everything about despicable Dane.

Dane gave me another cocky smile and walked away, with Amy behind him. I stared at them as they headed toward the exit. Just before they left, Dane turned back and stared at me. Not only was he selfish and mean, but he was the worst guy to ever walk the face of the earth.

It had been an eventful day at school, especially since the last ones were usually pretty boring. I constantly doubted whether to tell Maggie right away. No one was going to treat my best friend like that, but I had to think before ruining her day. I didn't want anger and impulsivity to drive my decisions. That was what had put Romeo in a tough situation in his own play. I tried to slow down and think. Should I go over to her house tomorrow morning? Should I trust Dane to tell Maggie? Should I look for signs of her dealing with heartbreak in the upcoming hours?

The more I thought about it, the less I knew what to do. I was sure of only one thing: I wanted to protect Maggie. Her crush for Dane had been going on for so long that I wondered how I could tell her without destroying her completely.

I gathered all my things and headed to the competition pool. She was surely there waiting for Dane, who obviously had missed practice. Perhaps I could give her a hint so the news didn't catch her off guard.

Once I got to the competition pool, I peeked through the door window. The pool was almost empty, and only one person was swimming laps.

I ventured inside, then quickly sprinted to hide under the bleachers. Getting caught by the coach would definitely get me into trouble even if it was the last day of school. Fortunately, a couple of people were leaving, and there seemed to be no one else there to notice me, besides the swimmer, who was doing their own thing.

Under the bleachers, the signs hanging on the opposite side caught my eye. *Go Sea Wolves!*, *Storybridge's Swim Team to the Lead*, and my favorite, the one I had made for Alex at the beginning of the school year: *Chlorine is our perfume.*

I thought about calling Maggie, but she would know something was off. Maybe waiting was the best strategy. Once the dust settled, and I hoped it would settle by tonight, I would call her.

Besides, even though I hated Dane, I had to give him space to end things the right way. It was their relationship, after all. The last time I tried to help Marian with her last boyfriend, we ended up not talking for a month, and it was the longest month ever. I only hoped Maggie was having fun and away from Dane, even if that meant hanging out with the wick-pops.

I was about to leave when the splashing stopped. It seemed like the swimmer, who I assumed was a guy, was about to get out. I didn't want to have a weird interaction with someone I probably didn't know. What would I say? *You are doing great. Nice jammers? I'm looking for Maggie's future ex-boyfriend?* Or something stupid like the usual things I said when I was nervous. I didn't have a logical alibi, so the best thing was to wait.

I was standing patiently underneath the bleachers when the

swimmer, who turned out to be a very hot guy, got out of the pool, looking like a model from a perfume ad. He had an amazing body highlighted by the water beading on his tanned skin. I couldn't recognize who he was, since he had his goggles and cap still on, but I couldn't stop staring at him, and part of me hoped he didn't have a date for the party. I hit my head on the metal as I looked closer. He looked my way at the sound but didn't see me.

The door opened, and Nichole came in. "Coach is looking for you," she said, and he nodded.

I couldn't stop staring at his well-formed abs. I leaned forward to get a closer look. He reached down to grab his towel and patted his torso. He was even hotter than my imaginary book boyfriends, like a literary Greek god. When he took his cap and goggles off, my eyes opened to their max, and I dropped some books. The sound of the spines hitting the metal base of the bleachers was impossible to miss. He and Nichole looked my way, and she started in my direction. There was nowhere to hide. I'd get in trouble. I grabbed my books and ran to the exit. As I passed them, I heard Alex's voice calling me as I pushed the pool doors opened, but I kept going.

I ran to the parking lot, looking for Maggie's car, but it was gone. Then I looked for Alex's blue Jeep, and once I found it, I ran to it, avoiding the cars that drove through the parking lot. Why had I become such a mess after that stupid song? I had to calm down, because Alex would be here soon. I sat underneath the shade of a beautiful oak tree closest to his Jeep.

Of all the competitions I had attended, of all the countless times we had both been wearing swimming suits together at the neighborhood pool, I had never felt out of breath from looking at his body.

My heartache felt heavier, like an anchor that had been dropped at sea. Before, he was only Alex, my buddy, my best friend. But now he was everything I wanted and couldn't have. My heartache was again about the same guy, and not related to one made out of words and imagination.

I took a deep breath and let the heaviness inside sink in. I had allowed myself to believe something would be possible between me and him. *Be positive,* I had thought. But this time it would take way longer than an evening of endless ice cream to forget him. The image of his body coming out of the pool, the way butterflies fluttered when I met his eyes in the morning. All these feelings weren't inside of me a week ago. Why did I have to open that stupid Pandora's box, and with a song I didn't even understand?

I looked through the books I had left, trying to focus on something other than an impossible love. Even if it was about improving my drawing skills or learning how to crochet. I didn't care, I needed something to take my mind off him, because he would be here any minute, and I couldn't tell him all this.

For the first time, I couldn't let Alex in. I wouldn't be able to tell him why I was acting so weird around him or why I would be spending the whole trip to the library staring out the window. I would have to endure the ride to the library acting as if my heart was not in pieces, acting as if it was not him, but a literary character, who had broken my heart this time.

As I browsed through the books, I realized I was missing one. I was sure I'd had it earlier when I emptied my locker. Then I hit my forehead with my palm. This day couldn't get any worse. I must have left it under the bleachers. I bumped my forehead with one of the hardcovers, repeatedly. Why did I have to become such a stupid girl when real boys were involved? That was the exact reason I preferred them fictional. Because they didn't mess with my life. They stayed between the pages. And when the story wasn't going to my liking, I could simply close the book and go back to my normal life. But now this was real, this was not fiction, and my life felt like a tragedy.

Alex showed up twenty-six pages later as I was immersed in learning about the different yarn fibers in a crochet book.

"I think you were looking for this?" he said and handed me the book I was missing.

I tried to pretend I was so immersed in my book I hadn't seen him. That would give my heart a couple of seconds to slow down to a steady beat. I stared at his signature untied sneakers and noticed his typical scent. It didn't matter that he had just taken a shower. He still smelled like chlorine.

I stood up and grabbed the book, thanking him as I stared at his signature damp frizzy hair. My cheeks warmed, but I blamed it on the Southern heat. He walked to the rear of the Jeep and swung the back door to the side. I stared at the bike rack over the spare tire. It had not been there last week.

"Is that new?" I asked, trying to avoid talking about the embarrassing moment of me stalking him behind the bleachers.

"Oh yeah." He seemed surprised by my question.

"Are you now a biker too? Is there anything else you are not telling me?" I asked, regretting how my passive-aggressive tone came out unexpectedly.

He stared at me, then ran his hand over his wet hair, making it even frizzier.

"It's for Edgar," he said, unsure.

I knew Edgar was anything but athletic, but I didn't want to get into that. Besides, it was taking all my energy to simply act cool. I left my bag and heavy books in the trunk, and he closed it. We were about to jump in the car when someone shouted goodbye at him from three rows down—Nichole.

I ignored her and got in and shut my door. I'd had enough of her. Alex jumped in shortly after and stared at me, but I refused to look at him. I tried to focus instead on how colorful my favorite sneakers were. He turned on the ignition, and the music blasted from the speakers, making me jump. He chuckled and lowered the volume. Any other day, we would both be laughing, but not today. I stared attentively out the window, which would be my focus point for the whole seventeen minutes that the ride was going to last.

The silence between us felt so weird. Especially since there weren't more than a few seconds of silence when we were together. I recognized some of the songs. He had even played a couple of them, but I still didn't understand the lyrics, because they were all in Spanish.

It wasn't the traditional Mexican music people usually thought about. It was easy pop with a lot of guitar sounds in the background and some piano, which made it sound romantic. I untied my braid again, trying to focus on anything other than songs.

"June," Alex said as we were on our way.

"What?" My tone came out defensive.

"We don't fight. That's just not what we do. We disagree on book reviews and flavors of ice cream. We disagree on music and what's considered the right or wrong amount of time to be actually late, but not *this*." He stared at me with a disappointed look on his face.

"Well, maybe it's long overdue. I mean, siblings fight, friends fight, so I guess it's our time now," I answered, looking out the window.

He was right. We never, ever fought. We joked, we disagreed and ignored each other for hours, but not this.

"June, come on. What is the real reason you're so mad at me? You don't want me to take Nichole? Is that it?"

The fact he was making me look like a jealous girlfriend

made me furious. And the last time I checked, we were *only* friends.

"Why did you lie to me when I asked if something was going on with Nichole?" I couldn't help it. The Nichole topic was really bugging me.

"I didn't lie. There is nothing going on between us. I thought we were going to the party together like always." He pointed at both of us. "But you went out with that weird friend of Maggie, and I thought you wanted that. You know I don't care about the stupid party, but you do. You care about pleasing Maggie so much you even had your first date with some random dude."

I didn't say a word, so he kept going.

"I'm an expert by now about your favorite book boyfriends. I've heard you talking about them for hours, and believe me, that random dude was very far from your ideal Romeo. The opposite, in fact."

I tried to be calm. But he knew me so well it was annoying. It left no room to hide.

"I knew you would go to that party, no matter who you went with. And I needed a date to be there for you. I just knew Nichole would say yes," he said with a hint of overconfidence.

Suddenly I felt I was with Tyler in the car, not Alex. The confidence in knowing Nichole wanted him was so unlike him.

"Hey, I know you, June," he mocked.

"No, you don't," I said, looking down, noticing how he shifted the stick as he drove.

He was right about everything, but I didn't want him to know it. I didn't want him to see how desperate I was to not lose Maggie, but by the way she totally missed telling me about her and Dane this morning, it seemed that no matter what I did, I was already losing.

"Is that what you want me to say? That you were right?" I asked defensively.

Maybe he just wanted me to say it. Some guys loved to hear

that, only caring about the words, rather than the pain that came from whoever said them.

He gave me a confused look. I was losing control of my words and my emotions, and I couldn't let that happen.

I set my arm on the armrest between us, trying to relax my shoulders, and stared out the window in silence. I shouldn't have cared about all this.

We reached Main Street, and Alex put his hand over the armrest as he merged onto the road. For a moment his fingers landed on top of mine. It was electric, and I didn't want to move. I could feel the warmth of his hand, and part of me wanted to hold his. I wanted to tell him I couldn't stop thinking about him since he sang that song. That I couldn't keep his messy hair and voice out of my mind. That these feelings had resurfaced along with a fear of losing him. Everything he represented was so against my imaginary Romeo, but still I wanted him.

He took his hand off and put it on the wheel. "I can't uninvite Nichole. She canceled on Brody to go out with me. He's not very happy about that, by the way," he said, as if what had just happened meant nothing.

"I'm not asking you to do that. I already have a date," I said, feeling annoyed at looking like I couldn't get a date.

Neither of us said anything for a while, him looking at the road and me at the trees.

"Why didn't you ask me first?" I asked, surprised the words left my mouth. "We always go together," I added, trying to sound more friendly.

"I don't know." He looked at me. "But it's OK. Don't worry. After the stupid party we can go back to normal and pretend none of this mess ever happened."

The mess. The only mess here was me. Whatever mess he

was thinking of felt totally different from the one twisting inside me. I couldn't go back to where I was before. You couldn't just turn on and off your feelings for someone. Once you named the feelings and put them into words, whether spoken or thoughts in your head, you couldn't escape from them anymore.

The only thing that had helped me in the past was time apart, and that would come soon, but not until after the party. And he'd meet new people at Arthsteen U, and then he would date new people. And I would lose my best friend forever. The spiral of thoughts was drowning me. I stared at the street signs as we got closer and closer to the library, but the tears wanted to come out. Once I was inside the library, surrounded by books, I'd feel better.

We arrived curbside at the library, and before he could turn off his Jeep, I opened my door, jumped out, and opened the back door, then rushed to take my books out. He came quickly and tried to help.

"I don't need your help," I said, taking the books out of his hands. I pulled one of them too hard, and it flew by and landed on the sidewalk. I stared at the book, worried that I had damaged a library book, but a pair of leather boots stood next to it and picked it up.

"Milady, what is the matter?" Tristan asked, and for a moment I let go of my anger. I focused on his British accent that always made me forget everything.

"Hi, Tristan. Nothing, I'm fine," I said, grabbing the remaining books from the trunk and walking toward him.

Once I stood by Tristan, he immediately grabbed my backpack and carried it for me. It was so nice of him. Alex came closer, and both guys stared awkwardly at each other before I introduced them. Tristan stared at Alex suspiciously but eventually bowed slightly.

"Tristan is my date for the party," I added, holding Tristan's arm.

The uncomfortable tension between them didn't seem to change after I introduced them. They still didn't seem thrilled with each other.

"Is he really your date to the party?" Alex asked, staring at Tristan's outfit, he was wearing his theater costume. At least his thick jacket was open in the middle, so it could pass for a retro one and not Grandma's old couch.

"Indeed," Tristan intervened proudly, staring at me with his gorgeous olive eyes. "I am the lucky man that will escort this beautiful lady to the party." His fingers interlaced with mine.

The look in Tristan's eyes as he stared at me gave me jitters. I couldn't believe he didn't have a date. It seemed too good to be true. It felt as if the heavy books I was carrying were suddenly as light as mass paperbacks.

I smiled and looked away. I didn't want him to notice me blushing. His fingers were cold, not as warm as Alex's. Perhaps he also suffered from cold library syndrome, like me. That would explain his thick jacket.

Alex stared at us with a look that I couldn't read well. "I guess I'll see you guys tomorrow at the party."

Tristan nodded and turned to me. "Milady, let me assist you with your books."

I felt all the weight lift off me, literally and figuratively.

I turned to Alex. "Thanks for the ride," I said, not feeling the big rushing anger anymore.

He turned my way and nodded but didn't meet my eyes.

"Farewell, Alex," Tristan added.

Alex got into his Jeep without looking back. I didn't know why I couldn't take my eyes off his blue Jeep as it drove away.

"Shall we, milady?" Tristan said, and we headed inside the cold library.

CHAPTER 10

BIKES, BUBBLES, AND ICE-CREAM LOVERS

I t was no surprise that as soon as we entered the library, Nora jumped on us and demanded that I should follow her immediately. It was especially embarrassing since Nora called my name louder than a normal person would speak inside a library. Apparently they were behind schedule getting everything ready for the library's upcoming celebration this Sunday. In my opinion, we still had time, but for Nora everything was urgent, and that poked my anxiety up a notch.

As I worked from the children's reference desk, I kept looking at Tristan, who was calmly reading in a corner. Every now and then, while I cut the bookmarks I had designed for kids to color, I stared at him sitting in one of the colorful chairs on the main floor. There was something romantic about watching a guy read in public. It made my heart skip a beat. It was so rare to find a guy interested in books, since most guys preferred screens. I secretly wished my future Romeo liked to read too.

Tristan shifted in his seat, and I looked away. He was hypnotizing to watch. I was glad he didn't seem to notice me, because I could stare at him for hours, especially when he wore his theater costume. He looked like a prince out of a fairy tale.

Even though my usual Romeo-like crushes were medieval-style, I never thought I'd be having a crush on a *prince-from-a-fairy-tale* kind of guy. He looked my way, and I blushed, then looked away, acting as if I was deeply immersed in my job rather than stalking him.

A moment later Tristan was coming toward me, and the fluttering inside of me increased. I noticed a ribbon that hung on his neck. The blue color meant he was a volunteer at this library.

"You are one of us now, huh?" I asked as he approached.

Tristan stared at me as if I were speaking another language.

"Your badge?" I pointed.

"Ah, indeed, I am. Lady Sarah made the honors." He bowed.

I always found it funny how even though we all learned grammar rules and spelling in elementary school, no one really spoke that proper. Unless they had learned English as a second language. Talking so well was one of Tristan's quirks, and I loved it.

He chuckled awkwardly, and I realized I was staring at him again. I immediately looked away, hoping he wouldn't notice my cheeks blushing.

"Milady, may I have a word?" Tristan whispered, getting closer to me.

I swallowed hard, trying to keep my body temperature normal. "Sure," I answered, standing up quickly.

"Do you recall your previous offer about providing me with assistance if I ever needed it?" His gorgeous olive eyes stared, hypnotizing. I nodded, trying to not get lost in his proper English. "I do not want to become a nuisance or create inconveniences, but is there perhaps someone who could wash my clothes?" he asked, not looking me in the eye.

I was so sure his mom did everything for him, so for him to ask for help must be a first.

"Yeah, you can come over to my house and you can . . . we can wash them . . . together. I mean, we'll wait for the machine to wash them for us." I smiled, trying to contain my stupid anxiety, which was through the roof. He thanked me with one of his bright smiles.

"What were you reading?" I asked before I could do anything more embarrassing.

He stared at the book in his hand. "Milady, mock me not. But of all the books I have encountered, this is perhaps the first one I have genuinely understood." He showed me the cover. It was *Don Quixote.* I couldn't believe a hot guy like him enjoyed the classics.

Nora appeared from behind and asked me to follow her. I waved at Tristan, still in disbelief that my imaginary type of guy actually existed.

I was almost done with the giveaway tote bags for the library party when Sarah came holding my bag. "I think your phone is in there, because it buzzed several times. I assumed it might be important."

I thanked her and checked. I had two missed calls from Marian. It was such a bummer to miss each other again.

"Do you carry rocks in there?" Sarah asked jokingly.

I laughed. "Sort of? I always carry a book, my electronic reader, and my lucky charm," I said, pulling out my *Romeo and Juliet* pocket edition.

"Oh my, that is gorgeous, may I?" she said, and I handed it over. She browsed through the pages "It *is* a unique edition."

"It was a gift from my sister, and I carry it everywhere with me. Never leaves my side." I stared at my bag. "Well, almost never," I corrected.

Sarah nodded. "I love collecting book treasures too. I have a soft spot for unique bookmarks. My most treasured one is the one my niece made for me. She's five." Sarah smiled and handed me my book back. "Are you done for today?" She looked at the neatly arranged pile of tote bags. "Because I think it's time for a much-deserved break," she said, handing me over a couple of coupons.

I looked at them, seeing they were for the local ice-cream place that had just opened a couple of weeks ago.

"Thank you!" I said as I checked the time. I could take the evening off, since I had finished everything Nora had asked me. Maybe Tristan would like to join me too. I'd love to hear whatever he had to say about Don Quixote and other literature classics.

"Enjoy, dear," Sarah said, patting me on the shoulder. "Just make sure you take your bag with you. I mean, I don't know if the coupons cover the eccentric ice creams they serve over at that store. My niece has told me all about the bizarre flavors."

I chuckled and thanked her again.

"Leave now before Nora comes back. I'll tell her you had to go do something important." She winked at me and then walked away.

If only Sarah could be my supervisor. That would make my summer much more enjoyable.

The look Tristan gave me when I told him we were going for a ride on my bike was surprising, to say the least. I assumed that no matter how spoiled he was, he must surely know how to ride a bike. It was like a childhood rite of passage. But apparently he didn't find it at all amusing and even acted as if my bike was too much for him. Perhaps it looked a little childish, being a neon teal color with bright-yellow rims and a white flowered basket. Will had been embarrassed to even ride along with me once on our way to school. But I loved how unique and different it was. Besides, it was also an environmentally friendly way of transportation too. I unlocked my bike from the stand since it had stayed overnight.

"Is it intended for two passengers, milady?" Tristan asked, looking over my bike.

"Ta-da!" I said, removing the cover on the back. "You can sit here, behind me." I patted the back seat that my parents had given me last Christmas with the intention of Will and me spending more time together once Marian was gone. It had not been used until today. "Just put your feet over those tubes and keep them there or you'll make us fall," I said, pointing at the back wheel and the footrests.

Tristan looked unsure.

"C'mon, where's your sense of adventure?" My tone came out overly excited, so I cleared my throat to seem more normal and secured his laundry tote in my bike's basket. "I'll be doing most of the job pedaling. You just have to sit and enjoy the ride."

He kept staring at my bike, and I was losing patience, since I was really craving ice cream.

"Milady, it seems not fair that you do all the work. Can I at least carry your belongings?" He pointed at my backpack. I nodded and handed it over. He carried it on his back and proceeded to analyze the handlebars and check the brake levers. His weirdness never seized to surprise me.

"I promise I'm a safe driver," I said, getting on and putting on my helmet. He shook his whole body as if he was preparing to jump, then sat slowly behind me.

"Let's embrace adventure, milady!"

We hadn't even left the library parking lot when I had to stop because Tristan's fingers were digging into my shoulders.

"Why are we stopping, milady?" he asked.

"Can you relax a little bit? I know this might not be your

preferred way of transportation"—I imagined he might be the typical chauffeur kind of guy—"but I promise I know what I'm doing." I had never ridden my bike with anyone else on it, but I wasn't going to tell him that.

Tristan nodded from behind and let go of my shoulders. Once I pedaled again, he held on to my waist. Not as tightly as my shoulders but still pretty tight. As we rode onto Main Street, I tried to focus on not losing my balance rather than on how the cutest guy in the world was holding my waist.

Main Street was beautiful, not only for its designated bike lane, which made me feel safer than on any other street, but also because of the shade from the canopy of pistachio and red oak trees. The foliage was so thick there was no direct sunlight. Tristan seemed to enjoy it, too, because I noticed his grip on my waist softening. I focused on the feeling of the breeze on my face as I rode my bike, one of my favorite sensations. We passed a speed bump, and I felt Tristan's hands hold on to me tightly again. But his touch softened, awakening the butterflies in my stomach.

We arrived at the ice-cream place, and Tristan was now an official fan of my bike, talking about how amazing and practical it was. Since he acted as if it had been the ride of his life, I wondered if he had actually never learned to ride one. It was uncommon, but I've heard of people who had never learned as kids and wanted to learn as adults. We got off and I locked my bike. Then we headed inside.

Once we got in, I stared, amazed at the huge variety of flavors. Tristan held his hand over my ear and whispered, "What exactly is ice cream, milady?"

I laughed, but when I realized it wasn't a joke, I stared at him, hesitant. His oddness was cute and all, but this was weird.

"It's similar to gelato," I said, hoping to appeal to his Italian side, but he remained clueless.

He stared at me with a straight face and then looked down. I felt awful. Perhaps I had gotten it all wrong. It was not that his parents wanted him to grow up; he must have come from an overprotective family and was desperate to experience the outside world. Maybe this whole exchange program experience was the only opportunity he had to leave a conservative community that was trapped in time.

I cleared my throat and whispered back in his ear, "It's a mix of frozen fruits that can also have milk, and it melts in your mouth when you eat it." I tried to use simple concepts, as I had back when Will was two years old.

"Do you have a favorite, milady?" he asked, still looking at all the different ice creams on the board.

"During the hot summer months, I tend to go with something fruity, like . . . that mango-passion fruit sounds good." I pointed at the sign with all the special summer flavors.

Tristan stared that way, too, but kept quiet.

Then I added, "You can never go wrong with lemon. Basic but always good."

His seriousness melted away, and he gave me a side smile. Maybe that was more familiar to him.

"You can ask to taste a few." I pointed at the sign on the counter advertising free samples.

He nodded and asked the girl behind the counter for chocolate chip, mango-passion fruit, and lemon. She seemed to click with Tristan right away. After anything he said, she would smile and giggle, and before I knew it, they were talking like they were old friends. She even let him try every single one of the ice-cream flavors in the store.

What started as cute was now turning a little annoying. The line behind us was growing, and Tristan's new friend was taking too long. I took out the ice-cream coupons from my backpack and handed them over to the girl as I ordered a scoop of the mango-passion fruit ice cream. Perhaps the coupon would make them stop flirting. The girl didn't seem pleased with my interruption, but I didn't care. I wanted ice cream.

Tristan asked for a triple scoop in a waffle bowl with all the different toppings. It was a little embarrassing. Not even Will behaved like that at any ice-cream shop. I assumed the coupons wouldn't cover Tristan's eccentric selection, but instead of us paying the difference, the girl said it was on the house. At least his flirting came with its perks.

We found a free bench outside of the store and sat together. Tristan closed his eyes and seemed to be lost in the summer breeze, while his hair moved with the wind. It was cute to see him enjoy the same simple things I did.

"You have to hurry and eat it, or it's going to melt," I said, pointing at his ice cream as I licked my cone.

He opened his eyes and stared at the waffle bowl. The ice cream was melting at a rapid pace, getting his fingers all sticky. I tried to help, handing him napkins, but Tristan laughed, seeming to be having the time of his life. He ate his ice cream slowly at first but then hurried until he squeezed his eyes closed. Now he was covering his forehead with one hand. I couldn't stop laughing.

"I guess I should've warned you about getting a brain freeze," I said, trying not to choke on my own ice cream.

He was smiling, even with his eyes closed tight. "Milady, this has been an extraordinary experience!" he said as he relaxed and opened his hypnotizing olive eyes to look at me.

Even as I felt the ice cream dripping between my fingers, I couldn't take my eyes off him. He was not only the most gorgeous guy I'd ever met, but he was incredibly funny, charming, and so out of this world.

With his eyes fixating on me, the world around us seemed to disappear. That is, until he looked away and frowned at something in the distance. I turned and found the cause of his annoyance. Several cars away, Alex was getting out of his Jeep and walking with Oliver toward other members of the swim team.

I turned around to look at Tristan. It was obvious they hadn't liked each other, and perhaps they were too different to have anything in common. Alex's messy hairstyle crashed against Tristan's perfectly arranged hair. And Tristan's theater outfit was totally opposite from Alex's unkempt style of cargo shorts and flip-flops.

Tristan stood up quickly, staring at the distance.

"Hey, what's the matter?" I asked, but he didn't answer.

He left his ice cream on the bench and walked away. I turned quickly to see where he was going. He was heading toward Alex and the swim team, who sat outside the smoothie place at a table several stores away. I had no idea what had gotten into him. Alex hadn't even noticed us. He was just sitting with his teammates, biting his thumbnail—a horrible habit of his.

I was too far away to hear what they were talking about, but Tristan seemed to say something to Alex that made the entire table laugh. Alex didn't laugh, though. He simply stopped biting his nails and looked away. Tristan kept talking, and Alex's annoyance seemed to be growing until he stood up and pulled Tristan away from the swim team holding him by my backpack. As Tristan stumbled, trying to keep up with Alex, I saw the zipper of my backpack breaking.

They were standing a few feet closer to me now, but something told me this wasn't going to end well. I stood up and headed toward them, since I could see Alex was losing his patience. But it was too late. Alex grabbed Tristan by his jacket and pushed him against a rock column.

"Hey!" I shouted at Alex, running toward them. "What the heck are you doing?"

"What am *I* doing? Ask this weirdo," Alex said, turning away from Tristan.

Tristan straightened up, looking ready to fight him back. People around us were looking our way.

"Tristan, what happened?" I asked, but he didn't seem to hear me. He stared at Alex, waiting.

Alex ignored Tristan, as if Tristan was just a boy looking for trouble. I was about to pull Tristan aside when he pulled Alex by the shoulder and punched him in the face. Alex tumbled against the wall behind him, his swollen cheek bearing the mark of Tristan's hit. Tristan stood there looking satisfied with what he had done, but Alex's swimmer arm swung through the air, and he punched Tristan right in the center of his face.

Tristan fell, along with everything inside my backpack. I knelt and gathered my pocket edition, my e-reader, and everything else scattered on the floor. The security guard vehicle was driving our way. Having to explain to my parents that hanging out with the exchange guy had gotten me into trouble was a scenario I didn't even want to imagine.

"What is wrong with you, Alex?" I said, anger boiling through my veins.

But Alex didn't answer. He just stared at Tristan, not even caring that blood was dripping from his nose. The security guards arrived and Alex backed up. Tristan opened his eyes, and I felt relieved. He looked at me and grinned with his bloody smile, as if nothing had happened.

"This was all your fault, Alex. I thought you were better than this." I was furious, and I couldn't even look him in the eye. All I saw was his shadow on the floor as he walked away.

Tristan and I walked back to our table, and I helped him sit on the bench, his ice cream completely melted. The girl from the ice-cream shop came right away with a bag of ice, a water bottle, and napkins. Tristan's new friend had turned out to be very helpful. I couldn't help thinking that Tristan's charm apparently worked only on girls, because it had obviously had the opposite effect on Alex.

I hesitated about taking him to a doctor, but he assured me that he had been in worse fights and that he was fine. Once he got all cleaned up, only the bruise remained. I still wanted to wait a little before we headed to my house.

Shortly thereafter he went back to his happy self and talked to the ice-cream girl. I sneaked out to call someone, because I needed to vent. I walked toward my bike and took my phone out from my back pocket. I called Maggie, but she didn't pick up. I called Marian, but the call went straight to voice mail.

My feelings twisted tightly inside of me. In just that day, I had been happy, jealous, jittery and now sort of angry. It was close to a mix of being anxious and overwhelmed. I couldn't believe Tristan had punched Alex, but the worst part was the feeling of mistrust toward Alex. I couldn't believe that even with his competitive swimmer training, he had completely lost it and caused pain to someone I had recently come to care about.

As we got on my bike, Tristan swore for the tenth time that he was completely fine and ready to go. We wouldn't have time to wait for his clothes to go through a whole cycle in the dryer, but at least we would be able to wash them. As I put on my helmet, he reassured me that he was prone to accidents, and this happened to him all the time. Which wasn't really reassuring.

Tristan did seem more relaxed on the way to my house, holding me by the waist as we passed over speed bumps. Something about Alex was bugging me. My recently discovered crush on him had gone from hopeful to heartbreak to anger and disappointment. Alex was not a troublemaker. He had never gotten into fights, not even with his brother when they were little. So why was he acting like that?

When we got home, the mere sight of Alex's old blue Jeep parked in his driveway tied my stomach in a knot. His Jeep and my bike in our driveways were our signals to show each other that we were home. But this time I left my bike hidden behind the shed at the back of our driveway.

While I grabbed Tristan's laundry bag I heard Miriam's voice, so I ran to my front door, where Tristan was waiting for me, and pushed him quickly inside my house. I had expected no one to be home, since Mom's car wasn't in the driveway, but what I didn't expect was Haiku's awkward reaction when he met Tristan.

Haiku loved guests, no matter who. Any visitor was an opportunity for cuddles or to play fetch. But when Haiku stared at Tristan, he tilted his head from side to side, not wanting to get close to him. I knew certain situations could trigger stressful memories for rescue dogs, but Haiku had never showed any signs of trauma, yet he was acting so weird. He didn't seem to be afraid of Tristan; it was like he couldn't figure him out.

"Here, boy." I knelt, hoping Haiku would relax, but he refused to come closer even as I showed him one of his favorite toys. "Don't you want to meet my friend?" Haiku stared at Tristan, still tilting his head from side to side.

I turned to Tristan. "Want to throw him the ball?" But Tristan stared at it with disgust. The ball was old and dirty. But still, it was obvious Tristan wasn't a dog person.

I turned to Haiku again. "Do you want to take a nap in my bed?" I hoped that by giving him the opportunity to do things that I wouldn't normally let him do, he would behave nicer.

"You sleep with animals? In your bed?" Tristan asked in shock.

I hesitated to answer his judgy question. It was clear Tristan wasn't a pet lover at all. "He doesn't normally sleep on my bed. He just likes to be in my room. It started when my sister went away to college. I guess I'm his second-best choice." I was rambling now, like I did when I was nervous, and I could see that Tristan wanted my dog out of sight, since he was standing behind me, hiding from him.

"Tristan, the laundry room is that way, next to the kitchen." I pointed to the far end of the house. "Why don't you go get your clothes in the washing machine while I take Haiku upstairs?"

Tristan didn't move until I held Haiku's collar and walked away.

After Haiku jumped on my bed, he seemed happier. I petted him right behind his ears, just the way he liked it. He acted more normal now, and I guessed we have found the only person in the world that Haiku disliked. I figured that if Tristan would want all his clothes washed, he would need something clean to wear as well. I grabbed the first oversize clean T-shirt I could find and baggy sweatpants that would work for now. He was more or less my size. I left my room door open in case Haiku decided to change his mind and join us.

As I entered the laundry room, I found Tristan with his head inside the dryer.

"You can be so weird. Have they told you that?" I joked, causing him to hit his head on the drum.

"Sorry," I said, feeling bad for scaring him. "Don't tell me you are one of those against using dryers for the electric bill?"

Tristan ignored me and stared at the buttons on the dryer.

I rolled my eyes. "Let's get your clothes clean, then," I said, opening the washing machine and realizing someone had left a load of laundry in there—and that it smelled.

Frustrated, I grabbed a basket and pulled the clothes out to wash after Tristan's load. My heart sank as I pulled out my favorite black scarf. It was ruined, as if it had lost a battle against a chlorine-based stain remover, white spots all over it. Even full sentences were gone.

"What is the matter?" Tristan asked, noticing my mood change.

"This was my favorite scarf. It had my favorite lines printed from my favorite love story." There was no way of saving it. "I guess it's laundry karma," I joked masking my huge disappointed, but Tristan didn't get it.

I left it aside, along with my frustration, trying to focus on getting Tristan's clothes done in time.

As I loaded Tristan's clothes in the machine, I tried to push back the tears that were building up. I knew it was *just* a scarf, but it was *THE* scarf.

"I brought you something to wear now so we can wash what you have on too," I said, giving him my clothes. "The bathroom is that way." I pointed to the hall outside of the kitchen.

He seemed to be in a hurry, because he began to lower his pants, and I had to turn around to give him some privacy.

I tried not to get carried away by a hot guy changing behind me. When I no longer heard the rustling of clothes, I asked him if I could look.

His hand took me by surprise when he held mine, and I turned around.

"Here, milady." He put the scarf Ty had given me over my palm. "It might not be a favorite, but it contains the raw material writers use to write stories."

I stared at him in surprise. "What?"

"Writers organize the alphabet in the correct order to form words and sentences. It's their tool to make stories. The ones that make us feel all sorts of things. If the story is well written, that is." His fingers touched mine.

His words were poetry. Not even in my wildest dreams could I have imagined a guy like him could exist and say such wonderful things. He was completely odd but had the right mix of book smart and street smart.

I stared into his eyes, but the bruise on his face grabbed my attention. The redness on the area between his cheekbone and nose would be hard to hide, and somehow I felt responsible.

Haiku came down barking, and I knew someone was at the door. I looked away, hoping he wouldn't notice how red my cheeks were, and focused instead on putting detergent pods into the washer. Before I closed the door, I realized it would take more than two pods to make his clothes smell clean, so I threw in a couple more. The Southern heat and his thick theater costume were just not meant for each other.

Mom and Will came into the kitchen while Haiku jumped around them, clearly avoiding Tristan.

"I was just helping my friend Tristan." I felt the need to clarify, since no normal person would just hang out with their friends in the laundry room. "I told him he could wash his laundry here."

"Of course," Mom said, and Will said hello to Tristan.

Tristan bowed at Will and walked toward Mom. "It is a delight to make your acquaintance, milady." Tristan held Mom's hand and kissed it. His Jane Austen obsession was getting out of control.

Mom seemed surprised, but she simply answered, "Likewise, you can call me Claire." Then she turned to me and said, "Your friend is . . . unique."

"He's in a drama club."

Mom's expression changed to concern as she stared at Tristan's bruised face. "What happened to you?"

I was not going to let Tristan tell the truth. "I tried to teach him how to ride a bike. Can you believe that he didn't know how?" I laughed, trying to slow down my talking speed to sound more believable. "But it turns out I'm not a very good teacher." The less my mom knew about the Alex–Tristan feud, the better.

Mom smiled. "Is there anything else we can help you with? Ice, perhaps?"

"You have provided me with more help than I could ask for," Tristan replied politely.

Will interrupted as he opened the washing machine. "No wonder I couldn't find where the smell was coming from."

Part of me wanted to slap him, but that wouldn't look nice in front of Mom. I grabbed my ruined scarf and put it in front of Will. "Was this your doing?"

"Oh no! That's terrible." Mom jumped in with her condescending tone, and as always, covered for Will. "How about we try to find you a similar one online?"

"It was part of a limited edition," I answered, annoyed. Part of me wondered if it had been Will's revenge for that day when I didn't get his uniform clean on time.

Will changed the subject, and like many kids who are completely incapable of being discreet, said, "Tristan, why do you stare at my sister so much?"

Tristan blushed and looked away.

I didn't know I could make a guy blush, ever.

Will continued his mocking, now singing an annoying tune over and over: "June and Tristan, sitting in a tree, k-i-s-s-i-n-g!"

"Stop it!" I was embarrassed.

Mom jumped in. "Will, how about we get a Popsicle and watch a movie? You can pick anything you want."

Will hesitated but gave in, though he still sang his annoying tune all the way upstairs.

With that annoying song now stuck in my head, I realized I had forgotten to start the washer. I added liquid detergent, closed the door, and pressed start.

We stood there in an uncomfortable silence, my hands sweatier than normal.

"Do you want anything to drink while we wait for your

clothes?" I asked Tristan as I poured water from the counter pitcher in a glass and chugged it all in one gulp.

Tristan settled for water, too, and we headed to the living room to sit on the couch. Both of us stared awkwardly at the wall.

Nothing in the hundreds of romance novels that I had read said anything about this uncomfortable moment. When you have alone time with your crush but there was nothing else going on to trigger a conversation. I tried to think of any of the things I wanted to ask him earlier, but all I managed to do was look all around me, staring at him every now and then, trying to act normal. I noticed he was still carrying my back pack, it was rarely visible since his jacket and the straps were the same navy color.

"Milady," he said, breaking the silence, "there is something I have been dying to say." His olive eyes stared straight at me and pierced my soul. Even after a whole glass of water, my mouth was bone dry, and I couldn't articulate any words. I nodded instead.

He hesitated, opened his mouth to speak, and then closed it again. "I just wanted to express my appreciation for your constant assistance. This experience would not have been the same without you."

He stared at my lips. I couldn't help but do the same. His lips parted in a soft smile, and all I could think about was how kissing him would feel. His hand landed on the couch, and he leaned in closer to me. Without thinking I mimicked him, the distance between us getting shorter and shorter.

An unusual beeping sound made Tristan jump, and I sat back and looked away. My heart was racing, but I couldn't figure out where the sound was coming from. It was similar to the beeping of the washer's end of cycle, but not quite that.

My hands sweating profusely, I stood up. "I'm going to check on your clothes. I'll be right back."

I grabbed my phone from my jeans' back pocket to text Maggie again, but as soon as I turned on the lights in the laundry room, I slipped, falling flat on my belly.

Damn it. I blinked repeatedly as I realized the laundry room was filled with foam and tiny bubbles. It was as if one of those bubble trucks for kids' parties had a hose straight into our tiny laundry room. Why did I always have to be such a laundry mess? Especially the only time I'd ever brought a guy home.

I tried to get on all fours to stand up but slipped again, and this time my glasses fell from my face. At least I had managed to find my phone and keep it in my jeans. I reached out, searching for my glasses, but I couldn't hold on to anything that wasn't slippery or slimy. Why couldn't I behave normal around Tristan? Why did I have to go the extra mile of stupidity and add detergent mindlessly? I was going to get into so much trouble. I couldn't see a thing other than white foam all around me.

I heard someone walking and I shouted, "Stop!"

"Milady, are you—" Tristan's words were interrupted by a *thud* as he fell to the floor next to me.

"Tristan?" I asked, reaching for him, but in all the bubbles I could only find his foot.

"Milady, are you hurt?" he asked.

"My glasses . . . please don't tell me you squished them." It wasn't only the brightness of the bubbles everywhere; it was that I couldn't focus. I had no clue what was happening around me, not that there was much to see, but still I needed them. I saw a shadow move, but I didn't know how far he was from me. Then silence.

"Tristan?" I asked, worried that he might still be hurt from earlier, but his laugh broke the silence.

"This is fascinating, milady!" He parted the bubbles, and I could see a silhouette getting closer to me.

His laugh was contagious. I threw bubbles at him, and I heard him spitting the soap out of his mouth. Then he threw a bunch of bubbles back at me. I tried to sit and slipped again on my back; then I felt Tristan's hand reaching out.

"Milady, there you are." His hand was rough but warm. He held my hand, and not in a *Where are you?* kind of way. It was more in a *I want to hold your hand forever* kind of situation. The butterflies in my stomach were fluttering all over, like the bubbles that surrounded us. I felt Tristan getting closer, and I could barely see his silhouette. Then he put my glasses over the bridge of my nose, and even with tiny bubbles everywhere, I could see his olive eyes a few inches from mine. I felt the warmth of his breath as his lips drew closer and closer to mine.

"Is everyone OK?" Mom asked, and I jumped away, hitting Tristan on the forehead with my head.

"We are OK," I said, rubbing my forehead as I heard another *thud*. It was so embarrassing to be so clumsy around Tristan. "I had a little trouble with the detergent," I added, taking the blame before Mom could come up with any theories.

"Wait, I'll go for some towels so you can safely get out. Don't move," Mom said.

I laughed, and Tristan did too. "Are you really OK, Tristan?" I asked in a low voice. I wished Mom had come a few minutes later, but I had to admit this had all felt kind of magical.

"Worry not, milady." His words, like him, were always weird. But this time it wasn't the word order that I focused on, but the soft tone of his voice. Maybe it was the bubbly environment, but for some reason his voice sounded . . . sort of attractive. It was so surreal it gave me shivers.

I tried to reach for his hand. This all felt right out of a romance novel. But as I heard Mom's voice coming our way, I let go of any intention of reaching out for him.

"I'm going to throw you guys a couple of towels. Place them on the floor so you'll have something to stand on," Mom said.

"OK, Mom," I answered.

"June, before you get out, please find a way to drain the washer and add a rinse cycle."

I knew that was just the start of my punishment for this soapy mess.

"Here it goes," Mom said, throwing a towel into the bubbles.

The first towel landed on Tristan's face, and I couldn't hide a laugh. He learned fast and caught the rest of them on time. As he handed me a towel, our fingers touched again, and this time it was electric.

I knew Mom was right there, so I placed a towel carefully next to me so the friction of the towel would allow me to get up. I used another towel to clear the bubbles, looking for the drain button. Tristan placed the rest of the towels underneath him, but the movement made the remaining bubbles fly into the air. The sound of squishing bubbles ended, and I saw him and Mom more clearly. She didn't seem as angry as I expected.

"Are there any of Dad's clothes that we could lend Tristan so he can have something to wear?" I asked Mom, since now everything Tristan owned, even the ones I had given him, wouldn't be ready before we had to head back to the library.

"I'll check," Mom said, handing me a mop and a bucket.

"Please allow me. It is the least I can do for all the disruptions I have caused," Tristan said, taking the mop from my hand. Mom smiled and went away.

I filled the bucket with water from the laundry sink and placed it on the floor. It was evident Tristan didn't know how to mop, even though he acted like he did. I was almost sure he had never done it before. Maybe his family had all sorts of help in their house. Or maybe his family fell into the typical stereotypes of women clean and men fix things.

I gently grabbed the mop and showed him how to do it

properly, and he seemed happier to know how to help. I could've done it faster, but I didn't want to take that tiny victory away from him.

Once the floor was not as slippery, I looked at my watch. "Would you like to take a shower before heading back?" I asked, looking at how his hair was now soapy, sticking out in all directions.

He stared at his clothes and nodded.

"Mom," I called through the stairs. "Would you mind if Tristan takes a shower?"

"Not at all," she shouted back. "Just show him how to turn the water on."

I walked with him to the guest bathroom. I pulled the curtain aside and explained to him some of the quirks of my old house.

"You have to open this one a little bit and then open the cold one a little at a time." I pointed at the faucets on the wall. "You have to slowly find the right balance, or you'll get burned."

He stared at me attentively, looking so cute. I took out a towel from the linen closet and left it over the toilet and closed the door.

Mom brought me some of Dad's clothes. I could hear the water already running, so I left them right by the bathroom door. Mom walked toward the laundry room, and I followed her to make sure the floor wasn't wet.

"I'm sorry, Mom," I said feeling terrible for always being such a laundry mess. Mom didn't answer. "Are you really mad?" I asked.

"No, honey." She exhaled deeply. "Not really."

I stared at her.

"I mean, I'm not going to lie. Having to ask your dad to help me move the washer and dryer to clean underneath is not my definition of fun. But I'm so glad you are making new friends, and I know all you wanted was to help him out." She smiled, looking as if she wanted to say something else.

She took another deep breath. "To be honest, I've been worried about you." She paused as if what she was about to say had been on her mind for too long. "With your friends going away, and Marian not coming back for the first summer ever, I thought you'd be terribly lonely. Your world has always revolved around Marian, Alex, and Maggie."

It turned out I wasn't the only one worried about all that. I remembered Marian's message. Perhaps Tristan was like Benvolio. I was having fun with him, and he was a new friend. But it also made me realize why Maggie wanted me to date. Perhaps I was really a loner.

"Besides"—Mom's voice took me out of my thoughts— "Tristan is"—she hesitated, as if she was taking her time to find the right word—"one of a kind."

I laughed. She was right.

"I guess what I'm trying to say is I'm happy to see you happy. Even if it involves another laundry mess." She laughed, and I smiled, feeling the impulse to hug her. As I held her tight, I thought of all the things I'd heard classmates say about their parents. Either they worked all the time and weren't involved at all or were so controlling and strict they were feared. I felt incredibly lucky that my parents didn't fit any of the above.

We heard Haiku barking, and I knew Dad's car had just parked in our driveway.

"Why don't you take a quick shower too?" Mom asked, pointing at the bubbles still clinging to my glasses and hair. I ran past the front door before Dad could ask anything about my appearance, and he was too busy greeting Haiku to notice anyway.

I took the quickest shower ever. I didn't want to take so long that Tristan had to interact with my parents. Mom knew how odd he was, but Dad had yet to discover it, and I was not ready for that, not yet. While I mindlessly browsed through different TV shows, sitting at the living room across from the guest bath, waiting for Tristan to come out, I thought about how unusual it was for a guy to take such a long shower. But then I heard the creaking of the door hinges.

I turned around and saw Tristan standing in the doorframe of the guest bath, wearing just a towel around his waist. Wet strands of hair framed his face. His well-formed body was impossible to look away from. He looked just like one of those practically perfect Italian statues.

Tristan simply smiled at me as he noticed the clothes neatly folded on the floor in front of him, and he went back in to change. I tightened my jaw to avoid opening it in awe and played with my damp hair as a distraction. Tristan was unusually charming, but after this evening, I realized I was falling for him. Somehow I felt my heart had been pierced by an arrow, and there was nothing I could do about it.

Even if they were damp, I quickly folded all Tristan's clothes. That way, as soon as he was ready, we could head over to the library. Dad was busy reading with Will before bed, which had worked in my favor since Dad couldn't do his signature move of asking never-ending questions to my friends in an attempt to bond.

Tristan came out and gave me my backpack, which was still covered in bubbles. Luckily the contents were still intact. I quickly passed the important contents to another bag. In the meantime, Tristan seemed to feel unwell. I helped him with his balance, thinking that perhaps the long hot shower had messed up his sugar levels. That happened to me often after a long bath. Mom got worried, too, like all moms do, and gave him some orange juice and an apple muffin freshly baked that morning, which seemed to help him right away.

Maybe it was not only the food but my daring gesture of placing my hand over his knee as I waited for him to feel better. There was something different in his smile, and I wondered if that was what Maggie was talking about when she said I was missing out.

Once we headed to the library, Tristan insisted on carrying my bag for me, since I was carrying his laundry for him—even if my bike's basket was doing all the work. But for some reason I found it hard to tell him no. He remained quiet all the way to the library, and even when we passed over speed bumps, since I took the longest way, he no longer held on to me like a scared cat.

We got into the library parking lot, and I locked my bike to the rack. I was about to say goodbye and head inside to help Nora close when he pulled me into the library garden.

"Milady, there is something I want to show you."

After we reached the big oak where the tree house was, he held on to the rope and began to climb. I checked that there was no one around us and followed him, awkwardly carrying his clothes with me. Once we were at the top, I traded his laundry bag for mine, but he barely noticed, since he was staring between the branches.

"What are you looking for?" I asked. Then I saw what he was talking about.

Storybridge was famous for having the most breathtaking

sunsets, or at least that was what they always advertised in their brochures. But as I stared into the orange-blue sky with hints of purple and pink, I was struck anew by the sight.

The contrast of the tree's dark branches against the bright colors made me realize how much I had gotten used to something so beautiful and so magical. Seeing the excitement in Tristan's expression made me appreciate it even more, as if I was seeing it for the first time too. In a way I was, because no sunset was ever the same. A few minutes later, I blinked, and it was bluer as the warm tones faded away.

"I don't remember ever seeing something so beautiful," I said.

"Me neither, milady."

Tristan's voice made me turn his way, and I realized he was staring at me. I felt thankful for the low light as the sun went down, because there was no way I could hide the rising heat on my cheeks, even with my long loose hair swaying with the summer breeze.

He took a step closer and held my hand, his fingers interlacing with mine. Even with no light to highlight the gorgeous color of his eyes, they sparkled just as bright. He took another step, and for the first time I was not clumsy around him. Perhaps his words were all my heart wanted to hear. Because right there, under the most beautiful sunset, in an old forgotten tree house, Tristan closed the distance between us, and I had my first kiss.

Time was something peculiar. It always moved at the same speed, yet it never felt the same. It all depended on what was going on at the moment, and it could feel very fast or very slow. But at that time, it felt as if it had completely stopped. At least until my alarm buzzed, reminding me it was 8:40 p.m. and I needed to wrap up whatever I was doing to help close the library. The distraction made me look away, and I noticed Audrey walking to her car in the parking lot. It was as if cold air punched my heart.

"Do you say these things often? I mean to other girls?" I asked, a little jealousy in my voice. I knew every girl he met fell head over heels for him, and it suddenly made me feel less special.

Tristan looked shocked.

"You once said your heart belonged to someone," I added and looked away from him. I had no idea why I had brought down the mood after such an incredible kiss. The fact was, I didn't even want to know the truth.

"Milady," he said, placing my hand over the middle of his chest. "Can you feel it beating?"

His charming accent was making me tremble. I swallowed hard and nodded.

"It beats only for you. It has only done so since the very first moment our eyes met. On that evening, surrounded by stories where you childishly threatened me with a book," he said, and I couldn't help but laugh. He grinned and put his forehead against mine. "There is nothing frightening about a book, at least not while it is closed."

His words always hit me like a spell. He was so perfect.

"Would you really come to Maggie's birthday party with me?" I asked. His smile got wider, but before he could say anything, I added, "I know you agreed before, but I hadn't told you the specifics. We're supposed to go with someone special, someone we like . . . a lot." I blushed but I didn't care. "Would you be my date?" With Tristan, I didn't feel scared to say all those things out loud.

"It would be my greatest pleasure, milady." He kissed my hand.

With every word and everything he did, I realized I was falling more for him.

We stared at each other, and he kissed me again, softly, but then my phone buzzed. It was a text from Nora asking where I was. I could always count on her to break any romantic moment, fictional or real.

I opened my bag and tore off a piece of paper from a tiny notebook. "This is the way to get there." I drew a quick map and wrote Maggie's address on the back. I also added a detailed route, making the library the starting point and showing things he would see along the way.

"Meet me there at seven sharp," I said.

He stared at the paper, nodded, and kissed me again gently on the lips. He was surreal.

"Are you going to stay here longer?" I asked, trying to force myself to leave, and then I reached for the rope.

"Indeed, milady. It is the stars' turn to shine now." He looked up, the sun completely gone. "But fear not, for even the moon and all the stars together hold no comparison to your beauty."

He kissed me again, and I had to take a deep breath to avoid having my legs turn to jelly.

"See you tomorrow," I said as I began to climb down.

He nodded. "A thousand times good night." He truly was a Shakespeare fan. And he had perfect timing for the right quotes.

"Make sure no one sees you when you get down," I said in a low voice. He nodded and waved goodbye.

Once I was at the bottom, I tried to contain my huge smile as I headed toward the library. Then, as I met with Nora and her annoying attitude, I realized nothing she could say or do could erase the smile on my face. Tristan was out-of-this-world incredible, like a dream come true. But a part of me couldn't stop thinking about Maggie and the Spanish ex who broke her heart.

Why was I falling for an exchange guy? Had I learned nothing about her experience? I had been there to help her pick up the pieces, so why was I headed down the same path? At some point he was going to leave—that was certain. But I didn't care. No logic could change how I felt about him. He had quickly become the best thing about my summer, and I just wanted to enjoy it, to be around him as much as I could before he had to go. Following Marian's advice hadn't been that bad. It had steered me to an extraordinary theatrical guy who called me milady, was the best kisser in the world, and liked to look at me the way one marvels at the stars.

CHAPTER II

THE PLUS-ONE PARTY

I t was the fourth time Marian and I had tried to have a video call, but her connection was still terrible.

"So did . . . reach . . . Maggie?" Marian asked.

"I tried, but it's impossible. I even accompanied Mom this morning to her house to drop off the cupcake tower for the party. But she was not there." I was getting impatient. I really needed to talk to my sister.

"Why wasn't . . . sh . . . sh . . . sh . . . there?" Marian's chopped voice was getting on my nerves. Maybe it was the heavy rain messing up with our internet. Or maybe it was her connection. Why did she always have to call me on the go? Couldn't she just be at home and give me some of her undivided time?

"She was not home because she dropped her phone who knows where, the pool or something, so she went to get a new one this morning," I said, thinking of how convenient Maggie's issue with her phone had turned out to be for Dane.

"Weird, that . . . brothers . . . not close."

I tried to answer what I imagined Marian had asked. "Her brothers are over ten years older than her, so it's not like they saw me hanging out at their house when we were little. I mean, they surely know me, but that's it. The brothers are close with each other, but not as much with Maggie."

Her silence made me wonder if she had asked me something that I didn't hear or if she was just not following our conversation. "I left her a note," I added, "but I didn't want to write down every detail, so I just wrote our emergency code."

If Maggie or I wrote the word or drew a jellyfish, it meant it was an emergency. We had to drop everything and meet ASAP.

Marian's face froze on my screen. This was impossible. I looked at the clock. It was already past five. Maggie hadn't responded at all, and I had to get ready. Any chance of Marian helping me virtually with my hair and makeup was out the window.

There was silence, and then a message on my phone appeared: *Call Failed.* Followed with a text message from Marian: We'll talk later. Why don't you wear my white dress? You'll look great in it, accompanied by a wink emoji. I rubbed my forehead in frustration.

"Is everything OK?" Dad's voice took me by surprise.

I exhaled, annoyed. "I hate koalas."

Dad chuckled. "Is there anything I can do to help you not hate them so much?"

"Can you travel back in time and make Marian interested in bald eagles instead?"

Dad laughed again. "I think my abilities don't go that far, but I'm sure if it's a hair problem, your mom can help."

I still remembered when I was seven and Dad had to do my hair because Mom and Carmian were out of town. I liked my hair in a tight high ponytail with every little hair out of my face. But Dad had to do it, and he was not very good in the hairstyle department. He tried different ways, but my ponytail broke loose before recess. I lost our volleyball game that day because I couldn't see the ball. I was so mad at Dad, but to be fair, he had tried his best. That was when I learned how to braid my own hair.

Mom peeked in, as if we had rubbed the genie's lamp, and Dad relaxed his shoulders.

"What's up?" Mom asked.

"Marian said she was going to help me get ready," I said, frustrated.

"Can *I* help you?" Mom was always down for some quality mom–daughter time. "I don't know much about what's in, but I bet we can figure out any video tutorial together."

As we approached Maggie's house, I took one last look at myself in the visor mirror. I had to give it to Mom, I loved the way I looked. I didn't look at all like Maggie's makeover. I looked even better, more like myself. There were no huge layers of makeup on my skin, no extremely long eyelashes or contouring, and my eyebrows looked natural. My eye shadow matched my colorful sneakers with pink on the eyelid, a little shimmer on the crease, soft blue under my lower eyelashes, and a touch of yellow in the inner corner of the eye. The colors were a nice subtle contrast to the whiteness of my dress.

Mom turned on her blinkers and stopped at a neighbor's driveway, the street packed with cars on both sides. I hugged Mom and thanked her for helping me turn this day around; moms had that healing effect. I told her Alex would give me a ride home once the party was over—he always did. The french braid to the side of my head allowed romeo to keep my hair out of my field of vision. I got out of the car feeling pretty and confident. Something I hadn't felt on my date with Tyler.

Once I was standing across the street from Maggie's house, I tried to take a few deep breaths as I watched Mom drive away. Just the idea of seeing Tristan any minute now made it impossible for me to be chill. There was a huge line building up by the photo booth in Maggie's driveway. I was thankful to be wearing comfortable sneakers, since every single girl complained about heels digging into the mud. It was unusual to have such heavy rain during summer, but with climate change, nothing was unusual anymore when it came to weird weather. Luckily for Maggie, the sky had cleared up, and there was no more forecast for rain, since the party was supposed to take place in her backyard.

I looked both ways, waiting for Tristan, while also hiding behind a tree to avoid having my classmates recognize me. I almost never used contacts at school, or put on a dress, or wore my hair loose. But still, standing alone and looking all dressed up outside the most anticipated party of the year was a little pathetic.

It was 7:20, and there was still no sign of Tristan, so I was getting restless. The line for the photo booth was still long. A huge, colorful balloon arch decorated the entrance with white and gold balloons. Maggie's house had turned overnight into a lovers' theme park. People held all sorts of fun props for the pictures. I couldn't wait to take mine with Tristan so we could go inside and Maggie could meet him.

I'd seen Maggie's house so many times before, but waiting outside made me focus on all the details I had overlooked. Dark trims contrasted beautifully against the white brick house. The flower beds on each side of the entrance gave the house a cozy feeling while blending with the modern straight lines, and the landscape lights made all these details pop. This house could easily be the front cover of a design magazine, especially with the big balcony on the top floor filled with flower baskets on the banister's rim.

Maggie peeked through the curtains of her room, looking at the long line of people on her driveway, and then it hit me. I still had to talk to her and tell her the truth about her despicable cheating boyfriend. But I didn't want Tristan to come and not find me.

I checked my watch as if my life depended on it, looking in all directions. I was getting so impatient my stomach was hurting. Maybe Tristan was unaware of the time, or maybe he was not used to *being* on time. I don't remember ever seeing him wear a watch, but I knew he didn't have a phone. I didn't care about his aversion to technology until it became inconvenient. I tried to focus instead on the people standing in line for the party. I'd wait for Tristan a little more and then go in.

Tristan was officially forty-five minutes late, and I was getting upset. Was he really going to stand me up after what had happened last night? He seemed to have enjoyed it, too, unless he was pretending. The longer he took to arrive, the more disappointed I felt. Maybe he really was a player, like all the other exchange students, and I had fallen for his trap. I couldn't take it anymore. I crossed the street, and just as I was getting closer to the photo booth, I heard a familiar voice.

I froze at the sight of Alex and Nichole walking in my direction, her long dark hair swaying from side to side. The obnoxious cat walk was a clear consequence of her sky-high heels. She wore a skintight green dress that showed off her swimmer's muscles. She hadn't seen me yet, so I ran to hide behind a bush. I could hear her arguing, and she sounded furious as she literally rushed through the line for the photo booth, complaining about being the last ones.

If she thought there was a way on earth to make Alex Marquez arrive on time, she was delusional. Even his coach would tell him an earlier time to make sure he was there before everyone else, especially for competitions. That was Alex's thing —he *always* arrived late.

My heart stopped as I stared at Alex. His hair was unmistakably messy but not as much as usual. Nichole seemed to be bothered by something regarding Alex's clothes. Apparently he hadn't dressed up to Nichole's standards. Maybe that was true. Alex always had a sporty vibe, since he preferred comfort over style—unlike Dane and his gang, who wore linen shirts with rolled sleeves to parties. But at least for Alex it was an improvement over his regular cargo shorts or baggy jeans and graphic tees. At least he had tied his shoelaces this time.

They were the last ones in line for the photo booth. I tried to ignore the fact that I desperately wanted to be there instead of Nichole. In fact, I would never give him a hard time for whatever outfit he chose or even for being late. If anything, I thought he looked really nice with his unbuttoned blue plaid short-sleeved shirt and a white T-shirt underneath. For the first time, his jeans were not ripped or baggy. They were straight, and he looked pretty hot, so different from the sporty Alex I usually hung out with.

Nichole got into the photo booth, and as they sat, she hugged him tight, pretending to kiss his cheek, and I had to look away. I stared at my phone as I stood up from my hiding spot and realized Tristan was already a full hour late. He had officially stood me up.

A couple of guys came out from the backyard gate, which was my way into the party without going through the photo booth. A mixture of anger and disappointment bubbled inside of me as I entered through the backyard and saw every single person with a date. It was more like a Valentine's party than a summer party. My thoughts bounced between Tristan and Alex, not knowing which one made me agonize less. Why did I have to care about real guys? As I made my way through the wet grass, I needed to keep my clumsiness to a minimum. One trip and the white would get stained with mud, and it would be embarrassing.

I tiptoed strategically toward the deck, but still my shoes ended up muddy. Once I reached the back door, I tried to clean my shoes against the doormat but eventually decided to take them off and carry them as I headed inside. Maggie would never forgive me for going into her room or the upper area with muddy shoes.

This was not the entrance I had anticipated, but at least I was in. I searched for her quickly on the lower level, but the more I looked at couples around me, the lonelier I felt. I couldn't believe Tristan would do this to me. He seemed to be different. He seemed excited about coming to this party with me, but perhaps I was wrong.

I ventured upstairs, passing people standing by the huge round staircase. Holding my shoes and Maggie's present in one hand, I knocked on Maggie's closed door. There was no reply, so I turned the knob to walk in, but Mia's face blocked my way.

"June, where's your date?" she asked, looking for someone behind me.

"Somewhere around, socializing," I lied, and took a step into Maggie's room. A wick-pop was not going to stand in my way. I looked around Maggie's room, but she wasn't there. Her bathroom door was closed, and the light could be seen at the bottom of the door, so I knocked.

"Maggie? It's me, June. I brought your birthday present. The one that finally arrived," I said, but there was no answer.

I pressed my ear against the door. Trying to block out the loud music coming from the lower level, I could hear her sniffling. Dane must have told her. At least that scumbag had kept his word.

I couldn't imagine how devastated she must feel. I was annoyed by Tristan and Alex, but it was no comparison to what freaking stupid Dane had done to her. I wanted to be next to her.

It was my duty as her best friend to stand by her side against all heartbreak.

"Maggie, I'm coming in," I said, trying to open the door. It was unlocked, but the other wick-pop blocked my way.

"Maggie can't talk right now," Alessandra said in a serious and somehow victorious tone. "You can leave the present on her bed."

Before I could say anything, she closed the door on me, and this time she locked it. I was speechless. I wanted to bang on her door so Maggie would let me in. I could hear her crying softly inside. But I wasn't going to push her. If Maggie needed space, I would respect that. I was still not going to leave without talking to her, so I'd have to wait around for her. I left the present on her bed and headed downstairs, hoping to find a familiar face among the crowd.

As I stood at the bottom of the staircase, looking where to go, my gaze stopped at Alex and Nichole sitting with a bigger group in the living room. It was almost torture to watch how Nichole acted around him. It was like she owned him, always trying to touch him or get closer. If it wasn't her knee bumping with his, it was her fingers accidentally falling over his or holding his shoulder as she laughed at an abnormal volume. It seemed like Alex didn't mind, but I was too far away to observe his expression. Could it be that he was going through the same thing I had with Tyler? No, it couldn't be. He had asked her.

Alex stretched with his arms over his head as he leaned on the backrest, and Nichole's head lay on his chest. I had to look away. The restroom was open, and I went in without thinking. I closed the door and sat on the closed toilet, taking my e-reader out. I had to focus on something else. I had to ignore the drowning feeling of having unrequited feelings for two guys.

It wasn't long before someone knocked incessantly. There was only so much time I could be locked in here avoiding the intolerable party. I put away my e-reader in my satchel, washed my hands, and headed out. I'd have to find another hiding spot to keep reading or force myself to make small talk with a familiar face while I waited for Maggie to make an appearance.

I scooted between groups of people scattered throughout different areas. Since I couldn't find anyone to chat with inside the house, I decided to head out to the yard. Besides, the low light would make it easier for me to hide while in plain sight.

The music was loud but not distorted. In fact, it was a nice selection, and some people were even dancing—well, more like swaying. I could barely recognize anyone, since the patio was illuminated only by string lights, and everyone looked so different dressed up. I had no idea who truly went to my high school, since Maggie was such a social butterfly.

The pool lit up in an array of colors, and it was mesmerizing. Maggie had outdone herself with all the details. If only Tristan had shown up, this would've been a date to remember. I shouldn't have put my hopes in a guy I had just met. There was a reason exchange students had a reputation, and I was blinded by his charm, thinking he could be different. All I wanted was to go back to obsessing about my book boyfriends, who never failed me. I pulled out my phone, instead of my e-reader, and opened the reading app. At least it would look like I had an online social life instead of an obsession with what was going to happen in the next chapter.

As I was deep into my book, leaning against the fence, someone bumped into me, even though I had strategically stood far away from the walkway. I turned to look, and his voice preceded him before I realized who he was.

"Well, well, well, if it isn't the hottest bookworm in town," Tyler said in a slurry voice.

"Hi Ty . . . ler," I mocked, staring at his hair, which was in that horrible man bun.

He laughed. "Such a pleasure to literally bump into you. Where's your date?" He looked around me, like every single person had done since I arrived at this freaking party.

"Mingling around," I lied, realizing fictional people wouldn't count.

"You couldn't find someone who wanted to come with you?" he asked, and I felt his words sting like lime on a fresh wound.

I needed to avoid engaging him with any conversation. Although he didn't sound as though he were mocking me. He seemed, like always, completely unaware of the impact of his words. I looked away, since I couldn't come up with a witty answer that would make me feel less upset.

"Hey, I didn't come here to bother you. I just wanted to talk to you about something." His voice was low as he came closer to me. "I sort of wanted to clear the air between us."

I took a step back, trying to maintain distance between us since I had no idea when the air hadn't been clear.

As I vaguely focused on Ty, I noticed Alex standing a few feet away, alone. Tyler moved closer to me and blocked my field of vision. Then I realized he was staring, waiting for me to say something. I wasn't proud of how little attention I paid to him, even if he had turned out to be a little nicer than I thought. I blamed my lack of attention on the loud music.

He cleared his throat. "I'm making a confession here, and it's not easy to say, bookworm." He took a deep breath. "I'm sorry."

"For what?" I asked, confused.

"It must be really hard to see me with someone else." He made a face that made me feel he was a little sorry for me. "I'm truly sorry things didn't work out between us."

"Don't worry about it," I said as I patted him on the shoulder, hoping I could walk away. But he stopped me.

"I just want to make sure you don't get hurt when you see me making out with someone else. 'Cause it will happen tonight." He gave me one of his practiced horrible smoldering gazes, accompanied by his revolting overconfidence.

"No hard feelings, at all. I promise. I wish you nothing but happiness with whatever girl chooses you," I said, trying to end our conversation. He nodded, and that was my cue to walk away.

I was just a few feet from Alex when Nichole shouted his name, and he hurried away like a puppy that knows he had done something wrong. Nichole walked past, staring at me from head to toe in a dismissive way. I ignored her and headed over to the drinks table. At least I'd blend in better if I held a cup, just like everyone else. Although I was sure mine would be the only one with no booze in it.

As I was serving myself, a familiar voice greeted me. When I looked up, I was relieved to see Oliver, holding two empty cups. I said hello to him and felt some relief at not being alone.

A freaky loud laughter, not a normal one that blended into the background noise, made us both look. Dane must have said something funny, or probably stupid, to the swim team group that gathered around the pool. Nichole laughed again, and I realized she was the one making that horrible noise. And she was holding Alex tight, her arm around his like he was a prisoner. I was grateful not to sound like a parrot being squeezed to death when something made me laugh that hard. Oliver seemed to have similar thoughts, judging by his raised eyebrows. We both laughed, and I looked away, pretending to refill my already-full cup.

Oliver seemed to be staring at someone in the distance as I

waited for him to take me out of my misery and be the one who started the small talk. We weren't used to talking to each other without Alex around. He stared at me longer, and then at someone in the distance. Maybe he needed to get back to his date.

"Hey, I know it's none of my business"—he paused, making me nervous—"and Marquez would kill me if I said anything. But I . . . I just think it's important that you know he didn't want to come with her." He looked at me, then away at his cup, avoiding my eyes. "I mean, he . . . he wasn't looking forward to spending time alone with her—I mean Nichole."

Oliver seemed nervous, and I didn't understand what he was trying to say.

A mix of annoyance and frustration bubbled inside of me. I definitely couldn't feel sorry for Alex, since he had actually gotten a date to come here. No matter how bad it had turned out. Besides, it was he who broke our tradition of us coming together to these parties, no matter the theme.

"I'm not the one who asked someone else out first," I blurted, still not completely over the resentment toward Alex. I took a sip from my cup and looked away. Years ago I would have been able to tell Oliver more, to talk to him as if he was my friend too. Back when Alex, Oliver, other kids from the neighborhood, and I used to play outside several times a week. But all that was before he'd moved to another neighborhood and joined the swim team with Alex. Then it was as if he became only Alex's friend.

There was an uncomfortable silence between us. I didn't want to talk about anything regarding Alex anymore, but I hesitated over whether we had anything else in common. I was about to walk away to perhaps hide in the bathroom again when he spoke.

"Wanna join us?" Oliver asked, pointing his head to a nearby group. I looked at the group and considered my options, then nodded and followed him, trying to cling to the only familiar face around. Marian had a point. I only had senior year left, and I barely knew other people outside of my closest friends.

Oliver's group stood by the old playground. It was shocking to see it still stood after so many years. Oliver gave Emma, a girl from my art class, a cup, and she seemed to have a sparkle in her eyes as she stared back at him. Perhaps Maggie's idea of having a couples' party had benefited more people than I'd thought. Still, I felt odd being the only single person in the group.

Everyone around me seemed to be happily in love or at least enjoying themselves. Mark from my science class held hands with John. Lillian from my history class seemed very giggly, flirting with Alissa's hair. Wherever I looked, everyone was flirty or in love. Even Tyler, standing yards away, seemed to be enjoying his date too.

I wished I could leave my cup and run, with no other explanation, but I couldn't go before talking to Maggie.

"Where's your date, June?" Mark asked.

I blushed, feeling all eyes on me.

"He's somewhere around," Oliver said, and I mouthed a silent *thank you* once no one was looking.

"That's unnecessary." Lillian pointed at the distance. We all turned to look. Tyler was making out with his date as if he wanted to explore every inch of her mouth, with no idea about how privacy worked. It was definitely not a pretty scene to watch, but he seemed to be enjoying himself.

"I still can't believe you went out with *him*," Oliver mumbled.

By the way he mocked Tyler's questionable flirting techniques, I caught a glimpse of the seven-year-old Oliver who wouldn't stop annoying Alex for not scoring a goal when we would play soccer. My genes gave me a high metabolism, so I was lightweight. Even though I was tiny for my age back then, I was an unbeatable goalkeeper. It was easy for me to jump high, and I was not scared of blocking any ball.

At least Tyler's make-out session gave us something to talk about other than the absence of my date. It was like all of us were watching a terrible telenovela, or a train wreck about to happen. Predictably, it ended with Tyler getting slapped.

Once Tyler was no longer our source of entertainment, Oliver, Emma, and I somehow found other topics to talk about. Suddenly the evening wasn't the worst. I found out Oliver would be going to the same summer program at Arthsteen U, but unlike Alex, he didn't need a scholarship to attend. He was already admitted and told me his upcoming five-year plan. Oliver was so different from Alex, way more organized and sarcastic too.

As I talked to him, I could see the little boy who was famous for telling jokes to all the neighbors. Which was before he moved and traded his soccer ball for goggles and a swim cap. I couldn't believe I was actually having a good time. Emma and I have had the chance to talk before, but she was nice and laughed at every joke Oliver told. The jokes were not that good, and they were kind of silly, but she seemed to be genuinely enjoying herself. It was as if their senses of humor easily matched.

The conversation switched to weird middle names. Alissa, who was now holding Lillian by her waist, couldn't stop laughing at John's middle name.

"I would never have picked Cattus." John tried to defend himself, but I couldn't help laughing, too, once he explained Cattus was Latin for cat.

Neither Emma nor Oliver had middle names. Then Alissa turned to me. "What's yours?"

"I actually have two," I said, feeling my anxiety rising as everyone from our group stared at me. But there was something nice about being part of a group rather than my usual party of two with Alex or Maggie.

"My parents wanted to please both grandmothers, so I got their names. Rose and Lynn."

Oliver looked surprised at that piece of information, given that we have known each other for so long.

"I prefer June, though," I added.

"You are lucky you are the only June at school," Alissa said, to which Oliver and Emma replied that having a unique name spared them from adding their last name to everything they signed. It made sense, since there were several Olivers and Emmas in our generation alone.

"Tell me about it. Alejandro Fernando Enrique Marquez is way too long." Alex's voice took us by surprise as he joined our group. "At least I don't have a double last name like some of my relatives, because that would be a nightmare," he added.

We all laughed, and Oliver teased him about having a telenovela name—one of those impossibly long names to say all together when a character was upset or wanted to start a fight. And it was nice to see Alex laugh, to be back to his normal self without Nichole hovering around.

"Where's Tristan?" Alex whispered, breaking my happy moment.

"He's . . . not coming," I whispered back, hoping the rest couldn't hear.

"What? He stood you up?" Alex's voice was louder than I would have liked. I shushed him, slapping him on the shoulder. Perhaps the music was loud enough to be a good cover for the rest of the group. "I'm sorry, June," he said softly, holding my shoulder, looking straight into my eyes.

"Yeah, right," I mumbled.

"For real, for everything. None of this would have happened if I had told you how I—"

"Marquez, five o clock," Oliver interrupted. Alex looked around and ducked. Then he tried to hide behind Oliver, unsuccessfully, and walked away.

"What the hell?" I looked around, and Nichole was coming our way. Oliver elbowed me and pointed at bushes next to the AC units. I stood still. Once Nichole realized Alex was no longer with our group, she changed direction and walked away. Then I headed toward the bushes.

"Alex? What are you doing?" I whispered, feeling ridiculous talking to an azalea bush. A hand pulled me through the bushes, and I was standing next to Alex, hiding from Nichole too.

"Have you seen Marquez? Have you seen my babe?"

We could hear Nichole's voice getting closer. Between the branches and leaves I could see her asking different groups about him.

Once she walked away, I said, "You've gotta be kidding me. You're her babe now?"

Alex shook his head and pulled his hair in frustration. It was sort of funny, but I tried not to laugh at his despair.

"This whole thing is getting out of control. I don't know why she calls me that when I already told her nothing is going to happen between us."

My eyes opened wide. "And how did *that* go?"

Alex shook his head and sighed in frustration.

"You must have known what you were doing when you asked her to be your date to *this* party. I mean, honestly, what did you expect?"

Even with the lower light, he looked a little embarrassed. "I just never expected her to turn into bridezilla overnight," he said. "It is not fun for me to have to hide and run around the whole place."

I secretly enjoyed his misery. That was what he got for bringing her as his date.

"Look, this was not the way things were supposed to happen," he added.

"Tell me about it," I mumbled, thinking of how his scenario

wasn't as bad as mine. "That's what you get for inviting her, knowing very well how she feels about you."

I tried to walk away, but Alex stopped me and shushed me. I followed Alex's gaze, looked through the bushes, and found Nichole coming our way, again. This was no longer funny; it was exasperating. If I was going to hide, at least I wanted to be reading.

I copied him and ducked, trying to be a good friend and keeping my jealousy at bay. He signaled me to follow him, and we tiptoed along the fence, away from the house. At least walking between the trees and the flower beds, where most of it was mulch, didn't make our steps squishy.

As I followed him, away from the people and the cute hanging lights, I thought of what Oliver had said. Something had ignited a spark of hope, and Maggie had not been so far off after all. But every time I tried to read Alex's facial expressions, I felt it might all be just a dumb idea stuck in my head.

Once we reached the old playset, we hid behind it. After Alex checked to ensure Nichole hadn't seen us, he relaxed a little. I just hoped we wouldn't get eaten by mosquitoes.

"What were you fighting about when you got here?" I asked out of the blue. Alex stared at me, surprised. Perhaps I'd forgotten to mention I'd waited a whole hour for Tristan outside.

"When I picked her up, she wanted me to go home and change because my outfit didn't match hers, but I refused. I told her that was my style, take it or leave it. You know, soccer T-shirts, ripped jeans, and sneakers, like always."

"Untied," I added, and he smiled. "Go on."

"I don't know what happened, but one moment I was refusing to change clothes, and the next I was arguing with my mom over the phone. She almost grounded me for not wearing decent clothes to take a girl out."

I tried with all my strength not to laugh so hard, but I

couldn't help myself as I imagined Miriam scolding Alex. To be fair, just imagining her raising her voice made me tremble.

"Laugh all you want, but today has been *the* worst," he said.

Something about his words made my smile fade away. Nothing was worse than being stood up. Besides, if I didn't get ahold of Maggie, it'd be like I was never here, just like a ghost.

"I have to go . . . talk to someone," I said, turning away. Perhaps with a little bit of luck I could avoid the wick-pops and actually talk to Maggie. But I had to move. I couldn't stand being here alone with him. We were too close, and I could feel my heart breaking again.

"Please don't," he said, holding my hand, and the warmth of his touch made me tingle all over. "I know Tristan didn't necessarily make your evening fun."

I froze. I felt completely torn between Alex and Tristan. Just because I'd had an amazing kiss with Tristan last night didn't mean that whatever I felt for Alex was automatically disqualified. Even as I gave him my full attention, he didn't let go of me. His mixed messages sent my heart pounding. His touch was gentle, and it was borderline torture.

"I would have never stood you up," Alex said.

I didn't know what I felt, but I didn't like the contradiction of wanting to kiss him while at the same time, feeling hopeless for him not knowing how I felt. He looked away, and it was a bit of a relief.

"Talking about your friend, I'm sorry for punching him. I don't know what got into me. It was stupid, and impulsive, and he is *your* friend, after all." His eyes met mine, and they were softer this time. It was as if he was trying to fix whatever was broken between us.

"He's OK," I managed to say, realizing my anger toward him was gone.

We heard Nichole's laughter again, and Alex dropped my hand. We both stood still, wondering if she was coming our way.

Once we peeked out and saw she was not around, that it was just her overly annoying laughter, Alex took a step closer.

"I'm sorry I didn't ask you to the party first. You are my best friend, and I would always pick you first." His words were sincere, but something about that made my heart break a little more. I just wanted to stop caring about Nichole, stop hiding from her as if we were doing something wrong. I just wanted to leave this freaking party.

Alex must have been able to read me, because he hugged me out of the blue, and it was comforting.

"What is going to happen now?" I asked, still hugging him back. The question held infinite possibilities. Perhaps he had a plan to stay away from Nichole for the whole evening, but I secretly hoped he would say something about our friendship before he left for his summer camp tomorrow.

"I'm not in love with Nichole, I can promise you that," he said, not hesitating at all, and it made me laugh.

But it seemed like he was not trying to be funny. There was no joke following his words or a tremble in his voice. He broke apart and looked at me, the same way he'd stared that evening when he sang that Spanish song on his front porch.

"Te ves muy guapa hoy," he said in a low voice, and my whole body shivered.

A couple walked by, distracting us both. I could see Alex was nervous. I didn't quite get every word he had said, but somehow I understood what he meant. Years ago, in that same posada, when Alex greeted his aunts, the ones he hadn't seen in a long time, everyone called him that: *guapo*. Later he explained it meant handsome. But it all added up to this moment, because something made me think we were no longer standing in the friend zone. I bit my lips so my smile wouldn't be so big across my face. He smiled, too, and there was something different about him. Some type of joy I hadn't seen since that time when he beat his own personal best swim time.

I didn't know what to do with myself. I stared back at him, at his hair that was now as messy as always. At how great he looked in that shirt, and how easy it was to be around him. I blinked several times, trying not to get carried away by my thoughts. He could walk away any minute or say something to send us back to the friend zone, but he didn't. We stood there in silence, and then he stared at my lips, just the way Tristan had before he'd kissed me. My heart fluttered as I realized what was going on. Maybe Maggie was right. Maybe we had both been afraid to say more, scared to lose our friendship. This felt surreal, a mix of excitement and fear. And to think this had all been triggered by a misunderstanding that had started with my date with Tyler.

His smile was sincere, and I played with my hair, trying to hide my nerves, my heart racing. Maybe the party mood had set the stage for us, or maybe it was us being away from the rest of the party, in our own little world. I stared at his lips, too, giving him permission to go on. He shortened the distance between us with every second. Then I heard Maggie's voice, calling my name through the speakers, and I had to pull away.

After Maggie called my name several times, the music grew louder, and the DJ switched to remixes of popular songs. People roared in unison as the evening transitioned from a backyard party to some sort of club. I found Maggie close to the DJ booth, tumbling with a cup in her hand. With no doubts, I walked in her direction, squeezing through groups of people trying desperately to reach her. My footsteps squished the wet grass underneath my sneakers, but I didn't care about the mud, or about anyone around me. I needed to get to her before she disappeared again, or she got so wasted she wouldn't remember.

Even as I pushed through the people jumping and dancing

everywhere, it felt impossible to get to her, like swimming against the current. This was yet another reminder why I was not a party girl. My happy place involved silent stories and PLEASE BE QUIET signs. I finally got close enough and called to her, but my voice was no match for the loud music. I reached for her arm but was only able to pull at her clothes.

She turned my way. "Hey, January! Where have you been?" Her words were slurred. *January?* She was drunker than I thought.

"I've been wanting to talk to you, but your friends didn't let me get to you," I said, resentful.

"It was not the right time." She shook her head. "But you above everyone wouldn't understand."

"Excuse me?" I said, my words swallowed by the loud music. I knew Maggie turned to a different version of herself when she drank, but I had no idea where this had come from.

"Where's your guy? You know, the guest of the hour," she said, looking around me and swaying in place, her bare feet covered in mud. At least she was not wearing heels in this squishy ground; that would be a disaster. She twisted her head like a confused puppy. "Did you get rid of Nichole?"

I turned and saw Alex standing behind me. I wished it was the time and place to tell her so many things. That she was right about Alex, that there was something going on, and that I also had my first kiss, even if it had been with another guy. But stupid Dane had to take priority over everything I wanted to tell her.

"I need to talk to you," I said, but she shook her head and pointed at her ear. It was impossible to talk or listen to anything other than the dance music that surrounded us. I grabbed her hand and tried to pull her aside, but we got only a few feet away from the speakers before she shook her arm free. I turned and saw her gulp half the contents of her cup. One second she looked dizzy, and the next her eyes opened wide.

I turned to follow her gaze and saw Nichole and Alex

dancing. Nichole behaved like the female version of Tyler, trying all her sexy dance moves with him. But Alex looked uncomfortable, trying to keep the distance with her wider than a foot. Alex stared at me as if he was begging me to help him, but I couldn't, not until I talked to Maggie.

"I need to tell you something important." I gathered all the strength I could to tell her something that would break her heart.

"That Dane cheated on me?" she said right away, not surprised at all. "Everybody said it would happen. I was stupid enough to think it'd be any different with me." Her words slurred again. She couldn't stand straight to keep her balance and could barely move in a straight line.

I tried to lock my arm with hers to help her balance, but she shook me off right away. She was now acting like the infamous drunk Maggie, someone I didn't particularly like. I wondered if it was too late, if she was beyond a point where she'd remember anything else I said tonight.

"Maggie, is something else going on? You know you can trust me," I said. Perhaps Dane had really broken her heart, but the BFF's sixth sense made me think she wouldn't get this drunk just for him. She'd be making out with a rebound guy by now, but not this wasted.

"No, I don't," she said, staring at her cup. I didn't know if she was trying to be funny or if she was messing with me. "The *wickish-pops*, or whatever you call them behind my back, told me something."

I frowned and straightened up, feeling very uncomfortable. The wick-pops would say or do anything to make me look bad. I just didn't want to end up being Maggie's punching bag for whatever she was angry about.

"Don't look at me like that. I'm not the one lying. Did you really have a date for tonight?" she asked.

People were turning our way, more interested in our conversation than their dates or the music.

I nodded.

"Marquez?" she asked.

I shook my head and tried to tell her what happened. The words *he stood me up* lingered in the air as one song ended and the next started. That brief moment of silence between us was all I needed to feel like a total loser, with everyone around me staring. Even the wick-pops appeared out of the blue next to Maggie.

I wanted to disappear somehow. No, I wanted to travel back in time and not come to this party. But I was stuck in the miserable present where seconds moved slower than normal.

"Why should I believe you?" Maggie said, looking angry.

I looked at her, confused and hurt. It was miserable enough to be stood up for this stupid party, and then dealing with drunk Maggie, who was known for being nasty and mean.

"What do you mean? I'm your best friend," I said louder than normal, making sure she heard me over the music.

Maggie took a step closer to me, stumbling. "They said you would never get a date, but I tried to help you with my friend Ty, and you ruined that too." Her words were like knives.

"Tristan. Didn't. Come," I said angrily and turned around, looking for Alex.

He had seen Tristan. He could tell Maggie I was not lying, that he existed. But Alex couldn't escape Nichole's reach. He couldn't come and save me. I looked at Maggie, wanting to tell her how miserable I had been that day with Tyler, but I kept quiet, since this was not the right time.

"I thought Dane liked me," she said and burst into tears.

I hugged her right away, feeling her weight leaning on me. "I know, he's a horrible person to do that on your birthday, and with one of the girls from the swim team," I said, closer to her.

She immediately pulled away. "You knew? You knew all this and didn't tell me?" Her drunkenness seemed to recede as the new information sank in.

"Maggie, I tried to tell you! I tried texting, even calling you several times. I've tried in every possible way I could think of, but you didn't answer. I even came to your house this morning," I said, frustrated as she stood there looking disgusted at me with the wick-pops behind her. "Ask your brother Nick. He knows about the jellyfish note," I said, betting on my last chance.

"How could you do this to me?" she said, her tears turning to anger.

This whole situation was fracturing slowly, like cracks in a dam. My heart broke a little more as I saw the pain in her eyes. Why had this party brought such complications? All this drama happened only in YA books or TV shows, but now it was happening to me.

Maggie looked down. I got closer to her and tried to hold her. But she pushed me away with much more strength than I could take. I fell in the mud, and my white dress was covered in it, as well as my hair. I tried to brush it away from my face, but some had landed in my mouth.

This was a new level of humiliation. I needed to get the hell out of this party. I tried to keep the tears in, but it was almost impossible. Alex came closer to help me stand. Once I was up, Nichole rushed to pull Alex away from me.

Maggie took a step closer to me, defiantly. "Leave."

I turned to look at the wick-pops standing close to her. They were sporting stupid victory smiles. It felt like they had something to do with this whole mess.

I felt anger at the injustice of it all. Even his brother had failed to deliver my message. I had done everything to tell her and still ended up looking like the villain. But now it was all crumbling down.

"GET OUT!" Maggie shouted, and I realized one of the wick-pops was recording it all on her phone.

This must be a nightmare—it was torture. But the mud itched on my skin, and I knew I was not dreaming.

"I don't want to talk to you EVER again!" she shouted. The way she looked at me signaled our friendship had gone to a place beyond repair. I stood straight, trying to keep myself from breaking entirely, to hold on to any piece of dignity I had left. I focused on my breath, tried to steady it. At least, covered in mud, no one could see my tears. Maggie took a step closer, and I instinctively took a step back. It was as if my best friend had vanished, and only a copy of the wick-pops remained in her place.

I turned on my heels, unable to stop the tears from pouring. My heart shattered into a thousand pieces—for Maggie, for Tristan, and for ruining Marian's dress. The humiliation, the mud all over me, the fact that Tristan was not around. But I knew I could count on Alex. As I headed toward the gate, hoping I wouldn't run into anyone on my way out, I waited to hear a second pair of squishy footsteps next to me, but there were none. I wanted to turn back, but I couldn't. The faster I could get out, the faster this would be in the past.

I heard a huge splash followed by laughter and screams while the music kept going, but not even that made me look back. I went through the gate and took a deep breath, realizing there were no other sets of squishy footsteps beside me. I was completely alone.

I crossed the street, looking all around me. I didn't know what I expected. Perhaps a tiny hope of finding Tristan outside, waiting for me to walk me home. But there was not a single soul on the street. I walked slowly, not caring about the direction. I desperately wanted to hear Alex's voice as he tried to catch up with me, but no one had followed me.

Nichole must have caught him, like she desperately had wanted all night long, and he hadn't managed to get away. Perhaps this had all been a stupid misunderstanding. If Alex was not here, it meant he cared more about staying there with Nichole than being with me when I needed him the most.

The neighborhood got quieter as I walked away from the music, replaced by the sound of cicadas and crickets chirping in the night. When I was far enough, I stopped and looked for my phone. The maps app would show me the way.

My bag was all messy and covered with mud. As I looked for my phone, I realized my pocket edition of *Romeo and Juliet* was gone. It must have fallen when Maggie pushed me. I shook my bag in frustration, as if it could actually change anything, but all I wanted was to scream. To let my anger and pain find a way out of me. It was supposed to be just a party, and it had become the worst night of my life.

I unlocked my phone, trembling. The angry tears wouldn't allow me to see the screen clearly. Somehow I expected to see a missed call. Alex wanting to know where I was to get me home like he always did, but nothing. There were no notifications.

I hated myself for believing stupid Dane, for trusting Tristan, for wanting Alex to be something more. I hated to have lost my tiny book and Marian's gift. I hated guys, all of them, and Maggie too. And I hated feeling so lonely.

I managed to open the maps app and found my way. Then I walked home, hoping the night breeze would dry my tears.

CHAPTER 12

SUMMER STAR-CROSSED LOVERS

When I opened my eyes, it took me a while to process why I felt as if I had stayed up really late or was hungover. I was dragging myself groggily to the bathroom to get ready for the library party when I saw Marian's dress hanging in the shower. Then it all hit me like a waterfall. I had tried desperately to wash Marian's dress in the sink last night, but perhaps shampoo was not strong enough for mud stains.

My mind wanted to pretend yesterday hadn't happened and focus instead on my day ahead at the library, where I'd try at all costs to avoid Tristan. Last night I had turned my phone off, something I rarely did. I had no mental space to deal with Alex or Maggie, in case they had reached out. Maggie was known for drunk dialing, and even though I had somehow messed up things with Dane, I still didn't deserve to be treated that way.

I thought about keeping my phone off for the rest of the day. Especially since the wick-pops might have already uploaded my humiliating video on social media. But I could avoid the tech world only so much, since I was sure Nora would text nonstop with last-minute details for the library party.

I ripped the Band-Aid off and turned on my phone, waiting for the notifications to build up on my screen with a series of beeps. To my surprise there were no texts, not a single one. Just one missed call from Alex, which seemed like too little after last night. Today he was leaving for the summer, and I had come up with the plan that as soon as I was done working at the library, I'd check out a ton of books and submerge myself in fictional stories until reality was a vague memory.

Marian's dress was stained but dry, so I hid it at the bottom of my laundry basket to deal with later. I let my hair air dry and went down for breakfast, where I tried my best to avoid my parents' party questions. With all my free time going to Tristan in the past weeks, I hadn't had as much time to read. But I faked excitement about a book I told them I was into. I made it all up, but by now I could come up with believable plots and characters just by taking bits of different books I had read.

When I couldn't find a way out of my own ideas, I lied about Nora texting me nonstop, needing my help. Which I hoped was believable, since Nora, like all librarians, was one step ahead and was always prepared beforehand. I blamed it on my absence yesterday, reassuring my parents that it had been an OK party with nothing interesting to report. I just wanted to avoid even thinking about that stupid party any longer. Mom mentioned they might be able to come by later after Will's soccer game, which I honestly didn't mind.

Then I switched the conversation topic to Mom's beautiful Bundt cake, which was neatly decorated with natural flowers on a plate over the counter. Mom said she had already finished with the pictures and offered us a piece, not without taking pictures of a single slice on a cute plate. We got to enjoy the results of her latest blog post.

"Five stars, Mom," I said with my mouth full. It was definitely the best version of blueberry lemon cake she had ever made.

When I headed outside and saw Alex's blue Jeep parked on the street, it hit me like a wall of bricks. I tried as best as I could to shake it off, get on my bike, and ride, enjoying the warm summer breeze. Sarah had mentioned that many new books had arrived for the summer, so I decided to focus instead on all the book boyfriends that might be waiting.

I have never been good at handling crowds, even as I stood comfortably under the shaded canopy of the library's booth. It had been more than a couple of hours since the summer reading club party had started, and we were in the peak of the summer heat. The loud music, along with the kids' joyful screams as the warm breeze blew the bubble truck's foam all around, was overloading my senses.

"June, have you already checked that the remaining totes have the correct items inside?" Nora's micromanaging was just the cherry on top.

I turned to look at her. "I checked them twice the other day when I was putting them together. I'm sure that little boy just wanted an extra pencil." She didn't seem satisfied with my answer. "Can I take a break? I think I need something sweet to drink. The heat is killing me," I lied, thinking of an escape plan since I knew there were coolers underneath the booth's table with water bottles.

Nora flared her nostrils. "Just don't take too long." She looked away, switching her mood instantly and smiling as she engaged with other patrons.

I was walking toward the Stories and Bridges Café booth to get an ice tea when, halfway there, I saw him. Tristan was working at the booth next to Audrey, smiling and giggling in a more-than-friendly way. I froze. How stupid had I been? Even with Maggie's exchange boyfriend drama last summer, it looked like I hadn't learned a thing.

Tristan seemed to be wild about me a couple of days ago, but perhaps it was my own wishful thinking getting in the way. Maybe he was just another careless exchange guy. I just couldn't erase overnight how much I had grown to care about him. How unique he was with his charming eyes, bright smile, and the way he would call me *milady*. It was fun to somehow be *his*, but perhaps it had all been nothing more than a game. It was easier to forget my feelings about guys when they were not standing in front of me being handsome.

"What's the matter, my dear?" Sarah's voice took me by surprise. "You look as if you've seen a ghost." She chuckled. Her motherly concern was sweet but just not what I needed.

"It's nothing," I answered, looking away.

"Does it have anything to do with Mr. Tristan, perhaps?" she asked.

If Mrs. Lib were here instead, I could tell her every single detail of my sorrows. How frustrated I felt because fiction couldn't be real, and she would tell me a similarity between my situation and a book. And then I'd read and obsess about that book and forget my despair. But Mrs. Lib was not here, another reminder of how miserable my life had become and how angry I was at myself for somehow believing guys like Romeo could be real.

"He truly is a peculiar character." Sarah's words interrupted my daydreams. "Yesterday evening he wandered all around the library, running through the parking lot like a wild person, even mumbling in another language. He seemed lost, which was strange since the library is a building known for having everything marked." Her joke confused me. If he was here, alone, then why didn't he go to the party? I had left him a map and directions. Besides, Maggie's house was only a fifteen-minute walk from the library.

"Young people, I swear, sometimes I don't get them." She stared at me. "Well, not all of them." She smiled as she rubbed my shoulder. "I'm sure whatever troubles you, it must be just a misunderstanding, dear."

Jim came by and asked her something, but I zoned out of their conversation. Then they walked away together, blending into the crowd.

Perhaps there was an explanation for last night. Maybe nothing was going on between Audrey and Tristan, like he'd insinuated before. But I couldn't understand why he had stayed here when I'd drawn a clear path on the map around the streets of Storybridge and told him a precise time to meet.

Perhaps I could allow him an explanation, just for my peace of mind. It was clear I didn't want any sort of relationship with any real guy anymore. I would need to talk to him later, when I wouldn't freeze at the sight of him. I turned toward the library's garden instead. I needed a break from the noise, inside my head and out.

I sat with my back against the trunk of a big oak tree and stared at the blue sky peeking through the branches. Even a beautiful view couldn't cure last night's heartbreak. I couldn't take my mind off that stupid party. Perhaps blocking out something was not the right way of dealing with it. So I allowed myself to be miserable for a while. Maybe then I could process it a little at a time and, when the time was up, go back to not thinking about it.

Last night's events played in my mind like a movie. Every single thing that could have gone bad had gone terribly wrong. If Tristan would have gotten there on time, there would be a picture of us to prove I had a date. I would have found Maggie and talked to her, and she would have met him. She would have seen Tristan with her own eyes, proof that I had kept my promise.

I had focused so much of my time on Tristan, trying to forget about Alex, that it all had backfired, and I'd ended up completely wrecked by both guys. The past couple of weeks had been a total mess.

I was getting by OK, as I was processing my rekindled crush for Alex even though he didn't have feelings for me. So I focused instead on having fun with Tristan, even though I knew he would be gone by the end of summer. But I didn't expect Tristan to kiss me or for Alex to want to do the same the following night and later leave me hanging while he stood by Nichole. I didn't need any of this. I hadn't even been able to enjoy the fact that I had my first kiss ever with someone as close as Romeo could get in real life.

The *should*s and *would*s were killing me, for I couldn't do a thing to change the past. I took my glasses off and closed my eyes, trying so hard to forget Maggie's expression when she realized I already knew about Dane. That was the worst part, losing my best friend who would help me out with all this guy drama.

"Hey." A familiar voice took me by surprise. I quickly put my glasses back on and saw Alex's untied shoes on the grass. I cleared my throat and looked up at his signature messy hair.

"Are you here to say goodbye?" My tone was defensive. I needed a minute more to lock the party drama back again in a box at the back of my mind, before I felt ready to deal with any of its participants. I couldn't shake off the anger and frustration as I stared at him. Perhaps I had expected too much of Alex.

"I . . . I wanted to see how you were doing." His tone was serious.

"Well, obviously not great. It was the entire opposite of the best night of my life," I said, looking away.

"I went looking for you. You know, after the whole mess of Maggie falling drunk into the pool."

His words shocked me. "What?!"

"After you left, she tumbled as she walked. The wick-pops tried to hold her, but she pushed them away. One of them fell into the mud, just like you." Alex laughed.

On any other day, I would have laughed, too, but not today. That scene was too fresh, and it hurt too much for me to laugh. He noticed I didn't react to his comment and kept going.

"Anyway, Maggie fell into the pool. At first we thought it was funny, but once we realized Maggie was not coming to the surface, I knew something was wrong."

I couldn't believe all this had happened just after I left. I remembered hearing a splash, but I was too ashamed to turn around.

"Please tell me you helped her." Even though I was hurt, I couldn't deny that I cared about her.

He nodded. "I did. I went into overdrive trying to save her, remembering the process from when I worked as a lifeguard at the city pool."

I felt relieved.

"I jumped in, got her out, did CPR, and before I had to blow air into her mouth, she responded, spitting all the water out at me. Easily the most disgusting thing that has ever happened to me." He smiled and I tried to too. "Her brothers called the paramedics and helped her out. She's fine now. I thought you might want to know."

Knowing Maggie was fine felt like fresh air in my lungs. I had been so immersed in the Tristan-Alex-Dane disappointment that the thought of something happening to her was unimaginable. Now that I knew she was OK, I could go back to being mad at her.

Alex scoffed, and I didn't understand why until I felt someone gently take my hand.

"Milady, may I have a word with you?" Tristan stared at me with his gorgeous olive eyes. At first I wanted to slap him, but the more I stared at him, the more my defenses crumbled.

"She's not *your* lady," Alex said, and I turned to look at him. "Can't you see we are busy?" He added.

"Scoundrel!" Tristan dropped my hand and turned to him. I didn't know if I should focus on his weird offense or the conflict that was brewing between them again.

"I'm not the one who didn't show up and embarrassed June in front of everyone." Alex's words still stung.

"You fool! On my word I did not." Tristan took a step closer to Alex. Tristan must have been practicing with the drama club.

Alex laughed cynically. "Don't tell me your busy schedule stopped you from going to the party?" He teased with a mocking smile. "Maggie's party is conveniently aligned with the arrival of the exchange students. I believe you guys are the main reasons for that party."

Alex was not entirely wrong.

"On second thought, it was good that you missed it. We got to spend some time together, walking under the lights in the garden. In fact, it was great." Alex grinned.

"Fire-eyed fury be my conduct now," Tristan mumbled, but only I got the *Romeo and Juliet* reference. Tristan must be memorizing the play. They were the same words Romeo said before killing Tybalt. I could see Tristan's hands clenching into fists, his knuckles turning white. I was not going to let this situation become another ice-cream incident. I had no idea what Alex was up to, but I wasn't about to find out.

"Stop it! Both of you." I stood between them, pushing them apart. "I don't care what your issues are, I work here and I will not let either one of you get me fired."

They stared at each other, neither of them wanting to move away, but then Alex took a step back. I stared into Tristan's eyes.

He had to calm down. His frown dissolved, and his eyes grew watery.

"Milady, my love. I cannot bear causing you any pain." His voice broke as he knelt and kissed my hand repeatedly. "Milady, you are too fair, too wise, wisely too fair."

Tristan's words made me blush as I noticed another *Romeo and Juliet* reference. Damn, this guy knew how to play me. Tristan's range of emotions was impressive. No wonder he liked drama club. He could go from being mad to desperate in two seconds flat.

I pulled back my hand, trying to not get carried away. "I need to get back to work."

Alex scoffed, "Don't tell me you are buying his theatrical crap. You'd never forgive *me* if I stood you up." His snobbish attitude was unlike him.

"Alex, just let him be," I said. Tristan was odd, but who did Alex think he was to bully him for being so passionate?

Alex ran his hand through his hair. "I'm not here to deal with Mr. Drama Freak. I came to bring you this." Alex took a tiny object out of his jeans' back pocket and gave it to me. "It's beaten up, but I tried to clean it as much as I could."

It took me a few seconds to realize what it was. He had found my pocket edition of *Romeo and Juliet*. Once I wiped the dry mud away, I realized it was in bad shape. The cover was falling apart, and the pages were all wavy from the humidity. I tried to open it, but a bunch of pages were stuck together, and some of the ink had even blurred.

"What is the matter, milady?" Tristan must have noticed my change in mood.

"It's ruined," I said, staring at it. I had seen videos online about people fixing books. Fanning out the pages and putting a cloth between each one of them. I hoped that would be enough to save it. Excitement and sadness mixed inside of me as I realized how pretty it was when I'd gotten it, and how horrible it looked now. Perhaps my lucky charm had lost its luck, but at least it was not entirely ruined.

"Alex, I . . . thank you." I took a step closer to him, wanting to hug him so badly, but I stopped myself.

"Milady, may I?"

I hesitated.

"I may know a thing or two about books. Allow me to help. I will do anything for your forgiveness. For us to resume our love story where it paused and to feel your tender lips on mine one more time," he said, holding my hands, enclosing my book.

"What did he just say?" Alex asked.

I got lost in Tristan's words, like they were some sort of spell. My mind had gone back to our first kiss and how amazing that moment had been, but it had led me to this messy situation.

"Nothing," I said.

"My lady June and I shared the most precious kiss," Tristan intervened proudly. "Your fruitless attempts are no match for our love. It will prevail until the end."

"Did *you* kiss *him*?" Alex asked.

"You fool, didn't you hear—" Tristan jumped in.

"I was not talking to you." Alex frowned at Tristan and looked at me. Now he was the one with tight fists and white knuckles.

I was glad Tristan hadn't gotten into any more details, but I didn't want Alex to know about my love life. "It's none of your business what I do with *my* life. Besides, aren't you leaving today? Does Nichole know you came to see me?" I said defensively.

Whatever moment Alex and I had had last night had been a misjudgment on my part. It took me over an hour to walk home, and he could have found me after helping Maggie. There was only one route to get to our street.

Alex looked away at the trees. "You are right. I have to go."

He pointed his head at Tristan. "I guess you prefer his stupid theatrical crap than honesty."

I rolled my eyes at him.

"Can't you see he's a fraud? He knows exactly what to say so you come to him. He memorized the whole freaking play." Alex's eyes narrowed. "He punched me outside the ice-cream shop with some shit about me biting my thumb at him!"

All I could focus on was his cheek. The bruise was still visible, but not green anymore. Now it was more in the soft-yellow tones.

"Well, he didn't go unscathed." I looked at Tristan's eye, and the bruise was also the same yellow tone.

"I can't believe you'd take his side." Alex's frustration was impossible to mask.

I avoided his gaze. Lately, everything Alex did generated a roller coaster of emotions in me. Either I wanted to be with him or I was furious at him. There was no middle. And now I no longer knew what was going on between us.

I turned to Tristan. "Do you really know about fixing books?" I asked, thinking he was smart and maybe knew something about it, since he also liked books. He nodded "Then fix it and we'll call it even." Then I looked at Alex. "Thanks for my book. I hope you have a great summer far, far away in Arthsteen U." I was furious. "Now if you can both leave me alone, I have to get back to work."

"Before I go, there's something else you need to know," Alex said, looking as if he had built a wall between us. He turned to look at Tristan, who was still standing next to me, examining my book. "Can you at least give us one minute?"

Tristan stared at me, waiting for a confirmation. "Go, Tristan, I'll find you in a little bit. Just promise me you'll take care of my book," I said to him. Tristan looked disappointed but nodded and walked away. I turned to Alex. "Can you be quick? I really need to get back to work before Nora thinks of a new punishment because I took so long to return."

Alex looked around, waiting for Tristan to be far away. Then he grabbed my arm and pulled me closer, as if to tell me a secret, which triggered different reactions inside me. Part of me wanted to punch him, to take my anger out on his mistakes, but I no longer knew how to act around him, especially when we were so close that his cologne—rather than his typical hint of chlorine— messed with my senses.

"After Maggie's diving incident was over, just before I left the party, I overheard the wick-pops talking about you."

That was not surprising.

"Apparently Mia is part of the exchange welcoming committee or something like that."

"I already know that," I said defensively.

"Well, the thing is, it turns out that there is nobody from all the exchange students this summer whose name is Tristan, first or middle name."

I scoffed. The wick-pops would lie and do anything to mess with me. But Alex's tone was serious, and that threw me off. "I did a little research of my own, and it turns out there's no one from England or anywhere in the UK. Not even Northern Ireland this summer at Storybridge's exchange program."

I wanted to laugh, since he must be trying to mess with me. But something inside of me knew that Alex wouldn't lie to me, not like that. Alex doing research of his own meant something else. I remained quiet. Perhaps I needed to stop fantasizing about Tristan and start asking the right kind of questions.

"I have to go. I still have to go back home and pick up my stuff." Alex stared at me. "Are you going to let me leave without a goodbye hug?" His tone dismantled my defensive reaction.

I stared at him, realizing I wouldn't see him at all until the end of July. None of our summers had been like this. But maybe time away from each other might allow our friendship to heal and go back to where it was before this whole mess started. I just didn't want to lose him, like I'd lost Maggie, when we had only one year left before graduation.

I gave him a weak hug, but his embrace was much stronger. "I don't like fighting with you, June."

All I could think of was that if last night Maggie had called me a minute later, perhaps we would have kissed, and today would have been very different. I couldn't stand the daunting weight of possibilities, how easily life could change in a single moment. I hugged him tighter. He was no stranger; he was my best friend. Then why had a single night messed up everything between us, especially when nothing had really happened?

His hug lasted longer than a normal goodbye hug. It was as if he didn't want to leave.

"Promise me you'll take care of yourself," he said, and I heard his voice through his chest. His voice had always brought me so much peace, but now it was wrecking me.

I broke apart, realizing now Nora would be really upset. "Have fun meeting girls from the college team." My tone had come out more bitter than I'd intended it. There was nothing friendly or supportive in my voice. It should be different. When he'd first applied to the summer program, I had been truly happy for him. It was good for his future scholarship plans. But now things had gotten weird between us.

He took a step back, and his dark eyes stared at me too long. Then he nodded and turned away. Next time we'd meet, things would be different. He would have met new people from college, and I'd still be his small-town childhood friend. I stared at how he walked away and blended into the crowd. He didn't turn back, not once. I saw him leave along with the idea of us being something more. I stared until I could no longer recognize him, not his height, not his messy hair.

I got back to the library booth to find Sarah and Nora chatting. Nora looked at me with disapproving eyes. Fortunately Sarah was there, and they kept chatting until Jim came to speak with Nora. At first I was hesitant, but she didn't look my way as she spoke to Jim. Honestly, it was a relief. Then they left, taking the empty containers with them.

Few patrons were coming to our booth. Most were in line for the food trucks now. Sarah encouraged me to walk around and have fun before it ended, which was really nice of her. I walked around, looking at the different booths, one for the fire department, one of local soaps, one selling honey from local beehives. I even ran into my parents. Will and his best friend, Sam, were beyond themselves, running through the bubble foam. It reminded me of the laundry incident with Tristan. Which made me realize I had not seen him at the café booth when I came from the library's garden.

I hoped trusting him with my precious book had not been another mistake. Something about what Alex had said still buzzed in my mind. Could it be that Tristan had been lying about who he truly was all this time? Could he be an exchange student from another school's program? There was only one big high school in Storybridge, and if Tristan moved around by foot, that meant he had to live around here. Maybe there was a local theater school around the area that I had no idea about and he was an exchange student from there. Or maybe he had parents with different nationalities in Europe and had entered the US using a passport that was not from the UK. He hadn't actually told me anything about his hometown or about his family.

There had to be another explanation. I had no proof other than his obsession for theater and that he spent a lot of time at this library, but I wanted to find out. By now I wasn't sure I wanted something to happen between Tristan and me. I was leaning toward not dating anyone real again. The past weeks Tyler, Alex, and Tristan had brought more drama than I could handle. If this was a book, I could just close it and forget about it, but it was real life, and I didn't have much more mental space left for boy drama.

The library party was finally over, the fire truck had left, people were packing up their booths, and I had not run into Tristan. I remembered the last time I found him he was at the tree house, so that was my next stop.

Once I was in the library garden and knew no one was around, I climbed up the tree at full speed. Once I reached the top, I found Tristan staring at my tiny book.

"Hey, you!" I said as I climbed the last steps. He didn't answer. He just flipped through the pages of my tiny book. I blinked repeatedly and stared at it. It no longer looked like the same dirty, beaten book.

"How did you fix it so fast?" I asked as I took it from his hands and examined it. The cover was fixed, and although many pages were now a grayish tone with no words at all, it looked like a book. Perhaps the ink they had used was the cheapest and had diluted in water. It was still wavy, but other than that, the book looked way better.

"Milady, I must confide in you. Lady Sarah once mentioned that if I ever faced any problem with a book or else, I should come to her. She was the one who provided the tape to secure the cover," he said with a hint of sadness.

Tristan was right. We could always count on a librarian to save the day, except for Nora. But now I was worried about Tristan. He seemed sad, and even with everything that had happened with him in the last twenty-four hours, I still wanted to cheer him up. And also go inside, since the heat was now killing me.

"What's wrong, Tristan?" I asked, no longer mad at him. I was grateful he had helped me with my book, and a part of me kept thinking how much fun we'd have had if he had come to the party. Perhaps he would have kissed me again, or maybe I would have gotten to know him better, but for now I just wanted to be around him, even if it was just as his friend.

Tristan seemed unsure. "Not sadness, but confusion haunts me, milady. Perhaps you might be able to enlighten me with your wisdom." He looked at my book. "Why have you referred to *this* as your favorite book?"

I stared at him, clueless.

"Its pages are completely blank. If anything, it resembles more an empty book to take notes," he said.

I laughed. "Yeah, I know some words are blurred out, but this is not a notebook, Tristan," I said, trying to follow his joke.

"Notebook is a great term for it," he added, acting surprised.

I browsed through the pages carefully. The end was all blurred out, which was a shame, but the beginning still had a lot of words clearly printed. Perhaps it had fallen on the back cover and lay in wet mud and grass for too long.

"Can't you see this?" I pointed at the prologue and showed it to him. But even as he squinted and stared at it closely, he shook his head, saying again that it was all just blank paper.

"This doesn't make any sense," I said, wondering if the heat had anything to do with him not being able to see it, or maybe he needed glasses. But I noticed his hands shaking, then heard his breathing accelerating, and I was suddenly scared of not knowing what was happening.

I turned to look at him, and tears were running down his cheeks. "Tristan, what's wrong?"

"Milady, more dark and dark my woes! More to add to my despair."

"What are you saying?" I asked, freaking out a little. Perhaps he was the best actor of his generation, but his suffering seemed real.

"Your book, the ball. You must believe me. I attempted everything, but I could not escape the library grounds to get to you. The hours lengthened, and I kept trying, just the way I did the first night we met."

He covered his face with his hands and began to cry unconsolably. I wanted to find a convincing explanation for what had happened. He came with me to get an ice cream, so it didn't make sense he couldn't leave. Could he be lying shamelessly to my face?

I had no clue what to tell him. I just did the same thing as when we were in this exact same situation. I patted his back and told him to breathe. He might be having an identity crisis after portraying so many characters. What would I know? I was a book fanatic. I knew nothing about theater. But I once heard about actors going mad after portraying certain characters.

Something flag-like caught my eye. I stood up and walked around the trunk to figure out what it was while Tristan finished weeping. The *flag* that I had seen was my dad's old polo shirt hanging from the branches and moving with the wind. Tristan's clothes, or the ones my family had donated and I had washed for him, were stuck to the branches as if they were drying. It took me a couple of seconds to process.

"Tristan, have you been living here all this time?" I asked, thinking over and over about what Alex had said earlier.

He uncovered his face and took out my koala handkerchief, then used it to dry his tears. At least he hadn't lost it.

"Milady, this is precisely what I must confess. The truth I have been hiding for too long." He was starting to freak me out for real. Who was he? "The world has been a prison. But your presence has made it bearable." He stood up, and I suddenly wanted to be talking about this at ground level and not at the top of a tree. "I have lived here since our stars aligned and we met that glorious night. Milady, you provided me with a safe place to sleep."

My anxiety spiked as I realized I might have helped a lunatic —or a thug—out of a mental facility.

I no longer cared where he was from. I needed bigger answers. "Who . . . who are you?" I asked, a little scared to know the answer. Tristan seemed to be scared himself to tell me the truth. I began to think it was not a good idea to scream for help. I'd get into trouble either way—for giving him the idea to stay at the top of a tree and for being in a forbidden old tree house myself.

"I know not who am I, milady. My identity is the root of my despair. I have tried to find the right moment to confess to thee."

"Should I be scared of you?" I naively asked, not wanting to be that nerd who got murdered by a serial killer in disguise.

"Milady, no!" He knelt and reached for my hand. "Since my lips touched your angel's lips, you have shortened my hours. This is my faithful vow of love."

And then it all came crashing down like a wave swallowing me whole. Every single detail about him fit in a puzzle that seemed impossible to exist. All the tiny quirks since I met him suddenly came to mind. How scared he was with lights and different sounds. How overly excited he was with a sandwich. How freaked out he was about getting into an elevator. How weird he acted about automatic doors and how panicked he was as he confused a bunch of cables for snakes. How he acted like he had never seen a bike before, how he didn't know what ice cream was. So many little things I had dismissed. Even Haiku didn't want to be around him, and dogs judged people better than we did. But Tristan living here, not knowing who he was, not being able to read his own play . . .

"It can't be. You can't be." I stumbled over the words, trying to convince myself that he could be real. I felt the floor wobble below me, and my feet could no longer hold me up. I stumbled and used the tree house wall to steady me.

"Milady, are you all right?"

"Romeo? It can't be," I mumbled in the weakest voice. Part of me thought this was a stunt or a game, and in any given moment he'd say, *I got you!* But he stared at me seriously.

"Milady, what did you just say?" he asked.

It just didn't make sense.

"Please say that name again," he demanded.

I said it and witnessed his expression go from shock to excitement as the sadness dried away from his eyes. "Of the house of Montague," he added, unsure at first, then beaming with happiness. "Oh milady, you have long known the answer!"

Technically, I didn't. But I began to think I was on my way to completely losing it. He came closer and held on to my waist, raising me up in the air. The scene was worthy of any rom-com, but all I could think of was how dizzy I felt being up in a tree house, plus the added height of him lifting me. It was getting too much for me to bear.

He put me down, and his smile reached the corners of his eyes. He was truly happy, an excitement I had never seen in him before, even with all his signature whirlwind of emotions.

He raised his hands in the air and shouted, "I AM ROMEO MONTAGUE!" His voice was so loud the birds flew away.

I shushed him. "Tristan, take it easy."

"Milady, let us rejoice in us knowing. I have spent weeks in ignorance. It is the first time I feel . . . real."

His words took me by surprise. For the first time I thought how hard it must be to lose your identity. A little part of me still believed all this couldn't be real, but with my experience as an avid reader, I had learned to put myself into someone else's shoes. For him to finally be able to understand something about the world around him must be mind-blowing. And, after all, he was here with me, his biggest fan in the whole world.

His happiness became contagious. He got closer to me and held my hand and waist, trying to dance, even with no music. I tried to stop, since dancing was not really my thing, but he made it all seem so romantic.

"Milady, it has been a terrible mistake of letting my emotions cloud my judgment."

No kidding, I thought but only gave him a weak smile. Something seemed different about him as I stared at his hair, his smile, and his perfect features. It felt as if I was getting to know him again for the very first time. He twirled me around and reached for me, and as I felt the warmth of his fingers interlacing with mine, I suddenly realized Romeo was a living, breathing guy.

"My love, milady, my savior. Let me feel your lips again." He held my face between his hands and kissed me. It was sweet and tender. My brain stopped, and I forgot even my own name. He pulled back an inch and I could see his smile so close to mine. I got lost in his olive eyes. His breath was so inviting, and all I could think of was kissing him again and again.

We had kissed before, but now it felt different. This time I was kissing the real Romeo Montague. This time I was starstruck. The probabilities of this happening were nonexistent. Yet I had to take a chance on having my wildest dream come true. Life couldn't get better than this. Reality was finally better than fiction. That was until a voice from below took us by surprise and we pulled apart.

CHAPTER 13
TIMES OF WOE AFFORD NO TIME TO WOO

"Who's up there?" someone shouted up to us. What was I doing? I was going to get in trouble. I peeked down and saw Jim. Oh crap. Even though he was nice and easygoing, I had no idea what his reaction would be to finding us alone, up here in a forbidden place.

As I climbed down, holding the rope, I thought of a way to hide the fact that I had gone up with a friend and come down with a boyfriend. These kinds of situations didn't look good to adults.

"Sorry, Jim. I know I shouldn't have gone up there. I was feeling nostalgic, that's all." I tried to act apologetic by accepting any consequences beforehand.

"Who else is up there?"

He looked up, and I knew I couldn't fool him.

"Come on, tell your friend to get back here now too."

I could sense the irritation in his tone.

Tristan greeted Jim from above and came down, too, much more agile than me. There was not much I could do to escape or lie about this situation.

Jim looked at me, unsure as to what to do. He could follow

his job description and report me, or take into account the many years of knowing me and maybe spare me.

"You are not a troublemaker, June," he finally said. I shook my head. He was right. I was a book nerd obsessed with libraries, not a wannabe Tarzan who made out with cute boys at the top of trees.

"Are you sure nobody saw you climb up there?"

The friendliness in his voice made me relax. I shook my head. The fewer words I said, the better.

"Good, now promise me you'll stay away from this place once and for all, or I'll tell Nora about it. I don't want you to get hurt like last time," he said, looking between Tristan and me. I didn't want to disappoint Jim, and I dreaded the thought of hearing Nora fuss about it.

I promised Jim I would stay away from the tree house for good, and he let us go. I was incredibly grateful for him sparing me this time but also wondered what would happen now. Tristan needed a place to stay, and we would eventually need to get up there to get his clothes. Fortunately, Jim hadn't bothered to remove the rope.

Tristan and I headed toward the library to cool down. I didn't have to go back to work, but I still wanted to check out the new books before they would be added to the New Titles section for patrons to check out. But something told me I'd be spending my summer's free time with my new crush rather than my fictional guys for a change.

"Were you the young person who fell from the tree?" Tristan asked, taking me out of my thoughts as we stood in the lobby. "The one you mentioned before."

Oh man, it seemed I wasn't able to avoid things today. "Yep," I said, walking a little faster.

"Milady, wait." He caught up with me before we crossed the library doors. "Is there perhaps something else you might be able to tell me about myself?"

I tried to not lose my cool now that we were in public. Public displays of affection were never really my thing.

I sat on one of the benches inside the lobby, away from the entrance and people. Our conversation would sound nuts to anyone eavesdropping. I didn't know where to begin. If only he knew what would happen to him or what he was capable of. Just the thought scared me. I mean, if he truly was Romeo Montague, things didn't look bright for him. But he was here, out of his time and place, and that would make everything entirely different for him. My lips pressed in a line, and I couldn't tell him what I knew.

Even with all the books I have read, I couldn't come up with a fake storyline that would make him feel better. Because in all the stories similar to *Romeo and Juliet*, at least one of them ended up losing. Like in *Tristan and Isolde* or *Westside Story*.

"Well . . ." I tried to think of anything that would bring him a sense of peace, but my mind went down a rabbit hole of literary dilemmas. What if authors were gods deciding their characters' entire fate for it to fit into a storyline? What if Tristan couldn't read his own book because we were not supposed to know about our future ahead?

Tristan held my hand, and I came back to the present. His warm fingers above mine made me think maybe I was getting ahead of myself, like always.

"Milady, anything will do. I expect not for you to know everything there is to know about me. We have barely yet to know ourselves in love. And the future lies in tomorrow, a place we can't see because we haven't arrived there yet."

Wow, he was deep. Any logical thoughts went out the window with his words. Why was he so irresistible?

"Italian. You are from Verona, Italy," I finally said. Perhaps that would soothe him enough for now. But if he was anything like me, he wouldn't stop until he found out everything there was to know. I'd have to carefully select each word I'd use with him, but something told me this wouldn't be the end of it. Besides, I was a terrible liar.

"Cara mia, hai dato un senso alla amia follia." He knelt and kissed my hand.

"Tristan, just because you rediscovered your mother tongue doesn't mean I have any clue about what you're saying." I took my hand away, noticing that people were staring.

"Milady, apologies. I only said that you have brought sense to my madness," he said with a bright smile.

He had done the entire opposite. He'd brought chaos to my boring small-town life. I was new at this dating thing, but I thought dating guys came with more fun and less homework. Tristan seemed to be wanting to be closer to me, and I was getting overwhelmed. Besides, I was sure Nora might appear any minute now, since she always had the worst timing.

"You know what, Tristan? I forgot to finish something, about work. Can we talk later?" I said nervously.

"I will be here waiting, milady," he said, standing along with me. It seemed that he could only walk away from the library *with me*, and we both knew it. But it felt odd. Why me? Could it be the fact that I was his biggest fan? Oh gosh, my obsessions were getting me into trouble, and I needed time alone to think. I'd sit at the quiet lounge as soon as I was alone and write all my sorrows away.

He walked next to me as I headed for the library's entrance but he stopped at the café. I crossed the library's main doors and immediately felt the temperature change. The extra cool air around me made me wonder if I was wild about him or delusional. I reached for the light scarf inside my bag. At least Tyler's present had turned out to be pretty useful in the summer months. Something about staring at the scarf made me wonder,

Could it be that my favorite black scarf getting ruined was not a laundry accident? What if Tristan's presence in this time and place had a consequence for his play? I remembered the meeting, the one where Nora blamed me for the terrible shape the collectible was in. That was it! The collectible was the book he must have come from!

I headed to the Timeless Literature section. It must all be in my mind, but I'd die if something happened to my favorite love story. I ran rather than walked to where I wanted to be. Some library staff gave me funny looks as I skipped two steps at a time, going up the stairs. No one in their right mind would be in a hurry inside a library, but I was. My nerves didn't allow me to focus well on the location of my favorite book, so I closed my eyes and let muscle memory guide me. I opened them and found the title on the spine, taking a deep breath.

As I opened the book, I realized the words were missing. I blinked and looked closer. This copy looked similar to my pocket edition. The beginning was there, but the end was all blurred out. How could it be? This copy had been safe and sound inside a temperature-controlled building. Oh no, oh no, this couldn't be real. I grabbed another of Shakespeare's works, *Hamlet*. It was completely fine. My hands shook as I realized the greatest love story of all time was fading. I couldn't let this happen. I returned *Hamlet* to its right place and grabbed *Romeo and Juliet*. I'd have to hide it somewhere where no one would notice. But I'd have to check the other copies too.

I walked down to the Adult Nonfiction section, where all of Shakespeare's works were, but stopped by the computers first. Maybe the collectible had had an effect on the copies nearby, and once Tristan went back to his book, everything would be fine. As I sat, the swivel chair moved away from me, almost making me fall. People sitting around looked my way.

"I need to check my grades urgently," I lied, and their eyes went back to their monitors. I could have used my phone, but I needed a bigger screen.

I typed in the words in the library's online catalog, nervously trying to steady my hand to avoid typos. I hit the enter key and waited. My eyes opened wide as the results came: *No titles found (0 hits).* I rechecked for a mistake, perhaps a double space or a period. That usually messed up the very sensitive library's catalog. But no, I had spelled it right.

Maybe someone had noticed and had taken it out of the system. But how? I opened another tab for Google. My fingertips could barely type the words *Shakespeare's most famous play.* I hit enter, and as I stared at the screen, the feeling of drowning became so overwhelming, I tried to gasp for air. Shakespeare's most famous plays were *A Midsummer Night's Dream* and *Hamlet.*

This couldn't be happening. Maybe a hacker had found a way into Wikipedia. I closed my eyes, trying my best to focus. I couldn't let panic win. Not when I was the only one aware of this situation. And maybe the only one who could do something to avoid this tragedy. At least I was the Romeo expert, so I could figure this out.

I looked for their names, their last names, every possible combination I could come up with for Romeo Montague and Juliet Capulet. But it was as if the characters along with the play had simply stopped existing. I couldn't let the them disappear, I'd have to find a way to send Tristan back to his book, but how? I had no idea why he had come here in the first place.

I logged out and headed back to the area where Shakespeare's works were. If any patron or librarian noticed a damaged book, the library would be in so much trouble we might kiss the grant goodbye. Librarians knew very well that keeping damaged books was a sign of an unkempt library.

I didn't even have to look for the classification number. I knew it by heart. I stood in front of the bookshelf with

Shakespeare's works, feeling like Sherlock Holmes in an investigation. I browsed through all the books, every single copy. The rest of the plays were fine, even the sonnets. It was just all the copies of *Romeo and Juliet* that were off. The beginning was there, but the title in the spine seemed to be fading, like sun damage. But no sun came to this side of the library, and there were special blinds to keep the sun away.

If only Mrs. Lib was here, I could tell her. I could trust her. But she wasn't, and I didn't know if I could trust Sarah enough to tell her what I had discovered. Suddenly kissing Tristan seemed like a terrible lack of judgement on my part.

Any part of me that debated whether Tristan was the real Romeo or just an actor went out the window. Now I'd have to make sure he was safe and unharmed. I'd have to protect him from even a paper cut. Nothing could happen to him, not on my watch. My once-boring summer had become a tireless mission to protect one of the most famous characters of world literature.

I found the closest library cart and pulled out all his play's copies. I couldn't check them out to keep at home, so I'd have to hide them somewhere where no one could find them. The storage room came to mind. No one frequented it, and I just had to make sure that if Nora or Jim came, it would look like no one had been there or touched anything.

Once all the copies were in the cart, I moved the cart to the elevator, but instead of clicking the upstairs floor to the storage room, I went down. If the play was gone, that meant everything about it was gone, including the movies and soundtracks inspired by it. So many composers and filmmakers had created their own versions of it, and I had to collect them all.

As I had anticipated, movies like *West Side Story* were also fading. This play couldn't disappear. It had made its mark on so many other works of art. I was thankful for my sweet obsession. I had read and researched all about *Romeo and Juliet* retellings, so I could easily remember them and find them inside the library.

From Media to the Teen Area to Children's Nonfiction, I managed to collect them all. The cart was completely full on both sides, so I headed to the elevator with a despair so big it crushed my heart.

Before the elevator closed, Sarah stopped the doors. "June, don't tell me you are working overtime again."

I froze. I couldn't manage a single word. I just wanted to cry like Tristan, unconsolably. At least my body was covering the cart, so Sarah couldn't see the contents. I gave her a tiny smile.

"Are you almost done?" she asked, and I nodded. "Make sure you don't forget to have fun. Remember you only get to be young once."

She let go and the doors closed. Her words stung like lemon on a paper cut. Romeo was young once, and that was the end of it, the end of his story.

When I thought he was an exchange student, I knew he'd leave. But it would be as a normal person taking a plane to go somewhere in the world. Now I was thinking that I was falling for a ghost or spirit. I mean, if he couldn't leave the library grounds, would some weird paranormal force make him leave? Would he just disappear before me? I rubbed my eyes, and the thoughts bouncing around in my head were spiking my anxiety.

I couldn't stop the whirlwind of emotions inside of me. What would happen to Tristan if he didn't die? Or even worse, what if he would die anyway, since Shakespeare hadn't written anything about him after he was sixteen? Would he live forever here stuck in time, never aging?

I opened the storage room and found some empty containers. The same ones we had used to keep things for the library party. Nora had brought them here, so I'd have to make sure to leave things just the way they were, so she wouldn't suspect anything if she decided to come in here. I took a picture with my phone and began to gather things.

As I placed all the books, CDs, and movies inside the

containers, I realized it had been stupid of me to think the play would remain the same when one of its star-crossed lovers had vanished from the story. There was no story without Romeo. Before he met Juliet, Romeo had already fallen for Rosaline, and she was also a Capulet, but his love for her fell apart instantly at the sight of another girl. So the whole tragedy developed as a consequence of one of Romeo's choices. The girl he had chosen to fall in or out of love with.

Romeo was the center of the play, and without him there was no story. Juliet would marry Paris, and that would be it. No feud, no dying Mercutio, no raging Romeo who would kill Tybalt. So no tragedy left to tell. I felt the tears coming as I kept the last copy, trying to reorganize everything to match the picture in my phone. I had never even considered a world where Romeo didn't exist, not even in fiction.

As I stood up, I noticed an odd piece of furniture at the back. I took the dusty sheet away and found an old beaten lounge chair broken at the seams. This would make a good enough bed for Tristan. I looked through the window. The tree house was somewhere close. He would have to make sure people saw him leave the building. But then he could come back and climb through the tree house to here. It was only a couple of branches away. I'd have to make sure opening this window wouldn't trigger any alarms in the library. I opened it and waited. If there was an alert connected to it, someone would come and check. I set a twenty-minute timer on my phone. That should be enough. Perhaps with a little bit of luck, this forgotten room was so neglected that even the alarm system didn't care for it.

I stood there in silence, staring at the minutes moving backward on my phone screen. I closed my eyes and let myself cry. I let all the tears that had been building up run loose. I cried for the joy of meeting the real Romeo, for the privilege of kissing him, but also for the daunting feeling of losing the one book that had taught me so much about love. At the bottom of my tears there was pain, the one that kept the tears coming. I cried most of all because I'd have to find a way to stop loving Tristan, to not allow him to be close to me anymore. Why did love have to be so cruel? I supposed I couldn't expect to fall for such a dramatic character and not experience my own tragedy.

The timer in my phone rang. I looked outside, and I didn't find Jim or other library staff looking around. No one had even bothered to come up here. At least I had found a way to keep him safe at night. He now had a place to sleep, and it was more comfortable than the tree house. I only hoped he was as agile as I thought and wouldn't fall. He'd need to climb from the tree house to another branch to reach the window, but at least Shakespeare had made him good at climbing balconies.

If only I could tell someone about this mess—Maggie, Marian, Mrs. Lib, or Alex. But they were all far away or mad at me. The mere thought of Alex still hurt. Why did I have to choose the wrong guys? If only someone could help me. But I was on my own. I had to find a way to fix the play, to keep Tristan safe, and somehow break my own heart along the way.

CHAPTER 14

THE RENAISSANCE EFFECT

It had been over three weeks since I discovered Tristan's true identity. At times I had enjoyed it, at others I had panicked. But now it was clear where his oddness came from, and I was able to understand his reactions better. Once I explained to him that the fact he didn't understand the world around him was not his fault, he seemed to relax. I wondered how much more of himself he had been holding back to not look so out of place.

I even felt more confident in asking him odd questions, and I had succeeded at not revealing that he belonged to a place and time four hundred years earlier. It seemed too much to take, and even worse for an emotional person like him. Knowing that people have been saying his name for centuries could either crush him or give him an ego I was not sure I was ready to deal with.

"So you are fine with computers but can't deal with elevators?" I asked, trying to keep a serious face no matter what answer he came up with.

"Indeed, milady, the boxes people stared at for long hours

inside the library seem to be harmless. Contrary to the, mmm, *elevators*, in which people suddenly disappear. Although I must confess, I do not understand people's fascination with either of them."

It was getting harder to keep a straight face. "But you do know people just appear on another floor?"

"Milady, who knows what happens between apparitions."

Even though he was a real sixteenth-century guy, it was still amusing to interact with him. But I had learned my lesson, I wasn't going to elaborate on how elevators worked. A few weeks ago, it had taken me over an hour to explain my plan for him to climb through the treehouse and get to the storage room window to sleep inside at nights. Mainly because he kept asking questions about what cameras were and how security alarms worked.

I had checked the storage room almost every morning, and was happy to realize he had followed my instructions to the T. I wondered if he'd be able to go unnoticed for the rest of the time he would stay here.

Today was going to be a different challenge though, I was about to risk getting Tristan out of the library. The plan was to make him feel homesick, something that hopefully would send him back to his book. I somehow felt responsible for him being here, and the guilt was eating me alive the longer he was here. There must be a connection between me and him, since he could leave the library's grounds when we were together.

"Where are we going, milady?"

Tristan's voice took me out of my thoughts as he pointed at the computer's screen. The browser was opened with my email, and I was supposed to be searching for the tickets.

"Perhaps somewhere where I can undo my mistake of leaving you without escort for that party?" he pleaded with a melodic voice.

He had insisted we should have some sort of a *do-over date* since he'd stood me up for Maggie's party. Even though I knew I had to keep my distance with Tristan, I couldn't help enjoying his company.

"We are going to a fair that's in town for the summer. I think you'll like it," I said as I stood up to retrieve the Renaissance Faire tickets I had sent to the library's printer. Since Marian isn't coming back for the summer, my parents were scared that we would lose our summer tradition of going out together as a family every other weekend. We were supposed to take turns picking out activities, but Marian always had the best ideas, so it was comfortable for Will and I not to have to participate in the planning.

But this summer, neither Will nor I seemed to agree on anything, except the fair. Mom and Dad were over the moon to discover our tradition was still alive and agreed to my plans without hesitation. They even encouraged us to invite friends along for the first time ever. Maybe the fact that Will and I had fought a lot lately also affected their decision. Anyway, using my dad's technical words, it would help me fix two bugs with one line of code.

As I walked toward the printer, a weird sound caught my attention. Someone was sobbing quietly. I looked around and saw Sarah sitting at the reference desk, holding a tissue under her nose. I slowly walked in her direction. "Everything OK?" I asked as I got closer to her.

She looked my way. "He's going to disappear."

My eyes opened wide and, instead of being cold as usual, I was suddenly sweating.

"Here." She turned her monitor around and showed me. She was reading an e-book on her computer. I knew librarians were not supposed to read on the job unless it was for book club.

"Is that for the upcoming book club?" I tried to keep my nerves at bay.

She nodded. "A ghost story with a surprising ending. I just

didn't imagine the key to his freedom would be his own book." She wiped her tears with the tissue. "Oh dear, I'm so sorry. You know how it is when a book gets to you."

"It's that good, huh? Or that sad?" I asked relieved and intrigued.

"I'm not going to spoil anything else in case you want to read it. The writing is great and it's very moving. It just took me by surprise."

I related to her, having read books like that.

"Lady Sarah, is everything all right?" Tristan's British accent was to die for. In a moment it made me forget everything.

"That's so sweet of you, Tristan. I'm fine. It was nothing more than a very emotional plot twist in a novel. I'm assuming you have plans for today?" She pointed at the printer a few feet away from her.

"Yes, we are going to the Renaissance Faire." The last part of my sentence came out in a lower voice.

"Oh, that sounds delightful! My sister loves to dress up for the fair. I bet Tristan would look incredibly handsome in a Renaissance costume." She smiled at me and the phone rang. She excused herself as she got back to work, and we walked away.

I hadn't thought of that, but it was a great idea. Maybe by fitting right in, he'd go back to his book tonight. I turned to Tristan. "I'm going to go get your costu—your clothes. You know, the one you were using the night we met. Why don't you wait for me in the lobby, and I'll meet you there in a few minutes."

He explained where I could find his clothes inside the storage room and bowed before heading downstairs.

I looked around me before opening the storage room. As usual, the area was deserted. I used my key and went inside. As I was looking for Tristan's clothes, something about what Sarah had said clicked. *The key to his freedom is his own book.* Maybe *I* was not the reason Tristan could leave the library. Maybe it was the proximity to his own book. It was the fact that I carried my pocket edition everywhere. I remembered when we went for ice cream, I'd offered to carry Tristan's laundry on my bike, and he'd offered to carry my backpack, and there was my book. It made sense.

I grabbed his clothes, put them in a library tote bag, and walked out of the storage room. I knew Tristan was waiting for me, but I had an idea that I wanted to check first. Nora wasn't working today, so it was my only chance. The library was not empty but not full, either, perfect for exploring incognito. I headed upstairs to the exhibit room. It was open, and fortunately no one else was inside but me.

I opened the cabinet and looked for a box of latex gloves, which I knew Mrs. Lib kept somewhere. I couldn't risk leaving my fingerprints around the case with the damaged play, especially with Nora's obsession with blaming me for everything. My anxiety made me restless, and I looked around every now and then to check that I was still the only one in the room. I took a deep breath and punched in the number combination I never thought I'd have to use, 1987. The case unlocked, and I held my breath.

My shaking hands held the book that had once brought tears of joy to my eyes. Nora hadn't specified what she'd meant by bad shape, but I had to see it for myself. I opened the book, and the beautiful marble end paper didn't seem as bright as I remembered it. But many times memories fade and the images change, and only the feelings associated with that memory remain. Perhaps I was getting ahead of myself and it had always been that pale blue.

I browsed the pages from the back to the front. The last pages were completely blank, like all the other copies of the play.

Then, more than halfway through, I found words printed on the pages. A sense of relief flooded my body. It was a scene before the masquerade ball where Mercutio, Benvolio, and Romeo were chatting. Romeo hadn't met Juliet yet, and it made sense, since without them meeting, there was no tragedy left to tell. But there was something odd on the page, and I took a closer look at the fine print.

Some consequence yet hanging in the sta

Romeo's line was incomplete. As I stared closer, I realized the letters were vanishing. Just like magic, the letters of the word *stars* faded with every passing second. I swallowed hard. It was one thing seeing the impact Tristan's presence had in the copies of his play, and a very different thing seeing letters disappearing right in front of my eyes. It was like staring at a ticking clock rather than just listening to it. Time was literally running out.

I heard voices outside the room and placed the book back in its place, just the way I had found it. I closed the case and waited for the lights to go back to green. Then I took the gloves off and kept them in my pockets. I grabbed Tristan's clothes tote and walked out of the room as some patrons were going in. As I headed for the exit, I felt the weight of my despair. With every step, I felt more and more out of breath.

It made sense—this was a symbiotic relationship. Without its characters, there was no story to tell. But without a story, the characters had no place to exist. If Tristan needed his own play to walk around, that meant a character's source of life was his own story. Looking at the old collectible had made me tremble. If the play was the reason Tristan existed and it was fading away, that meant he would eventually encounter the same fate once there were no more letters to his book.

I couldn't bear a life where *Romeo and Juliet* didn't exist, or even worse, when only I knew what humanity had lost. A work of art like that couldn't just disappear. Even if it was hundreds of years old, people still understood what it was about by just hearing the word *Romeo*.

The weight of the world fell on my shoulders. The clock was not only ticking, but ticking backward. Tristan couldn't know that his book would set him free. If he knew, he would roam around town to explore, and do it alone. He could get lost, and just the thought of not being able to find him made me want to faint. What would happen if I came to the library and he was missing? I couldn't imagine the panic. Or what if he got hurt, since he didn't understand the modern world we live in? Even though we lived in a small town, bad things still happened. But Tristan was not dumb—maybe too trustworthy and naive, but never stupid.

I reached the bottom of the staircase and stopped before crossing the automatic doors to the lobby. I took a deep breath and tried to hold it together. I couldn't succumb to panic. I tried to think happy thoughts, as Peter Pan would say, and walked out to meet Tristan. I'd have to persuade him that the sixteenth century was way cooler. But first I had to convince him to get into my mom's car to get there.

Tristan's monologue as to why Gutenberg's press was way more sophisticated than the library's printer was nothing compared to all the opinions he had about cars. They weren't as elegant as carriages, they were suffocating, they were loud, and he didn't trust me being a professional driver. I felt our different centuries colliding for the first time. Maybe he was fine with riding on a bike with no motor, but he kept insisting that if he couldn't see the horse, or what made the wheels turn, he would never trust a car. When I joked, asking if he would like to drive, he hesitated, and I wondered if his mistrust had anything to do with me being a girl.

Our different mindsets were crashing and for the first time, his charm wasn't working that well one me. Nothing breaks the spell of a cute guy like making you feel incapable because of your gender. If I'd let him, he would have gone on and on complaining about cars for longer than I could bear. But we were already late, and Dad hated when we arrived separately—even worse because they would have to wait for me since I had all the tickets.

Finally, he had agreed to get inside the car, which was progress, but then he refused to close the door or wear a seat belt, which meant we were back to square one. I haven't encountered such a stubborn character in all my life. If we had left after he finished changing, we would be halfway there by now.

I even considered putting my weight over him to buckle his seat belt, but that would barely work, since my weight was not significant enough to restrain a guy.

"Tristan, we can't get to the fair if you don't put on your seat belt." My annoyance was noticeable. He shook his head and crossed his arms, and I had a flashback to when Will was a toddler. Perhaps many of the troubles between me and my brother had begun back then.

"What is it that you don't agree with? It is just a strap across your chest. You know it's supposed to keep you safe."

"It is a retaining cord. That is what it really is. A form of prison, milady."

Maybe this had more to do with him feeling like a prisoner at the library than a gender thing. "Fine, then get out and I'll go without you." I hoped my menacing attitude had been enough for him to change his mind. It seemed to work, since his expression changed. "Look, I promise we're going to have fun, and the car is harmless. In fact, it's comfortable, and you know I'm a good driver, since you rode behind me on my bike," I said, trying to keep calm.

He stared at me for a moment and held the seat belt to put it on. I closed the door before he changed his mind and did a tiny victory dance as I walked around the car to the driver's seat.

"Thank you," I said as I sat inside and put on my own seat belt. I turned on the car, and Tristan screamed, almost giving me a heart attack. The AC blasted at him. I should've predicted that. I turned it off and tried to rub Tristan's shoulder to calm him down. "Sorry, my bad. It's just air. You'll like it once the car cools down."

"Milady, you mentioned the car ran on horsepower. Where are the horses?" His tone was accusatory. "Florence is never going to forgive me."

Perhaps this had been too much technology for him, or maybe he had totally lost it, because I knew the play by heart, and there was absolutely no character with that name. "Who the hell is Florence?"

"My horse."

For the first time I considered the possibility of characters having real lives beyond what we read on the page. I had once read a novel about that. "You have a horse?" I asked, but I answered myself before he could. "Never mind, of course you do." He came from a rich family, so he had everything he wanted.

Once we were already on our way, Tristan seemed more comfortable and began to enjoy the commodities of the present century, like AC and portable music. I had been careful to select a musical playlist that matched with his century, and he didn't complain about it. Predictably, he kept looking around for the musicians, but I didn't have the patience to explain how recorded music worked.

"How is Florence?" I asked, grateful he had stopped complaining about cars.

"She is the ultimate—majestic, even tempered, and knows me very well." His smile faded. "But she will never forgive me for riding a mechanical horse." He was getting upset. I was rooting for a homesick Tristan, not a depressed one.

"Hey, it's OK. She doesn't have to know. I mean, you know what they say, *out of sight, out of mind.*"

He looked at me with sad puppy eyes, and I couldn't take it. "My mom's car is just a method of transportation, and we are going to see horses at the fair. Then you'll have some stories to tell Florence."

He grimaced but seemed to cheer up a little. I wanted to say something to cheer him up. "I'm glad you are remembering details about your life, though."

His eyes lightened up. "It is all because of you, my love."

I took a deep breath, trying to focus on the road and not the touch of his hand whenever we were at a traffic light.

Once we entered the parking lot, I saw my family standing by the ticket booth, looking for me. We parked close by and walked in their direction, but before my parents saw us, I stopped in front of Tristan. "Look, there are a lot of people here, and not everyone is well intentioned. You have to stay close to me at all times. I mean it. Do you understand?"

I hoped my motherly attitude wouldn't smother him and cause him to run away.

He raised an eyebrow, giving me a suspicious look, but nodded anyway. "Whatever you demand, milady."

"Remember, I *am* the reason you can leave the library." I felt horrible lying. It had been so much better when I hadn't known about the distance between his book and him. Ignorance really was bliss. I wanted to tell him about the book and its relationship to his freedom, but he had gotten upset before for not being able to read it, so I decided against it.

My bag was extra heavy. To be prepared, I had gone through my house and gathered all the copies of his book—my pocket edition, my old favorite edition, and my parents' copy. At least that preparedness gave me some sort of peace of mind.

Mom found us among the crowds and waved. I could feel the sweat rolling down my temples, and it wasn't even that hot yet.

"Tristan, just one more thing. Please try to be cool with my dad."

He gave me a big bright devilish smile, and a part of me wondered if this had been a terrible idea, but I kept in mind the whole point of coming today was to make Tristan homesick to save his book.

If everything went well, he'd go back to the library tonight, missing the familiarity of his time and place, and I wouldn't see him again tomorrow. That thought made my heart skip a beat. Would today be our last day together? I didn't have time to think about that anymore. From the moment my dad saw Tristan, I knew he wouldn't be able to keep his thoughts to himself. I just hoped I could survive the evening without dying of embarrassment.

"Wow, I have never seen such an authentic costume!" Dad said as we got closer to them. "You must be the famous Tristan." He extended out a hand for him to shake.

Tristan shook his hand. "I was not aware that my fame preceded me, my lord."

Dad raised an eyebrow at the title, and thankfully Mom jumped in. "It's not every day an exchange student creates a detergent-bubble party at our house. It's nice to see you again, Tristan."

"Lady Claire, always a pleasure." Tristan took Mom's hand and kissed it. I wondered if anyone would notice my ability to turn all shades of red at the same time. Then Tristan turned to my dad. "My lord, I have been looking forward to this day."

I was unsure if my dad was uncomfortable or about to laugh. "The fair? Yeah, I can tell."

Mom bumped Dad with her elbow.

"I mean, why? What day is it?" Dad asked.

"The day that I declare my intentions of marriage. I am in love with your daughter and would like her hand in marriage, with your and Lady Claire's blessing."

Tristan bowed.

I cringed, almost choking on my own saliva. "He's kidding, Dad. He's in character. He loves theater."

Dad seemed too confused to say anything.

"Why don't we go in?" I said as I pulled out the tickets from my bag and grabbed Tristan by his jacket, then headed us toward the entrance. Like I imagined, Sam and Will burst out laughing behind us.

"Please tell me you are joking," I whispered to Tristan as I handed our tickets to the lady at the entrance.

"Milady, why would I joke about love? I believe my romantic intentions have been clear." He seemed perplexed. "Doubt not my intentions, my love, for they are honorable. Milady, your hand in marriage is all I dream about."

He seemed dead serious. Damn it, one more thing I should have seen coming. Romeo and Juliet kissed, and that was as far as they got before marriage was involved. This was going to escalate quickly.

"Let's talk about this later, please. There are certain traditions here in Storybridge very different from your time—I mean, your town, of Verona."

He seemed unsure but looked away. This day was going to be more complicated than I thought.

We entered the fair and Dad, like always, explained the plan for the day. I couldn't organize the family activity and then ditch them to see if Tristan loved this century better, so I'd have to play along.

"Our first stop is the costume-rental booth," Dad announced. "Sam and Will want to be knights, and inspired by Tristan's commitment to the fair, I think we should hop on the train as well." Dad smiled at Mom. "Milady?"

Mom smiled back at him and wrapped her arm around his as they walked into the costume booth. I covered my face, hoping the earth would swallow me whole.

"Shall we?" Tristan extended his hand.

I let out a long breath. I'd have to be fully on board the Renaissance boat, anything to make Tristan go back to his play and stop talking about marriage.

"Why not?" I grabbed his hand and we walked inside.

Dad said to not focus on the price of the costume at all. He insisted that I pick whatever I liked. He must have really wanted the family outings to continue this summer. I just wondered what I could do to keep Tristan away from my dad for the day. Dad wasn't particularly the chill kind. Marian's first boyfriend had been the victim of endless interrogations during their first month together, and Tristan was already peculiar enough.

At first I thought about getting just a flower crown, but within minutes of us browsing around the booth, at least ten people complimented Tristan's attire. If only they knew it couldn't get more authentic. Tristan, like always, bowed politely to every person who greeted him. At least we were finally in a place he fit in, even by the way he spoke.

I focused instead on finding a dress that went along with Tristan's attire. I had once been obsessed with a French musical about *Romeo and Juliet*, where the Montagues wore blue and the Capulets wore red. For one day I wanted to be Juliet, not for the dying part, but for being able to experience a literary love story. And although I knew the purpose of today's adventure was for Tristan to leave, I still wanted to enjoy every single moment I had left with him.

I found a gorgeous red carmine dress with long flowy sleeves. They were made from a lighter fabric so I wouldn't boil in the summer heat, and they would match the flats I was wearing. The center of the dress was ivory with golden damask details. I grabbed it and headed to the dressing room.

As soon as I closed the curtain, I felt someone standing behind it. Before I could say that this dressing room was taken, someone spoke.

"Is this distance close enough, milady?" Tristan's voice coming from behind the curtain was some sort of spell. It was charming how he wanted to please me by following my requests, and that way he'd be safe too. I weakly said yes and tried to focus on getting changed, but it seemed an impossible task as I stared at his silhouette through the curtain of the dressing room.

Once I was done, I stared at my reflection in the mirror, undoing my usual side braid. Then I slid the curtain aside and Tristan turned around. His eyes met mine, and without words I understood how much he liked the way I looked. A part of me wanted to hold back and focus on the task of making him homesick, but it felt impossible. Maybe it was my loose wavy hair that made me look so different, or the mood of the fair. But being the book nerd that I was, I felt as if I was living in a fairy tale, especially with Romeo by my side, and I didn't want to miss a single second.

A lady who worked at the costume-rental booth approached

us. "Can I suggest a hairpiece to complement your outfit?" she asked.

I nodded, and as she went for it, Tristan stared at me in amazement as if I were a work of art in a museum.

The lady came back with a white flowered crown that had a red veil on the back. "May I?" she asked.

I nodded and she put it over my head, attaching it with pins. "What do you think?" She held a mirror for me to see.

I looked like a princess out of a fairy tale. I turned to Tristan right away. He quickly held my hand and kissed it. "The all-seeing sun never saw a match since the first world began."

Even the booth lady clapped.

My face must have turned the same color of the dress. I smiled and looked away as I recognized lines from *Romeo and Juliet*. Even though I was desperate to be part of a book, or better yet to be like Juliet, I felt the wrong kind of Juliet. I was not the girl who would end up with Romeo. He would say those words to another girl.

Reality crashed in as I remembered he had to fall in love with someone from *his* century, not with me, but he was making it so, so hard. I thanked Tristan for his words and headed to the register. Dad had already paid, so I left my clothes at the booth and got a token instead. Which was convenient, since I didn't have to carry my clothes around the fair, along with the three books already in my bag.

Tristan insisted on me holding on to his arm as we walked, but once I spotted my parents, I tried to let go of him. He didn't seem to agree, since he held my arm a little tighter. It had been a good thing, since only a few steps out of the booth, I tripped with the uneven grass and the long dress. If I hadn't been holding on to Tristan, I was sure I would have ended up in a similar situation as I had at Maggie's party, but with less mud.

Mom stared at us as I held on to Tristan's arm for balance. Something about romantic PDAs made me really uncomfortable, especially in front of my parents. Before we reached them, Mom had already taken out her fancy camera and was snapping pictures of us. Fortunately Tristan already had experience with cameras and didn't freak out.

"Wow!" Dad said as we reached them, and I blushed again. "You look gorgeous, kiddo, like always, and I can't believe after all these years you finally agreed to dress up for the fair."

"Tristan, you have been an inspiration to us all," Mom added as she took more pictures. "I mean, his attire is worthy of a prize too."

Tristan blushed.

As we all posed for pictures, I heard Will whisper to Sam, "I never want to fall in love. It makes you do weird things."

Sam giggled, and they both made vomiting gestures. So immature.

I tried to smile for the pictures, but I had a battle going on inside me between my head and my heart. I never imagined I would meet the real Romeo, much less have to force him to go away.

"Next stop, the Dragon Fire's Pass for a glass-blowing demonstration," Dad said, looking at his map. Sam and Will complained, but it couldn't be a better place. Everybody would face the same direction in silence, with no talking and no interacting. All boxes checked.

As we walked, I tried to stay behind my family. That would allow less opportunities for my dad to try his dad jokes on Tristan. Which I was sure his sixteenth-century mindset wouldn't allow him to understand, leading to uncomfortable conversations. Mom was more laid-back, which was nice, but Dad wasn't.

"Is this some sort of cheap silk?" Tristan asked as he analyzed the fabric of my sleeves.

"I guess it's fake? It's just a costume," I said, trying not to laugh at his expression, since I knew he was being completely honest.

"Once we are married, milady, you will have the finest fabrics to dress."

Suddenly my corset felt a size too tight. I smiled uncomfortably as we entered the glass-blowing booth. Once we sat, he held my hand, and I didn't fight it. For once I tried to live in the moment and enjoy it, however imperfect the moment was.

Dad was pleased with the glass demonstration—Will and Sam, not so much. Once out, we approached a timetable sign to decide which show to see next. My parents couldn't agree between the *Birds of Prey* or the *Miniature Circus*. I definitely could tell Tristan wouldn't react well to trained rats walking along a tightrope. While my parents debated, Will held on to his toy sword, trying to fight Sam.

Tristan raised an eyebrow as he stared at Will's plastic sword. "Hey, lads, would you be interested in learning how to duel?"

Will and Sam shouted their enthusiasm.

"Very well indeed then," Tristan said, letting go of me.

I tried to stay close to him. I must look like a possessive girlfriend, but I didn't want to know how long the distance between him and his book had to be for something to go wrong. Will handed over his sword to Tristan, but he looked as if he was not sure he wanted to touch it. Then he looked up and around, searching for something.

We were standing close to another costume booth, so Tristan grabbed an authentic-looking metal sword and seemed content. Then he showed the boys how to stand and hold the sword properly. Both were mesmerized by everything Tristan did. All I could think of was that no matter where he was or what he did, he was really something unique to watch.

A guy walking by seemed interested in Tristan's skills and stopped to watch attentively. He was dressed in a similar costume and stared at Tristan's feet as he worked with the sword. Tristan met his gaze, and the guy raised his sword and pointed it at Tristan. I knew he must be one of the stunt guys or part of a show, but I was afraid Tristan was not aware of that.

Tristan's expression changed in a second. He was prepared to fight. He pulled Will and Sam behind him and stood like he was born ready. The scene looked so real that people gathered around to watch. The problem was that only I knew that one of them wasn't pretending at all.

As they moved, it was getting harder and harder for me to be close to him. We were about to find out just how long the distance between him and the book had to be for him to be safe. Fortunately the people who gathered around created a circle, so we were close enough.

Tristan showed off his excellent fencing skills against his opponent. If this were a real fight, Tristan would be winning, without a doubt. His movements looked effortless, and he seemed so light on his feet. There was not a second that he appeared to hesitate or doubt his next move.

I could see fear in his opponent's eyes, and I wanted to shout at Tristan to slow down, that this was all pretend, but he wouldn't be able to hear me with all the people around us cheering them on. Including Dad, who now seemed to be a true Tristan fan.

Tristan forced his opponent out of the circle and cornered him against a rock wall. I tried to move as close to them as I could, but the growing audience was making it hard for me. I had no idea how the magic between his old collectible and the library worked, but I doubted three vanishing copies of his play had enough strength to keep him going for much longer.

Tristan stumbled, and his opponent advanced. I knew he was getting tired, but I wondered if it was the heat, the duel, or the distance from his book.

They jumped to a nearby hill, and the distance between us had never been so long. There was a moment when Tristan tripped over the uneven rocks and my heart skipped a beat. I knew they were fencing with props, but I doubted they were entirely harmless. His opponent was about to attack when Tristan's face became pale, his body didn't seem able to hold on to his own weight, and he fell to the ground. I ran to him, pushing the people around me with all my strength. I was just a couple of feet away from Tristan when his opponent got closer. Tristan came back to his senses and seemed to recover right away. He stood up faster than a spring and cornered his overly confident opponent against a tree.

"There's nowhere for you to go, you filthy peasant!" Tristan threatened.

The guy seemed genuinely scared, and I had to do something. This must all seem so real to Tristan.

I stood on top of a rock and shouted with all my strength, "The winner of this performance is Tristan!"

The spectators cheered, and Tristan seemed unsure as to what was happening.

His opponent raised his hands as a sign of defeat and lowered his sword. "You are very good, mate. Well played."

He held his hand out. Tristan seemed confused and still gripped his sword tightly.

I ran next to him and whispered, "This is all pretend. It's a game."

Tristan looked at me, confused, and reluctantly turned to his opponent to shake his hand. He patted Tristan on the shoulder and bowed to the crowd. Tristan copied him, still holding on to his sword. Perhaps it had been a very bold idea to bring him to the Renaissance Faire without a little context.

As the crowd cheered, Tristan seemed to relax. They both

bowed again for the audience, which went wild clapping and whistling, especially my family.

The opponent bowed to Tristan. "Great technique, man. It was an honor." Tristan looked like he still didn't know what was happening around him and nodded several times without uttering a word. "I haven't seen you in other fairs. Ben is my name."

I introduced myself and Tristan, since he didn't seem to process what was happening around him. I squeezed his shoulder gently and whispered in his ear, "Tristan be friendly. He's just an actor."

Tristan smiled sideways, looking a little more comfortable.

"I must return to the stage for my next show, but it was a pleasure. Hope to battle you again sometime." Ben laughed, patting Tristan on the shoulder again. "Perhaps I'll win next time." Ben bowed in our direction and left.

I held Tristan's hand tight, hoping the proximity to his book would recharge his energy, or maybe that was just wishful thinking. But I had to find a way to make him carry one of his copies. This had been risky, and I didn't want it to happen again. What if he had fallen over a rock or next to a bonfire?

We walked together to return the sword to the costume booth, but people still followed us, wanting to take selfies with him. He posed for all the pictures with a crooked smiled, clearly uncomfortable.

"Are you OK?" I asked, rubbing his back once there were no more fans around us. "I should have told you there are tons of actors in this place."

Tristan shook his head and stared at me. "His name . . . it was familiar."

I waited for him to elaborate.

"I think I have a cousin named Benvolio."

He seemed excited and frightened at the same time. It was as if a waterfall of information had just fallen over him. Perhaps having bits of his identity coming back to him was a good sign—

or maybe not. I was unfamiliar with characters who wouldn't stay within the bounds of their books.

If only I could call Mrs. Lib, because she would know how to handle this situation. I took a deep breath and tried to calm myself. Since I had no logical answers for him, I hugged him instead, hoping that would help somehow. It must be a lot of centuries to process all at once, and even if he was in a familiar setting, he didn't seem to feel at home.

"That was amazing!" Will and Sam shouted as they came toward us and we broke apart.

"Outstanding, quite a show!" Dad said excitedly. "I am quite impressed, Tristan."

My dad's words seemed to cheer him up more than I could. "How about we walk around and then head over to the *Birds of Prey* show. The next one is in an hour." Dad pointed at the fair's pamphlet, and we all followed him.

As I predicted, Tristan was not amused at all by the Miniature Circus. In fact, he was repulsed by the rats walking the tightrope, and he didn't believe me when I said that some people had them as pets. He wanted to stand as far away from the circus as he could, and I had to do the same for the sake of his book.

On the other hand, he was mesmerized by the *Birds of Prey* show, which was predictable. But when he wanted to volunteer for the owl activity and walk by himself on stage, I knew I had to find a way to give him a copy of his book ASAP. Fortunately they had picked Will and Sam over Tristan. I kept thinking of how to slide him a copy of his book without him noticing. I couldn't lie about being cold, intending for him to give me his jacket, since it was a hundred degrees. Then I purposefully spilled water over him, hoping he would take his jacket off so I could slide the book inside. But I was not considering Mom would suggest that, with this heat, it would dry out right away. I suspected Mom, and me, too, wanted him to keep his entire costume on, which was admirable in this heat.

It was time for lunch, and although everyone in my family expected Tristan to be the first to order a turkey leg, it was far from what Tristan wanted. To everybody's surprise, Tristan was mesmerized by pizza. I had to explain to my dad that his parents had a gluten aversion and wouldn't allow him to eat pizza. I had no idea how much of that they believed, but I was getting tired of justifying all of Tristan's quirks.

Before continuing on, the boys wanted to pee, so Dad took them, and I was alarmed when Tristan wanted to go too. My dad and Tristan in an enclosed space was not a good combination, but there was no way to justify me going with him to the restroom. As they walked away, I followed, feeling like a possessive girlfriend, something I had never ever wanted to be.

"Tristan, wait!" I shouted and ran to him before he went into the restroom. As I hugged him, I slid my pocket edition inside the back of his shirt. Hoping naively that he wouldn't notice.

"What was that for, milady?" He seemed to be surprised by my sudden display of affection.

"Nothing, I just felt like giving you a hug," I said, feeling awkward.

Then I watched Tristan walked inside the restroom doors. I tried very hard to not obsess about the conversation Dad and Tristan must be having.

Ten minutes later, they came out, and I felt immense relief that they seemed comfortable with each other. We walked to the next event in my parents' agenda, and I hugged Tristan sideways to feel if my book was there, and fortunately it was.

We stopped to watch a passing parade. People played the bagpipes, and we found Ben among the crew. He even waved at us when he passed. Toward the middle came the queen's carriage, and everyone took pictures. Tristan even bowed as Mom explained who was on the fancy carriage.

Then came the knights, who were my and Will's favorite part. As I looked at the horses' costumes, I noticed one dressed in green that refused to cooperate in the parade line. The more the rider tried to pull him to follow the horse ahead, the more anxious it became. People around them were getting scared and trying to move away. The rider even tried to take him away from the parade, but the horse became even more agitated. Tristan rushed toward the horse.

My heart stopped. I couldn't bear him getting into another risky stunt. Will and Sam stood up on the closest table to see him better, and I ran a little closer to Tristan. As he approached the horse, it rose up and threw its rider to the ground. Tristan walked in circles around the horse and put his hand in front of him while looking away, like waiting for permission to touch him. After a few seconds, the horse calmed down, and Tristan reached for its face. The horse seemed to like him, and I wondered if his charming Romeo effect applied not just to women but to animals from his time. Everybody around was clapping, even my parents.

The horse seemed to calm with Tristan's gentle touch as he pulled him to the closest water stand. He unbuckled a part of the costume that seemed to be making him uncomfortable. A guy from the stand gave him an empty bowl and filled it with water. It was as if Tristan were a horse whisperer, and being gentle with animals was one more quality to admire about him. But it made me think about Haiku's weird reaction toward Tristan.

Once the horse had finished drinking, Tristan tried to return him to the parade, which had gotten ahead, and the horse seemed perfectly fine with Tristan riding him. Maybe he actually had a special bond with horses, and maybe Florence had something to do with it. A part of me was mesmerized, since it was like seeing Prince Charming riding his horse—and even more special since I knew he literally had come out of a book.

We walked behind the parade, and at least this time I didn't have to be extra worried about the distance between me and Tristan. Mom chatted with Sam and Will, and Dad came closer to me. I doubted that was a coincidence. Part of me wanted to know what they had talked about in the restroom, but I wondered if men actually did such a thing.

"The fair is just as I remember it," I said, trying to avoid the uncomfortable questions I was sure Dad was thinking of.

"Every year feels different with you and Will, and, well . . . now your friends." He didn't have to say it—the hole Marian left behind was evident, although we had all been somehow distracted by Tristan's quirkiness. "I like your friend. He is . . ."

"Weird? Unique? Like out of his time?" I desperately wanted to say those words out loud.

Dad chuckled. "I have to admit he's quite a character, definitely unusual. But I always knew you would date someone out of the ordinary, kiddo."

I decided to take that as a compliment.

"I think now I understand what your mom said about him being old fashioned."

Dad's laughter made me smile. He put his arm around me and talked in a lower tone. "Although when he asked me for your hand in marriage, well, that threw me off, but I'm pretty sure he was just joking. Part of the costume and drama club, right?"

Dad's hesitation seemed more like a question than a statement.

"Right." My answer seemed to give him some sort of peace. I mean, it must be daunting to have your daughter's weird foreign guy friend asking him for his teenage daughter's hand in marriage after they just met. But to be fair, he didn't know who Tristan really was or where he came from.

"What did you tell him, Dad?" I asked.

He took a long breath. "Well, I told him marriage was entirely your decision, but that I thought you were still very young. I know your mom and I don't have much say in your life anymore, but we want you to feel fulfilled in whatever you decide to do with your life first."

Dad's gaze was sincere. This was not an order or a brainwashing tactic. "I believe you should travel and date as long as you want before even thinking about marriage. There's no rush."

I knew his words were honest, but I couldn't stop thinking about my sister. "Like Marian?"

He shook his head. "No, not like her. I want you to be *you*," he said, looking straight into my eyes. Perhaps he had always known I acted like Marian's shadow, but now I didn't feel like that anymore. "Look, now more than ever, women are free to do what they want. I have always been a firm believer that if the world were run by women, it would be a better place for everyone. But I guess you already know that." He winked at me.

I read once that we choose a partner based on the similarities between them and our parents, and Tristan was so far away from what my dad was. It might be that he had a five-hundred-year-old mindset, but still. It made me realize how much I didn't want to marry someone like Romeo.

"I mean, look at your mom. I love everything about her, especially the way she succeeds at everything she sets her mind to, even with life's setbacks."

He smiled at Mom, who was way ahead of us. I wanted what my parents had, the way Dad looked at Mom even after so many years together. "She has her own successful business, which makes her happy, and it shows from within. I want that for you too."

There was something about parents' pep talks that worked.

"I want that too, Dad," I said, hugging him tighter. I could see his smile reaching his eyes. It was also a relief for him to know that I wouldn't marry soon.

We reached the jousting arena, which was where the parade ended. We found Tristan chatting with the queen, which wasn't surprising for me, but it was for Mom. The queen greeted us and excused herself to her special balcony.

"At what time does it start?" I asked.

Dad looked at his watch. "Ten more minutes."

"May I ask what *that* is, my lord?" Tristan pointed at Dad's wrist.

"It's a new smartwatch," Dad said, showing off his latest acquisition and all its features. He might as well be talking to himself, because Tristan stared at it like it was a recently discovered animal species. Tristan's face made me wonder why even watches had to be smart nowadays. I mean, before watches had all these smart features, no one thought watches were dumb. In fact, they usually gave a smart look.

"It is indeed very practical to have it attached to your wrist," Tristan added with a fake smile, staring at it.

"Tristan is into old, old watches," I intervened. "Like the ones that are attached by a chain."

Both my parents nodded, somehow convinced. It was exhausting trying to anticipate Tristan's every move. With every tiny thing he said, he revealed more and more about his awkwardness. A normal person would know what a watch was, even what a smartwatch was. There were only so many times I could explain away his quirks as Tristan being antitechnology. Honestly, you could be against technology, but you couldn't act like you lived under a rock. Perhaps it was the heat, the dress, the risk of taking him here. I was getting tired.

When it was time to pick our seats at the jousting arena, Tristan won the evening. Because of his heroic horse saving, the queen had invited us all to her balcony, which had the best view for the jousting tournament. Will couldn't stop thanking Tristan enough for being a horse whisperer.

"From which order are you, brave knights?" The queen asked Sam and Will as we all sat behind her.

"I'm the noble knight of the order of the . . . ," Will started.

"Silliness?" I mocked. Will frowned and stuck his tongue out at me.

"Dark rose," Tristan added.

"A rose? I want something more impressive than that. Maybe a dragon or a lion," Will said cockily.

"You underestimate the power of simple things, my noble knight," Tristan said in a serious tone. "Roses might appear common, but a dark red rose can be a sign of power and beauty. We might be aware of the power a lion possesses, but a knight of the order of the dark rose has a deeper impact and some mystery to it."

Tristan talked with his hand in the air, like he was reciting poetry. Just the way I imagined Romeo would speak under Juliet's balcony.

"You are right," the queen added, "it is like a legend waiting to be uncovered, a story of love and hate fighting over something as beautiful as a dark rose,"

Tristan turned and winked at me.

Since even the queen was impressed with Tristan's

monologue, I understood why kids begged Sarah for Tristan to be the one to narrate the books during story time at the library.

Will and Sam agreed, and the queen crowned them symbolically. Tristan, just like Romeo, had a hypnotizing way with words. If I weren't scared of his novel disappearing, I would be flying on cloud nine, thinking he was a dream come true.

Mom and Dad brought us all drinks before the joust started. Tristan looked intrigued by the soda can, but eventually opened it—something I assumed Audrey had taught him.

Tristan stood up. "I would like to make a toast," he said with his drink high in the air.

We all raised our soda cans, even the queen, who held a fancy cup. I only raised mine slightly, since I was scared of what he might say next.

"It is usually the gentleman who saves the damsel in distress, but Lady June has done more for me than I could ever ask for, including save me repeatedly from insanity."

People around laughed as he stared at me with his charming olive eyes.

"Milady, you are my reason to live, my very own princess. But not one that needs to be saved or trapped in a tower, but the kind that could start wars between kingdoms."

The heat was rushing to my cheeks, his public words making me feel unsettled.

"It is with proudness that I share that the queen herself has given us her blessing for marriage."

I looked away, trying to keep my composure.

"A woman like yourself is at wedding age, and I believe I can be the man to protect you. And perhaps one day be blessed to carry children of our own."

I wanted to throw up. It was as if the villain from *Beauty and the Beast* was speaking.

"Milady, it has been the ultimate privilege to meet your family. I hope to be worthy of your hand in marriage whenever you considered the time to be right." He raised his drink higher, full of a confidence that felt unbearable. Then he looked straight into my eyes. "Even if that eternity cannot come soon enough."

My parents raised their drinks uncomfortably, and all I could think about was the closest exit. Why did love have to make me feel so uncomfortable?

The jousting tournament was about to start, and the queen stood up to give her own speech through the microphone. Tristan wanted to hold my hand, but I stood up to go to the restroom. Now I was the one who needed the longest distance between him and me. He could wait an eternity, but he didn't know how brief that eternity could be.

On our way back I was grateful we had come in two cars. That way it would only be me and Tristan again, with no more marriage nonsense to talk about in front of my parents. But then I saw Sam running away.

"Where is Sam going?" I asked, worried as a woman approached him.

"That's Sam's mom," Mom said calmly. "After this morning's soccer practice, we mentioned your dad's car was at the mechanic and you had taken my car, so she volunteered to give us a ride here."

This couldn't be happening. The last thing I needed was more time with my parents and Tristan. It was getting harder and harder to avoid telling Tristan that a marriage was never going to happen. It was my fault. I should have foreseen this scenario given that I knew his play by heart.

"What's your address, Tristan?" Dad was the last one to get into the car, and he opened the maps app on his phone. "I'm assuming close to the library, right?"

Damn it, I hadn't thought that through.

"The library indeed, my lord," Tristan said, and Dad turned back, confused.

"He takes walks every night, Dad, to exercise. The library is fine." I was getting more and more desperate.

"Whatever you say, kiddo," Dad said, turning the ignition of the car and backing out of our parking space.

I had strategically sat between my brother and Tristan to minimized unsupervised interaction, but thankfully Will seemed to be more entertained with the pictures he had taken at the fair with Mom's phone than talking to Tristan.

After a while Tristan seemed to be intrigued with the pictures as well. He asked all sorts of technical questions about how pictures were taken and stored, but he eventually stopped after Dad's long, technical explanations.

"What's this?" Will asked, and a second later I heard Alex's voice, singing. My whole body had an immediate reaction, one I hadn't felt all summer long. It had been close to a month since I last heard from him. I looked at the tiny screen and saw Alex singing the same song he'd sung that evening on his porch.

I took the phone away from Will immediately. "You shouldn't be peeking into Mom's private things!" I said and gave the phone back to Mom.

"There's no problem," Mom responded. "I texted Miriam earlier, asking how things were since we haven't seen each other lately. She replied saying that they went over to Arthsteen U to see Alex. And she shared this video of him practicing for his live gig."

"He's good." Dad said.

There was a tense silence, and I could feel Tristan's mood shifting despite the darkness in the car.

"I thought you knew," Mom added.

"I did." I lied feeling banned from Alex's life.

His gig was next weekend. I had promised him I'd be there. Excitement and anxiety mixed inside of me. Could I tell him about Tristan's true identity? No, that was a terrible, terrible idea. I knew very well by now that mixing Tristan and Alex in the same place and time was a recipe for disaster.

"Do you play any instrument?" Mom asked Tristan.

"No, Lady Claire, I am afraid being musical is not one of my qualities." His tone was different, more serious.

I had to say something before Mom invited him to Alex's gig, because that would evolve into a different kind of cold war.

"OH MY GOD, DAD, TURN THE VOLUME UP! THAT'S YOUR FAVORITE SONG!" I shouted, making everyone in the car jump. I had to try anything to change the conversation.

He turned the music up and sang out loud. For once I was not embarrassed about how Dad or I sang. I tried to sing along with him, not caring if I hit the right notes. In fact, I didn't know the lyrics very well, but I had to say anything to steer away from the Alex topic of conversation.

It worked. Mom kept her phone and was now singing along with us. The only one not singing was Tristan, and I knew it had nothing to do with the fact that he didn't know the lyrics.

Dad stopped the car in the drop-off bay at the library and shifted into park. The doors unlocked immediately and Dad pressed a button which opened the side door of Mom's minivan. Tristan got out as fast as he could. I tried to follow him but by the time I got out, he was already by Dad's door talking to him. I couldn't hear what he was saying. I whispered to Mom, who was sitting in the front seat, if they wouldn't mind waiting for me while I talked to Tristan alone. Mom nodded, and a second later Tristan stood next to me, kissing my mom's hand as he said goodbye.

Tristan then said goodbye to Will, and walked away faster than I anticipated. I caught up with him as we turned around the closed library and entered the library garden. I knew he was upset, but other than listening to Alex's voice, I had no idea why he was so angry. I had managed to avoid the marriage topic during the whole ride.

Once we were sitting at a bench in the library's garden, he turned my way. "Milady, is your male friend the reason you will not accept my proposal of marriage?"

I took a deep breath. I knew no matter what I said, it would upset him. "No, Tristan. This is not about Alex."

His eyes softened and he listened to me attentively.

"Here in Storybridge, things are very different, you know? We do many things in our teenage years, like study, but technically we don't marry. Not yet." I was rambling, which happened often when I lied. "Look, all I can promise you is that no matter what happens, I won't leave you alone."

We stood in silence, and a part of me wondered if this was goodbye. He seemed calmer with my answer. There had been some truth in what I had said. Whether this moment together was our last or not, I would be there for him until the very end.

He came closer to me, his forehead touching mine. "My love, my lady. Forgive me for letting jealousy guide my actions. I am willing to wait an eternity, if necessary, for your hand in marriage."

This was supposed to be really romantic, the type of thing that every girl wants, but all I could think of was how much of his play was left, and if this outing had been enough for him to go back. Besides, by the rate at which the words of his play were vanishing, I doubted his idea of eternity meant the same as mine. Once Mrs. Lib told me that when you had nothing nice to say, silence should suffice, and I took that advice. I remained quiet, avoiding saying anything that would get me into more trouble.

My phone buzzed, and I knew it was Mom. "I have to leave, Tristan. My parents are waiting."

Before I could say anything else, he kissed me, and for the first time, it tasted bittersweet. Perhaps it was the overbearing marriage proposal, or maybe it was my heart retreating because part of me knew that if today had been a success, this was our last goodbye.

CHAPTER 15
EL MARQUÉS

When I opened my eyes, I felt rested. Something I hadn't experienced in a long time. Everything was rainbows and sunshine, until I realized today was Alex's gig. Then the rainbows dissipated and everything felt cloudy. My Renaissance Faire plan hadn't worked, and Tristan was still here. With every passing day my anxiety grew a little, and even more since today would be the first day that I wouldn't see Tristan. I wasn't worried about him getting bored or missing me, it was more about not having someone watching over him.

I took my time before getting up trying to calm myself down. He'd be OK, it was only one day. What could go wrong? My phone buzzed, and I reached for my glasses. It was Alex.

Going to load the Jeep, are you coming?

There was something joyful growing inside me after reading his text. Alex was here, and that brought a big smile to my face. I got up pacing up and down the room. What would I wear? I decided to get my bag ready first. I reached for it and put my e-reader inside, just in case.

As I looked through it, my heartbeat accelerated. I dumped my bag's contents over my bedspread and realized my pocket edition wasn't there. I tried to think of the last time I had it with me. I hit my forehead with my palm as I realized that I had slipped it under Tristan's shirt last weekend. That meant he could leave the library, especially today since I wouldn't be there. That is if he knew about that possibility.

That couldn't happen, he couldn't know about the freedom his book could give him. I had to go to the library and fast. Just the thought of him not being there was making me want to faint. But I didn't have time to panic. I grabbed the first scrunchy I found on my dresser, tied my hair into a ponytail, and rushed downstairs. Mom's car was not in the driveway, so I grabbed the first shoes I could find and headed to the back door instead.

As I pedaled out of my driveway on my bike, I noticed Alex's blue Jeep parked in his driveway, its back open. I should've been helping him load his equipment, like I always did, even if I couldn't carry much and had no clue about audio equipment. But I had to make sure Tristan was OK first. I'm sure Alex would still be here when I came back. I pedaled like no time before, the faster I could recover my book, the better. On my way, my mind returned to when I saw the collectible's lines disappearing. How long did I have before the rest of the play disappeared? I took a deep breath—first, I needed to find Tristan.

I parked my bike without even caring about the lock. The sooner I could make sure Tristan was safe and sound, the sooner I could get back. I entered the cold library, realizing that wearing pajamas had not been the smartest choice. My avocado shorts were cute but couldn't pass as anything other than sleepwear, and my T-shirt had holes in it. I refused to get rid of it, since it had Edgar Allan Poe's face with the words *I have no desire to fit*

in. In short, I looked like a mix between cutesy and goth, but the only thing I cared about was locating Tristan and recovering my book.

The more time it took me to look for him, the more my fears grew. Like I feared, he was not in the usual places, like the café, the garden, or anywhere inside the library. I'd run out of my house so fast that I had forgotten my badge with the storage room keys. I headed over anyway to knock on the door. Could he be taking a nap? I was about to knock as Jim came out. I got to peek inside before he closed the door, and nothing seemed out of the ordinary. Jim stared, cocking his head as I came up with a white lie about not having time to change, since I feared I had lost my library badge. He suggested I should report it as soon as possible, but I added to my white lie, saying that I had forgotten to check my mom's car.

On my way out, I ran into Audrey. I tried to act cool even though I knew she was a fashion diva and I had picked the worst day to run out of my house without checking in the mirror first. She stared at the words on my shirt and chuckled respectfully, but unfortunately she had no idea about Tristan's whereabouts. My anxiety was spiking. How could I have been so reckless?

I sat on a bench by the library's entrance, trying to think of any possible places he could have gone to, when someone across the street staring at the establishment's flower beds seemed awfully familiar.

I crossed the street, avoiding the passing cars. "Tristan, where have you been?"

"Milady, what a pleasant surprise! I was collecting flowers for you, my love," he said with an innocent smile. It was the cutest gesture, but I doubted plucking flowers out of private flower beds was a good idea.

"That's so thoughtful of you, but I'm afraid you can't do that. People plant those, and I'm sure they would be upset if they find you cutting their flowers." He seemed disappointed, but he nodded and took a step away from the flower beds.

"It's too hot. Can we go back inside?" I pointed behind me, but he refused to move. If he was outside of the library's grounds, it meant he had my book with him, and he knew.

"Also, I forgot to ask." I laughed, trying to sound cool but failing. "Can I have my book back? I mean my notebook. You know, the one with the blank pages."

My tone came out weird, but the look in his eyes told me everything I needed to know. The usual gleam in his eyes vanished. He knew what I was really asking. I was asking him to go back to being a prisoner. I didn't want him to be miserable, but I couldn't risk him getting hurt or lost without supervision, and I couldn't miss Alex's gig today or bring Tristan along with me.

We crossed the street in silence. Once we were in the library's parking lot, he pulled out my tiny book from his pocket and gave it back to me.

"This... this notebook is magical isn't it, milady?" He asked.

I took a deep breath thinking of a logical answer for him. "Yeah, but it would only keep you safe if I'm with you." I lied feeling terrible. Having this power over him didn't feel good. I didn't want to be the villain in his story. I would be miserable, too, if I felt locked up.

"We can go out again some other day, I promise." I said, trying to make him feel a little better, but failing at it.

During this past week we had barely talked about why I wasn't coming today to spend the day with him. He kept asking questions about it. I kept avoiding them by changing the subject and saying how happy his presence made me. Which was true, I mean, hanging out with Romeo was a dream. I just didn't want to give him any reasons to be unhappy.

I reassured Tristan that Alex was *just* my friend, and that being a day apart wasn't a reason to be sad. For the first time, I realized that even when I was Romeo's number one fan, perhaps he loved me more than I did. Since I was OK spending one day apart.

He stared at me with his gorgeous eyes, looking sad and placed the cut flowers in my hand. I stared at the colorful bouquet, it was gorgeous. He gave me a quick kiss on the cheek and walked past me back to the library without saying a single word.

I came home sweating, even in shorts. The trunk in Alex's Jeep was full, and he stood there staring at it. As I reached my driveway, the sound of my bike's chain made him turn around. I wanted to run to him and give him the biggest hug. I had missed him so much, but so many weeks had passed. He must surely have met so many people in his college program, and surely So. Many. Cute. Girls.

I walked over him and stopped. He stared at my outfit and smiled. At this point of the day, and after running into so many people, I no longer cared about what I was wearing. I was just happy Tristan was safe and I had my pocket edition back.

There was something calming about seeing Alex smile, or even his Jeep. He brought some peace that I had craved all summer long.

"Hey," I said, feeling a little awkward. "You didn't wait for me to load up the Jeep?" I joked.

He laughed. "You do know that you're more like emotional support than actual help."

"Hey!" I answered, a little hurt. "How is life at Arthsteen U?"

"Fun, real fun. You'd know about it if you had texted me at all."

Ouch. In my defense, he could have texted me too. But

something told me the furthest I could stay from the Tristan topic, the better. "Are you ready for today?" I asked.

"I am now."

I smiled hoping my presence had something to do with that answer. We heard a car park close by, and we both turned. Dad's car was parked in my driveway, and after the door opened, Haiku sprinted in our direction. He ran past me and jumped, barking, at Alex with a contagious excitement. Their interaction was totally opposite from Tristan's.

Alex knelt and gave Haiku a belly rub. "I missed you too, buddy."

I wished he would have said those words to *me* and not to my dog. I tried to look away. Being jealous of Haiku was the proof that being around Tristan had made me a little off this summer.

"Alex, it's so nice to see you!" Mom came closer and hugged him like she'd found her lost son. Dad joined us, too, and chatted with Alex about the latest World Cup matches.

Will came last, looking sharp in a new soccer jersey. I knew it was new because the tag was still hanging from his armpit. "Ready when you are." Will stared at Alex with confidence.

"What is he talking about?" I asked Alex. *I* was going with him, not my annoying little brother.

"I thought you were not coming. You didn't answer my text," Alex replied.

Damn it. I totally forgot to text him back. I was about to justify my forgetfulness when Will spoke.

"There's only one free spot in his car, reserved for *me*."

The little prick's attitude was putting me in a terrible mood.

"Mom, can I borrow your car?" I asked before they left.

"Sorry, honey, we just left it at the mechanic for an oil change, and we have that dinner tonight, remember?" Mom said with a disappointed look.

How could I forget about her best friend's fiftieth birthday party when they talked about it at dinner every night for the past week. It was the reason they couldn't join Alex's parents to see Alex play.

Maybe if I was dressed and ready, I could fight Will and get in the copilot seat before he noticed, forcing him to fit in the back with the rest of the equipment. But I was a mess, and I desperately needed a shower.

My parents wished Alex good luck and headed back home. Haiku had trouble detaching himself from Alex, but he eventually did when my dad made his special loud and authoritarian whistle—the one he always used when Haiku misbehaved.

I stared at Alex. I had imagined this reunion to turn out differently. But one way or another we were going to spend the whole evening together.

"I'll get there. Soon," I interrupted Will as he talked about the World Cup opening ceremony. Before Alex could say anything back, I turned around and headed home.

I stared indecisively at the back door of El Marqués restaurant. Whenever my family came to eat at El Marqués, we entered through the main entrance. But if I came to eat here with Alex, I always entered through the staff door at the back. And whenever Alex had any informal gigs, like at his teammate's houses, family get-togethers, or elsewhere, I always arrived with him to help him out. Now, I had come alone for Alex's gig, to El Marqués to eat, yet I had no idea which door to choose.

As I stared at Alex's Jeep parked by the back door, I wondered if I could keep my bike on his rack, since there was no parking rack in the front. But maybe Edgar wouldn't be OK with that, since the rack was his, and he and I weren't particularly close. I peeked inside the Jeep and noticed all Alex's equipment had already been unloaded. I looked up and saw someone staring at me from the backdoor window. I must look like I was about to break into the Jeep. Two seconds later, the door opened wide, and Miriam was there.

"I told Alejandro that he was grounded for not picking you up. Where are his manners?" Miriam's strong accent and high volume was recognizable everywhere. She came closer to me and hugged me so tight I felt like the victim of a boa constrictor. Once I explained to her that it hadn't been Alex's fault, that it was me who was not ready, her expression softened, and she went back to talking nonstop, like her usual self.

Miriam treated me like a daughter of her own, but at times I could understand what Alex meant when he said Latin families could be overwhelming. I could barely keep up with all the topics she was talking about. She insisted on getting my bike inside the restaurant, I appreciated the gesture, but managed to find a close-by post thick enough to chain my bike to.

We entered through the back door, and Miriam wanted to rush me to where Alex was, but after pedaling in the peak of the summer heat, and this morning's outfit fiasco, I wanted to take a moment to refresh my look, so I excused myself to the restroom.

I walked through the kitchen doors and into the main part of the restaurant. The Latin music surrounded me. It was not the traditional mariachi music anyone would expect at a Mexican restaurant. It was more like easy pop, kind of like if Ed Sheeran were Mexican. I passed the hostess, who recognized me right away, since it was one of Alex's cousins. I greeted her quickly, pointing at the restroom before she could get me, as she was also a big talker.

I stared at myself in the mirror. Even with the breeze on my face pedaling my way here, the little makeup I had on was smashed. For once I understood why Maggie complained about mixing Southern summer heat and makeup. Just thinking about her made me miss her, even with all the mess of her birthday party. But she had taught me a few tricks, and I had come prepared with extra makeup to fix it before I ran into Alex.

As I stared at my reflection, even all tidied up, I still felt jittery inside. Even if I had worn my famous literary quote T-shirts, jeans, and colorful sneakers, Alex wouldn't mind at all. But this time I wanted to look great, since today was a big deal. I wanted to show that I had put in effort without it being over the top. I wished Maggie and I were on speaking terms so I could have video called her before coming here. She would know the right thing to say to give me confidence in my outfit and calm my nerves, especially if a guy was involved.

Earlier I had spent a good amount of time going through Pinterest. My final outfit choice was a white ruffle armhole top tucked inside a flowy lemon skirt above my knee. The denim jacket along with the white sneakers kept me warm inside the cool restaurant and toned down my look, making it sportier. Which on one hand was more comfortable and also made me look cute without looking desperate to flirt with him. I had to remind myself that we were just friends, but I couldn't ignore the rediscovered nervousness I felt around him.

I stared again at my hair, worried about the complicated low bun I had tried to pull off. I was nervous and wanted to come up with a pep talk for myself. What would Maggie tell me? Or even Marian? Although I had given up on counting Marian as part of my immediate support system. But either one would tell me to relax and have a good time. I untied my hair and let it loose. Why did it feel like I was trying too hard? This was the reason I always wore my hair in the exact same way. My outfit selection was only about which literary T-shirt I felt like wearing every day. Even if I looked like a cartoon, I didn't have to waste time with these silly decisions.

Maybe deep down it had nothing to do with the way I looked and everything to do with being around Alex. We had never been apart with so little contact—not when he had traveled to Mexico

City to see his extended family, and not when my parents had taken us camping in the middle of the woods a couple of years ago. Perhaps I had been kidding myself, allowing the whole Tristan drama to overshadow my crush on Alex. 'Cause even after all this time apart, just being around him made me realize my crush hadn't disappeared or diminished at all. Once I saw him on stage, I was sure my heart would get all fluttery, and I would long for him hiding in the dark, while he had the spotlight right on him.

Focus, June, focus. I took one last deep breath. All I came here to do was support my best friend. So as long as I smiled and cheered for him, everything would be fine. Besides, he had *always* been there for me, so it was the least I could do. And if I found my crush to be back in full swing again, I would push it to the back of my mind and ignore it until the night ended. There was ice cream at home, and I could eat my troubles away. It wasn't like I hadn't done that before.

Perhaps it was silly of me to think that I would find Alex right away. The restaurant was now packed, and I couldn't even find Miriam. I shouldn't have taken so long in the restroom. I pushed my way through the people. Fortunately I had been at this restaurant enough times to know my way around it, as a patron and an employee.

Before crossing the kitchen doors, I realized there were a bunch of reserved tables by the stage. It looked like Alex's gig was not just any other entertainment on a regular Saturday night. The entire Marquez family was coming. I had to find Alex, who must be biting his fingernails away.

Once I entered the kitchen, Miriam spotted me like a highly trained eagle. Her voice rose above all the other people shouting orders and ingredients at one another. Like every time I saw her, she offered me food, but I had to pass, the anxious knots in my empty stomach making it impossible for me to eat anything. Hopefully, once Alex started playing and the main event of the evening was already going, I'd be able to relax and devour whatever Miriam put on my plate. Because everything here was always finger-licking good.

Miriam walked me to the back, and I followed her like a puppy, since the kitchen was in full swing and I didn't want to get in the way of any cook. The sounds of pots and pans clinking and people asking for orders flooded the kitchen, and I realized for the first time that Miriam's bossy tone was even scarier than Alex's dad, Alejandro Sr.

As I walked by, people waved at me. Every person in the kitchen was related to the Marquez family in some way. A couple of them recognized me and came to say hello. I tried my best to follow the Mexican way and kiss them on the cheek, but truth be told, I had never gotten used to that tradition. Even less when it was the first time I'd meet them.

The smells of familiar foods and beverages drew me in. The aguas frescas table had lined up pitchers of hibiscus water and horchata, with its recognizable pinch of cinnamon. Next to it I could smell the tamarind pods boiling on the stove, to be made into a refreshing drink too. Also on the stove were pots of pozole, my favorite Mexican soup that could be different colors and came with the signature hominy corn.

The smell of freshly made tortillas along with the famous house salsa verde also flooded the area and were the signature items of the restaurant. The Marquez family used it in everything from enchiladas to sopes to tacos. People usually thought of tortilla chips and salsa as the staple of Mexican cuisine, but it went beyond that. I had been guilty of misjudging that before, but it took only one bite of each different tortilla dish to taste the difference in texture and flavor.

Next to the mole section, which in my opinion was the

strongest of scents and the most flavorful sauce in Mexican dishes, was the dessert area, and my mouth watered. The fridges were filled with little flans in tiny plates, multicolored gelatin cups and tres leches cakes. And close by, I could smell the cinnamony hint of the arroz con leche pot that had just been made. I had to focus on finding Alex, but my stomach was telling me that maybe I was already ready to eat. The tamales that had just finished cooking were calling my name, and I called dibs on one of the sweet pink ones. Will and Edgar passed by with a soccer ball, and Miriam shooed them out of the kitchen right away.

A server reached Miriam, and I could sense the frustration in her voice, even in Spanish. She turned to me, smiled, and pointed to the door at the far end of the kitchen. I walked slowly in that direction, trying hard to stay out of the way of the passing cooks.

I pushed the door open, leaving the loud noises of the kitchen behind me. At first I had no idea where I was. I had never been in this area of the restaurant. I pulled aside a thick black curtain and realized I was backstage, if that tiny section could be called that. I walked a little closer to the stage and found a couple of stools at the center and a bunch of black containers piled up against the backdrop, which was another black curtain.

As I opened one of the containers to help Alex set up, even if I had no idea which cable was plugged where, I felt someone poking my back, making me jump. Alex's laughter followed after I turned around and tried fruitlessly to punch him in the shoulder, as I couldn't contain a smile too.

"Aren't you supposed to be set up by now? You know you can't run late, especially *today*," I said once he stopped laughing. He took a step closer into the light, and I realized Alex was all dressed up. I had to bite my lips to avoid smiling or opening my mouth in awe. I had seen him in all sorts of clothes—just woken up with ripped pajamas, sweaty and muddy after playing soccer, even in his swimming suit at competitions—but this was a different Alex. This was rock star Alex.

His style made it impossible for my heart to beat at a normal rate. I couldn't look away. His perfect slicked-back hairstyle was a first—I thought I'd die before seeing his hair so neatly styled. His tight wine-color T-shirt underneath a rolled-up, opened, denim shirt gave a cool vibe. And the leather cuff on his right wrist was just the finishing rock star accent. Even his sneakers were perfectly tied, and for once his black jeans were not ripped. I knew how much Miriam annoyed him about the shabby way he normally dressed, and I wondered who had been responsible for this transformation. In a single moment, my bubble popped. A girl must be behind all this.

"What do you think?" Alex asked, turning slowly.

I bit my cheeks, anything to focus on something other than this torture. "You, you look different," I managed to say.

"Good different?"

I nodded and quickly looked away. If this change had been because of one of his new college friends, I didn't want to know. But also, I didn't want to jealously blurt that out at him and burst his confidence before his most important gig. I swallowed hard and tried to make myself useful by taking cables out of their containers, even without knowing what I was doing.

"Hey, I forgot to tell you how beautiful you look tonight." Alex's words were the opposite of what I needed today. I rarely wore skirts or dresses so he would surely notice. Why couldn't I keep my crush for him locked away?

The door swung open, and a few seconds later Oliver came in, holding hands with Emma. I hugged them as if I had missed them more than anyone else, just to break the tension I was feeling with Alex. We caught up quick and they both seemed happy—and in love. Something that annoyed me for no reason.

Emma helped Oliver out right away, and it looked like I was the only one who didn't know anything about setting up audio equipment. Maybe Alex was right. I was just here for emotional support. Oliver and Emma seemed to be inside their own world as they set up a keyboard.

"Who is playing that?" I pointed in their direction.

"Oliver is. Didn't you know that?" Alex asked, as if my question was stupid. He handed me a mic stand, and I held it there awkwardly.

"So you've been busy, huh?" Alex asked as he took out the microphone.

"Well . . . it's been more like filled with literary moral dilemmas," I said, which was a vague way of portraying my current problems.

"You've been immersed in heavy books again?" He laughed, and I ignored him. If only he knew that losing a literary character wasn't just any problem.

"How about you? Have you met anyone fun? Any girls?" My questions came out in an accusatory way. Maybe I was getting too hangry.

"I have. In fact, I met this girl who has helped me see things in a different way." He smiled, and it was agony. Damned friend zone. I knew he couldn't come up with such a great makeover by himself. "We both have met lots of people." He pointed at Oliver. "I can't wait to graduate from high school and attend that college full time."

"We're still missing senior year." My words came out bitter. The rest of the world could have him, in a year's time.

"Did you know they have a library studies program there?" he said with excitement.

I raised an eyebrow. I remembered something about it, but once Marian graduated from college and chose Australia over a master's at Arthsteen, I didn't see the point of going there anymore. "Where are you going with this?"

"I'm just saying that it would be great if both of us went to Arthsteen U." His smile was sincere as he stared into my eyes. I felt a mix of excitement and despair. I couldn't follow him and see him fall in love with someone else.

But something in his smile seemed different, more confident, more relaxed. Maybe it was being outside of a small town. I only hoped it had nothing to do with his *new friend*. He stared at me for a second too long, and I wondered if I could talk to him about my summer problems too. Because if anyone would believe that Romeo was wandering around in the twenty-first century with me, it would be Alex. But something stopped me. Every time I had mentioned being with Tristan around Alex, it had ended up bad. So I smiled and looked away. Today was *his* day, after all.

Someone peeked from underneath the closed curtain—Edgar. "Mamá says you're up," he said and disappeared again.

Without my realizing it, Alex, Oliver, and Emma had set up everything in no time. Emma kissed Oliver good luck and came toward me.

I stared at Alex and hugged him as tight as I could. "Good luck," I whispered, and he hugged me back. His cologne masked his usual chlorine smell, and I sort of missed it. I didn't know if we were back to being best friends again, but I enjoyed his huge embrace, trying to process one moment at a time. I let him go and turned, following Emma away from the stage. At least I'd be able to eat now.

I assumed I would sit with Emma but she sat in one of the small reserved tables with Oliver's parents. Miriam insisted that my seat was already ready in the Marquez's cousins table. She pointed at an empty spot at the end of the table next to Edgar. I guess now was the time to make small talk about bikes. Before I could ask him anything, the servers surrounded us. Some poured hibiscus and tamarind water in the empty glasses as other brought big plates with appetizers. I dove right in.

The *esquites*, or prepared corn, was one of my favorite snacks. Alex liked to add mayo and chili, but I liked them with just a little bit of lime. I always tried whatever dish Miriam served, even if I was hesitant at first. Who knew mushrooms and pumpkin flowers were such a good filling for quesadillas—things people wouldn't imagine being part of Mexican cuisine?

As the lights lowered and the curtain drew open with one of the Marquez cousins at the center of the stage, the sound of the public diminished. That was until she said Alex's and Oliver's names. Then the people went wild, as if this was a festival rather than the musical entertainment at a restaurant.

"Good evening, everyone. *Buenas tardes a todos*," Alex said, holding the mic like a pro.

He introduced himself and Oliver, and shared with the audience the type of songs they would be playing. "We want to start with a song that means a lot to me. I hope you guys like it." Alex looked at his guitar and played it like it was an extension of himself.

Alex's melodic voice and guitar filled the room. As soon as the song started, I recognized it right away. It was the same song he had played that day on his front porch, and he played it flawlessly.

There was something hypnotizing about the spotlight's glow over him. Alex looked like everything I had ever dreamed of. I looked away, trying to fight the knot in my throat, and I focused instead on my plate, savoring the different spices. I was here *for* him—that was all that mattered.

The whole Marquez family roared as Alex finished the first song, smiling wide and blinded by the lights. I had been to all his smaller gigs, but today he was the headliner. Something in his presence, his stance, and his voice had the winning combination. There was something about him being on a stage, with people shouting at him, that let me see a side of him that I had never had the chance to witness.

Some girls from a nearby table, not related to the Marquez family, screamed at them like groupies, and I realized for the first time that Alex's destiny was much bigger than mine. While I excelled at libraries, words, and books, he was meant to be a people person, a leader, a rock star. He'd make people feel things with his songs, while I just wanted to feel through somebody else's stories.

They sang a few more songs, alternating between slower and more upbeat tempos, sending chills through my body as the music grew in intensity and volume. It was not only that those songs by themselves were catchy, but they made them better. They even brought some people to their feet.

Sometime during the tenth song I realized Alejandro Sr. was already sitting next to Miriam. He held his hand over his mustache and beard, covering his mouth. He frowned as if he was analyzing how good his son could be, not realizing how amazing he already was. The servers took the empty appetizer plates away and replaced them with big ones. Just like always, Miriam sent a tamal to my place, and I was in heaven.

After a few more songs, Alex and Oliver took a break, and the lights went up a little. I expected to see them coming out any minute now, but they must have stayed backstage.

"So, Alex told me you are into biking now," I said to Edgar, who was mindlessly staring at the ice cubes in his glass. He immediately looked my way, confused. "The rack on the back of his Jeep," I clarified.

He shook his head. "What? He told you that?" He laughed.

"Aren't you?"

"No. I don't care about sports unless it's soccer." He looked at me with hesitation. "Let's just say he got it for the *one* that means the most to him," he said.

Another Marquez cousin came by, changing the conversation

to soccer, like always. Could it be that Alex had gotten it secretly for me? It had turned out to be useful at school and would be useful later today. Maybe my friendship did mean a lot to him.

I looked around, waiting to see Alex, but only found Will. He was very entertained with Alex's younger cousins, playing games on their tablets. At least I didn't have to babysit anyone today, not even Will.

Alex and Oliver came out of the kitchen doors and headed toward our table, but a bunch of girls stopped them to take selfies. I never thought I could be jealous of strangers. Emma cut between the groupies and gave Oliver a strategic kiss, marking her territory. It was sort of cute. I stood up, trying to get to Alex, but Alejandro Sr. beat me to it. Alex's expression changed, losing all playfulness. His dad put a hand over his shoulder as he nodded. Alejandro Sr. smiled; it was a first. Then Alex looked my way, but our eyes didn't meet, and Miriam rushed him back to the stage. A few minutes later they appeared back up there.

The spotlight shone again over Alex and Oliver, and people clapped. This time Alex sang more songs in Spanish, and even though I had heard him speak Spanish lots of times before, his singing voice was absolutely hypnotizing.

We finished dessert when the gig was about end. Alex and Oliver thanked the audience for being patient and amazing with them all evening. The Marquez family went wild whistling at them like this was a soccer match.

"This will be our last song." Even with tiny drops of sweat flowing down his temples, he looked hot, and now his hair was messier, more like him. "I have never been as nervous as today. Not only because we got to play for you, but because I'm about to share something I have never shared with anyone." The groupies clapped and shouted at them. "Thank you. So I wrote a song."

My eyes widened. WHAT? Had he finally done it? Although part of me was hurt he had kept this secret from me.

"I wrote a song inspired by my best friend. It's called 'Walking in the Dark.'"

Me? No, it must be about Oliver. I tried to keep my breath steady, but just having something to do with this made me jittery. Even after all these weeks apart, it was nice to know he had missed me or that at least I had been on his mind.

"June, this one is for you," Alex said in a low tone.

The sound of my name through the speakers broke all doubts and I couldn't help but smile. The beat was up tempo, catchy, and I got lost in his words.

So many years, so many stories
We've been through thick and thin
Failures and glories
We've never been this far apart
Life's not fun without you, that's a fact

There are so many things I haven't said
You know, since secrets are better being kept
I've tried to hide it, deny it, disguise it (oh oh)
But words keep trying to escape

What if we're more than random stories,
What if we're two people
that connect and intertwine
Tell me, I'm not the only one
Who misses a heartbeat
when we're together side by side
Let's find out, let's see what happens
If we dare to walk together in the dark

Perhaps I was driven by fear
Perhaps you were too
Risking something like what we have

Brings doubts in me too

There's no one else who gets me like you do
Even when you're mad,
even when we're far apart
You're always in my mind, day or night
Say you're not scared, it'll all be alright
If we both try together, at the same time

What if we're more than random stories,
What if we're two people
that connect and intertwine
Tell me, I'm not the only one
Who misses a heartbeat
when we're together side by side
Let's find out, let's see what happens
If we dare to walk together in the dark

These are the words, I've been keeping, fighting
Wondering when would be the right time
But then I thought, why not?
Pour my heart out, into a song

What if we're more than random stories,
What if we're two people
that connect and intertwine
Tell me, I'm not the only one
Who misses a heartbeat
when we're together side by side
Let's find out, let's see what happens
Let's walk together (in the dark)
Let's walk together (in the dark)
Let's walk together (in the dark)
You and I (you and I)

In the dark, in the dark

The music stopped, and Alex looked down at his guitar. The public clapped like no time before. I tried too, but the happy tears in my eyes made it hard for me to join the madness. Such romantic things happened only in books and movies, and it was happening to me in real life.

Oliver and Alex bowed together, and even though I felt a few people staring at me, I didn't care. I was on cloud nine. I jumped and screamed like his favorite groupie, because this was what dreams were made of. The curtain closed and I could barely focus on what was going on around me.

All those years of having a crush on him, all those times anticipating heartbreak, thinking Alex might be in love with someone else. They had all been complications but eventually had led us to tonight. This magical and romantic moment that I'd never forget. I didn't know whether to go and meet him backstage or wait here. Emma was nowhere to be found, so I assumed she was already waiting for Oliver backstage.

As I walked toward the stage, Edgar stopped me. "June."

I was surprised he had something to say to me now.

"Please don't break his heart again, OK?"

He patted my shoulder and left. His words brought so much confusion. When had I done that? My cloud nine vanished, and suddenly I was at ground level. I had to talk to Alex. He had to know how much I'd wanted to be with him.

Trying to get backstage quickly, I avoided the kitchen route and climbed clumsily, trying to not pull the heavy black curtain of the closed stage. Then I felt someone helping me up—Alex. Once I stood, I realized Emma was there, too, hugging Oliver. Alex stared at me with a smile I hadn't seen before, a shy cute smile.

"Alex, that song was amazing. I loved it," I said, standing awkwardly and not knowing what to do. Maybe my expectations of him kissing me were wrong, since it had taken him so long to tell me how he really felt, and maybe I was to blame too. Things would have turned out differently if we both had been honest about our feelings.

"I'm glad you liked it," he said, staring at me.

I couldn't stand still any longer and hugged him with all my strength. "I'm so happy to have you in my life, Alex." I could feel his warm arms around me. Oliver and Emma got closer, and I congratulated Oliver too. Apart from the amazing love song at the end, it had been a cool gig.

"I didn't know you played keyboards," I told Oliver.

"Well, I have been playing piano since I was five, mainly classical. This summer we got to practice together at Arthsteen and even met some of the music majors. It's pretty cool."

I would have never taken Oliver for a classical pianist kind of guy, but apparently there were many things about him I didn't know.

"I hate to be the party pooper, but we have very little time left to pack up and head home," Alex said.

"Please tell me we have time to eat," Oliver added, and we all laughed.

The four of us chatted while we packed up everything, and Emma and I got to have a second serving of dessert as the guys ate. I didn't want the night to end. For the first time I felt part of a group, and it was such a novel and lovely feeling.

Oliver had to take Emma back before her curfew, and he volunteered to take most of their equipment, since Alex had to take me and Will back home. Alex skipped dessert so he could teach me how to dance a little bit of salsa. The feeling of his hand on my lower back sent chills through my spine as we both realized the dance genes were clearly missing from my DNA. He had the moves, which I attributed to his Latin genes. But our lesson was cut short when Will began to get cranky, and Miriam practically rushed us out of the restaurant so we'd be home before midnight, as she had promised my mom.

Once we got my bike on the rack and got in the car, I was sure Will would pass out right away, but I was wrong. He seemed to have gotten a second wind and was talking nonstop.

"Did June tell you about her latest laundry mess?" Will mocked. I tried to intervene right away, saying there was nothing out of my ordinary clumsiness. But Will kept going, and there was only so much I could come up with to stop him. The moment he mentioned Tristan's name, I noticed Alex's knuckles turn white as he held the steering wheel. And the part when we kept falling on top of each other definitely put Alex out of his happy mood. Apparently Will had witnessed everything that happened in the laundry room.

"You've missed so much, dude," Will added, and all I could think of was how much I hated having to share my friends with my annoying little brother.

"Will, I haven't seen Alex in a long time, do you mind?" My tone was menacing. He took the hint and stared out the window in silence. It didn't take long before he fell asleep in the back seat.

The air between Alex and me soured, and us not talking during the summer wasn't necessarily helping. If I had told him what was going on with Tristan, maybe he'd be acting more normal. But I hadn't, and things felt weird between us, even after the song.

Maybe it was the right time to tell him the truth. "Alex, I'm sorry I didn't text you or call you in the past weeks. It's just that Tristan—"

"I don't really want to talk about your British friend," he interrupted. He took a hard right turn, and I could feel his annoyance.

The evening had been lovely. I almost had forgotten about the whole play-disappearing issue. But ignoring it for a couple of hours didn't mean that it had disappeared.

"Alex, can I ask you something?"

"Anything." His tone was friendlier.

"What's my favorite love story? I mean, the one I always obsess about and have read over thirty times."

He laughed, taking longer than I expected to answer. It seemed as though he knew but hesitated to say it. That was when I realized something was wrong.

"Come on, you out of everyone should know," I pushed, but the longer he took, the more the despair filled me. If Alex couldn't mention Romeo right away, it meant it was only a matter of time before I would forget about the famous star-crossed lovers too.

"I . . . I don't remember. I know it but"—he raked his hair—"ours?"

His words took me by surprise. I put my hand over his on top of the gear shift. I wanted to be in the present moment, to enjoy how amazing Alex was, but all I could think of was how long Tristan had left.

"Come to Arthsteen tomorrow with me." He looked at me while we were at a red light. "I can drive us tomorrow early. It's Sunday, so you don't have to work at the library. We can spend the day together walking around campus. We can even check out every inch of the college library and ask about its library studies program. We can have an early dinner, and then I'll drive you to the bus station so you'll be back home before nine."

The light turned green, and he looked ahead. "Girls are not allowed in the boys dormitories, if that worries your parents."

He was not asking me to come with him. He was begging me. But I couldn't leave a lost literary character alone.

We got home, and he parked on my driveway as the door opened. It was exactly midnight. Dad came out, greeted Alex, and helped carry sleepy Will to his bed. I knew I had to say good night to Alex, but Dad whispered that I could have a little more time.

We took my bike down, I kept it and joined Alex in the front porch, looking at each other, and all I could think of was how much I hated feeling trapped in the in-between. I would go with Alex in a heartbeat, and I knew my parents would give in with some convincing. But I couldn't leave Tristan alone. I couldn't waste one more day without attempting to send him back into his book.

"June, now can you answer me something?" he asked as he leaned against the door frame.

I nodded.

"Is Tristan the reason you won't come to Arthsteen with me?"

I froze. I was not expecting that. Would he believe me if I told him about Tristan's real identity when he couldn't remember who Romeo was? I desperately wanted to tell him everything, but I doubted he would take me seriously, with a character out of a book he couldn't remember. I took too long to answer, and my silence told him everything.

He looked away disappointed, kissed me on the cheek, and walked to his Jeep. I wanted to say something, because this moment had played out differently in my head. I expected our first kiss to happen tonight, but it didn't, because real life rarely worked out as planned. I had messed up the best night of my life, all because of my inability to send a guy back to his book. Why did love have to be so complicated? Why did it had to turn the simple into complex?

I fought against my desperate need to run after Alex. What good would it do? I wanted nothing more than to tell him everything about the disappearing play, but I didn't even know how to fix the situation myself.

As I closed the door behind me, I felt my heart break even

though I'd just had the greatest night of my life. This night was supposed to be about new beginnings, so why could I only feel like things were ending? I knew deep in my heart I wanted Alex more than anyone in this world, no matter what Tristan did or who he really was.

I headed up the stairs to my room, and through the open door of my parents' room, I saw Dad kissing Mom on the cheek, and he covered her with a blanket as she lay asleep with a book on her lap. I wished someday I'd be lucky enough to find someone to share the same love my parents had found in each other. I wondered if I had already found it and had just ruined it.

CHAPTER 16

OPERATION RESTORING SHAKESPEARE

Tristan, with his not-so-subtle insistence for my hand in marriage, was driving me up a wall. I was so tired I even mentioned Juliet, an amazing girl who was going to change his world once he met her. But he insisted that he longed only for me, so it was fruitless. At one point I even had to ask Audrey to keep him more occupied at the café, since he was interfering with my work. I had already misplaced several books while trying to reshelve them before the library opened.

Nora was in the worst of moods lately. Even with the summer programs running smoothly and taking a couple of days off work, she still seemed more bitter than normal. I wondered if her mood had anything to do with her bad sunburn. But I was hesitant to ask where she had gone, since I was afraid of getting one of her annoying looks, which would curse me and turn me into stone. At some point I considered gifting her a sunscreen or an after-sun lotion, but I backed out, since I didn't know if she'd take it as a gift of peace or a reason to fire me.

Her bitterness was contagious, especially today. It had been three weeks since that night at El Marqués. I knew I had broken something before giving it the chance to begin, since Alex barely replied any of my texts. If I was going to wreck my love life, at least I had to save my beloved play. I had come up with a great idea to get Tristan back into his book, but I needed Nora to take her usual long lunch break on Thursdays. It'd better be worth it, because it was costing me my relationship with Alex.

The evening story time was over, and I couldn't keep a smile on my face any longer. I had used all the positivity I had left in me to make Heather Hare, the library puppet, enjoyable for the kids. I missed Marian. She always had a way of making me forget my sorrows when I became bitter June.

I also needed a break, so I crossed the street and sat on a shaded bench under a big oak tree. Maybe it seemed mean, but it was the only way in which Tristan couldn't come close, even if he found me. Just as if I had summoned her, my phone rang, and it was a video call from Marian.

"Happy birthday to you, you belong in the zoo. With the tigers and lions, 'cause the monkey is like you!" Her silly song brought a smile to my face. "It's already your birthday over here." She had a party hat and all.

"I miss you." I needed her to know it.

"Me too, Sis. Have you been enjoying your gift?" Marian asked.

The pocket edition had actually turned out very useful. I nodded. "If you only knew how much."

"Yay!" She smiled wide. "Is everything ready for the Capehart Fest?"

I nodded. My birthday celebration was the unofficial annual get-together for our whole family, plus my friends. It was always nice to see my little cousins and all, but this year with Marian, Maggie, and Alex not coming, it was going to be the lamest birthday ever.

"Is Tristan going?" she asked.

"How . . . what? Do you know about him?" It had been so long since we'd talked that I wondered if I had told her anything about him, since I tried to avoid the Tristan topic with any family member.

"You can't expect Dad to get a request from an exchange guy for your hand in marriage and not say something about it." She laughed. This was embarrassing. "Just beware, he might mention it again at the family party." Marian had a point, and I only hoped Dad still believed it was only a joke. "But I must say, I'm happy to hear you are meeting new people, Sis. It's good for you."

I gave her a fake smile, like the ones I had perfected when I dealt with the wick-pops.

"I have to go now, but I hope you have a great day," she said, looking away, and I could tell people had arrived at her apartment.

"Are you coming for Christmas?" I was desperate to know when I'd be able to see her again.

"Already got my ticket. Love you."

A hint of excitement triggered inside of me. "Love you too, Sis."

I hung up. As I looked away from my phone, I noticed Tristan waiting patiently on the other side of the street, the library's parking lot side. I took a deep breath. I liked him, but the more I thought about his book disappearing, the more desperate I felt. And the more he insisted about marriage, the more I questioned why I once wanted so desperately to have him for myself. I guessed I was ignorant to the actual-century mindset differences between us.

Nora's car drove by, which meant she was gone for lunch. I stood up immediately. Operation Restoring Shakespeare to fix the collectible was now in motion. I had only close to forty minutes, and my plan better work, because I was about to risk my job.

As Tristan and I went into the exhibit room, we encountered a complication. A pair of silver-haired ladies seemed to be taking forever to examine all the books on display.

"Did you hear about the damaged collectible?" one whispered to the other.

"Yes, such a pity. And have you noticed the empty shelves in the Shakespeare section? This library is desperate for some funding, or I'm afraid we're going to have to look for another library to go to," the other one answered.

The two ladies seemed to be the kind of people who thrived on small-town gossip, but something of what they said had stung. *I* was responsible for the empty shelf, and if patrons were talking, that was a bad sign. I needed them to leave, but I couldn't rush them, especially since I worked here.

I stared at the time on my phone. I had a little over twenty minutes left. I tried as discreetly as I could to explain that we would be closing the exhibit for lunch but would reopen in an hour. They didn't seem pleased at all, but after they stared at my badge, they complied and left. The blinds were already down, which was unusual, but I couldn't risk another patron coming in, so I locked the door.

I punched the combination numbers on the keypad, and the display beeped as it unlocked. Recklessly, I didn't care if my hands were perfectly clean. The book was already damaged, and time was ticking. I opened the case, trying my best to hide how much my hands were shaking. The cover looked even duller than before. It was no longer a faded blue; it was brown as a dead autumn leaf.

Tristan stared at me, and all of a sudden it hit me—this was our goodbye. After a roller coaster of a summer, it was time to part ways. I was going to miss his quirkiness, but he needed to go back to meet his Juliet. As I took the book out, I wondered why I always ended up crying when I held this book. This was our last moment together, but it didn't seem like there was enough time for a proper goodbye.

"Milady, are you all right?" His accent made my heart shrink. He had been my first kiss, and even before I met him, he had been my first love. But I was no longer in love with him, and he deserved someone who would die for him.

"Everything's fine, Tristan," I said, trying to distract myself as I browsed carefully through its pages. All the other copies had whole blank pages, but this was the only one with letters that disappeared one at a time. This was *his* book, *his* home.

Only one scene from the first act remained. It was the very beginning of the play, where Montagues and Capulets fought on the streets of Verona. The prologue was there, but I knew it meant we had very little time left.

"Tristan, hold this," I said, fighting the knot tightening in my throat. He took a step back, afraid. "I promise, nothing bad is going to happen," I reassured him, although I knew he was going back to a fate that was anything but pleasant.

"Milady, your admiration for blank magical books never seizes to amaze me." His charming accent was killing me.

I chuckled but kept quiet, since I couldn't say anything without my voice breaking. This was supposed to be a quick, efficient mission, not a long heartbreaking one. I brought the book closer to him, and he grabbed it carefully. Once the book came in direct contact with him, its main character, he'd have to go back to it, and everything would be over. Or at least that was my plan.

"Milady, this is a lovely edition. Distressed, but much closer to the ones I remember seeing at the Montague house."

I nodded. Surely an edition from the seventeen hundreds

must be more similar to the ones he was used to. So many of our magical moments came to mind, like when he complained about the plain and boring modern editions at this library, and we agreed about how old books possessed an irreplaceable charm and beauty.

The anticipation was killing me. Tristan looked back and forth between me and the pages of his book. I didn't know what I expected to happen. Perhaps some sort of magic or even sparks, but nothing. Maybe it wouldn't happen in front of me. Maybe he had arrived when no one was looking.

"Goodbye, Tristan," I whispered as I turned and closed my eyes. Any minute now he'd be nothing but a memory.

"Milady?" Tristan asked a few moments later. I opened my eyes and turned to look back at him. Nothing. He was looking at the book. I didn't understand why it was not working.

Maybe there was a magic phrase or something. Since the scenes where Romeo appeared were gone, I had to rely on my memory to remember his lines. I covered my forehead with my hand and tried to remember.

"What is happening, milady?" Tristan's voice was fearful, but nothing seemed to be changing.

"Tristan," I corrected. "Romeo, I need you to repeat after me. *Did my heart love till now?*" I said, trying to remember Romeo's exact words.

"Milady, I knew you would accept our marriage eventually! Our love is my greatest blessing," Tristan exclaimed as he closed the book.

"NO!" I said loudly, and Tristan stopped.

"Please, Tristan, just repeat the words, *Did my heart love till now?*"

He seemed to doubt for a moment, but then said the words. Nothing changed.

I tried to remember another of his famous lines. *"For I never saw true beauty till this night."*

He gave me a confident smile. I was not flirting with him. I was trying to save him. "Please, say it!"

He did, and it sounded like he meant it, but nothing happened.

"No, no, no, please. OK, one more." I tried to remember a line of his before he met Juliet—maybe that was it. He hadn't met her yet. He had met me, a Rosaline in his life, the one before his big love. "I'm going to say something, and you are going to reply with *Not having that, which, having, makes them short.* Understood?"

He nodded.

"What sadness lengthens Romeo's hours?" I asked, and he replied word by word what I had asked him to say. I was about to lose my mind. "This can't be happening!"

"Milady." Tristan tried to take a step closer, but I stopped him.

"Don't. You can't come any closer. You have to stay away from me."

He frowned in confusion.

"Please." I said. He needed to be with Juliet, not me.

All the hopes I had of restoring my favorite love story vanished in front of my eyes. It got even worse when someone tried to open the door. I took the book from Tristan's hands and stared at the cover. There were no more engraved letters, no title or author. The fore-edge painting had become a faint mark.

"Why is this door locked?" Nora's voice on the other side of the door made my heart race. We had run out of time. "Jim?" she called.

I looked around. There was nowhere to hide, and I was about to lose my job.

"Tristan, say it one more time with me, louder," I begged him. I no longer cared if they knew it was us inside, as they were about to find out anyway. His tone was sadder, more convincing than before, but nothing changed. I heard the sound of Jim's huge key chain dangling, and instinctively I put the book inside its case and closed the lid just as the door opened.

"June!" Nora's tone sounded as if I was already fired. "What do you think you are doing locked up in here? Who closed the blinds?"

Tristan and I stared at each other. Then he took a step forward. "Lady Nora, it has been *I* who asked Lady June to—"

"You do NOT work here." Nora's interruption was anything but polite.

Tristan was familiar with my complaining about whatever Nora blamed me for doing or not doing, so I appreciated his help covering for me. But this time it wouldn't be enough.

Nora walked closer, and the way she looked at me, I began to think I might not be far off comparing her to Medusa or any other scary mythological creature. She stared at the display behind us, and we both realized the LED lights were not green, like always. I had forgotten to close it.

"You opened the case? Did you take the damaged collectible out?" Nora's tone was frightening. "Answer me!"

Out of nowhere a familiar voice intervened. "It wasn't her." I turned around and saw Sarah by the door, coming toward us. "I called the respective association and was even on the phone with them." She sounded totally convincing, but how could she save me? I was actually breaking the rules this time. "The reception was bad, and I had been on hold for over an hour, so I had to rush outside for the call not to drop."

Nora took a moment to think. "That does not explain why the blinds were closed."

"They suggested less light, so I closed them."

They had been closed when we got here, but I was sure I had been the one to open the case. I began to doubt my own sanity.

"And what are you going to say about the locked door?" Nora crossed her arms, but Sarah didn't respond. She just shook her head and shrugged. Then Nora frowned my way.

"Things have not been working properly, Nora," Jim added. "That's what I've been telling you about the library needing the grant."

Both Sarah and Jim had become like guardian angels now that Mrs. Lib was away, but this had gone too far. I had risked too much.

"I'm sorry, Nora," I said before this got out of hand. "I wanted to show Tristan the exhibit. I really didn't want to cause any trouble. You know I have tried to follow your instructions to the T in everything." That part was true. I had no idea if she believed me, but I couldn't take the full blame of opening the case, not now.

Nora pointed at me. "Your position at this library does not entail rushing patrons out so you can have a private showing with your boyfriend."

I knew the ladies would be trouble.

"Luckily for you, I can't fire you, since Alice Libbengood has to approve any staff changes."

I had no idea how Mrs. Lib was going to take this, but something told me that *hosting a private exhibit*, as Nora had said, would be nothing compared to losing an old collectible borrowed by an association.

"What I *can* do is put you on leave," Nora added "Alice Libbengood will hear about this, and every detail regarding your poor performance during the summer. Make no mistake about that."

Her index finger was getting too close to my face, so I took a step back.

"I don't want to see you around this library until Alice comes back, understood?"

I nodded and headed to the door before she could say anything else. "As for you, Mr. Tristan, I will respect your volunteer status, just because you are going to be gone soon, like the rest of the exchange students. But be careful, sir."

Tristan froze at her accusation. At least he didn't fight her like he had against Tybalt.

I came closer to him and pulled him from his shirt so he'd follow me. Just as we were exiting the room, I heard Nora criticizing Sarah for leaving the case open, even to take a call. I felt horrible, because it was all my fault—since the moment Tristan appeared, and every disaster that followed.

As I walked out of the library, heading toward the garden, I realized I couldn't take losing anymore. I was tired of seeing my favorite things in life breaking apart. First Marian and the long distance, then my friendship with Maggie. Now Alex was barely talking to me, and I was about to lose Romeo, his play, and my favorite job. Tristan tried to cheer me up, but I couldn't see the sunny side of life, not today. He hugged me and I cried, for I knew I was about to lose him, too, forever, and for all humankind.

I knew I had to leave as soon as possible, but I still worried about Tristan. Now we wouldn't be able to hang out at the library, and the heat made it impossible to be outside for very long. I thought about inviting him over to my house, but I wondered if he needed to be in proximity to his book for him to go back. I got an idea that was also a trust exercise for Tristan. He reassured me that he would do whatever I asked him to do to make me happy. I knew he would. I just felt bad having so much control over him. This was not what I expected a relationship to feel like.

I was unlocking my bike to head home when I felt someone tapping my shoulder.

"I didn't have time to wish you a happy birthday." Sarah was standing next to me with a bookmark in her hand. "We made these in one of our programs. I hope you like it." She hugged me and gave it to me. It was a beautiful collage bookmark pressed with dried flowers.

"Thank you so much, Sarah. I love it." It looked so well made, as if she had bought it in a store.

"June, I have to say, I know you love old books, but please don't try to do anything of that kind again."

Her words froze me. She knew I had opened the case.

"I will help you with Alice when she comes back, so it won't interfere with your plans for library school. I know you are a good kid and have been coming to this library since you were little. You know we all are very fond of you."

I knew that *we* included Jim as well.

"I'm really sorry," I said. Part of me wanted to ask if she still remembered *Romeo and Juliet*, but I couldn't do it. Because if she didn't, I would stress even more.

"Also, I should let you know"—she looked at me with a soft smile—"that I changed the combination of the display. I thought it was best to remove any temptations."

I nodded. What else could I do? I had flown too close to the sun this time, and I had gotten burned.

I thanked her for helping me so much during the summer and headed home. I wanted to lock myself in my room and read for hours. That had always made me forget any bittersweet reality. Maybe I'd use my new bookmark and enjoy the silence before my whole house would be filled with family.

CHAPTER 17
SEVENTEEN WISHES

I paced the entryway, waiting for Tristan just the way Haiku did when he wanted to be let out and we had been gone for too long. No, even worse. I came to the conclusion that if Tristan was going to either linger here forever, disappear, or whatever fate he was going to encounter, I wanted to make his last days enjoyable, so I'd given him some freedom by lending him my pocket edition.

I also told him that the magic within my tiny notebook, as he called it, would keep him safe as long as he held on to it at all times, and would only go to the specific places I had pointed out to him. I knew it was controlling, but I needed him to be a little fearful and not be his reckless self and do something stupid. The problem was that now I was cursing at the technological advantages, like instant texting, that weren't possible with him.

Last night I had stayed up until midnight, like I did every year, to get a call from Alex or Maggie, but none came. I wished I could have called Tristan, to have someone be the first other than my parents to wish me a happy birthday. Since I needed some sort of a messenger pigeon to get to Tristan, and since I was banned from the library, I had thought of someone who had a phone and was close to Tristan—Audrey.

I thought that was a brilliant idea. But now it had turned out to be even more frustrating, since perhaps I shouldn't have picked someone who had a crush on him and discreetly disliked the girl he had fallen for. She wasn't answering my texts about how long Tristan had been gone from the library, and I was sure one more text would ban me from the café too.

He was taking too long, and I was getting desperate, imagining the worst. I had given him a map with clear paths on where to cross the streets and explained to him what a traffic light was, but my anxiety was spiking to the roof. Besides, the whole Capehart clan was already here, and my house felt unusually loud. Totally different from its normal quiet, at least when Will was not around. But not being able to hear someone knocking at the door made me agitated enough to open it every few minutes. Mainly because I was sure Tristan would surely freak out at the doorbell, since, thanks to Dad, was one more smart thing in the house.

I was about to go wait for him outside when I opened the door and found him. A wave of relief flooded my body. "You are safe," I said and hugged him quickly. I knew I shouldn't be getting any closer with him, but I was worried. "What are you wearing?" His black T-shirt gave rock star vibes but showed the face of Audrey Hepburn.

"Lady Audrey reassured me it was, in her words, *fashionable*." His smile was wide. All I could think of was that it might as well be saying *Property of Audrey*. Perhaps my getting banned from the library had been a happy thing for her. I didn't care. I only cared that he was safe and here.

"Tristan, there are a lot of people here. Can you please not mention the marriage thing? Please? Just not today," I begged him with puppy eyes.

He seemed disappointed but agreed.

"Milady, I have something for you." He pulled out a gift. "I got this for you at the fair but thought today was the right day to give it to you." I definitely had not expected Romeo Montague to give me anything on my birthday. He handed it over and kissed me on the cheek. My face went so red I thought I might be mimicking the roses in the vase at the entrance table.

I untied the string carefully and stared at the brown paper. Under all the layers was a beautiful handmade leather book. I opened it and realized it was a notebook, since it had thick, yellowish paper. The sheets were blank, but there was something written on one of the first pages.

> *Milady,*
> *May your smile be forever the brightest and your mind be always the smartest.*
> *With all the love that I possess,*
> *Tristan, R.M.*

The words almost made me cry with happy tears.

"It seemed like a fitting gift for your obsession with blank notebooks," he said sweetly, with a big smile.

There were not enough words to tell him how much his gift meant to me. I hugged him instead. "Thank you," I tried to mumble, but it came out as a weird squeak as I hugged him again. I was going to cherish the book forever.

As he hugged me back, I realized his embrace was different. His arms didn't feel as tight around me. I hadn't hugged a lot of guys before, but all I could think of was how different it felt from hugging Alex. Tristan was definitely skinnier, and he didn't have a recognizable smell. I imagined he'd smell like paper or old books, but he didn't. But still, I hugged him tight, because I didn't know how much time he had left.

"June, my favorite bookworm!" Aunt Melissa's loud voice

reached us before she did. She was short with long blonde hair. I broke apart from Tristan, clearing my throat to force my emotions back. I introduced them and was surprised to see Tristan had followed my instructions. Instead of kissing hands or bowing, he waved his hand in the air. It was comforting for me but seemed extremely awkward.

"How's your job at the public library?" she asked.

I lied, saying it was all great because no one would believe I could get kicked out of a public library. "When are you going to come visit me in New York? I'm sure you'd love to come with me to work one day."

"Maybe one day," I said. She was the relative who'd sent me the most books. Mainly advanced reader copies, since she worked in one of the biggest publishing houses. I was sure that if I convinced my parents to let me spend a summer with her, she'd get me an internship, but I was not very comfortable with the idea of getting into publishing. I'd read all sorts of horrible stories about it, and my personality fit best in a quiet library, which was the job I ultimately wanted.

"I know it's far from here, but you'll love the Big Apple and my flat too. Besides, New York is closer to England than here." She winked at me. At least I knew Tristan's story of being an exchange student from the UK was still what my parents were telling everyone.

"Have you been to England, Lady Melissa?" Tristan asked.

I smiled nervously, waiting for her answer. She was known for being nosy, and I just wanted to avoid any of her uncomfortable questions. Fortunately, I had explained to Tristan before that, for his identity purposes, the UK and England were commonly mistaken as the same place.

"Lady Melissa?" She laughed loudly. "I have been to England. It's lovely there, although too rainy for me." She stared at him closely, as if she was analyzing him. "From which part are you from, exactly?"

"Verona, Italy," Tristan responded with all the confidence in the world, bowing his head.

My aunt stared at him, raising an eyebrow.

I just wanted to head outside and mingle with my little cousins, who wouldn't ask complicated questions. But I jumped in nevertheless: "He was born in Italy but has spent most of his life in an itty-bitty forgotten town closer to Stratford-upon-Avon." I emphasized the words *forgotten town.*

"How unique." Aunt Melissa nodded. "You seem to be quite a character, young man." She pinched his cheek, just the way she did with me and all my cousins, but Tristan looked excruciatingly uncomfortable.

We needed an escape plan. "We're going to head outside now, and Will is going to teach Tristan to . . ." I suddenly remembered a detail about soccer, that it was Europe's most-watched sport. It would be illogical if Tristan didn't even know what the game was about. ". . . to refresh Tristan in his soccer skills. He hasn't played in such a long time." I tried to push Tristan away from my aunt.

"I'm sure he'll remember as soon as his feet touch the ball. After all, you say he's sort of English!" Aunt Melissa laughed out loud.

Thankfully, Mom brought out snacks, and Aunt Melissa got distracted by them, which was our cue to exit.

Once we were out in the backyard, Tristan whispered, "Milady, what exactly is soccer? Or that which your aunt was referring to? You know I am Italian, not English."

His accent proved otherwise. But it got me thinking. Now that I knew who he really was, I wondered if the reason for his English accent was because the play had been originally written in English. Or maybe it could be because Shakespeare was English. That thought opened a can of worms. Were characters always bilingual? Meaning, were they able to speak the language of their author or creator as well as the one from the place their story took place?

"Milady?" Tristan asked, and I shook my head, coming back to the moment.

"Right, soccer." I quickly thought about an easy explanation. "Soccer is another name for football. You use your feet to kick the ball into your opponent's net." I pointed at the goal. "You can use your head or knees but never your hands."

My cousins ran immediately toward us. They couldn't care less who Tristan was. They only cared that they needed an extra player to complete their soccer team. Will was the first to call dibs on Tristan, which helped him seem more confident.

To my surprise Tristan learned the game pretty fast. He must have gotten beginner's luck, because he even scored a goal. Of course, his size and strength worked to his advantage while playing with a bunch of seven- to twelve-year-olds. I could finally relax, knowing no one would ask him any uncomfortable questions while he played.

Tristan tried to hit the ball with his forehead but failed and fell to the ground. My immediate concern was that my pocket edition had fallen out of his clothes. Every time Tristan ended up on the ground, which was often, I stood up. Instead of a girlfriend's normal reaction to him getting hurt, I felt like a mom taking care of her firstborn toddler.

They finished their game when it was time to eat. Fortunately, they had tied. Will was a pretty bad loser, and I didn't want him to ruin my birthday with one of his tantrums. Dad finished grilling just before the soccer game on TV was about to begin. Even when the World Cup had ended last weekend, there was always a game going on around the world. Half of my family was glued to the TV in the living room waiting for the game to start. The rest, mainly my little cousins, watched the game on the patio TV while questioning Tristan.

They were all incredibly surprised as to why Tristan had never tried a hot dog before.

He seemed to be happy enjoying the attention and trying the different toppings my cousins suggested. The funniest part was his reaction to trying french fries on top of a hot dog. He was now obsessed.

Mom waited for halftime so the whole family could redirect their attention to singing "Happy Birthday" to me. As she was placing the candles in the cake, someone rang the doorbell. Haiku, like always, got to the door first. He barked incessantly, not letting me hear who it was. My jaw dropped as I opened the door and saw Alex standing in the doorway.

"You're here," I said, utterly surprised.

"I'm here," he said seriously with his hands behind his back, giving me the weakest smile. Haiku barked until Alex petted him. I wanted to hug him, but I stopped. Then I realized I was tired of waiting, tired of holding back and overthinking every step. I hugged him, because after all, it was my birthday. I got lost in his scent, and even the fresh cologne couldn't mask the subtle smell of chlorine, which brought joy to my senses. He had come for me, and he was hugging me back.

When we broke apart, he wished me happy birthday and gave me a colorful bouquet of gerbera daisies, my favorite flowers. Even though the flowers were gorgeous, all I could think of was the happiness I felt that he was here. It was as if everything was right with the world, and nothing bad could get to me, not even my own worst thoughts.

His expression changed to annoyance when we heard Tristan's laughter coming from the living room.

I stared at the flowers and smiled at Alex. "I'm so happy *you* are here," I said, and at least I was still able to change his frown into a smile.

Will came running to the front door. "What's up, dude!" He jumped and landed next to Alex, bumping their fists together.

Alex took an envelope from his back pocket. "I found it."

"No way, for real?" Will's voice was louder than normal as he rushed to open the envelope. "How did you get it?"

"I have my ways." Alex clicked his tongue with confidence.

Will hugged Alex. "Thank you, dude!" He couldn't hold his excitement. "I'll be right back. I have to put it on right now." He ran up the stairs.

"What am I missing?" I asked Alex.

"He only needed that one stamp to fill his World Cup album."

I smiled at him. "Wow, so you are Super Marquez," I joked.

"It's no big deal. I mean, it was not easy to find, but it was important for him." Alex looked up.

Mom was coming toward us and greeted him with excitement. "Just in time for the cake," she said.

As we followed her into the kitchen, I wondered if he just happened to have an extra or if he had gone through the trouble of finding it for him, no matter the cost.

My entire family gathered around a multilayered cake in the shape of stacked books. It was the most beautiful cake I'd ever seen. As I sat in front of it while my mom lit the candles, I realized she had written the titles of my favorite books on the spines. But something bittersweet made my heart ache as I realized *Romeo and Juliet* was not among those titles.

All the excitement Alex's presence had brought seemed to deflate as the central conflict of my summer came to mind. Mom took several pictures of me, and I felt someone's hand land softly over my right shoulder. I turned around to see who it was and found Tristan's gorgeous olive eyes staring at me. I felt another hand over my left shoulder and turned the other way—it was Alex. My heart and my mind felt awfully divided.

Mom started singing, and the rest followed. I knew both guys wouldn't have the biggest smiles in the pictures, but at least both were here, and both meant a lot to me in different ways. While everyone sang the "Happy Birthday" song, I could hear Tristan's voice the clearest, since he enthusiastically tried to follow the words. I tried to focus on Alex's voice, which was softer but the most melodic and sweet of them all.

"Make a wish," Dad said as they all finished singing, and I closed my eyes.

A birthday wish. Something supposedly simple, but I couldn't pick only one. My heart desperately wanted Alex, for him to sing me his song over and over again. To hold his hand and laugh and find happiness just being around him. But my mind desperately wanted to save my favorite Shakespearean love story.

I thought of the seventeen candles lit up in front of me. Could I ask for seventeen wishes instead of just one? That way I could ask for everything I wanted to get fixed in my life. For Maggie to talk to me so we could fix things. For Marian to come back or at least call me more often. For Mrs. Lib to be here so I could tell her the truth about the collectible and maybe together find a way to fix it before it was too late. For Nora to stop making my life so miserable at the library. For the wick-pops to stop trying to destroy my friendship with Maggie. For me to gain weight and not be so skinny. For my summer to be more fun and have fewer worries. But mostly for my heart to get what it desperately desired.

I felt the weight of Alex's and Tristan's hands equally over my shoulders but I could have only one wish come true. I blew out the candles and thought of the wish I wanted more than anything in the world.

The second half of the game was almost over. I walked away not caring about the final score and helped Mom transfer the different layers of the cake to separate containers. I heard everyone's disappointment as the game ended and Liverpool lost.

I saw Alex standing outside annoyed with the score. He seemed to redirect his frustration as he showed off his soccer tricks to Will and the rest of my cousins. He kicked the ball to his knees, then to his head, and balanced it on his nape. Alex was unbelievably talented. He could do all sort of things, from sports to music, even writing heartfelt songs. I got lost daydreaming about that night at El Marqués when he'd sung his heart out to me in front of everyone there.

"Milady, wasn't your friend already gone far away?" Tristan's voice took me out of my daydreams as he acted like a jealous boyfriend.

I turned to look at him. "Tristan, don't start. You know he's my friend, and it is *my* birthday." He didn't seem too happy about it.

"Even the dog prefers him," he said bitterly and pointed at Haiku, who was jumping around Alex as he showed off his soccer tricks. It was kind of funny how jealous he was, but he had a point. Ever since Alex had arrived, Haiku hadn't left his side.

"You truly care for him, right milady?" Tristan asked, sounding worried.

I was not going to get into that. Not now, not with him, and not with my mom behind us listening. "Tristan, promise me you'll stay away from Alex. Promise me you won't get into any trouble with him."

He hesitated but accepted.

Dad came by and offered him a soda. "So when is Maggie going to arrive to complete the JAMs?" Dad asked me.

That name rang different now. A long time ago Alex, Maggie, and I were so close we called ourselves the JAMs for our initials. But those days seemed far in the past.

"We don't call ourselves that anymore, Dad," I answered, and a pinch of nostalgia struck my heart, making it break a little. Maggie hadn't congratulated me on my birthday, and it hurt. It really hurt.

I knew Tristan would ask about the JAMs, but luckily he had to use the restroom. I was not in the mood for him asking me any more questions about anything.

As he walked away, Dad pointed his head at Tristan. "How are you doing, kiddo? Everything holding up?"

"What do you mean?"

"I mean that the summer is almost over and I don't want you to be unhappy once Tristan goes back to his home country. No parent wants to see their kid suffer and it took you quite a while to smile again when Marian left."

Another tear in my heart. I had completely ignored the fact that Tristan's absence would wreck me in unexpected ways. Perhaps that was the problem with heartbreak. Even as I'd read a lot about it in romance novels, it was inevitable. And no amount of logic or preparedness would keep you from feeling the pain.

"I'll be OK, Dad. I know his time is up and there's nothing I can do," I said, feeling defeated after I had tried everything to send him back.

The one thing that I had learned this summer was that life was constantly changing. And as time went by, all I would have left would be memories. Soon Tristan would be one, too, that was if *I* still remembered him.

I went outside looking for Alex. The sports commentators debated over replays of the game. I watched Alex and my dad taking about the game. Alex's arms were over his knees, bouncing his left leg anxiously as he bit his nails. Maybe I stared at him for too long, because he turned my way. Our eyes met, and he smiled at me for a moment. Until Will shouted upset about his soccer ball going over the fence.

Tristan came out to the patio, and I switched my gaze between Alex and Tristan. Both guys had somehow stolen my heart, and I felt torn. Not because I doubted who I wanted to be with, but because I cared enough about both to not want to hurt either one of them.

Our neighbor returned Will's ball and I watched Alex and my cousins play soccer together.

"Milady." Tristan said sitting by me sounding upset.

I turned, and something in his face looked pale, not OK. "What's the matter? Are you feeling all right?" I was genuinely worried about him. Had something happened to his book? Was he going to disappear right here in front of everyone?

"Worry not about me, my love. But there is something I need to say." He pointed at Alex. "Every time *he* is present, I cannot battle the rage inside me."

Will kicked the ball and it headed toward me. But Alex blocked its path and stopped it from hitting me. He fell gracefully backwards landing very close to us.

"I know you asked me to not talk about marriage, but I am dying inside. Will I ever get my answer, milady?" Tristan asked.

I didn't want to break his heart here, not when there were so many people around us. But I had to tell him the truth—we would never get married because there was not a future together. There was barely a future for him on his own. I shushed him instead, not wanting Alex to hear our conversation. He stood up threw the ball back at Will and left through the gate. Something was off.

"Wait for me *here*," I told Tristan and rushed after him.

"Hey, Alex!" I followed him but he didn't stop. "Where are you going?" I asked, but he was already on the sidewalk, heading to his house. "You can't leave. It's my birthday," I shouted, desperate for him to stay. It worked, because he turned around.

"I know it's your birthday. That's why I drove four freaking hours this morning just to be here for you." He rubbed his face in frustration.

I walked toward him, but he wouldn't meet my eye. I put my hand on his arm, hoping he would focus on me, but he closed his eyes and then pushed my hand away. I knew there was something special between us. I just didn't want it to break before it had a chance to begin.

"I can't do this anymore," he said, running his hand through his hair and making it messier, like always, but this time I found it irresistible. "I'm tired of waiting for you, June."

I could see the sadness in his eyes.

"Alex, what are you talking about? I've had a crush on you for years."

He laughed and shook his head. "Then why didn't you tell me?"

"I . . . I don't know. I thought you didn't feel the same way. That night at the posada, years ago, your mom told me you loved me like a sister. What was I supposed to do?" He stared at me in silence. "You friend-zoned me, Alex."

"Are you punishing me because I asked Nichole out for Maggie's party? Is that it? Because you were the one who started out dating her setup guy. Everyone could see you were not into him, but still you were all cuddly at the mall. It was like you were someone else."

"Do not judge me when you went out with Nichole, knowing very well how she felt about you," I said defensively. Not everything was my fault.

"I offered to take you instead, and you said no. I didn't care about canceling with her."

"You are acting childish and jealous." The frustration was clear in my voice.

"And why do you think that is?" he asked, his arms spread wide.

I opened my mouth, but no words came out.

"Do you know what it's like to hear you talk about fictional guys for years? To realize I could never compete with your imaginary book dudes? Because you should know authors make them perfect so you buy more books. I thought you would eventually realize they could never be real people. But then that English brat came out of nowhere and said the right things, so you followed him everywhere."

"I didn't *follow* him," I said dismissively.

"June, I don't really know what I am to you anymore, or what *we* are," he said, motioning between us. "I thought we had something . . . special and real."

He was right. Alex had always been something more than my best friend. He was my safe place.

"But that night at El Marqués, I felt like I put myself out there, and you didn't meet me halfway." He frowned.

"Alex, I did. I texted you, and you barely answered me back all these weeks."

"Yeah, because texting is the same as writing a song."

"What did you want me to do? I didn't know you had

feelings for me, not until the song. Before that, I had to act indifferent when girls who had a crush on you asked me all about you. While I should be OK with just being your best friend." My anger was such I felt the knot in my throat tightening. "But it's so easy for you to blame me for this mess, when you could have said something before. Before Tyler and before Tristan. I had to watch you leave, knowing you'd meet tons of people to then come and tell me about this *special* college friend?" I stopped trying to catch my breath. "It's you who have been sending mixed messages all along."

He looked down, then stared at me and tried to reach for my hand, but stopped. I wanted him to hold me, to at least give me a hint that we could solve this together. But something stopped him, and I didn't know what.

"Will talks to me. Maybe you don't know about it, but he does," Alex said softly. "I know that you went to the Renaissance Faire with him, how you got a full costume to match his. Remember when we used to go and you always refused to even get a flower crown?"

I hated when my little brother messed things up.

"If you're in love with him, just tell me. I know how to lose. Because if he's asking you to marry him, then maybe I'm just blinded by what I feel about you."

"I'm not in love with him, Alex," I said, realizing for the first time that I meant it.

"What is it then? Because it somehow feels like you are waiting to see which one of us you prefer. Or are you waiting for him to leave to be with me?"

My heart was racing, and it was getting harder and harder to fight back the tears. "No, Alex, why would you think that?"

"Because you always pick him over me. Not even when I wrote you a damn song and poured my heart out in front of everyone." He looked up to the sky. I knew he was fighting back the tears too.

"Alex, I loved the song. It was the most romantic thing in the world, but you can't be mad just because I couldn't ditch my life to go with you on a whim."

He laughed. "It was a Sunday. You can't be working every day at the library." He stopped. "Never mind, I don't know what game you're playing, but I don't want to be a pawn anymore. I can't be here watching how you fall for another guy, because this time he's not fictional."

I felt trapped by a secret that was about to turn into my worst nightmare. "He is. *That* is the problem!" I felt so relieved to say those words out loud. "I can't tell anyone because nobody remembers the story he came out of. Nobody recognizes *Romeo and Juliet* anymore. I asked you the other day about the love story I was obsessed with. The one I read over thirty times, and you above everyone couldn't tell me the title."

Alex stared at me, confused.

"You have to believe me. His play is disappearing, and I had to do something. I still do. I can't let Shakespeare's biggest play go into oblivion. That's why I couldn't go with you to Arthsteen U."

The front door opened, and we both turned. Tristan came out of the house.

"Milady, I heard someone shouting."

For the first time I didn't find his English accent charming.

"Have you been raising your voice at my betrothed?" Tristan accused Alex and rushed angrily toward him.

Alex took a step forward, ready to fight.

Tristan stopped inches away from Alex's face. "I am going to kill you," Tristan said with a menacing tone.

"I want to see you try," Alex replied cockily.

Tristan threw a punch at him, but Alex dodged it and pushed him to the ground. Tristan rolled on the grass, and I saw my pocket edition coming out of the back pocket of Tristan's jeans.

"Alex, stop!" I shouted as I tried to rush to Tristan. "My

book, no, no, no." I grabbed my pocket edition and put it inside his front pocket, but Tristan was not responding.

"Please, Tristan, please. Wake up," I said, slapping his cheek.

It took longer than normal, but he came back to himself. As soon as he opened his eyes, I stood up and ran after Alex. He was already getting into his Jeep.

I ran to the passenger side, which was closer to me, but the door was locked. "Alex, you have to believe me. He's going to disappear, and I can't lose *Romeo and Juliet*. I just can't. I can't let this all be my fault."

Alex refused to look at me and turned on the ignition.

I hit the copilot's window repeatedly. "I am not lying. He's Romeo Montague, and you'd know him if his play wasn't vanishing."

Alex stared at me. Then he looked away and drove in reverse out of the driveway.

I walked back and found Tristan swinging on an old swing in the front yard.

"Milady," he said, standing up.

"I asked you to stay inside, Tristan," I said, not looking at him. I was trying so hard for my mind and heart to stay in one piece.

"My love, I could not accept him treating you that way. The thought of that scoundrel even raising his voice at you."

"Tristan, don't," I said, looking up at him.

"Milady, I cannot allow someone to disrespect you." He tried to get closer to me. "I have vowed to always be by your side to protect you."

I held up a hand to stop him. "But you won't be, and that is the whole tragedy."

He stared at me, confused.

"Remember the book I made you touch at the library's exhibit? The one you claimed was blank?" He nodded. "Would you believe me if I told you that you came out of it? That it is disappearing because you are here?"

Tristan laughed. "Milady, that seems impossible."

"I know, I had trouble believing it at first too. Until I saw the words slowly vanishing from its pages. I've been obsessively trying to help you get back, but your book has less than a scene left." My eyes filled with tears again.

"Milady, perhaps the heat has gotten to your head."

"Tristan, I am used to the heat. I was born here!" I was at the end of my rope. "You're the one who doesn't get it. You're supposed to live in the late fifteen hundreds, not in the twenty-first century!"

He sat back on the swing with his hands on his forehead. I took a deep breath and tried to calm myself. I couldn't scare him away.

"Tristan, just think about it." I knelt next to him. "Have you never wondered why you get overwhelmed by elevators, bicycles, cables, or cars? Why you've never heard of such common things as ice cream, pizza, or hot dogs? Why you need my magical notebook to leave the library? Please tell me you find that odd."

He looked at me and then away, seeming unsure what to do with himself. Perhaps it had been too risky to dump all this on him. I didn't want him to stop trusting me or run away. I tried to get closer to him and put my hand on his knee to calm my nerves.

"I'm sorry, Tristan. You must know I care about you, a lot. I'm just scared of something happening to you." I tried so hard for my voice not to break. "You have to believe me when I say I've done everything in my power to keep you safe."

"I do believe you, milady." He looked at me, calmer but still hesitant.

"I know this might be too much to process, but you have to understand how big of a character you are. Imagine this: you are so famous we've been saying your name for centuries." My words didn't seem to impress him at all. "We have to find a way for you to go back. I don't know what will happen to you if you stay. But I know that if you return, you'll meet someone who will love you more than I would ever be able to."

He looked at my hand over his knee. Then he stood and helped me up. "Milady, my love, there is no place or person I'd rather be with than you. You possess all of me, for eternity."

It was sweet, but I realized convincing him to go back had become a lost cause.

"That's the point, Tristan. I can't be so selfish to keep you only for myself. You belong to every person who has ever believed in love. You are an inspiration, an ideal, and it's because of you that people are looking for their own Romeo."

Tristan held my gaze. I knew part of him was freaking out, and maybe it had been a bad idea to tell him everything I knew about him. But if I was going to disappear from this earth sometime soon, I'd like to know everything there was to know about me.

"Milady, then believe *me* when I say our love is stronger than any obstacle ahead of us." He interlaced his fingers with mine.

Romeo would say that. Romeo would believe that love was strong enough to bear any storms. Because, after all, he believed marrying Juliet would be enough to solve their families' longtime feud. He was being true to himself, but that wasn't going to save him. Sometimes loving someone wasn't enough to keep them from harm.

"Milady, I want you to remember that no matter where I am, I will love you until my last breath," he said, and broke apart from me.

"Are you leaving?" I asked, shocked.

"Milady, I will never leave you. But the bugs, the noise, and the heat are all dreadful. I am going back inside for something cool to drink."

Perhaps he had finally come to love the commodities of modern times.

"Want to join me?" he asked.

"I'll catch up with you. I just need a minute alone." He nodded and went inside my house. I sat at the bottom of the tree trunk in the front yard and looked up, closing my eyes. I focused on the feeling of the grass on my bare legs since I was wearing shorts, and the loud white noise of the cicadas to drown my sorrows.

As I stared at the clear blue sky through the branches, I wondered if I could always remember him. If there was a way to keep his story alive somehow. I tried to forget about all the movies and other books inspired by his play that would disappear forever. It was a huge loss for the art world. I thought of the people who would never be able to enjoy the play as I had. Why did my favorite love story have to be a tragedy in and out of its own book?

I stood, about to go into my house, when someone called my name.

"Are you June Capehart?"

I turned around and saw a guy holding a bouquet of flowers and a basket. He was wearing a uniform with the same colors and logo as the delivery van parked on the street.

"Yes, I am," I said.

"Can you sign here?" he said, giving me his clipboard. In the sender's field for the basket, I found Maggie's name. There was some relief inside of me after so much dread. Once I signed, he handed me the basket and then the bouquet.

"There's a card on the flowers as well. Happy birthday!" he said, then got into the van and left.

I looked at the basket. There were cookies, a bunch of them, in shapes of different books. They were a work of art. There was also a card. Even with all the mess of the party, Maggie hadn't forgotten my birthday. I'd take my time to read the card once the party was over.

Then I looked through the bouquet and found a tiny card.

My dearest June, Happy Birthday!

I can't wait for you to tell me all about your summer. I'll be back on the thirtieth.

With love,

Mrs. Lib

There was something calming and at the same time nerve-racking about Mrs. Lib coming back in eight days. Things were about to get real. Whether I'd be able to tell her that the play was safe, or that I had lost it forever, at least I wouldn't have to deal with Nora anymore.

As I headed to the house, I heard some cracks and looked around. Will was tiptoeing to the front door, stepping on dried twigs on the front lawn.

"What are you doing?" I considered possible reasons for him being here. "Were you spying on me?" This was just the cherry on top of an emotionally exhausting birthday.

Will looked at me with a guilty smile. "No . . . yes?" He shrugged. "I didn't mean to. I saw Alex leaving. I had no idea what you had done to him this time."

I stared at him with zero excitement for his comment. Why couldn't he be *my* brother? Why couldn't his loyalty be for me?

"So, then?" I asked him.

"I saw you and him fighting. I had locked myself out and couldn't get in until you finished. But you took *soooo* long."

I had no patience with anyone else today. My little brother listening to all my sorrows didn't help. "Can you just pretend you didn't hear anything? I'm sure you have better things to do than annoy me on my birthday," I said as I reached for the doorknob.

"I can help you, you know? I mean, getting Tristan back to his book."

His words made me stop dead in my tracks. It was one thing for him to be listening to Alex and me talking about our problems and another to have heard everything I told Tristan.

Will stared at me with a mischievous smile.

I ignored him and tried to act as if I hadn't said anything incriminating. "You're only eight. I'm sure you have no idea what we were talking about." I tried to laugh with confidence but failed.

"I know a thing or two about characters getting out of their books. It happens to Captain Jacquotte all the time." I stared at him, hesitant. "Besides, I do know what you are saying. I can't remember your favorite book, either, and Tristan's weirdness makes so much sense now. The way he talks, why he fought so well at the fair and has no idea what a World Cup is."

Could it be that he truly believed me? It was possible. He was constantly reading books with talking animals, animal detectives, and pirate stories. If anyone believed in magic, it would be him.

"Let me help," Will repeated, getting closer to me and peeking at my basket of cookies, which I immediately took away. "Or you can just lose Tristan and his book all at once. Your choice."

"How do I know you're not just tricking me?" I knew Will and his prankish mind.

"You're going to have to trust me on this one. I don't think you have much of a choice." He smiled, so proud of himself.

"Wait, how much is it going to cost me?" I asked him, since there was always a catch.

He gave me a mischievous grin. "Four tickets to the pirate exhibit at the science museum."

He was out of his mind. The answer to my problems was not in a museum downtown. "Who are the tickets for?" I asked before agreeing. Maybe he was just setting me up to pay for him and his friends.

"Are you in or not?" he asked cockily, taking advantage of the fact that I was desperate.

I hesitated. I had nothing else to lose. I had earned enough money this summer and had barely spent any. "Fine," I said.

"Cool! OK, then we'll tell Mom and Dad that we're going to the pirate exhibit by ourselves next weekend. They will be so happy that you're taking me somewhere, they won't even ask about it." He had a point. "All you have to do is take Tristan to the museum at noon and wait for me there."

"But how are you going to get there without me driving?" I asked.

"June, you know what? Sometimes all you have to do is trust."

CHAPTER 18

DELUSIONS OF ROMANCE

"Why on earth would I be interested in knowing about pirates?" Tristan asked as he read the big sign at the museum entrance. "They are despicable people."

It made sense—to us they were history, to him they were a menace.

"I thought you'd like to see more of the world. We are going to a modern museum." I tried to sound excited without actually knowing if he knew what I was talking about.

Tristan gave me a side smile, not happy at all with my selection of the activity for the day.

"Who are we waiting for, milady?" he asked as we stood by the fountain at the entrance.

"Just some friends," I lied, trying to find Will in the crowds. I had no idea whom he had invited.

The second I spotted Will walking toward us, I froze. Why on earth did he think having Alex and Tristan together was a good idea? It was going to be an even more challenging day with both guys constantly bickering with each other.

Will ran in our direction, greeting Tristan enthusiastically. I moved closer to Alex but didn't say a word. He looked me in the eye, and all he said was, "Hey," the coldest greeting he had ever given me. I wondered if Will enjoyed having *his* friend Alex around.

Obviously Tristan and Alex didn't seem to be happy to be part of the same group. They didn't even say hi to each other.

"Do you have the tickets?" Will asked.

I took my phone out, and the lady at the entrance scanned the tickets. This was going to be the longest day of the summer.

As we walked through the museum, looking for the room with the pirate exhibit, Tristan stopped at every display. It was getting harder to find ways to excite him about pirates when I knew how much he hated them.

When I found the opportunity, I pulled Will close and whispered in his ear, "So what's the plan?"

"You'll improvise, Sis," Will said confidently.

"What? I thought you had a plan." The anxiety was killing me. Trusting my little brother to actually have a strategy might have been asking for too much.

He pointed his head at Tristan. "I know what needs to happen for him to want to leave and return to his book, but I can't control other people. So we wait for the perfect opportunity," he said and rushed next to Alex.

If I hadn't made any progress with Will's plan, or things heated up between Alex and Tristan, I'd call Mrs. Lib right away. She would be landing sometime today since we were meeting the following morning.

The lady at the entrance of the pirate exhibit handed us a map. We were supposed to walk through the different halls on a scavenger hunt. Will was all for it, and he had already called dibs on any treasure we'd get at the end. I didn't care, but if they had any chocolate coins, at least one was mine.

We walked into the first hall and found ourselves surrounded by the sound of calming waves and seagulls. The floor was glass-like and underneath looked like a beach with sand and scattered objects, like an old, ripped map—a compass, a lost boot, and a few coins. It felt as though I were on a movie set. On one side of the wall was a projection of how diving expeditions worked, and on the other were items on enclosed displays that had been discovered in sunken ships. Even if four tickets had cost me a tiny fortune, it was definitely worth seeing.

There was a lady sitting by a table with ancient coins retrieved during expeditions. Will ran immediately in that direction. When we approached, the lady explained about the coins, but I barely listened, since I secretly stared at Alex. With his shoelaces untied, loose ripped jeans, and a T-shirt of Arthsteen University, he looked really hot.

"Tristan, hold these," Will said, putting a bunch of coins in his hands.

Tristan did, and Will stared attentively at him.

"Really?" I whispered to my little brother. "They're not going to be magical, just old."

"It can't hurt to try," Will replied before returning the coins to the lady and heading to the next part. I knew that getting Tristan back to his book was not going to be that easy.

The next hall was a complete opposite setting from the first. The sound of a stormy sea filled the room. Through the speakers, waves crashed and thunder crackled. The big ceiling fans created strong winds that made the pirate flag wave. No matter where we looked, it felt as if we were in the eye of the storm.

This part of the exhibit was about the abilities sailors and pirates needed to sail on tumultuous seas. Several posters explained the factors that influenced the handling of the ship. The sea currents, along with the weight of the cargo, affected the speed of the ship. There was another poster explaining how the wind currents and sails worked. All referring to the things a captain needed to know to manage the crew. Will was loving it, and I had to admit that it wasn't boring at all.

We stood in line for an interactive section that allowed us to experience what it was like when a ship sailed through a storm. While we stood in line for our turn, Alex told a couple of pirate jokes. I found them really funny. Tristan, not so much, which seemed to encourage Alex to tell even more. When he ran out jokes, he started talking like a pirate, even though we had just learned that the typical pirate accent had been manufactured by Hollywood. Still, Will and I were cracking up.

"Do you find it amusing to imitate such despicable people as pirates?" Tristan asked in a dismissive tone, and Will and I straightened up.

Alex ignored him, as if Tristan's words dissolved in thin air. Luckily it was our turn now.

We stood in a section of the boat that moved. It was like a 4D experience with the sound, the wind, the movement, and even the mist, which was supposed to be rain. Once we walked out, there was a sign at the front of the ship that even had a skeleton tied to the front. Will corrected me as I pointed at it. Apparently it was not the front. It was called the bow of the ship. I knew all about books, not boats.

The sign read *To continue on your journey, you must walk the plank. Or use the ramp on the back.*

"We are not using the ramp. Let's go," Will said enthusiastically.

Tristan was going first but seemed unsure, so Will pointed at the people in front of us. It wasn't that big of a fall. And at the bottom was a pit with foam cubes for a soft landing.

"The things men do for love," Tristan said, and I laughed.

He was about to jump when Alex jumped on the plank and Tristan lost his balance. He managed to do a somersault in the air and landed gracefully on the bottom. Alex's expression was anything but pleased as Tristan bowed to us, and we clapped from the top in return.

"It's going to take more than that to hurt me, you fool," Tristan told Alex as he climbed out of the foam pit and Alex stood on the edge of the plank.

Alex ignored him and jumped, landing effortlessly at the bottom. He was about to get up while I got in position. Out of nowhere Will pushed me and shouted, "Look out!"

Alex turned around and caught me, and we both fell into the foam pit. My heart fluttered as I pressed so closely against Alex.

"Did I hurt you? Are you OK?" I asked, and it was hard to conceal my smile.

"Never better," he replied and helped me climb out.

The lady at the top of the plank asked Will to be more careful, which, from the way he jumped into the air, had little effect on him.

Once we were all out, we got to the third and last room. We climbed up a rope ladder to get to the main deck. The soundtrack from the movie *Pirates of the Caribbean*, along with all the props that filled the area, made it feel like we were really aboard a pirate ship. Next to the walls were mannequins that showed how pirates really dressed in their time. And on the walls were posters with portraits of real pirates.

Will looked at his map. "We need to find a pirate associated with a color . . ."

"Blackbeard," Alex said before Will could finish.

Tristan stared at the posters on the walls. "Barbarossa means 'red beard' in Italian."

"That's it! Tristan, you got it! Find a pirate associated with the color of blood," Will said excitedly as he wrote it down.

Alex exhaled angrily. "You're not the only one who's bilingual, you know? I could have solved that easily." Alex's ego seemed to have gotten hurt.

Tristan stared at Alex defiantly and turned to me, holding my face between his hands.

"Amore mio, nemmeno il mare azzurro può brillare come i tuoi occhi oggi."

I took a step back, uncomfortable. "Tristan, I didn't understand a word of what you said." If I hadn't managed to understand a little Spanish even around the Marquez family, Italian was sure to be even worse.

"Milady, I just said that not even the bluest sea can shine as your eyes do today."

He kissed my hand, but I nervously took it away. I knew Alex and Will were also staring at us.

I couldn't fall for his excess of attention for me, not this time. I smiled instead. "Let's keep going." And we all walked ahead.

At the very end was an interactive reenactment of a pirate battle. The sound of swords and cannons elicited a whole different mood. We needed to stand in line as pairs.

"I'll battle my sister," Will said, holding my arm.

I smiled at the guys and turned to Will. "Are you out of your mind?" I whispered. "You can't make *them* fight." All I could think of were Tristan's amazing fencing skills as he dueled at the fair.

"Trust me," Will said.

"I'm beginning to doubt my choices," I said as we watched Tristan and Alex put on a protective fencing vest.

The museum guy explained the rules. Once the sword touched the vest, a string of LED lights on it would turn red. That meant we were dead and had lost the game. We had ten minutes to fight, and a timer was on each section. Since there were four in our group, they put us in the biggest section, the one at the quarterdeck or poop deck. Will cracked up at the name, and I was shocked to learn that part of the boat was really called that.

Tristan held on tight to his sword, his knuckles almost white around the grip. I knew the swords were props, but I was also aware of Tristan's violent tendencies, especially when he was hungry for revenge.

The clock had barely started when Tristan struck first. He was careful enough to not touch Alex's protective gear, but it seemed all he was trying to do was humiliate him.

"If anything goes wrong, it'll be your time to save Alex," Will said to me.

"What?" I answered. Was this his master plan?

"En garde," Will said, taking his position as I barely figured out how to hold my sword. The fencing gear was a size too big.

On the other side of our section, Tristan didn't hesitate to attack Alex. With every chance he got, he found a way to corner him. All the agility Alex had in soccer and swimming stood no chance against Tristan's skills with a sword. They were no longer playing within the fair limits of our space; they were all over the quarterdeck. I didn't know if it was lucky or not that the museum people couldn't see us. I stared at the timer. We had eight minutes before our time was up, but I was sure Alex wouldn't last that long without getting hurt.

Tristan used his body to sweep Alex off his feet. Alex didn't have enough time to use his sword to stop him, and Will and I heard a thump on the floor.

"Take it easy, dude!" Alex said, but it only made Tristan happier.

This was the part of Romeo that nobody thought about when people heard his name. He was known for being romantic, passionate, and even dreamy. But he was also reckless, impulsive, and unable to control his emotions. Just like in the play when he killed Tybalt and Paris, Juliet's fiancé.

Will hit me with his sword, and the lights turned red on my vest. I stared at the blade of Will's sword. I knew since they were props, they weren't dangerous, but then I realized they had an almost invisible plastic sheath. No wonder we didn't hear the typical sounds of metal clashing.

I looked to Tristan's starting point and found the plastic sheath on the floor. He had taken it off. I felt cold as I saw Tristan jumping over a barrel and swinging his sword at Alex, cutting his arm below the shoulder. Turning to look at the bloodstain on his torn sleeve, Alex didn't see the punch coming. Tristan's fist connected with Alex's jaw, making him tumble. This was getting out of hand. I shouldn't have trusted Will's fiction-based plans.

Tristan advanced, trapping Alex's neck against the mast with his forearm. Even if Tristan was shorter and skinnier, Alex couldn't escape. I almost called for help, but if we were going through all this trouble for Tristan to leave, Alex had to keep fighting. Although I had no idea if Will had told him anything about Tristan.

Even though Tristan had Alex trapped, he was not breaking any rules other than being out of our original zone and Alex's vest hadn't lit up red either. We were all trapped until something happened, hopefully with Tristan. I stared at the timer. We had five minutes left.

I rushed to where they were, making my way around ropes, pieces of wood, and barrels. Seeing how Tristan pointed his sword at Alex's face made me move faster, but I tripped over a rope. I looked up and saw Alex's sword on the floor. Tristan could hurt Alex—nothing was protecting his face.

I got up, holding my sword tight. At first I thought of getting behind Tristan and pulling him back to make him come to his senses. I didn't want either one of them getting hurt. But I knew he wouldn't reason, not in that state, and not even with me.

I did the only thing that came to mind. I grabbed a rope tied to the mast.

"Hey, Tristan," I called from behind, and he turned my way taking a step back releasing Alex. I held on to the rope and jumped, swinging through the air and landing in between them. I pulled Alex away and removed the plastic sleeve from my sword, pointing it at Tristan.

"Milady?" Tristan stared at me, confused. "What are you doing, my love?" He tried to get closer to me, but I brandished my sword at him. "Milady, he is the problem that stands against our happiness." His expression became more serious. "Let me finish him, once and for all."

"The problem has never been *him*. If you want to fight someone, you'll have to fight *me*," I said firmly, the point of my sword just inches from his chest.

"Go, Sis!" Will shouted from behind.

Tristan looked at me in shock. I had hurt him, but it hadn't been with a blade. As I stared at him, the disappointment in his eyes made me realize a crucial detail I had been missing. Tristan didn't want to go because of *me*. As long as he believed there was a possibility of us being together, he would stay here. It had all been my fault, from the very start until the very end. I was mad at myself for not freeing him sooner.

"Tristan, I won't marry you and never will. You have to go back now," I said, not lowering my sword, not even an inch. I had to somehow break his heart, figuratively. Who would have thought *I* would be the one breaking up with Romeo?

Tristan looked at Alex and then at me. "You choose *him* over me?" he asked with tears filling his eyes.

Before today I had no idea how to handle a sword, but I felt an indescribable strength inside of me to fight him, or whoever dared to hurt Alex.

I took a step forward, my sword touching his vest, the LED light turning red. He stared at the light and took the protective vest off.

"It's over, Romeo," I said, taking a step back. "I am in love with Alex, and there's nothing you can do to change that." I never imagined that in the same summer I'd meet Romeo, I'd be pointing a sword at him too.

"Milady, no. It cannot be." He put his hand over his chest, as if my words destroyed his heart more than any blade could.

He fell to his knees and sobbed. It was painful to watch, and I wasn't proud of how it all ended, but it needed to end. He needed to refuse being here.

The sound of Tristan's sword falling to the ground made me feel relief. He was not going to fight any of us anymore. I lowered my sword and turned to look at Alex. His eyes went wide as he pointed somewhere behind me.

"June, look!" Will exclaimed.

I turned back to Tristan and couldn't believe my eyes. Tristan hadn't dropped his sword. His hands were disappearing right before our eyes. He no longer had fingers, and his palms were almost gone.

"What . . . what is happening, Lady June?" Tristan asked in panic, staring at where his hands once were.

My heart raced. Had I been too late? Was he going back? I ran to the place where I had left my things and looked through my bag. I opened my pocket edition and browsed desperately through its pages. It was completely blank, nothing but a plain notebook. I looked at the other copies I had brought, and they were the same. There was no prologue and not even the character list at the beginning. No more cover or anything else. Time had run out.

"No, no, no. It's gone. It didn't work," I said and ran back to Tristan.

Will's plan had been my last hope, and now I wondered if Alex or Will would also forget about him soon.

"Calm down, Sis," Will said, getting close to me.

Never in history had those words ever made anyone feel calmer. "How can I be calm? You told me it was going to work!" I said in frustration.

We all stared at Tristan, who now seemed like a ghost. Only a faint silhouette of him remained. The timer rang just as the museum guide was coming back.

I stared at Tristan, becoming nothing more than thin air. "Goodbye," I mumbled as I looked at the place where, just seconds ago, he was holding his sword. This was, for real, the last time I would ever see Romeo Montague.

The guide walked in just seconds after we witnessed Tristan disappear.

"Hey, where's your friend?" he asked.

We all stared at each other.

"He left," Will said.

"Too bad. Did y'all have fun?" he asked.

I couldn't answer. I took my vest off and started to collect my things. Alex and Will asked me where I was going, since Will still had to get his scavenger hunt prize. But I didn't care. I had no strength in me to stay after what had just happened. I grabbed my things and headed toward the exit. Alex and Will called my name as I walked away, but I didn't listen. Nothing was going to make me look back.

CHAPTER 19

MIA

M rs. Lib texted me to meet her at noon today. As I locked my bike on the rack at the library's parking lot, I stared at the garden. The forgotten tree house was there, and nothing had physically changed, yet everything felt different. I wondered if this was what a breakup felt like, but it was mixed with grief and disappointment, so I couldn't really tell. It was my first real heartbreak, after all, so what would I know?

Last night I had packed everything related to *Romeo and Juliet* in a box inside my closet. Some memories were just too hard to deal with. Since I had failed at saving Romeo, I decided to rewrite the play, since I knew the plot by heart. The problem was trying to remember word by word the phrases other characters said in the play. Juliet came easier, but the rest, not so much.

I wanted to remember Tristan as more than just a memory. I had his handwriting on the notebook he had given me, but still, I wanted to remember his exact words and his beautiful turns of phrase. The most popular of Romeo's phrases came easily to mind, but the long monologues were getting harder and harder to remember. The fight with Tristan and Alex was still fresh in my mind, and it had been such an emotionally overwhelming experience that maybe that was the reason I couldn't sit down and write the whole play in one sitting.

As I was remembering the lines, I would write them down in the notebook Tristan had given me for my birthday. Even if I was riding my bike, reading, or even walking, I'd stop to write them down. Nothing I ever wrote would be as well written as Shakespeare's plays. But I desperately needed to write whatever I remembered before I would forget too.

I closed my notebook and walked inside the library. The cooler temperatures gave me chills, and I waved them away. Something happened when you were sad. Other common things didn't bother you anymore. I punched the key combination on the STAFF ONLY door and walked inside. Just the sound of Nora's voice coming from Mrs. Lib's office tied my stomach in a knot. I prepared for the worst.

As I walked in, mixed feelings bubbled inside of me as I saw Mrs. Lib after such a long time. Her silver curls still bounced as she stood up to greet me. Her red glasses bumped with mine as we hugged. There was something about her embrace that made me feel like my broken heart could be rebuilt again.

I greeted Nora more dryly and sat in the empty chair. There was a big container on the table, and I felt a new kind of despair when I thought Nora had found Tristan's clothes from the storage room. Now I was not only fired, but I could kiss any recommendation letter goodbye.

"You know what we have called you for, right, June?" Mrs. Lib asked.

I nodded. The less I said, the better.

Nora opened the container, and I was relieved when I saw books. Nora took them out one by one, and I started crying. Each and every copy of Tristan's play, along with all the books, movies, and music inspired by *Romeo and Juliet*, were there, covers and all. I felt like I could finally breathe.

"Alice, a lot of patrons complained this summer about an empty section in the Shakespeare shelf," Nora said in a dismissive tone. "I believe you'll agree with me that it is completely unacceptable for June to benefit from her position at this library to carry out such an immature prank, hoarding these valuable books. Her obsession took a wrong turn."

My obsession had saved the play, but Nora would never be able to realize that. Mrs. Lib stared at her the whole time, which was anything but reassuring. I had to shed my tears in silence, but deep down I couldn't contain the happiness and relief inside of me.

Nora took out the last book, which was the *Romeo and Juliet* copy from the Timeless Literature section.

"Crying will not make us feel pity for you, June. In case you are trying to trick us," Nora said, and I wanted to scream at her. If only she knew everything I had gone through to save a beloved work of literature. But nobody would know about it. People usually complained when things went wrong, but when they turned out right, no one was there to notice.

Nora went on to enumerate all my offenses that summer. From being disrespectful to Tyler to wasting time flirting with my boyfriend instead of working. And eventually to the big one that got me banned from the library—me opening the case of the damaged old collectible. Nora complained, frustrated about not being able to recover the security camera's recordings of that day. And she made a fuss about why the updates to the security system had been done at the library's peak hours of operation.

Mrs. Lib explained to her that Jim had been by the exhibit that day, which made it a safe time for the updates. It would be illogical to run updates at night, when no one was around. She had a point. Something about Nora not being able to prove I had been the one to open the case gave me infinite joy, but it also raised a lot of questions. I knew nothing I'd say would work in my favor, so I stood in silence, trying to bite my tongue.

Mrs. Lib remained quiet, nodding every now and then at Nora's accusations. Once Nora had nothing else to complain about, Mrs. Lib asked her to leave us so we could talk about the consequences of my choices. Nora made an unpleasant face. It seemed like she wanted to hear Mrs. Lib fire me, but at least she wouldn't get that satisfaction.

Once Nora closed the door behind her, Mrs. Lib grabbed her desk phone and dialed an extension, asking for someone to come in, but I didn't know who. Someone knocked on the door shortly thereafter. The doorknob turned, and Sarah and Jim came in. Jim held a big trash bag, which he put on top of Mrs. Lib's desk. I could tell by the lack of noise as the bag hit the desk that the contents of the bag were soft, like old clothes.

I swallowed hard as I realized I was not only going to get fired but was about to lose the love and respect of the people I cared for the most at this library. Mrs. Lib dumped the contents of the bag on her desk, and as I suspected, all Tristan's clothes spilled out, including his original costume and my koala handkerchief. I stared at my fidgeting hands instead, since I was scared to face Mrs. Lib's disappointed gaze.

She cleared her throat and I looked up at her with guilt in my eyes, waiting for her to say the first word.

"June, are you aware of the gravity of the situation you put yourself through?" she asked.

I panicked. I had no idea how to answer that question. I didn't know if she would believe me now that the play had been restored and it looked like nothing had happened.

"First of all," Mrs. Lib said, taking her glasses off, "I want to thank you for the bravery needed to face this situation."

I frowned. Was she perhaps talking about me being brave for coping with Nora's insufferable attitude during the summer?

"The MLA came by this morning to retrieve the magical

copy of *Romeo and Juliet*." My eyes opened wide in disbelief. "I wanted to let you know in case you wanted to check on it. But I would suggest, if you ever encounter that book, to never open it again. We now know, as well as the MLA, that you are the key."

"The what? MLA?" I asked in disbelief. So many words of that sentence didn't make sense.

I felt someone's hand over my shoulder, and I turned to look.

"You did it! You saved Romeo!" Sarah said in a low voice.

Jim stared at me and winked.

"Am I dreaming?" I asked "I'm not fired?"

Mrs. Lib, Sarah, and Jim chuckled all at once.

"No, you are not. But by my instruction, you are to take the month of August off work. Nora and I are going to have a serious conversation about not overworking part-time staff or interns at this library. I know you are here for the experience more than for the pay, but I don't want her to do that again," Mrs. Lib said, smiling at me.

It was such a relief to have Mrs. Lib be my mentor again and not have to deal with Nora anymore.

"How . . . how did y'all know?" I asked. It was still hard to believe that Sarah, Mrs. Lib, and Jim knew all along who Tristan was.

"Did you think the new rope at the old tree house was just a coincidence? Or the security cameras' recordings disappearing just as you opened the case and made Tristan touch the magical book?" Mrs. Lib said. "And you know Jim wouldn't allow someone to live at the old tree house, even just to check on it."

I stared at them. They were like secret agents working from behind the scenes, knowing all along that Tristan was real.

"Why didn't you say anything?" I asked Sarah and Jim.

"The one responsible for bringing out a character from a book must be the one to send it back. If we had interfered, horrible things would have happened to that play," Jim added.

"Are you all part of the MLA?" I asked.

The three of them nodded. So Jim was more than just the superintendent, and Sarah was more than a librarian here.

"Great things are mostly accomplished in teams," Mrs. Lib said with a smile. "I can't be prouder of the team I left in charge."

"Wait, you knew before you left? Was this a test? I have so many questions," I said.

"And all will be answered. First, let me explain. MLA stands for Magical Library Association. You and I have talked about it. Books are special, perhaps the ultimate proof of magic."

I nodded, wondering if the term *magical* had always been literal for her. Because it had been figurative for me until now.

"Some books are more magical than others, and the MLA is responsible for safekeeping them in its secret library somewhere in Washington, DC. There was a rumor that a magical copy of *Romeo and Juliet* existed. This copy, the one Tristan came out of, was the one the MLA suspected to be magical. I told the MLA that I might have found the right bookworm who was the key to open the book." She smiled at me. "I was supposed to be here all along to support you and intervene in case you fell in love with each other, making him not want to go back."

"But you had to go with your daughter," I said, feeling bad for not asking her about that first. It was shocking to realize that I had been the one to fix it all on my own. "Were you checking on me from afar?" I asked.

She nodded. "I almost came back when Sarah told me the Renaissance Faire outing didn't work out."

"Sorry if this comes out weird, Mrs. Lib, but it was very risky of you to trust me. I had no idea what I was doing, and you know I have been in love with Romeo for so long," I said.

"I know it was risky, but I've known you for a long time, and I knew you loved the play more than you could ever love a guy with such a retrogressive mindset."

She had *that* right. I was once in love with his paper version, but the human one turned out to be more challenging. Still, the amount of trust Mrs. Lib had for me blew me away.

"What did you mean by 'should I encounter the book again'?" I asked, wondering whether that was even a possibility but immediately regretting it, since Tristan had turned out to be clingier than I imagined.

"Well, since you have turned out to be the key to that book, the MLA is offering you a position there—when you finish college, that is. As long as you choose a career related to books, it never expires," she said, taking out a pretty light-blue envelope, which had a subtle shine to it. It was the same type of paper Mrs. Lib had used to send me the letter with the call number to find *Tristan and Isolde*.

I couldn't believe there was even a possibility that I could have a job related to magical books. I couldn't wait to graduate from college.

"Mrs. Lib, can I keep that?" I pointed at Tristan's clothes.

She nodded. "And please take the rest to the donation bin in the parking lot. Any more questions?"

"Just one more. Do you have a picture of your grandson?" I asked, and her smile was the widest.

"Here, let me show you," she said as she took her phone out. "He's not even a month old, and I'm already making him book lists of the best picture books."

Dropping the clothes at the donation bin brought a sense of relief. Now that the literary issue was solved, I felt like the circle was complete. It didn't feel exactly like a circle, though, because it somehow felt rough around the edges. But at least I had a sense of closure I never thought I'd get before this morning.

I walked toward my bike through the library's garden. This place felt totally different now that I knew he was safe. Or as safe as he could be knowing his play was a tragedy. There would always be a part of me that would miss him. I'd be left with an imaginary shadow and the memories of him scattered all around this library. But knowing he hadn't died—well, at least not here in the twenty-first century, but for the reasons Shakespeare had originally planned—made it all feel OK. And every time I would open his play, he'd be there, alive. At least before he met Juliet and started making reckless decisions.

Before I took off on my bike, my phone pinged with a text. I opened it and saw a GIF of a jellyfish from Maggie.

I called her immediately. Ever since I read her letter the night of my birthday, I realized that all friendships go through the motions. Some feel like a wreckage but even then, there's always something salvable. Besides we needed to catch up before school started the following week.

She picked up right away. Listening to her voice was a type of therapy.

She asked me if she needed to come over to my house with ice cream, now that she was back from her trip and heard all of the exchange students were gone. To her, Tristan was back to England.

"Forget ice cream at home. Let's go out!" I said with more excitement than I could contain.

CHAPTER 20

ROMANTIC AFTERMATH

Mom's obsessive paparazzi phase was in full force every first day of school, but it was particularly bad today since it was my first day of senior year.

"Just one more, with Will," Mom said, making us stand next to her cupcake tower.

I needed to hurry if I wanted to meet Maggie before class. When Mom was satisfied with the pictures, she kissed me with a tear in her eye, just the way she had with Marian. I put the orange juice back in the fridge as Will played with his toy sword, the prize for the scavenger hunt at the museum.

"Hey, I never got to ask you," I said as I closed the fridge and mom walked out of the kitchen. "What made you think your plan would work?"

Will stopped playing and stared at me. "Because no one really changes unless they want to." He pointed his sword at me. "Just like a character in Captain Jacquotte's books, Tristan didn't want to change until he saw that you only cared about Alex." He swung his sword at me, poking my belly playfully. I poked my tongue out on one side and closed my eyes, pretending to be dead.

He laughed. "Your dead face is kind of dorky," he mocked. I pushed him gently, and at least I didn't feel as annoyed by him as before. Out of nowhere I hugged him, as I hadn't had the time to thank him.

Will seemed surprised at my unusual show of affection. "You can let go of me now," he said, and I stepped away.

"Lucky for us Alex only left the pirate exhibit with a bruise and a torn shirt," I whispered.

Will nodded, and Mom returned to the kitchen and shoo us out the door so we wouldn't be late for school.

Since I wanted to take my bike, getting to school would take me longer than the bus. But I enjoyed the cooler morning breeze on my face—if eighty degrees could be considered a cold morning for the South in August.

At the rack in the school parking lot I secured my bike with a new lock, a gift I had given myself after my whirlwind summer. Mainly because I wanted to get rid of any annoying things in my life. Now that I no longer had to work with Nora at the library, I figured I no longer wanted to deal with any unnecessary stress.

Ever since I realized the play was safe and back to normal, I had a happiness I couldn't contain. Well, maybe making up with Maggie also had something to do with it. The only thing I was missing was Alex.

At first I thought he wasn't talking to me because he was giving me space. But then days passed, and now it had been a full week without even a text. I knew he was back because of the blue Jeep parked on the street. But for every day that he didn't look for me, I began to wonder if he had fallen out of love.

I kept obsessing about the reasons. Was he punishing me for our argument at my birthday? For the way Tristan had fought him at the pirate exhibit, even though I had saved him? Had he realized he liked his college friends more than me? I waited impatiently for Maggie, standing next to my locker. I needed something to take my mind off Alex, so I used the extra minutes to read.

As a resolution for my last year of high school, I promised myself I would no longer obsess about a single book. If this summer had taught me anything, it was that there wasn't enough time to read all the books I wanted to read. And if I kept obsessing over and over about the same one, I would never get to discover all the new stories waiting for me.

Maggie arrived a couple of pages in. She greeted me with a big hug, and I knew that even with everything that had happened between us before the summer break, nothing had really changed. I saw the wick-pops walk by, but I no longer felt jealousy or anger. I was glad that I didn't have to hang out with them anymore. They were Maggie's friends, not mine, and we were both OK with that.

Once I read Maggie's card, I understood why she had acted odd at her party. I just wished she would have told me about it sooner. I could understand why being around me was hard for her. My family has always been close, and her parents were on the verge of a divorce. Unfortunately for me, Alessandra's parents had gone through the same, so Maggie felt closer to her than me.

Maggie apologized for taking so long to reply to my jellyfish urgent message and thanked me for my thoughtful birthday present. She promised she would never treat me that way again, even if she got drunk. We had already caught up on the events of the summer. Like the cool places she had visited on her trip as well as Alex's song and my days with Tristan. But I left out the detail about where Tristan was really from—I wanted to keep that part to myself.

"Have you seen Marquez yet?" she asked.

I shook my head. I had to run into him today, with luck by my first class.

The first class Alex and I had together was Mr. Grooms' world literature. After talking about the class syllabus, he started where we left off last school year, talking about *Romeo and Juliet*. I wondered what the class would be about if I hadn't managed to send Tristan back.

I paid very little attention, since I'd had an overload of Romeo during the summer. But also because I couldn't stop thinking about Alex. He sat a couple of rows away, and I felt his gaze constantly. But every time I would turn toward him, he would look away. The whole class became a Ping-Pong game of stares. I stared, then turned away when he stared my way. It was somehow fun, but it must have looked ridiculous.

"Do you agree, Ms. Capehart?" Mr. Grooms asked me.

I stared at him, clueless.

"I asked for your opinion about destiny versus free will. How much of Romeo and Juliet's situation was written in the stars, and how much was about choices?"

Before answering, I thought of everything Tristan had taught me as a literary character, and as a real person during the time he was here.

"A little bit of both, I think," I answered, trying to come back to the present. "They chose each other, but also Romeo is reserved for Juliet, *and Juliet only*." I felt relaxed since he was no longer my responsibility.

Mr. Grooms seemed like he wanted more from my answer, but thankfully the bell rang. As I was busy packing up my things, I realized Alex had already left with Oliver. We had been in the same class, and he hadn't said anything. Now I was really upset.

If I had learned anything from Tristan, it was to go after what I wanted. So once my classes were over, I headed to the swimming pool. I needed to set our relationship status straight ASAP. The girls' team had just finished training, so there was no sight of the boys' team, but still I went inside.

"He's not here," Nichole said as she got out of the pool, patting her face with a towel. Somehow her attitude wasn't as annoying, or maybe I just didn't care anymore. I looked around as if I hadn't listened. I heard voices coming from the boys' locker rooms. I've never felt jealousy, anger, sadness, and love for the same person all within a couple of months. But I had for Alex.

"You can't go in there," Nichole said, but I didn't listen.

Without an ounce of logic, I stormed in.

I knew Alex was there somewhere. I just had to keep looking. I recognized his silhouette from behind, but I was not counting on seeing his naked butt. I turned around and closed my eyes.

"Alex, are you covered? Can I turn around?" I asked, so embarrassed that I wished I could magically disappear. But all I could hear were whistles from the guys around us.

"Yes, June, what are you doing here?" Alex said nervously.

I peeked before turning completely. He was wearing only boxers. The feeling of empowerment before coming in here had vanished. Suddenly I felt very hot. It might have been the humidity in the room, but I doubted it.

"Why haven't you reached out?" I asked, trying not to get distracted by how sexy he looked with wet strands of hair falling over his forehead.

"Can we talk about this as soon as I'm out?" Alex answered, looking a little red on the cheeks. I didn't know a Latin guy could blush like that.

"You had all week and chose not to," I said in a defensive tone.

"I was giving you space." He stared as the whistles around us grew louder.

"Space for what?"

"For you to deal with your breakup. To mourn your boyfriend?" He hesitated over the last part.

Everybody stared as if we were the main attraction. We had drawn too much attention, because I could hear the coach's voice becoming louder as he grew closer. *Damn it!* I had to leave. I was not getting detention on the first day of school. I turned around, annoyed and ready to leave.

"June, just wait for me. Please," Alex said.

I nodded and walked away. How ironic that now *I* would wait for *him*.

As soon as I heard him coming to his Jeep, I stood up straight. It hadn't even been ten minutes, but the sweat fell from my temples like raindrops. It might have been the burning heat of the last days of the Southern summer, or maybe my nerves.

"Was that really for me?" I asked him, pointing at the bike rack on the back of his Jeep.

He nodded. I still had no idea why he had to lie about it.

He helped me get my bike securely on his rack, and we got into his car. We drove out of the parking lot in silence, which was unusual and uncomfortable.

We both talked at the same time, and things felt so . . . weird between us, so tangled.

"So he's truly gone, huh?" he asked, blowing the hair out of his face. "I can't believe he was the real deal."

"I know." I blew out a deep breath as I stared out the window. "I'm glad he's gone, though. The play is back to normal, just like nothing had happened."

"I . . . I didn't wanna be the rebound guy," he said.

"You were never the rebound guy, Alex!" I said, surprised. "You were the reason I needed Tristan to leave as soon as possible." I had barely finished that sentence when I felt his hand over mine. All sorts of butterflies fluttered in my stomach and then migrated to my cheeks.

"I knew you would only fall for *him*. Weird he became real," he said, giving me a side smile that made me melt.

It was nice to know someone other than library staff knew what I had done in the name of world literature.

He made a right turn onto Luna Road, our street. "Do you remember what Mr. Grooms said today?" he asked.

I nodded.

"Do you think our fate is written somewhere? Like in the stars or something?"

"Maybe," I said, looking at the trees as we drove by. "I think our lives are a blank notebook. And we write one page each day. Do *you* think we are meant to be? Like fate?"

He parked on the street outside my house and turned off his Jeep. The AC was now off, and the heat felt immediately stronger.

He turned to me, "I believe it was destiny for us to meet. But it was my free will to fall in love with you."

His words left me breathless. I tried to get closer to him. I wanted to kiss him, but he opened the door and climbed out of his Jeep as fast as he could. He always did stuff that threw me off. He walked around the Jeep to my side and opened the door. He held my hand and pulled me out. In an instant I felt his hand on my lower back and the other on my cheek. I stared at his dark eyes, enjoying being so close to him and feeling so calm. His lips were inches from mine, and then he closed the distance.

My heart had longed for him for years. Our kiss was soft and sweet. He pulled apart and smiled at me. How I loved looking at his smile. We were the perfect fit. If only I had known how good it felt to kiss him, I would have done it sooner.

His breathing merged with mine, and we kissed again, this time stronger. He had my heart, all of it, and I had his. His lips were tender and sweet. It was like a fairy-tale ending minus the fairy part. Because this time it was no longer fictional. This time it was for real.

ACKNOWLEDGMENTS

Neil Gaiman once said that *"a book is a dream that you hold in your hands."* It's entirely true. Like many dreams, a book is built on many parts that create the whole. This book wouldn't be what it is without all the people who helped me along the way, from all the authors whose books have taught me new things about storytelling, to the people who have helped me master the craft.

First things first, I want to thank the following people: Lisa Poisso for helping me learn to be a better storyteller by asking the right questions and having the right answers. James Gallagher of Castle Walls Editing for changing my words into the best version of themselves. Dane Low and his team at Ebook Launch for an incredibly gorgeous cover. To Debbie Vavra for her invaluable feedback as a librarian. To Bonnie Jay, Marangely Granados and Andria Seward for their time, support and feedback. To my fellow writers who inspire in me a feeling of community, since every writer spends most of their time in solitude.

I want to give a special heartfelt thank-you to the people who mean the world to me. Without them, this book would be only a lost idea in my head.

To my mom, who is my biggest supporter and has always believed in me. Since my first stories crafted in lines and circles when I didn't yet know how to write, to my unique short stories in my family's first computer at nine years old, to the prized poetry I wrote at sixteen. Te quiero mucho, mucho, Mami.

To my dad for sharing books and art with me, and for always

taking me to book fairs and getting me every book I wanted to read. Gracias, Pa.

To Johann, my first reader. You've heard all the different versions of this story. Even late at night with little to no sleep after the kids went to bed. Thank you for always believing in the uniqueness of my characters and falling in love with mine. I love you forever and always.

To my best friends Andria and Kristen who heard me talk about this book and its characters for years. Thank you for cheering for me and always making me laugh. I always feel understood and supported by you.

To my favorite people in the whole wide world, my son and my daughter. You are the brightest lights in my life. I wake up every day wanting to become a better woman, mom, writer, and human because of you. You have taught me what unconditional love is and what life is truly about. I love you more than words will ever be able to express.

But most of all thank you to you, the reader. Without knowing me, you chose to pick up this book and read it all the way to this point. Whether it was bought, borrowed (hopefully not stolen), or checked out from your local or school library, thank you for taking the time to read it and share it with the people you care about the most. I'll see you on my next literary adventure.

ABOUT THE AUTHOR

Carmina started her career as an engineer, but then she realized she was much happier writing stories. She has lived in three countries and visited many others, always taking inspiration from her travels without forgetting her Mexican roots.

When she's not writing about imaginary people, reading, or finding pretty books at a public library, she can be found at home, baking or crafting with yarn or fabric. Most of the time those crafts become toy versions of her characters or beloved toys for her kids.

She lives in Dallas, Texas, with her husband, two amazing kids, and two hairy dogs.

To learn more, visit:
carminaesquivel.com

instagram.com/carminaesquivelbooks
tiktok.com/@carminaesquivelbooks